PRAISE FOR RACHEL

"A fresh voice in crime fiction."

—Lee Child

"Devilishly clever . . . Hall's writing sizzles and pops."

—Meg Gardiner

"Hall slips from funny to darkly frightening with elegant ease."

—*Publishers Weekly*

PRAISE FOR *WHAT FIRE BRINGS*

"Rachel Howzell Hall is a master of the psychological suspense thriller. *What Fire Brings* delivers shocking secrets, surprises on every page, and a killer twist that will leave you breathless. A must-read!"

—Melinda Leigh, #1 *Wall Street Journal* bestselling author

"This one will keep you guessing! Hall's considerable talent is on full display as she expertly deploys misdirection and subterfuge in a riveting tale of intrigue and suspense where nothing is as it seems. The past collides with the present to forever alter the future while the twists keep coming until the final shocking reveal. If you love an intricate plot with well-crafted prose, incisive insight, and complex characters, do not miss this propulsive mystery by a superb storyteller!"

—Isabella Maldonado, *Wall Street Journal* bestselling author

"Crackling wildfires, dark secrets, and a serial killer on the loose. Rachel Howzell Hall's *What Fire Brings* is a captivating and creepy thrill ride through the California canyons, right up to the final and fiery twisty end."

—Wanda M. Morris award-winning author of *All Her Little Secrets* and *Anywhere You Run*

"Rachel Howzell Hall is simply one of the finest crime writers of her generation, and *What Fire Brings* is her most assured novel yet . . . and one that hits a little close to home for everyone who puts pen to paper or finger to keyboard. Tense, illuminating, and filled with surprises on every page. A masterwork that will leave you flipping pages to see what you might have missed."

—Todd Goldberg, *New York Times* bestselling author

Praise For *What Never Happened*

"Rachel Howzell Hall does it again. *What Never Happened* blends blade-sharp writing and indelible characters with a suspenseful story that pulls you in and won't let go, as a seeming paradise grows dark with storms, suspicion, and murder. I couldn't put it down."

—Meg Gardiner, #1 *New York Times* bestselling author

"*What Never Happened* opens with a gut punch and doesn't let up from there. Rachel Howzell Hall's twist on the you-can't-go-home-again story is smart, dizzying, and thrilling. She not only handles the mystery elements expertly, but she honors the grief and rage of our past and present."

—Paul Tremblay, bestselling author of *The Cabin at the End of the World* and *The Pallbearers Club*

"Rachel Howzell Hall has crafted her own genre of slow-boiling, powerfully emotional thrillers. Her realistic characters are ordinary people, haunted by past horrors that won't stay buried, forcing them to face pure evil to find their own redemption."

—Lee Goldberg, #1 *New York Times* bestselling author

"In *What Never Happened*, Rachel Howzell Hall seamlessly weaves together the past and the present, decorating her breakneck plot with dark secrets and unexpected reveals that glitter like jewels. I couldn't turn the pages fast enough."

—Jess Lourey, Amazon Charts bestselling author of *The Quarry Girls*

"*What Never Happened* is superb. Beautifully and smartly written, it is an engrossing thriller with an ending that will leave your head spinning. It is deliciously creepy and perfectly crafted. In a word, stunning! Don't miss this one!"

—Lisa Regan, *USA Today* and *Wall Street Journal* bestselling author

"Rachel Howzell Hall's *What Never Happened* is a spine-tingling twist of a roller coaster that keeps you on the edge of your seat to the very last page and will have you saying 'Thanks a lot, Rachel, for my lack of sleep.'"

—Yasmin Angoe, award-winning author of the critically acclaimed Nena Knight series, *Her Name Is Knight* and *They Come at Knight*

PRAISE FOR *WE LIE HERE*

"*We Lie Here* is another fast and surprisingly funny thriller from Rachel Howzell Hall. I was on the edge of my seat through all the revelations, twists, and turns in a fast-paced third act. Get this book and relax with the knowledge that you are in the hands of a fantastic crime novelist."

—Adrian McKinty, Edgar Award–winning author of the Sean Duffy series

"In *We Lie Here*, Rachel Howzell Hall gives us a tight, lean, eye-level look at the Gibson family—flawed, normal, abnormal, and each affected by a deadly secret left buried for years—while weaving a page-turning tapestry of dread, cold-blooded murder, and nail-biting tension. What a ride. What a wonderful writer. More, please."

—Tracy Clark, author of the Chicago Mystery series

"Rachel Howzell Hall continues to shatter the boundaries of crime fiction through the sheer force of her indomitable talent."

—S. A. Cosby, author of *Blacktop Wasteland*

"*We Lie Here* is definitive proof that it's impossible to be disappointed by Rachel Howzell Hall, who just gets better and better with each book. She has tools and tricks to spare as she pulls you to the edge of your seat with her razor-sharp plotting and keen eye for the darker side of human behavior that's too easily obscured by the California sunshine."

—Ivy Pochoda, author of *These Women*, a *New York Times* Best Thriller of 2020

"Loaded with surprises and shocking secrets, and propelled by Rachel Howzell Hall's magnificent prose, *We Lie Here* is a captivating thriller that I couldn't put down. It's very clear to me that Hall is one of the best crime writers working today, and she keeps getting better. *We Lie Here* is a can't-miss book."

—Alex Segura, acclaimed author of *Secret Identity*, *Star Wars Poe Dameron: Free Fall*, and *Blackout*

"Rachel Howzell Hall continues to prove why she's one of crime fiction's leading writers. *We Lie Here* is a psychological-suspense fan's dream with both a heroine you'll want to root for and a story you'll want to keep reading late into the night. A must read!"

—Kellye Garrett, Agatha, Anthony, and Lefty Award–winning author of *Like a Sister*

PRAISE FOR *THESE TOXIC THINGS*

An Amazon Best Book of the Month: Mystery, Thriller & Suspense

"This cleverly plotted, surprise-filled novel offers well-drawn and original characters, lively dialogue, and a refreshing take on the serial killer theme. Hall continues to impress."

—*Publishers Weekly* (starred review)

"A mystery/thriller/coming-of-age story you won't be able to put down till the final revelation."

—*Kirkus Reviews*

"Tense and pacey, with an appealing central character, this is a coming-of-age story as well as a gripping mystery."

—*The Guardian*

"The mystery plots are twisty and grabby, but also worth noting is the realistic rendering of a Black LA neighborhood locked in a battle over gentrification."

—*Los Angeles Times*

"Rachel Howzell Hall . . . just gets better and better with each book."

—CrimeReads

"Rachel Howzell Hall continues to shatter the boundaries of crime fiction through the sheer force of her indomitable talent. *These Toxic Things* is a master class in tension and suspense. You think you are ready for it. But. You. Are. Not."

—S. A. Cosby, author of *Blacktop Wasteland*

"*These Toxic Things* is taut and terrifying, packed with page-turning suspense and breathtaking reveals. But what I loved most is the mother-daughter relationship at the heart of this gripping thriller. Plan on reading it twice: once because you won't be able to stop, and the second time to savor the razor's edge balance of plot and poetry that only Rachel Howzell Hall can pull off."

—Jess Lourey, Amazon Charts bestselling author of
Unspeakable Things

"The brilliant Rachel Howzell Hall becomes the queen of mind games with this twisty and thought-provoking cat-and-mouse thriller. Where memories are weaponized, keepsakes are deadly, and the past gets ugly when you disturb it. As original, compelling, and sinister as a story can be, with a message that will haunt you long after you race through the pages."

—Hank Phillippi Ryan, *USA Today* bestselling author of
Her Perfect Life

PRAISE FOR *AND NOW SHE'S GONE*

"It's a feat to keep high humor and crushing sorrow in plausible equilibrium in a mystery novel, and few writers are as adept at it as Rachel Howzell Hall."

—*Washington Post*

"One of the best books of the year . . . whip-smart and emotionally deep, *And Now She's Gone* is a deceptively straightforward mystery, blending a fledgling PI's first 'woman is missing' case with underlying stories about racial identity, domestic abuse, and rank evil."

—*Los Angeles Times*

"Smart, razor-sharp . . . Full of wry, dark humor, this nuanced tale of two extraordinary women is un-put-downable."

—*Publishers Weekly* (starred review)

"Smart, packed with dialogue that sings on the page, Hall's novel turns the tables on our expectations at every turn, bringing us closer to truth than if it were forced on us in school."

—Walter Mosley

"A fierce PI running from her own dark past chases a missing woman around buzzy LA. Breathlessly suspenseful, as glamorous as the city itself, *And Now She's Gone* should be at the top of your must-read list."
—Michele Campbell, bestselling author of *A Stranger on the Beach*

"One of crime fiction's leading writers at her very best. The final twist will make you want to immediately turn back to page one and read it all over again. *And Now She's Gone* is a perfect blend of PI novel and psychological suspense that will have readers wanting more."
—Kellye Garrett, Anthony, Agatha, and Lefty Award–winning author of *Hollywood Homicide* and *Hollywood Ending*

"Sharp, witty, and perfectly paced, *And Now She's Gone* is one hell of a read!"

—Wendy Walker, bestselling author of *The Night Before*

"Hall once again proves to be an accomplished maestro who has composed a symphony of increasing tension and near-unbearable suspense. Rachel brilliantly reveals the bone and soul of our shared humanity and the struggle to contain the nightmares of human faults and failings. I am a fan, pure and simple."
—Stephen Mack Jones, award-winning author of the August Snow thrillers

"Heartfelt and gripping . . . I'm a perennial member of the Rachel Howzell Hall fan club, and her latest is a winning display of her wit and compassion and mastery of suspense."
—Steph Cha, award-winning author of *Your House Will Pay*

"An entertainingly twisty plot, a rich and layered sense of place, and most of all a main character who pops off the page. Gray Sykes is hugely engaging and deeply complex, a descendant of Philip Marlowe and Easy Rawlins who is also definitely, absolutely her own woman."
—Lou Berney, award-winning author of *November Road*

"A deeply human protagonist, an intricate and twisty plot, and sentences that make me swoon with jealousy . . . Rachel Howzell Hall will flip every expectation you have—this is a magic trick of a book."
—Rob Hart, author of *The Warehouse*

"*And Now She's Gone* has all the mystery of a classic whodunit, with an undeniably fresh and clever voice. Hall exemplifies the best of the modern PI novel."
—Alafair Burke, *New York Times* bestselling author

Praise for *They All Fall Down*

"A riotous and wild ride."
—Attica Locke

"Dramatic, thrilling, and even compulsive."
—James Patterson

"An intense, feverish novel with riveting plot twists."
—Sara Paretsky

"Hall is beyond able and ready to take her place among the ranks of contemporary crime fiction's best and brightest."
—*Strand Magazine*

WHAT
FIRE
BRINGS

OTHER TITLES BY RACHEL HOWZELL HALL

WHAT FIRE BRINGS

A THRILLER

RACHEL HOWZELL HALL

 THOMAS & MERCER

Published by Thomas & Mercer, Seattle

www.apub.com

Amazon, the Amazon logo, and Thomas & Mercer are trademarks of Amazon.com, Inc., or its affiliates.

ISBN-13: 9781662504174 (hardcover)
ISBN-13: 9781662504167 (paperback)
ISBN-13: 9781662504181 (digital)

Cover design by Caroline Teagle Johnson
Cover images: © Anton Watman / Shutterstock; © Magdalena Wasiczek / Arcangel; © Beth Rooney / Getty Images

Printed in the United States of America
First edition

For Jessica and Clarence. This one was hard.
Thank you.

I can't go back to yesterday—because I was a different person then.

—*Lewis Carroll*

FORGET ABOUT ME

1.

Some things are unknowable.

I blink and—

Stop!

—slam my foot on the car's brake pedal. The Volvo skids to a stop on the side of the road. My heart booms as I try to catch my breath.

What . . .

Not paying attention on a twisty road while listening to this podcast about . . .

What . . . ?

I jab the stereo's power button, dropping the cabin into silence. Since I'm stopped, I close my eyes. Force my pulse to slow. Force my hands to unclench the steering wheel and for my lungs to take deep—

A knock on my driver's-side car window.

I yelp, jerking away as far as I can.

An old Black man is stooped outside the car, his knuckles still resting against my window. "Hey, you okay in there, young lady?" he asks, concern and sweat bright against his grizzled face. He wears a black baseball cap and a black satin jacket. A writing pen is clipped to his shirt pocket, and his gold tin badge—Russell Walker–Privatas Security Patrol—should also say "Marshal–Dodge City," that's how fake it looks.

"I saw you swerving just now," Russell Walker says. "You're lucky you didn't go flying off this mountain."

I gape at him, my mind still revving.

"You okay in there, young lady?" he asks again.

Am *I okay in here?*

I'm breathing so . . . *I guess?*

My purse sits on the passenger seat. My phone sits in the cup holder. There's gas in the gas tank. So . . . *yeah?* An envelope addressed to Bailey Meadows sits atop my purse along with a postcard-size invitation:

JOIN US

Emerging Writers Reception

May 12, 2021, 5:00 pm

61147 Old Topanga Canyon Road

Topanga, CA 90290

RSVP to Margo Dunn

Masks Required

I force myself to smile at Russell Walker–Security Guard, and through the small crack in the window, I shout, "I'm okay. All good, Mr. Walker."

Beyond the old man, there's chaparral and old thick trees and hill-sides covered with more chaparral and old thick trees. To my left, there are orange skies and the sun sinking behind a hill already lost in shadow. In front of me, there's a battered Wagoneer with a PRIVATAS SECURITY PATROL sticker on its rear and a bar of orange lights on its roof. Those orange lights are now swirling.

Swirling lights signal danger.

I want to write all of this down, capture it in the here and now because Topanga Canyon is a mystery to me—I've never visited this part of the county before today. It's too far from my home in South Los Angeles—thirty-nine miles—for a casual visit. This road carved through the Santa Monica Mountains is too twisty for a casual drive. A population of eight thousand people lives nestled around these parts. I roll down my car window and smell sage, wood, wildflowers. That sky, colored blue-orange-yellow—

"Where you trying to reach?" Russell Walker asks.

"Umm . . . I don't . . ." I swipe through my head for the address, then nervous-laugh. "Let me look . . ." I peek at the invitation and then peek at the directions on my phone now dangling from its charger between the cup holder and my knee. "I'm trying to reach . . . 61147 Old Topanga Canyon Road."

Some things are unknowable.

And you'll never know enough, even if you know everything.

Why am I thinking about the unknowable—

"Oh, I know *exactly* where you're going," the old man says, his head bobbing. "You're going to the Beckham place, ain't you?"

I swallow—my throat feels lined with sandpaper. "Yes. That's right." I grab my phone to confirm that, yes, I missed a right turn off this main road. There's a text message banner still sitting at the top of the phone's screen:

Some things are unknowable.

Ah. My eyes had left the road for just a second to read that text, and just like that . . .

"People always pass these turnoffs," Russell Walker–Security Guard says now. He chuckles, then adds, "Happens all the time if you ain't used to it. You from the city part of LA, ain't you?"

I nod. "Yes, sir."

"Uh-huh. It's gonna take you a while to get used to how they do things up here, then. The Beckhams' driveway is almost hidden. Like everybody up here, the family likes their privacy. Margo shoulda told you to slow down once you passed that first turnoff with all them trash bins."

"She may have," I say. "She probably did, and I still missed it." And now, that sandpaper sensation travels from my throat and up to my mind, *scratch-scratch-scratch.*

"But now, you got me, young lady," Russell Walker says, "and I'm not gonna let you wander 'round here for too long, heh-heh. They don't like it when Black folks wander up around here for too long."

Up around here. Down around there. No one likes Black folks wandering around too long.

The old man's gaze now pecks at my outfit. "Look at you!"

White floral-printed top, matching white floral-printed skirt, a mustard-colored trench coat.

Nice but not expensive. It's giving . . . writer with a day job but on a budget. The bold-colored coat stands out. Flair.

Cosplay.

Russell Walker gives a slight nod, father-proud. "You look real classy. Like you belong up here. Like ladies dressed back in *my* day. Some of them guests down there at the house are wearing jeans and those"—he waggles his fingers—"ancient-times sandals. You know, them Jesus sandals. At a cocktail party, can you believe it?"

I say, "Ridiculous."

But good to know that I'm passing, that he thinks that I belong up here.

The old man sucks his teeth. "We'd *never* be invited to a fancy party ever again, showing up in some Jesus sandals."

"Right?"

"But they do things different up here," he says, scratching his temple.

Privacy like this—can't see a driveway from this road, can't see a house from this road, trees hiding everything—is a luxury. Things, *people*, disappear in forests like this, disappear and no one would ever know, or even figure out where to start looking.

That's why I'm here. To continue looking for a disappeared woman, this time, in the forest north of Hollywood—and at the same time, moving one step closer to completing six thousand hours to become a licensed investigator in the state of California.

"If you're ready to roll," Russell Walker says, "just follow me back down the hill. I'll lead you to the driveway, so you won't miss it again. Heh, don't want you swerving off into the canyon, heh." The old man tips his baseball hat, then strides, Fred Sanford–style, back to the Wagoneer. He climbs behind the steering wheel and takes a moment to fasten his seat belt.

As I wait for him to lead me to my destination, the cell phone vibrates in my hand.

An email from avery.turner@gmail.com to bailey.meadows93@gmail.com.

I tap the notification.

> Deep breath in. Deep breath out.
>
> You're gonna be okay.
>
> You said you were ready for this, but I'm on the record. You know how I feel. But you've made it this far, which means that you're doing GREAT. You're a pro. I've never doubted that.
>
> So go to the reception and be as charming as you can be. Be as naive as an emerging writer would be in this environment—not so simple since you're not an emerging ANYTHING. But in this case, TRY YOUR BEST.
>
> I don't have to say it, but I will: All things (including our communications) must remain confidential.
>
> You are a writer working on your first novel, title: 39 Miles. We've gone over the synopsis sixty times, so you're good to go. The application and cover letter

are in your purse (Yes, you memorized all this, too, but it's always good to have a backup). CAPTURE THE FACTS IN YOUR JOURNAL. Dates, timelines, events, people. This is very important. (Again, you know these things—just going on record. You always say that I'm extra. I call that being thorough.) The smallest misstep could destroy all the progress we've made.

It won't look odd, you scribbling things down. I hear writers like journals. Give me an old-school steno pad any day.

Don't forget to use the pen—it records video and audio. Just double-click the top and it will start doing its thing. I know that you like Bics, but Bics can't record video and audio. Adjust and enjoy this new tech. You'll fall in love with it just like I did!

And to answer your question: Yes, California is still a two-person-consent state when it comes to record-ing devices. But there are exceptions, including pos-sible criminal activity. So, we're good.

Also remember to take a few personal items—tooth-brush, hairbrush, anything that would have DNA. Be sure to drop anything you take into a paper bag to preserve it!

REMEMBER THE ULTIMATE GOAL: FINDING SAM!

This leg may not be the final one of the journey, but it will get us closer. Learn as much as you can.

Little things may be important—little things actually turn out to be the answer to an impossible question. Don't make shit up for drama's sake. You're not there to force situations. Just let whatever happens happen.

To make sure all is well, I will sometimes text you a phrase that only you know the response to. It is vital that you respond. I wish that panic button was more reliable, but the mountains screw up its connectivity. So DON'T PANIC. ALSO: DON'T RELY ON TECHNOLOGY.

More about that: Wi-Fi and cell phone reception are unreliable up there in Topanga. From what I've been told, reception's always been shitty, but it's extra-crunchy shitty now and won't get better any time soon. So again I say: DON'T RELY ON WI-FI OR CELLULAR SERVICE!

Finally: Remember that you are not alone. I'm here for you. We all are. You've done this before, and I know that you can do it again. I'm so proud of—

The Wagoneer's horn toots—Russell has now pulled across from me, his vehicle headed in the opposite direction. He points to the road behind him. "Just do a U-turn up there—should be enough space."

I shout, "Thank you," then drop my phone back into the cup holder. I look in my purse and find the black writing pen. *Don't rely on technology.* But until that technology fails, though . . . I double-click the top of the pen. A small blue light above the clip brightens—it's ready to record.

I turn the stereo on again and plug my phone back into the car's charger. The podcast auto-starts, picking up where it left off. The female host drones on about the biggest lottery fraud in US history. Her voice must have lulled me into that liminal space that makes you zone out, makes you auto-drive, makes you forget why you entered a room, distracts you as you drive twisty canyon roads.

I hate when that happens. I go all short breathed and sweaty, and my blood rushes through my veins and my head *boom-boom-booms*. I snap out of this trance only when someone taps my shoulder and says, "Miss?" Although now, younger people say, "Ma'am?" which is even more unsettling than being asked to move up a space in the grocery store.

I'm only forty years old.

When did I become a "ma'am"?

I missed *that* turn in the road, too.

Let's U-turn. I slip the pen back into my purse and put the car in drive. Once I pull forward to the crest of the hill, I pause, intentionally this time, to appreciate that view . . .

To the east, skyscrapers cluster against the mountains and sparkle like jewel-colored Jolly Ranchers and . . .

To the north, the valley lost in brown haze while car taillights and headlights shine red and white and . . .

To the west, the Pacific Ocean, now a gleaming thread of silver beneath the setting sun and . . .

All around me, the canyon, with all its greens and browns, rolls on and on . . .

I'm glad that I'm here. Not about the *circumstances* that *led* me here but because I'll have context, and I will know this space better, and I'll be gaining the experience I need, moving me from training into full-fledged PI. Almost driving off the cliff—the work of an amateur. Fortunately, Avery's not looking over my shoulder. No one has to know that I nearly *Thelma & Louise*'d into a canyon.

Down the road, that dusty white Wagoneer waits for me, its orange lights no longer swirling.

No more danger. All is well.

"Sorry," I shout, even though Russell Walker–Security Guard can't hear me.

I take a few pictures with my phone, and then I follow the security Wagoneer. I think about nothing else *except* following the security Wagoneer. Don't want my mind wandering again, don't want it pondering that text message . . .

Some things are unknowable.

Up ahead, Russell Walker–Security Guard drives the Wagoneer like we've been flooded by mud and molasses. His right wrist pokes through the top of the steering wheel like a bracelet while his left elbow pokes out the open window. He's comfortable driving on this twisty, two-lane highway.

Not me. I clench my jaw as tight as I clench the steering wheel. My knuckles would be white from holding on to it so tight, but they're as brown as the trunks of these canyon trees. My stomach is tight, then wobbly with worry. Sweat dampens my armpits.

You're gonna be okay.

You are not alone.

Such lovely assurances from Avery that aren't helping me in this moment, since I'm obviously alone and a little lost and now, trusting this old man to lead me back to where I was supposed to be. In this, I've already failed. What if I fail even more, like forgetting a detail or some random thing that will make someone figure me out and I'm busted and then what?

Don't panic.

Because there's no panic button.

The Wagoneer's red brake lights brighten, and the turn signal tells me he's turning left. But we're both waiting as an orange Saab coming from the opposite direction hangs a right into this hidden driveway.

Russell Walker–Security Guard makes the left turn.

I make the left turn.

The old man drives a short distance, then pulls to the side of the driveway. He sticks his hand out the window and waves for me to pass.

I stop beside him and roll down my right passenger window. "Thank you so much for finding me. I'd still be trying to figure it out."

He asks, "You strong enough to handle this?"

I smile. "The ancestors are with me."

"Yes, they are." He tips his baseball cap. "You have a good evening. Be safe, Miss Meadows."

My eyebrows dip. *Did I tell him my name?*

He's watching me now. "You better get goin' before they eat all them little meatballs." He points to the road ahead. "Just keep going, you won't miss it now." He pauses, then says, "Know that you ain't gotta do this. You can always turn back."

Are they gonna eat me down there? Burn a cross? *Burn a cross and then eat me?*

I give him a thumbs-up. "I'm good. Feeling brave. Thanks, again."

And now, I'm off. Creeping down this coarse gravel private drive-way like it's made of TNT and cracked glass, this coarse gravel private driveway flanked by trees that hide the sky, passing through shrouds of dirt made by the tires of that orange Saab.

Up ahead, a young man wearing a white dress shirt and a red vest waves a cone-shaped flashlight. As I slowly roll past him, he says, "Just park by the Saab."

The orange Saab is an obvious car against the rows of already-parked, dark-colored Beemers, Priuses, and Teslas.

I snap pictures of the cars with my phone. Don't know why but it seems like the right thing to do.

The driver of the Saab has ruffled brown hair and wears a rumpled checkered shirt, wrinkled chinos, and an ill-fitting brown corduroy jacket. "Untidy" is his thing.

I quickly park beside him and then check my own reflection in the mirror. "Untidy" is *not* my thing. "Elegant" is my thing. Glossed lips and a flat-ironed bob, bronzed cheeks on brown skin, smoky eyes, this white floral-printed silk set—*my gawd, dressed for the ages, yes, kween* and all that.

Not bad for a forty-year-old PI-in-training "ma'am."

I reach into my bag to grab my journal, but my fingers first touch something else.

Cold. Hard. Rigid.

Glock 9.

Breathless, I peek into my purse, and I stare at the gun like I've never seen it before. I sit there, unmoving, for hours it seems, until I gain courage to *respectfully* pluck the weapon from the bag. Then, I pull back on the Glock's slide to check the chamber—a round. The indicator on the side of the gun sticks out. *Loaded.* I push out a breath, set the gun back in the bag, and grab my journal. This little book is almost as dangerous as that gun. My last entry:

I'm trying to breathe naturally and not pass out. I'm about to walk into the lion's den. Once I'm there, I can't turn back. Avery keeps asking if I'm good, if I'm ready. I have to be.

I find the next clean page and use the recording pen to document all that's happened in the last ten minutes—from the missed driveway and meeting Russell Walker to appreciating that vista of Los Angeles and dealing with a wobbly stomach.

All caught up, I climb out of the Volvo and step onto the gravel path with my red purse, invitation, and cell phone in hand. I dry my sweaty hands on the trench coat. I'm kinda shaky standing in my red ankle-wrap sandals, but I manage to march in the same direction as

Untidy Man with my head held high and my eyes fixed on the bending road ahead of me.

Pay attention to everything.

At that bend, I cross over a small bridge that traverses a dry-bed creek.

Low plucks from a standing bass, muted toots of a trumpet, the wail of a saxophone, and the shushing of a brush against a snare drum. A jazz combo.

These are a few of my favorite things . . .

Then, another kind of music that isn't as rhythmic or as wonderfully confusing as jazz rolls over me: the conversations of people dressed in jeans, Jesus sandals, and maxi dresses, holding martini glasses or wineglasses, beer bottles or clear plastic cups filled with bubbly drinks. Masks either cover the lower halves of their faces, cup their chins, or dangle from their wrists. They roll their eyes or throw back their heads to laugh. Some stand at high tables, not laughing but staring or glaring. Masked servers in white tuxedo shirts move through the crowd with trays in their hands, offering guests triangle-shaped things or meat chop–shaped things or those little meatballs shiny with glaze.

I'm the only Black person here. Avery didn't mention that, but I'm not surprised to learn that there's no one here to give "the nod." No one to share an eye roll or a sigh. No one to team up with if the revolution begins, and this makes me just as lightheaded as swerving off the road and almost flying into the canyon. I automatically stand out—my bold-colored trench pushes me closer to being tied to that burning cross and a server's platter.

Be cool. You got this. Knowing how to manage unexpected events during surveillance? That's on the PI test. I'm one step ahead—standing out on a Wednesday evening in a fancy part of Los Angeles is not *entirely* unexpected.

Behind the guests, a large hacienda-inspired house rises two stories, its windows aglow like boozy eyes, its eaves hidden beneath twisty oaks and climbing bougainvillea.

So beautiful. So . . . *wow!*

I could see myself living here and relaxing in that swing tied to that oak branch and thinking king-size thoughts.

I could see myself eating here, enjoying a sandwich or a steak on the green lawn that overlooks the rolling canyon.

I could see myself *thriving* here in this house off Old Topanga Canyon Road.

But I'm not here to do any of this. I will *never* do any of this, at least not *here*.

Untidy Man has stopped at a black-draped check-in table filled with name tags, bottles of hand sanitizer, and boxes of disposable face masks. This table is managed by two young maskless women with dazzling eyes and blushing cheeks. Untidy Man says a few words to them that makes their blushes burn brighter. The blonde—her name tag says SAOIRSE—hands him a sticker, then says, "We're so happy you're here. Jack can relax now. Congratulations, again."

Untidy Man slaps the tag onto his jacket, then turns away from the table. He smiles at me—not a polite smile, but the smile of the expectant. *You should know me.*

My eyes dart to his name tag.

Skylar Orion.

No clue who you are, sir, but that's one helluva name.

I approach the check-in table.

The young women beam at me, then say, "Welcome," like they're twins.

The redhead's tag says PHOEBE, and she asks, "Name?"

I say, "Bailey Meadows."

Saoirse runs her fingers along the leftover name tags on the table.

Phoebe consults a printed spreadsheet and then taps an iPad.

Both hold their fingers to their lips as they check and recheck, as they shake their heads, then flip through the binders and envelope boxes.

Fuck. Did Avery forget to RSVP?

"Sorry," Phoebe says, "the Wi-Fi's . . ." She rolls her eyes and shakes her head.

"Technology," I say even though my breath hangs in my chest like a weight. I want to explain, but what would I say? No clue—my name not being on the list is a for-real unexpected event. No, I won't utter one word—let these lovely ladies figure it out.

So . . . what?

The jazz combo launches into this classic.

In the original band, Miles Davis played trumpet. John Coltrane played tenor sax. Bill Evans on piano. Paul Chambers on bass. Cannonball Adderley on alto sax. Jimmy Cobb on drums. My child-hood Sunday afternoons, this song *always* played as I folded clean laundry and listened to the clink of dinner dishes and the clicking of the gas burner turning on to warm the pot of lima beans. A portrait of my boring, uneventful life.

Like I did as a child, I focus on Paul Chambers's bass question—*ba dap ba dap ba dap bah*—and the horns' response—*soooo . . . what*—instead of thinking the worst: that I'll soon be denied entry into this fancy party with people named after constellations.

Phoebe goes, "Ooh! We have signal."

My cell phone vibrates—signal!

This is an automated notification to
keep you informed about STEALTHScribe
and our cloud capabilities—

I don't tap to read the rest of the message because Saoirse is now shifting from one foot to the other. She looks at me, her blue eyes glistening with dread, her thin lips even thinner. She hates the words she's about to say—and it's not about wonky reception.

Any person standing at the entrance to any party *anywhere*, especially in Los Angeles, hates to hear these words . . .

"I'm *so* sorry," Saoirse says in a tiny, injured kitten voice. "You're not on the list."

Swirling orange lights. Danger.

And for a moment my mind goes blank and then—

Margo!

I offer my printed-out invitation for the two check-in assistants to see that I'm not trying to crash this party, that I *belong* here. *Always bring receipts.* And now, I say, "I was told to ask for Margo."

Relief washes over the young women's faces, and they clutch their bright-pink necks and exhale, all *phew, that was close.* Saoirse grabs a walkie-talkie from the table and winks at me. "Give me a moment?" She steps away from us, toggles the button, then says, "Hey, Margo?"

Phoebe grins again at me. "Did you find it easy?"

I blink at her. Find *what* easy? "Oh, the drive?" I give her an itsy-bitsy shrug.

"Lemme guess. You missed the driveway," she says, smiling warmly.

"Guess I'm not the only person to do that?"

"Nope. Cute outfit, by the way," she says. "Love that yellow against your skin."

"Thank you." I move away from the table once a pale-faced man and woman wearing matching black slacks, black Gucci face masks, and turtlenecks come to check in.

Their names are on the list.

My heart jitterbugs in my chest. After pushing out a breath, I check the pen in my bag—the light is still blue, *still recording*—and then, I swipe over to Google on my phone. The last tab I opened was a research paper titled "Dissociative Fugue Symptoms in a 28-year-old Male Nigerian Medical Student: A Case Report."

A Nigerian medical student had been experiencing tremendous stress. He'd been studying one night, and two days later he discovered that he'd traveled to see his sibling in another part of Nigeria. The medical student didn't remember making this trip. He was diagnosed with dissociative fugue, a condition that causes people under great stress or experiencing trauma to lose their identity and impulsively wander away from home.

Just like Sam Morris had . . . maybe. And she wandered away from down there in Los Angeles to come up here. Possibly. Sam had sent Avery an email—Headed out! Wish me luck—and left her condo with a travel mug of coffee—just like any other day. And like the Nigerian student, she'd been stressed out—but then, she was almost always stressed out, and she *seemed* to be okay . . . until she failed to return to her condo at the end of the day . . . and then at the end of the week . . . month . . . What happened to Sam, and how did it happen? I've been researching and have come up with one theory: dissociative fugue.

My job: to move "possibly" into "definitely."

Knowing how to analyze critical facts to come up with conclusions that refute or support claims? *Definitely* on the test to become a private investigator.

You can do this. You got this. Focus. Breathe. You are Bailey Meadows, investigator-in-training, who will complete her six thousand hours of paid work over the next two years and will pass that two-hour exam—not even getting one wrong—and will earn her license—

People clap, interrupting my internal pep talk. The jazz combo falls silent as a woman with a silver shag haircut and wearing a purple wrap dress takes the stage. "Welcome—"

"Bailey?" Saoirse has returned, and she's still smiling. "Margo will be with you in just a second."

"Great," I say. "Thank you."

"Until then? Have a glass of wine. The meatballs? They're yummy. Like, I can't stop eating them."

Saoirse hasn't eaten a meatball since my arrival.

My phone buzzes.

A text message from AAT.

Avery!

SAM?

I tap back:

I don't see her

But you're okay now?

Yep just got here

Will catch you up later

My phone's background is a picture of me, my arm around the thin shoulders of my mother attached to a mobile oxygen tank, still smiling even as sick as she is. She's wearing a purple Lakers championship T-shirt that nearly swallows her. Smoky-lavender Barbra Streisand rosebushes grow behind us—those roses her pride and joy, other than me. Our house is redbrick with two stories and needs a new coat of paint on the eaves and window frames. She knows that I'm searching for Sam—but she doesn't know that I've gone deep undercover to do that.

Initially, I'd been assigned a typical cheating-husband case—follow, take pictures, watch the client cry and cuss—but then, when Sam sent that final email . . .

After waiting a few weeks for her return—and not hearing back—Avery reached out to Sam. No answer. I hadn't worked a missing person case yet, and so Avery tossed me this one. Then, I emailed and followed up with calls to the few phone numbers that we had for Sam.

The number you have dialed has been changed or disconnected.

Since November, we've searched for Sam up and down the state of California. Six months have passed, and now, I'm here, in Topanga Canyon, posing as an emerging writer looking for answers this way because the traditional method—asking sketchy people questions and getting sketchy answers in return—hasn't yielded any useful answers. Not surprising. The person asking determines the truthiness of the asked.

Untidy Man bounds up to the stage. He futzes with his glasses, pacing as he then futzes with a paperback novel.

Someone shouts, "Woo-hoo," and the crowd laughs, except for the pale-faced couple in the matching beatnik costumes.

Untidy Man—oh, right, his name is Skylar Orion—leans closer to the mic stand and says, "I'll be reading from my debut thriller, *Catch*."

Another "Woo-hoo," and a smattering of claps.

"Jasmine held her breath," Skylar Orion reads, *"as she opened the back door. Her blonde locks were matted to her forehead and her shirt clung to her skin, beads of sweat dripping down into her eyes, stinging them. The dark clothing of the night wrapped around her like a cloak of the dead, and she was swallowed by it."*

A hand touches my elbow.

Startled, I spin around.

"Bailey?" The woman has a tanned, heart-shaped face and wild strawberry-blonde curls. Her neck and cleavage are covered with an explosion of freckles. She smells of tangerines and cigarettes. "I'm Margo Dunn. So happy to finally meet you."

I grin at her. "Pleasure to finally meet you, too!"

She holds out her elbow. "Since, technically, we shouldn't be hugging even though we're outside. COVID-19 hasn't left us yet, right?"

"No, it hasn't." I bump my elbow against hers. "New variant, too. Spreading like wildfire."

"The application process for this residency was already bonkers," Margo says, rolling her eyes, "but with a pandemic, it just got—" She gives me a raspberry and goofy eyes. "You're here, though. Finally!"

I grin. "Finally!"

"As you can see, we're having this outside," Margo says. "We don't want people calling this a super-spreader event. We spread joy through *art*. Good books are the only contagious thing here. And Jack gives all the ladies a different *kind* of fever. Ha!"

Onstage, Skylar Orion continues to read. *"Jasmine's ears filled with the sounds of jangling keys and the crunching of gravel beneath the tires of the walkers' feet. Her heart jumped into her throat."*

"Can I get you a glass of wine?" Margo asks. "Some sparkling water?"

"Umm . . ."

Margo plucks two glasses of rosé from the tray of a passing server, then offers me one. "Your 'umm' sounded like 'yum.' So 'yay for rosé'!"

I take the wineglass and clink it against Margo's. "Yay!"

"Let's walk," she says.

We slink toward a garden away from the stage and the guests. Here, the air is warm, but the breeze is cold. There are enormous plants with broad, thick leaves, and trees that are large and old, their dark branches grabbing at the sky while their roots hold the earth back, freshly turned earth that smells of flowers and sage and horses. There is quiet here along with birdsong, rustling leaves, the crash of falling fruit or acorns or whatever grows on these trees and their high branches.

A lacewing with golden eyes and luminous green wings rests on Margo's shoulder. "Do they really make noises with their abdomens?" I ask, peering at the insect. My hands and mind are tingling to know, and I resist reaching for my phone to find the answer.

"Do *who* make noises?" Margo asks, her voice forcing the lacewing to flee. "I was *saying* that when there's no *event*, the Beckham estate is one of the most peaceful places in LA County. Which is perfect for what you're here for."

Find out what happened to Sam.

Margo settles on a wood bench.

I perch beside her.

"OMG, Bailey, your résumé and your sample," she says, shaking her head. "During the review process, we were *so* impressed with your awards and with your writing. As you know, this writers-in-residence program is committed to helping marginalized and traditionally underrepresented groups break into the publishing industry in an Olympian way. A *meaningful* way."

I sip my wine, then say, "Right. Beyond the typical performative gestures."

"We weren't familiar with some of the organizations that awarded you. Probably because we're *genre* people." She snorts. "And now, *you* will be *genre people*, too. Welcome!"

"Excited to be here," I say.

Margo continues. "Your biography and statement of purpose, ohmigod, girl. You're *perfect*. That's why we want to modify the offer."

I blink at her. "To what?"

"How would you like . . . *a cowriter credit?*" Her eyes sparkle and her nose wriggles like a bunny's. "Of course, you'd be compensated, and like the earlier offer, room and board are still covered. But with this opportunity, your career would move you from 'emerging' to 'established' overnight. He's really committed to being an ally—and he's done this before, working with emerging writers on stories, using his platform to introduce new novelists to his fan base. Patterson does it. Clancy does it, too . . . well, Clancy's no longer with us, but his *brand* lives on. Really: Can't you see it? Your name beneath Jack's—of course, it can't be *above* Jack's. He *is* the *New York Times* bestselling author here."

I chuckle. "Of course."

"And then, when it's time to pitch *your* book, you'll have this publication and experience and a champion in Jack Beckham."

Margo taps my knee. "Sounds like a lot, I know. But you can handle it. It will be a helluva first novel for you, right? It would *totally* legitimize you." She stands from the bench. "Want to see more of the property?"

I drain my glass. "I'd love to."

2.

Holding my breath, I follow Margo to a sunroom, restlessness working through me like those vines and tree branches reaching for the sky. On the other side of the windowpanes, I glimpse light-colored wood floors and cream furniture, a floor lamp shaped like a chrysalis, and my reflection in a hexagon-shaped mirror.

Margo hooks her arm through mine, forgetting that we're supposed to be only touching via elbow. "So, were you to say yes to my newest offer, you'll be responsible for planning the novel once Jack gives you the overall plot. You'll help in drafting, transcribing, editing, providing sensitivity reads . . . this is a total collaboration between you and Jack. Like I said: bestselling authors like him are doing this more and more."

She sips from her glass of wine. "Your writing extension instructor, Avery, couldn't stop *raving* about you, and telling me just how *splendid* you are. Oh my gosh, girl, speech writing for the mayor and president of *Stanford*? Prose editor at that small press—can't remember the name cuz it's tiny but impressive. Contributor to that magazine and that other magazine. Avery sent us a few tear sheets to ooh and aah over. I'm so glad that she recommended you."

She leans closer to me and whispers, "It helps that you aren't problematic on social media. Didn't see one antisemitic, homophobic, or flat-earther comment on any of your posts. Jack can't be associated with that, know what I mean?"

"Totally," I say, nodding. "My social media presence is far from offensive."

Especially since my profiles are all fake, created for this project. Some stuff is made up—my interest in bowling and *WRITUALS*, that literary magazine that I edited. Some posts are real and were taken from my digital photo album. Eating ice cream. Standing at the rim of the Grand Canyon, arms spread. Yoga pose in the waves of the Pacific.

Avery *did* warn me that some last-minute details of my experience had been exaggerated. Up until I'd accepted this glass of blush wine from Margo, I didn't know that I wrote speeches for the mayor. Of what city? Los Angeles? Palo Alto? No clue. Hopefully Avery didn't tell them that I swam the English Channel last year because . . .

You belong there. Believe that and everyone else will. Hope she's right. If not, I'll be back to following cheating husbands to hot-sheets motels.

"Now, *this* is my favorite place on the estate," Margo says.

We approach a patio on the north side of the house. The sky has softened to violet, the hills and trees and more trees glow in this lavender tinge. Really: my anxiety and worry melt away, and a peace that I haven't felt in *months* washes over me, and I want to bask on this lawn and drink more of this blush wine and grab a platter filled with meatballs and . . . and . . . *be a writer.*

As she leads me into the house, Margo natters on about the other applications she received—*he didn't spell my name right . . . she called me "Dear sirs" . . . stories from some MFA writers are so predictable.* Here, the light-wood floors are spotless white oak. Good art not found in IKEA, even as prints, hangs on the walls. The scents of garlic, butter, and sugar are the scents of heaven in any belief system—and that's what it smells like now in this house. All the cooks and servers wear black masks, goggles, and black gloves as they plate food, fill plastic glasses with different-colored liquids, and dust powdered sugar over pastries.

"Don't worry," Margo says. "Everyone working gets COVID-19 testing every day."

With her arm still hooked through mine, Margo leads me down a long hallway. "We just started hosting events again—tonight is the first. Skylar is an alum of the residency program, and he just published his first novel, and we couldn't let that pass without a small celebration, pandemic or no."

We enter a library with floor-to-ceiling bookcases that smells of potpourri and old ladies' minty purses. The shelves are so tall and so wide that sliding ladders have been installed to reach the top ledges.

"According to Avery," Margo says, "you are a true-crime fanatic."

"Absolutely," I say, gaping at the books around me. "I find crime—the reasons why people do what they do—fascinating." The most authentic bundle of words I've spoken tonight.

"Well, remember," Margo says. "You aren't writing true crime *here*. You're making shit up. Not that there's not a smidgen of truth in fiction. But we're here, first and foremost, to entertain."

I nod. "Oh, yeah. Totally."

"What's your favorite true-crime podcast?" Margo's eyes pull at me.

Is this a test? My hands shake and I clear my throat. "I'm listening to one in the car right now. Can't remember the name. It takes place somewhere around here—"

"Here in Topanga? Or down in Laurel Canyon? Runyon Canyon? Benedict Canyon?"

"Possibly." I squeeze my eyes shut. *Crap.* I wrote it down six times to imprint on my brain. I was just listening to it in the car. Fraud . . . and . . . and . . .

Margo inspects her fingernails. "Probably Laurel Canyon. People are *always* dumping bodies around Laurel Canyon. I mean . . . you have the Manson murders. Then, there was the Hillside Strangler. Nothing but artsy-fartsy types and wildfires here in Topanga. No bodies. *But!*"

She squeezes my arm. "You like true crime and that's all that matters. While the book you'll be working on is fiction, Jack tries to be very honest in his depictions of the victims, the investigation, all of that. We honor truth in this residency. And authenticity. Being from a marginalized community, you know firsthand the effects of crime. You have a story that needs to be told, Bailey, and I'd be lying if I didn't say that Jack needs you more than you need him."

I snap my fingers. "I remember it now. *Criminal.*"

She gasps. "That's one of my favorites, too."

I ease out of Margo's grasp, then wander to the closest bookcase. The shelves are filled with hardcover and paperback novels written by J. D. Beckham.

"That's Big Jack, his father." Margo spreads her arms. "Fifty novels. If you ever watched TV in the nineties and early aughts, you know Big Jack's work. He was the Boy Wonder back then. Published his first novel in 1985, when he was twenty-one. Instant bestseller."

City of Exile was adapted for screen *twice.*

Shot of Fear was made for TV and won a bunch of Emmys.

Hidden Alley, adapted as a nighttime soapy crime drama, starred that woman from *Falcon Crest.*

Into the Mirage won an Edgar, an Anthony, book awards from newspapers, and a spot on a few US presidents' summer reading lists.

"Big Jack's books have sold more than four hundred million copies," Margo recites, "and have been translated into more than fifteen languages. He was awarded a lifetime achievement award by the National Endowment for the Humanities."

I say, "Incredible," and that's the truth. Also the truth: Big Jack Beckham was a sometimes-violent, hypermasculine, self-destructive narcissist whose personality inspired the creation of every villain in his novels . . . as well as villains in novels written by other authors. "Stubborn drunk" was a compliment compared to the other on-the-nose insults whispered about him.

Margo runs her fingers along the spines of Jack Beckham thrillers. "Though Jack Junior is no slouch. He was published first in 2010 when he was twenty-seven years old. So *not* a Boy Wonder like his dad, even though he looked like a baby. All Beckham men look stupidly young. I think they've hidden a mirror in the attic and drink from a fountain of youth in the cellar. I hate them. *Ha!* Anyway, Jack's written *ten* novels, six of which were adapted to film and television."

Pales beside his father's fifty, though. But then, I haven't heard any rumors about Jack Junior being a narcissistic alcoholic.

Margo pulls a hardcover novel from the shelf and hands it to me. "Your first assignment: read this if you haven't."

Old Topanga Road.

The cover art is a washed-out, bloody photograph of twisty blacktop that disappears into a blind curve of chaparral-covered hillsides.

"You and Jack will write the . . . it's not really a *sequel* but more . . ." Margo wrinkles her nose. "*On the story vine.* I'm a manager, not a writer, can't you tell?"

I open to the front flap with the novel's description.

After two separate car crashes, two years apart, two women wander the canyons of Topanga in a daze before stumbling to the home of a once-famous, now-reclusive writer. One woman wants to remember. One woman wants to forget. Both women are separated by time but are together as they run from their lives—and soon, run for their lives, forever changed. Because now, they will soon stumble into the crosshairs of the Hiker, the monster lurking in the forest that surrounds a town known for peace, love, and—

"Awesome story, right?" Margo has those sparkler eyes and that bunny nose again.

"Definitely." I hold the book to my chest.

Margo claps. "Let's go get your things. You'll be in the cottage out back. It's the cutest spot in the world. Like I explained in the acceptance letter: Topanga isn't the easiest drive—you probably noticed that, huh? And the Wi-Fi and all that . . . apologies up front. People keep complaining about it, but nothing will be done. Also, there aren't hotels or inns up here. The good people of Topanga don't mind *that.*"

She waits a beat, then adds, "*Everyone* thinks that Inn at the Seventh Ray is a true inn. Nope. It's a restaurant. Anyway, we don't want you wasting any time on the 405. Use that time for writing and exploring."

"You must be Bailey." A man's voice bounces from behind me—he sounds like whiskey-laced molten lava cake.

I look over my shoulder to see the face that belongs to that voice. He's tall, lean, and blond with sparkling gray eyes. His suit is sleek in that "Italian soccer coach" way, and the white shirt's cuffs are stiffer than a priest's collar. Unlike Untidy Man, not one wrinkle exists anywhere on this guy. No crow's-feet. No laugh lines. No forehead creases.

Bro-tox?

Probably. His face . . . it's kinda freaky in its marble-like smoothness.

He holds out his hand—no ragged cuticles. "I'm Jack," he says with a firm pump of my hand.

I force myself to stop staring at his skin and take his hand. "Hi, yes. I'm Bailey."

"Tell me, Bailey," he says, "and be honest. I bet that whatever you were doing last Wednesday wasn't as thrilling as what you're about to do in the next several weeks. Am I right?"

I squint at the man towering over me. "*Actually*, I was . . . rappelling off the north face of Mount Rainier last Wednesday."

He watches me, then Cheshire cat grins.

I hold my serious face. "No. Really."

"Oh." He blushes, then eyes Margo.

Margo blushes.

I finally relax into a smile. "Okay, so it wasn't Mount Rainier. It was Everest, but I didn't want to brag." I laugh.

He laughs.

We laugh together.

I have questions to ask. Can't come off as Angry Black Woman. I need them both to trust me, not see me as a threat.

I dip my head and say, "I don't remember *what* I was doing last Wednesday, but you're probably right: it *wasn't* as thrilling as this."

Jack takes my hand again. "You were meant to be here. No worries, okay? I got you." He squeezes my hand, and his touch feels warm and familiar.

"Tell me about the novel you're writing," Jack says.

My face warms as I clear my throat. Avery said that I was smart and that I was fast, and Margo has no doubts that I'm splendid and that I'm authentic, so I must be splendidly smart and authentically fast . . . starting right now.

He notices my silence and smiles. "No need to be embarrassed. We're all on the same team here."

I push out a breath. "It's titled *39 Miles*, and it's about a woman who disappears in the Santa Monica Mountains. The police aren't helping to find her, so her sister starts her own investigation. Her search takes her to a place she's never been. A place that's just thirty-nine miles away from where they grew up." I jam my lips together and hold my breath.

Jack grins and nods. "I like it. The title?" He waggles his hand. "But that's nothing. You're in the right place. Don't know if you know but . . ." He whispers, "I have a little experience in this area. Only ten books. Instant bestsellers. And I have a few connections to important people in publishing *and* in Hollywood. Not that I'm bragging."

Margo snickers. "He's bragging, *ha!*"

I squeeze my hands. "I'm terrified if I'm being totally honest. I came here to become a writer—"

"Become?" Jack's eyebrows lift. "Are you writing now?"

"Yes, but it's not—"

"Then, you *are* a writer. And we all worry, Bailey. Worrying never, ever goes away."

Margo scrunches her nose. "Jack is a master worrier."

He chuckles. "Skylar Orion? The guy who read tonight? He worried, too. But then, I helped him land his first agent, and I got him a bigger advance. Seven figures. And I want that for you, too. Your book will be *fire*, I already know."

31

Except I'm not writing a book . . . *yet*. I'm searching for a colleague of Avery's, a partner of the agency, who *did* disappear, possibly in or near this forest.

Last summer, Sam came to Topanga Canyon to search for her mother, who'd gone missing years ago. She was seen wandering the trails near this estate—and may have bumped into Jack Beckham.

Before being assigned this case, I didn't really *know* Sam, and I didn't know she'd disappeared until Avery told me. That's mostly because Sam and I were primarily social media friends. Like a post here. Leave a comment there. Avery would promise to have us meet face-to-face—*What about this weekend?*—but we never connected because life happens. And now, I'm here, looking for someone I know but have never met.

"It's true," Jack is saying now. "It's a lot of pressure and all this is so new to you. You can handle it, Bailey. And never think that you're the only writer who's ever doubted themselves. *Everyone* experiences impostor syndrome."

I nod and smile and nod some more.

Little does he know . . . I *am* an impostor.

3.

Now that they're hopped up on crime fiction, french apple cake, and Aperol spritzes, guests leave the Beckham estate with a signed copy of Skylar Orion's debut thriller, *Catch*, and cellophane-wrapped shortbread cookies that bear the book's cover. The wheels of departing cars crunch against the gravel, and taillights bob in the dark like chupacabras, rolling threats to the city south of this canyon.

A few stragglers inspect me with daggers in their eyes. They'd kill to stay behind, to hold a narrow glass of chocolate liqueur in their hands just like I'm doing *right now*.

One woman with squirrel's-nest hair even whispers to me, "You're so lucky. I've applied twice to this residency, and he's *never* chosen me. All this DEI shit, no offense. If you want my advice—"

"Please," I say, blinking at her, "give me advice that I don't plan to follow."

Squirrel's Nest snorts. "That was bad Edna St. Vincent Millay. The quote is actually, 'Please give me some good advice in your next letter. I—'"

"Yeah, okay." I swivel away from Squirrel's Nest and munch on the last portion of my book-cookie—yeah, I'm supposed to be nice and agreeable, but "DEI shit"? Fuck this lady.

A chilly breeze sweeps through the canyon, and as I tromp back to my car, my breath puffs in clouds. I wince—all this tromping and wandering has made my right side and lower back hurt. A hot shower, a glass of tawny port, and another slice of french apple cake—in my very own cottage, even better—sounds like the perfect ending to this weird evening.

"Bailey," Margo shouts from the three-car garage, "just park over here."

I throw her a thumbs-up, then pop the trunk of my Volvo. I've brought along an overnight tote and a large suitcase. I unzip the tote and dig through its contents to search for a pair of flip-flops.

Computer . . . cosmetics bag . . . files . . .

"Margo tell you that you can park in the garage?" Jack says, cruising toward me.

I quickly zip up the tote and close the trunk. "Yes, she did, and I'm about to move my car right now."

He grins at me, then knocks on the trunk. "I'll help you with those."

I hurry to the driver's seat. "Yes! But let me move the car first. Don't want you carrying heavy bags farther than you need."

I'm behind the Volvo's steering wheel again. My heart vibrates so hard that it can power the car, and it pounds in my chest louder than the crunch of the car's tires against the gravel. The thudding ache in my lower back draws tears to my eyes, and the garage looks wet and wavy as I slip into a space between a maroon Honda Civic and a gray Porsche.

The gun in my purse is the ugly part of this job, and I'm not sure if it's required, but I've had some weapons training—not that I'm certain guns will be on the investigator's license test. The gun reminds me that I'm actually working on foreign soil, trying to figure out what went on here—and how it may relate to Sam's disappearance. Will I use this gun? I hope not, but if I must—last resort and cornered, my life threatened, unable to escape otherwise—I will.

In this hot-white garage light, I notice the red posies on my skirt set—but the red posies between the blue lilies and green mums aren't posies at all. Those posies are . . .

Splotches of blood.

My blood.

Another reminder that this is real, that I can get hurt again if I'm not careful.

Margo knocks on the Volvo's passenger window, giddy as a kid in the parking lot at Disneyland, *C'mon, Mom* energy. Jack knocks on the trunk of my Volvo, ready to grab my bags.

I try to swallow my anxiety, but it sticks in my throat like the largest fish bone. My hands shake as I pluck the trunk-release button, then open the car door. I drop my car keys into my bag, force myself to smile, then climb out of the car.

Will Jack or Margo notice that my red posies aren't posies at all?

Will they ask me what happened?

They may not even notice—the shade of the dried red blood matches the shade of the posies. And there's not enough blood anyway to alarm anyone or draw attention.

Margo hooks her arm through mine.

I wince as my side—the source of the now-dried blood—screams from her jostling.

"So," she says, "Jack and I were talking about schedules and next steps."

"I want you to do some reading for the next few days," Jack says, his hands loaded down with my things. "*Old Topanga Road* first. Then, there's the local newspaper, *Topanga New Times*. A couple of articles and interviews I wrote and were written about me—you should read those, too. None of this is me ego-tripping, okay? It's just so you get my voice, understand the environment. We'll take a few field trips around Topanga—the markets, the parks, the fire station. Then, on Sunday, we'll start on the outline. I'm a plotter, not a pantser."

A what, not a who?

"I'm a list maker and box checker," I share. "Digital and paper. I have to write things down over and over again, like how kids had to write standards on a chalkboard? That's the only way things stick in my brain." True.

Margo gasps and pulls me closer. "Me too!"

Pain flares in my side again, and I bite the inside of my cheek, stifling my wince with a chuckle.

"I am *addicted* to the FranklinCovey system," Margo continues, breathless. "All the little spaces and tabs and—"

"Okay, Margo, we know, we know." Jack playfully rolls his eyes, then returns his attention to me. "Bailey, I want you to succeed, and to succeed, you need to know this place so that you can convincingly *write* about this place."

"Makes sense," I say.

"Where are you from?" he asks. "Apologies if you've already told me this."

"South LA," I say. "The Baldwin Hills area." Also true.

Jack nods. "I know that part of town. Beautiful houses, beautiful views." He turns to Margo. "Historically Black neighborhoods in that area. Ladera Heights, View Park . . ."

Margo says, "Ah. Got it."

"After the uprisings in '92," Jack says, "I actually went down to the Crenshaw area and helped clean up. My family foundation donated money to support community organizations and rebuilding efforts. I love this city, *all of this city*, so it felt like the right thing to do."

"A philanthropist *and* a publishing phenom," Margo says.

Jack blushes. "I pay her to say that."

We laugh.

"Seriously?" Margo says. "He won't tell you this, Bailey, but Jack also founded a juvenile offenders writing program."

Jack's head bobbles. "Helping kids learn how to express themselves without resorting to violence . . . I mean, that's what all writers do, right?"

Except for his dad—if the rumors are true. He peers at the moon above us. "I want people to be seen, to be . . . *acknowledged*. For their experiences to be . . . I don't know . . . *validated*, I guess."

The three of us round the corner of the main house, then drift along a gravel walkway.

There, nestled in the trees, is the cottage now lit from the outside like a dollhouse on center stage. With its blond wood door and jumbo picture windows, the cozy house offers direct access to the swimming pool and views of the gardens and hillsides.

"Isn't it the *cutest*?" Margo buzzes ahead of Jack and me to open the front door.

Jack stops at the cottage's threshold and bows to me. "After you, Miss Meadows."

Margo steps backward into the tiled lobby. "Welcome home, Emerging Writer. At least for however long it'll take you and Jack to whip up a bestseller."

My eyes goggle at the wood-beam ceilings, at the narrow dining room that bleeds into a kitchen equipped with stainless steel appliances. In the small living room, there's a fireplace on one wall and a television bolted to a perpendicular wall. A bronze wax warmer with an etching of an oak tree in its belly sits on the coffee table beside the television remote control.

I glide down a short hallway to the only bedroom, a generous space with gray walls, white curtains, and a desk and chair. Another bronze wax warmer sits atop a distressed wood dresser. Two sets of windows. Those to my right survey the eastern canyon—tomorrow, I will see the sun rise. The windows to my left offer a view of the pool and patio. The bathroom boasts a frosted window, a tub with jets, and a shower with a small bench.

"Like they have in those fancy Greek hotels," Margo says.

Back in the living room, Jack stands near another writing desk that looks out to the garden. There are stacks of unopened Rhodia notepads of every size on the desktop, Pentel pens still in packages, a MacBook, a separate keyboard, and a large desktop monitor.

"I'm sure you brought your own computer," Jack says, "but when you're working on our project, I ask that you use . . ." He taps the MacBook.

"Of course," I say.

"I know this cottage is a little small—"

"Are you kidding me?" I ask, eyes wide. "This is an incredible . . . I mean . . . the quiet will help me think." Another true statement. And if I *do* end up writing a book about this experience? My time here . . . *priceless.*

"I know the cowriting thing came at you last minute," Jack says, "but I do hope you say yes. I'd *love* to share everything I know about the craft, and to be honest? I'm looking forward to learning from you, too."

My cheeks flush. "I'm not . . . anyone to learn from."

Jack levels his shoulders. "Oh, but you are. I'll explain after you say yes. You can give me your definitive answer tomorrow. Luann, my chef, has filled the fridge and cupboards with sweets and meats, cheeses, and fruit. A few bottles of wine. If you need anything else, start a list, and we'll get it for you tomorrow. It's been a pleasure meeting you, but I'm beat—all this talking and being pleasant to seventy-five people has sapped my strength. I gotta get used to the commotion again."

Margo and I nod and agree, *Yeah, all this socializing is* hard.

"I'm heading to bed. See you tomorrow, Bailey," Jack says. "And don't ever be afraid to tell me how I can support you, okay? I have a lot going on, but for you, I'll stop and help any way I can."

I touch my heart. "Thank you, Jack."

He winks at me. "No problem." Without saying another word, he ambles out the door and back up the gravel walkway to the main house.

Margo presses her hands against her flushed cheeks. "You've probably heard he's pretty much a recluse. But he's not like Howard Hughes with the long nails and jars of pee. Jack's already shy, and then, throw in the pandemic, and all of that just makes his worst tendencies . . . worse. *But!*"

She grasps my shoulders. "He *likes* you. He runs hot and cold—he's been through a lot these last twenty years, and he won't connect with people unless he has to. Whatever. You come highly recommended, and so you *must* say yes." With praying hands and her gaze to the ceiling: "She pleads to the universe, pretty please, amen."

A knot pulls loose from my stomach and works its way up my throat. "I'll think hard on it."

Margo gives me a strained smile. "Trust me: it will be *incredible*. Oh! So. Tomorrow, we'll handle the business stuff. I'll need to make copies of your driver's license or passport, and you'll need to complete a W-9 form. You know, all that normal stuff so that we can pay you."

"Got it," I say. Every piece of identification is all ready, including a grocery store rewards card and a library card.

"Come here." She pulls me into a hug. "We're so glad you're finally here."

Silver stars pop before me from the intensity of her hold.

"Glad that I'm here, too." I nudge my way out of her grasp. Immediately the pain softens.

"Down for a nightcap?" Margo asks.

I make a sad face. "I'm exhausted, so I'll need to pass tonight. I gotta come down from all the excitement. Blame the writer-introvert-in-a-pandemic thing I was just talking about."

She points at me. "Tomorrow, then?"

I give her "okay" fingers. "Tomorrow. See you in the morning."

4.

Alone again, my shoulders relax. I'm not scared, which is good. I won't be able to think clearly if I'm scared. I slip off my heels, and the cold tile delivers relief to my bare feet. I exhale and let my head fall back.

Long day.

So quiet here . . .

No helicopters or police sirens. No squealing cars or revving motorcycles.

Just my heartbeat and breathing, the low thrum of the refrigerator, and chirping crickets and the wind whistling through the trees and across the canyons.

First thing to do: create a floor plan and map of this estate. As I discover more, I will add to the map. That way, when it's time, I can accurately describe this new world to whoever needs to know.

I open my red handbag.

That Glock . . .

No matter how many times I shove it into the bowels of this bag—and it's a nice-size satchel, big enough for a pair of ballet flats and a thermal mug—the gun rises to the top. The still-recording spy pen is nestled in the bag along with two MAC lipstick tubes, a lip balm tub, the Bible-size journal, a tissue pack, a wine-colored leather wallet, a roll of twenty-dollar bills, and six Visa gift cards. There's also a sheath of folded and stapled papers.

I flip through the pages of the journal, passing older entries like:

LAX MONTANA 10:33 a.m. UNITED

And:

JEWEL GENESIS head of Congregation of Sacred Harmony

Find out re timeline

I unfold the stapled collection of papers.
My résumé.

BAILEY R. MEADOWS

PROFESSIONAL SUMMARY
Creative and driven communications specialist with 3+ years of experience. Captivating storytelling skills and a nose for the truth as well as an excellent track record as a ghostwriter and media writing (blogs, digital news, etc.). Seeking to leverage skills and experience to write fiction with a true-crime edge.

There's Stanford University on my résumé (". . . to highlight university's engagement with community in Palo Alto and beyond . . ."). There's *Los Angeles Sentinel* (". . . the only weekly African American–owned newspaper in Los Angeles . . ."). There's a link to writing samples.

The paper is worn, speckled with fingerprints, ink, and some kind of red sauce.

The next sheet:

AFTER-VISIT SUPPLEMENTAL INFORMATION

There's a handwritten note:

Sam,

*This may help you further understand what may be happening.
Let me know if you want to talk further.*

-MB

The first page details dissociative fugues (". . . purposeful travel or bewildered wandering . . . amnesia for identity or for other important autobiographical information . . . overwhelming situation . . . primary psychological defense . . ."). I'd printed this definition from the National Institutes of Health website just like I'd printed the article on the Nigerian student I was reading about in my car earlier today.

I've handwritten notes on a printed copy of this same piece:

- *NCBI*
- *Confabulation aka honest lying*
- *Generate false memory w/o intention of deception*
- *Believes it's true*
- *No known exact mechanism (biological) in confab.*
- *Provoke conf = dates, places, history. Discovered by direct questioning, prompting false memory*
- *Spontaneous = memories w/o external trigger. Explain situations. Day to day*
- *Confab ≠ delusion*

I like this word: *confabulation.*

I look back at a screenshot of my last communications with Sam—I'd commented beneath a picture of a bottle of sparkling red wine against a sunset.

Yes! Please send me a bottle. I'll Cash App you!

Avery had actually been the person who'd first reported her missing—but the police weren't interested. Sam was an adult with free will, they said. She could pick up and move to Mars if she wanted, they said. That was her right, they said. But Avery has already lost her daughter, Jodie, to the great unknown, and she couldn't bear to lose another person she loved. Sam wouldn't have intentionally vanished—Avery swore to this—and so we launched our own investigation.

Every theory we've had about what happened sounds plausible . . . until another theory comes to replace it.

I've set up a Google Alert for "Sam Morris," but nothing accurate or related to *my* Sam Morris has landed in my inbox. Sometimes for hours, I'll search newspaper archives of papers in Los Angeles, Antelope Valley, Las Vegas, Oakland, and San Diego, the crime sections especially in case she was found dead or alive. I've studied photographs in case she'd become a Jane Doe. No luck. I've followed leads that have taken me all around California, places where Sam planned to visit or was last seen. And now, I'm here, in one of those places.

As the handwritten notes on this printout suggest, Sam had just seen a psychologist about her weird, brief episodes where she "went gray." She also identified the trauma that was overwhelming her so much that then caused her to flee from her everyday life, both physically and mentally. Did any of that trauma stem from something that happened here, either at or near the Beckham estate?

Possibly.

Sam has no other family. She has no partner. She's *ours*, and Avery and I are the clients. *Someone* besides us must miss her . . . I hope.

The next page in this collection is a photocopy of a slick brochure for The Way Home. The trifold piece features pictures of a smiling family hugging each other. Another page has the copy of the brochure's inside—the mission statement for The Way Home. *Helping to reconnect families with their missing loved ones and rebuilding all that's been lost.*

ABOUT US

The Way Home is a nonprofit 501(c)(3) organization dedicated to helping families find their missing loved ones. While we are not a private investigation firm, we do coordinate and consult closely with the Los Angeles Police Department—Missing Persons Unit. We also provide resources and support for families—from personal security and referrals to private investigators around the Southland to education and awareness.

Serving as a bridge between families and law enforcement, The Way Home works to truly realize its ultimate mission: to bring ALL the missing back to their loved ones.

LEADERSHIP

Cheyanne Carroll, president of TWH, started her career as a detective in LAPD's Missing Persons Unit. After 25 years on the force, Carroll retired but still saw a need for savvy and connected individuals being a bridge between families in stressful situations and a police force that serves millions of people. That's why she launched The Way Home in 2000.

Sam Morris, vice president of TWH, had only one dream: to reconnect families. Together with Cheyanne and the small but mighty TWH staff, she's helped to bring hope and healing to many families—solving 106 missing persons cases since its founding in 2000.

Sam is a do-gooder.

Bad guys absolutely hate her.

Did she come up against one of those bad guys?

Even though I have that Google Alert set up, I still type *Samantha Morris* into my phone's search bar.

About 28,200,000 results, the first being a researcher studying stem cell and developmental biology.

That's not my Sam.

A lacrosse player. *Not her, either.*

A basketball player. *Not anymore.*

None of the results on this first page are new or related to my Sam. I'll continue to dig deeper for do-gooder Sam Morris, who won't publicize every move she makes, considering the job she does.

Give me time, Sam. I'll change that, and the whole world will know your name.

Before I do anything else—and while events are fresh in my mind—I grab the pen and journal and record all that's happened since leaving the car. Then I refold the collection of stapled documents, close the journal, and shove everything deep down into my handbag.

I scowl as I carry my tote and suitcase into the bedroom and then close the curtains. Don't want anyone watching me from across the canyon. From the cute mesh bag beside the wax warmer, I select a lavender wax cube and drop it into the warming disk. I reach into the tote bag for the May 1 issue of the *Register-Guard*, published in Eugene, Oregon; the slot machine voucher dated October 6, 2020, for $305 from MGM Grand Hotel and Casino—Las Vegas; a take-out menu from Café Eritrea D'Afrique in Oakland—each are places Sam was last seen. I also grab the chargers for the pen and my phone. After plugging in both, I text Avery.

Settling in

I'm being very pleasant and friendly and my cover seems to be believable.

No one's lied to me yet

They seem nice

A little nervous but I have my Austrian friend with me!

Just hope I don't have to make her go POW!!

Each text is tagged DELIVERED, but none are tagged READ. It's almost ten thirty. Maybe she's putting her kids to sleep. Maybe she's greeting her partner at the front door. Maybe she's out walking her dog.

I swipe over to voicemail in case she called and I didn't hear the phone ringing over the noise of the book party. Ah—there's a red bubble marked "1."

A message left by a caller with a 541 area code. *"Hi, this message is for Bailey. This is Tina over at the La Quinta Inn and Suites? Someone found your wallet and a planner in the room. How should I get this back to you? Gimme a call."* Crap. Must be Sam's wallet and planner—Avery gave both to me once we launched this investigation. I flipped through Sam's belongings, trying to figure out her movements, and must've . . .

Ugh. Since I can't return to that hotel, maybe Avery—

My phone rings in my hand.

I answer.

No one responds. Dead air.

I say "Hello?" again.

Silence.

"Someone there?" I ask.

Silence.

One last time: "Hello?"

Nothing.

Anxious now, I end the call.

The light shifts in the bedroom—a shadow has crossed the bright lights shining around the pool area . . . *maybe.* My eyes are tired, my bones creaky, and I've lived three lives today and—

Footsteps tap somewhere up in the living room or kitchen. *Definitely.*

My spine straightens and I'm now fully alert.

No one should be in here with me—

Scraping. Like a pitchfork being dragged across the roof of the house.

My eyes roll up to the ceiling and follow that scraping until . . . quiet. Before I can exhale, though, footsteps tapping again.

I shout, "Hello? Margo? You out there?"

No answer.

Heavy breathing.

Who's breathing?

Oh. *I'm* breathing.

I want to grab the Glock from my purse, but if it's Margo doing something innocent, I'll scare her, and then folks will know I'm packing, and they'll want to know why.

Empty-handed, I creep down the hallway and shout, "Hello?"

No answer.

Closer . . . closer . . .

And one more step . . .

No one is standing in the living room or kitchen. The front door's locked.

I creep back to the bedroom and peek under the bed.

No one is hiding beneath the bed.

I throw open the closet door.

No one is hiding in the closet.

I tiptoe to the bathroom—and gasp.

The narrow window is open. Someone must've opened it earlier in the day to let in fresh air. And now, the bathroom is colder than the rest of the house.

I slide the window closed. Then, I listen . . . and listen . . .

No scraping. No footsteps. Just me, heavy breathing in this close space.

I find the courage to ease off my gold trench coat and hang it up in the closet. Back in the bathroom, I twist the "H" shower knob, and frosty needles burst from the showerhead.

I unwrap my floral top and . . . *crap*. Bloody white gauze taped against my brown skin.

How am I still *bleeding?*

Beyond the bandages, plum-colored bruises darken my abdomen. Those aren't as surprising, though, as the bright-red blood. I grab the hand mirror from the counter and turn away from the bathroom mirror to see the reflection of my lower back.

Bruises there, too.

I close my eyes and squeeze my mind tight . . . tighter, not wanting to remember being mugged, but *needing* to remember in case the police or Avery caught that mugger and I'm required to testify in court.

Crouched over me . . . my pink pants . . . sidewalk . . . the man . . . his dirty gray hair . . . He had a round face and a scar across his eyebrow. He swung a knife. I blacked out and woke up in a hospital room. It's because of that assault that I carry a gun.

But this is why Avery was reluctant in moving forward with the assignment even though there's no one else to help her. Now that I have a weapon and experience, though, I have more than hope to back me up.

Steam from the shower's hot water now covers the mirror, and I can no longer see me. I resist the urge to swipe the glass—I'm not ready to see me again. *Stitches . . .*

I retreat to the kitchen and search the cabinets for . . .

This. A roll of Saran Wrap.

I wrap plastic around my torso—to keep my stitches from getting wet—and grab from the tote bag a pair of striped silk boxers, my black satin hair bonnet, and a pink tank top.

Back in the bathroom, I adjust the water temperature, then climb into the shower. Steam envelops me, quiets my mind as water pounds against my skin. Instead of blood and guns and missing friends, I try to think minor thoughts like . . .

The taste of amberjack and charcoal and mushroom lemonade.

Like . . .

Tom Brady's retirement from football and college players being paid for their names and likenesses.

Like . . .

Every single thing, every single experience, every hurt and pain, slight and celebration, God and sex and death and cars and tacos and geese mating rituals and Mennonites and ectoplasm and ouzo and lacewings and Glocks.

Above the beat of the water, my phone vibrates and dings from the bathroom counter.

Please let that be Avery!

Done with showering, I rewrap my wound with new gauze and tape, then reach for my phone, the screen now bright with three new notifications:

Sale on hair products from Extensions Plus. A fundraising email from ASPCA. A CVS customer service survey.

No Avery.

My last texts still say DELIVERED.

My fingers tap the phone's keyboard.

WHERE ARE YOU?!

No ellipses bubble on the screen.

As I dress, an owl hoots. *Hoo-huh-hoo.* Just like the hoots in the movies. Deep. Soft. Spooky.

I peek past the bedroom curtains and out to the night—

A mountain lion slinks past the swimming pool, a collar on its neck and a raccoon in its mouth. The puma's amber-colored eyes reflect the dark as it looks over to me, no fucks to give, and then it disappears into the brush.

I'm breathless. Not because I'm scared of the big cat, but because . . . behold, the apex predator, the most dazzling, sexy, unbothered creature out there living a life, being monitored from afar, but *here.* I stay at the window, willing the big cat to return.

It does not.

Wait.

What if. . . ? What if Sam and a mountain lion met on a trail in the woods? Sam would certainly lose that fight.

Or . . . what if the lion *didn't* kill Sam, but something or someone else did, but the lion scattered her remains all across the Santa Monica Mountains?

Yet *more* theories—and like the others, I write both new theories down in the journal to debunk or confirm. Then, on the next clean sheet, I draw boxes that represent the first floor of the main house, and then I draw another box to represent the cottage.

Oof, I am *not* an artist or an architect. These "drawings" are *so* not to scale. Like my earlier sketches of the road map to Topanga (crooked lines, scratches for mountains), and the inside of Sam's left-behind Toyota 4Runner (a lopsided radio and an air freshener plugged into the front vent) . . . like the man who mugged me (forehead too big, eyes too close together).

The bedroom now smells of warm lavender, a relaxing scent that helps me come down from the highs of pretending to be someone I'm not and knowing that a semiautomatic is waiting in my purse.

I flip open the wine-colored leather wallet to confirm that I didn't leave my new identity at La Quinta Inn and Suites. There's my driver's license: Bailey Rose Meadows, 45625 Don Felipe Drive, Los Angeles. Born April 25, 1981. We kept my real birthday and address in case someone searches for me on the internet. Also, that's one less thing for me to remember. My host writes twisty murder stories, and so he thinks *a lot*. If I want to succeed, I can't jack up the simple stuff.

In my toiletries bag:

Face creams and washes and ointments, hyaluronic this, peptide and collagen that.

Chanel No. 5 parfum, not cologne. Parodontax toothpaste. More gauze and tape along with a tub of Percocet—white circular pills— and a tub of ibuprofen—white oval pills. Prescribed on May 10 by a drugstore pharmacy up in Oakland. Doctor's name: K. Sawyer. No refills available for either drug. Pain management for the wound in my side, courtesy of the thug captured only in my journal.

I also packed two near-empty vials of Sam's medications: Zoloft, an antidepressant, and Ambien to sleep. She hasn't refilled either drug since last month. How is she doing now, unmedicated?

I open the Percocet tub and count sixteen pills. Four to six hours' dosage. I've taken four since the pharmacy prepared them. Ibuprofen— thirty count on the label. Too many to count by just eyeballing, but enough to last me for at least a week or so.

Tight now, the wound that lives beneath these bandages is livid and violent enough to require Percocet, a helluva drug. I take one along with ibuprofen. The Perc will help the pain—but that same drug could snarl my mind, slow my thinking. After tonight, I won't take any Percocet.

I hope I won't have to break that vow.

Hair brushed and bonnet on my head, I grab *Old Topanga Road* from the ottoman in the living room and carry it with me as I switch off all the lights in the cottage, except for the light above the stove—I switch *that* light on. Leaving the bedroom door open—I've never been comfortable sleeping with a closed door—I click on the nightstand reading lamp.

A pair of black binoculars sits on the shelf above the bed. I pluck the field glasses from the shelf and wander to the canyon-facing windows.

I want to find that mountain lion. I want to find Mercury at its highest point. I want to see a shooting star. I want—

"What the *hell*?" I whisper, fiddling with the binoculars' focus knob. Finally, I hold the glasses to my face and see . . .

Russell Walker–Security Guard crouching in the darkness, slinking around the perimeter of the estate. He isn't carrying a flashlight, and yet he's creeping in the darkness like it's high noon. He stops moving, then looks that way, and then that way, and—

He's looking right at me!

Too late to duck.

Maybe he'll think it's too dark for me to see him.

He continues sneaking north.

My breathing quickens as I watch him disappear into the high grass.

What the *hell*? Why is that old man out there? Do Jack and Margo know that he's skulking around the estate? Is he working as a security guard right now, or . . . or . . . ?

Does he know about Sam? Has he *met* Sam? If he has, did he do something . . . ?

A pebble of fear forms in my heart. Why would I think that?

Because he's sneaking around in the—

The right side of my pink tank top catches my eye.

Oh no. Another bright-red posy.

9-1-1 Transcript from November 2, 1993, 10:50 AM

Dispatcher: 9-1-1, what's your emergency?
Caller: I need somebody. I need them ASAP.
Dispatcher: Okay, sir, give me the address.
Caller: I'm driving on Old Topanga Canyon Road and I've stopped at someone's house. We're seeing a fire near the water tower.
Dispatcher: Okay, what kind of fire?
Caller: Brush, I guess? It's burning a lot of dead grass and trees. This stuff is pretty dry.
Dispatcher: Are there any structures in danger?
Caller: No, but the flames look mean. Like they can't wait to burn some shit down.

5.

It's not the new sunlight bursting through the window that pulls me from sleep. The sun's bright-gold rays pound at me, yes, and even with closed eyes, I still have to squint. That sunlight, though, pales in comparison to the aurora-alert chime dinging from the nightstand.

I blindly grab my phone and groan as my sore elbow pops and creaks.

It's seven thirty on Thursday, May 13.

A banner: one new voicemail message.

The phone rang?

When?

While you were deep in the middle of a narc-infused sleep.

The caller has an LA-based area code. *"Hey, this is Quincy. Your new stuff is ready. It's about two-k. Call me."*

Quincy . . . Quincy . . . I've met so many people since this search for Sam began. What stuff is he calling about? Drugs? Information? Red pandas?

I grab my journal and search for any mentions of Quincy.

Trip to café—had cappuccino

IDed woman Vanessa has more info

Cherry or grape tomatoes?

Quincy ID master

And I'd scribbled down his number along with:

Passport if needed maybe MT DL

As I tap his number, I keep flipping through the journal.

Trina La Quinta between 7-7

Room check-in 2014 according to BOFA.

Trina . . . Trina . . . Oh! Trina left me the message about the left-behind wallet.

Quincy's line keeps ringing and ringing . . . ringing and ringing . . . until it decides to end the call without the courtesy of a voicemail prompt.

I toss the journal to the carpet and swipe the phone screen to clear out old notifications and then lie back in the bed again.

Up on the wood-beam ceiling . . . no sagging cobwebs. No ants or silverfish. *Old Topanga Road* sits open on the pillow, its cover facing up.

Last night, I didn't read past the epitaph—*If you don't know where you are going, any road will get you there, Lewis Carroll.* My mind thought its last thoughts—*Russell Walker, sneaky man, mountain lion, owl, huh-HOO, huh-HOO, I'm in the canyon, Sam was in the canyon*—and then, my mind went *whoosh.* The Perc kicked in and I closed my eyes.

I grab *Old Topanga Road* and turn to the last page. The novel is 413 pages long, not counting the acknowledgments.

Divide that by three days . . .

I'll need to read 137 pages a day by Sunday, and I'll skim some of those pages. Maybe there's a SparkNotes or something online to buy and download onto my own computer. For now, though . . .

I open the novel to the prologue.

A month had passed, and the Rosenblums hadn't realized that a murderer had been hiding out in their pool house.

That murderer knew that the old couple no longer swam, so they had no reason to come to the hut. The Rosenblums were also mourning the death of their granddaughter. He knew something about that, too. He'd shot that granddaughter one time, point-blank, with his Austrian-made Glock, given to him by the police chief himself back in the day. Yes, Chief Rusty Coleman thought that he still ruled Los Angeles.

No, I do. I rule this city. I'm the one the newspaper had named the Hiker.

That moniker lacked imagination.

That moniker lacked . . . *grit.*

He deserved better. Something like the Canyon Coyote . . .

But there'd been the Canyon Creeper years ago. Too similar . . .

I like this story so far. Will Prologue Dead Girl be the detective's wife, girlfriend, or ex-wife/ex-girlfriend?

How do novelists make this shit up?

To be perfectly honest, Axel Fletcher hated Los Angeles, even with that sunset and those perfect breakers rolling in from the other side of the world.

Sometimes, seaweed wrapped in fishing lines and plastic washed up on shore. Sometimes, a body.

A body like Priscilla Murillo's. Just twenty-two years old. Just starting out in life. She'd been shot first and then tied to concrete blocks. Then she'd been dumped from a boat by her drug-runner boyfriend. But Bad Boyfriend had dumped her too close to shore to disappear her forever.

It took some time, two weeks to be exact, a Thursday to be specific, but Priscilla Murillo finally rolled onto the beach, freed from concrete anklets. That had been the same day his daughter, Kinsey, was born.

The circle of life. He'd thought that was some bullshit made up by Elton John and Disney . . . that is, until he held his baby daughter in his arms at 10:16 that Thursday morning and then found Priscilla Murillo twelve hours later.

Fuck the ocean.

The canyons weren't that much better. Lately, the forests had also presented Axel with the dead. Months ago, he'd been called to the woods and to the death site of Jane Doe #88—white, brunette, about twenty-four years old. Tattoo of a butterfly on her thigh. Another tat—this one, a white rabbit on her shoulder. She'd been found off the trails in Topanga wearing nothing but a backpack over her head.

That backpack over the vic's head.

His signature.

The Hiker.

Sick, twisted bastard.

Always used a JanSport bag.

Expensive.

A profile of the Hiker theorized that he was strong and handsome—his looks and physicality were his primary lures—but not so muscular that he wouldn't appear safe. Maybe he faked an injury. He was familiar with this part of the world, this forest and its trails, especially. He was white. Could've been anyone in Southern California, then.

Four victims.

A serial killer.

Axel hated the Hiker more than he hated a thousand Edgar Castanedas who shot their girlfriends and dumped their bodies in the Pacific.

Crime wasn't supposed to happen here. Not here in Topanga Canyon.

I will catch you, Axel thought then.

And now, as he turned away from the bluffs that offered that view of the Pacific to the west and the Santa Monica Mountains to the east, Axel wondered about the dead young woman now lying before him.

A red JanSport backpack this time.

Did the color matter?

Did the Hiker choose that color just for her?

Why did the Hiker choose her?

Did a psychopath need a reason—

My phone vibrates, interrupting my reading.

A calendar alert.

TRIP TO SANTA YNEZ FALLS.

Yep—I'd printed out a map, and it's somewhere in my bags.

I kick off the comforter, sitting up with a wince as my body reminds me that I'm—

Wait. *Waitwaitwait.*

I stare at the bedroom door. I stare at the *closed* bedroom door. The closed bedroom door that I *intentionally* left open last night.

My face numbs as I stare at that closed door . . . Maybe I got up for a glass of water. Maybe I rose to adjust the thermostat. Maybe this is like . . . like . . . noticing a bruise on your leg but not remembering how you got it.

Percocet, man, so who knows.

Stop. Focus. Breathe.

My pulse flies through my body at supersonic speed, and I hold my breath and then, slowly, exhale. My swirling blood stops swirling, and my mind stops revving, and I am almost a jellyfish floating through calm waters.

There's a perfectly banal reason this door is closed.

Ghosts.

Okay. So. Unless the pain hits seven on the scale, I will skip the Perc and take only ibuprofen.

With deference to my injury, I scoot out of bed. The white oak floors are warm even though, outside, silver clings to wild grass. I open the bedroom door, telling myself that there's nothing on the other side of this door, that there's no one waiting and ready to jump me again.

And I'm right.

The hallway is cold and silent.

This is why I didn't bring every single document related to this project. What if someone snoops in my things while I'm away? I'd be so busted. Sure, most of this stuff can be explained away as "research" and "plot points," but do I want to take that chance? No, I don't. If I can close a bedroom door in the middle of the night, I can certainly forget and leave police transcripts and evidence lists in the bedsheets.

The side pockets of my tote bag are stuffed with envelopes of all sizes and colors, each marked with black-inked handwritten words—SITE,

ROSTERS, OIR. *What the heck is "OIR"?* I pluck a printout from the white envelope marked MAPS.

Printed back on April 20, according to the header at the top of this page. Hopefully nothing has changed in the last three weeks. I had also highlighted a trail, and then, with black marker, I wrote:

2.5 miles away from B. estate

Old chimney 100 yards across from creek that leads down to waterfall

Came here in the 90s—

Someone knocks on the poolside bedroom window.

I yelp and spin around, caught.

Margo stands on the other side of that window, waving, her face nearly pressed against the windowpane. Her strawberry-blonde curls are way too cheerful this early in the morning. "Ready to start the day?" she shouts through the glass.

I give her a thumbs-up.

She points to her right and shouts, "Coming in."

I shout back, "Okay."

I predict: Margo plans to be my friend during my stay here. Her homie-wino. Her *Cosmo* bedside astrologer confidante. But . . .

I don't want to be any of this. Still, I must be agreeable so that once I start asking questions, Margo will give me authentic answers as rosé sloshes from her wineglass.

I will drink thirty Aperol spritzes every day, all day, if that means Margo talks without hesitation.

6.

"So, are you our new cowriter?" Margo, wearing a hot-pink pantsuit, is already standing in my kitchen, now warm with sunlight.

My kitchen—I've already claimed this radiant space now catching every free sunbeam. The magnet on the refrigerator says PEACE LOVE TOPANGA, but I don't feel any of that right now. Not only is Margo standing in *my* kitchen, she is also standing over platters of cut fruit, bagels and schmear, and strips of crispy bacon that weren't there last night.

Did the food fairy visit me as I slept?

Margo's eyes peck at my head. "Ooh! Bonnets really exist in real life?"

I tap my head—the satin bonnet is still protecting my crown. "Yeah. Why would we make that up?"

"No idea," Margo says. "Looks weird, though. I'll pretend it isn't there! And . . . *good morning!*" She presents the food, her arms spread like a model on *The Price Is Right*. "Did Luann do good?" She plucks a slice of perfectly sized and fried bacon from the plate and chomps it in half. A greasy bacon crumb falls onto the lapel of her hot-pink blazer.

That bacon crumb looks weird. I'll pretend it isn't there.

"BTW," she says, eating the second half of the bacon strip. "I love-love-*love* your Pinterest board. And I *also* love cabins by the lake! And your Yelp reviews! I never tried that fried-chicken place. Sounds horrible. Thanks for saving me a trip."

I shrug and smile.

"Also!" Margo says. "Not that you have yet, but . . . we would appreciate it if you didn't post any details about your time here. At least, not yet. Since you're working with Jack on his next book." She squints at me. "Is that okay?"

I shrug and smile again. "Of course. Whatever you all need me to do. Or *not* do."

Margo's eyes narrow, and she clasps her hands together as though she's praying. "I hope you don't mind me looking at your socials."

"Nope. Not at all."

Because there's a larger problem.

"How . . . how . . . ?" I now stutter, hornets buzzing around my stomach. "I thought I locked the front door."

Margo plucks another strip of bacon from the plate. "You *did* lock it. But that's to keep *strangers* out. And yes, while this is your residence, we still work here. Luann has to feed you, and Azealia cleans twice a week. Since I run everything, I also have a key. Jack, though, will *never* just *barge* in—he was raised right. Me? I was raised in Fontana. *Oh!*"

She plucks a face mask from her pocket. "Do you want me to . . . ?" She waggles the mask. "I've already been vaccinated—I have a preexisting condition. And thanks so much for sending in your results and vax card."

Before I can respond, though—

Margo holds out a thick silver key fob. "This is *pour vous.*"

I take the fob, still perturbed that *strangers* will have access to my stuff, to *me*, without warning. Yeah, and now I'm *really* glad I didn't bring everything. The fob feels heavy and magical in the palm of my hand, and I think about those green seeds that James dropped into the soil and that peach growing large enough to house a human-size centipede and ladybug.

"Can we limit the random pop-ins?" I ask, not so agreeable now. "I know life is different here in the TC, but where I'm from? We don't just . . . *drop in on people.*" I pause, then add, "You can get killed easy that way."

"Of course," Margo says. "My bad. Just remember, though. You *are* in TC. We live differently up here."

No banks. No nightlife. Flammable trees. More land for your money. Flash floods. Not overdeveloped. Rattlesnakes. Unobstructed views. Hippies. Isolation. The forest. Vibes, man, vibes.

If this was South Los Angeles, I would've heard police helicopters by now. Police sirens, booming car stereos, the screech of tires, the screech of feral parrots.

Strangers entering my temporary cottage in the woods without warning is charming and small-town kitschy, and I guess I should welcome this kind of safety.

"Oh no!" Margo points at the dried brown blood on my tank top. "You're bleeding!"

"This?" I touch the stain, then manage a smile. "Nosebleed. No worries."

Margo says, "Phew," then flips over two coffee mugs that Luann also placed on the breakfast counter. "Shall I remind you," Margo says, beaming, "while we are not writing nonfiction, we don't need you to actually *be* a thriller heroine? All imaginary, okay? Promise? Just know enough to write about it. Make the rest up. *Ha!*"

Why didn't I hear Luann living a whole life without me knowing?
Closed bedroom door and knocked out by Percocet, remember?
Vibes, man, vibes.

"Speaking of true things," I say. "What's the craziest crime that's happened up here?"

"Hmm." Margo grabs the filled pot of coffee from the coffee maker. "There's the married couple who got in a big argument about a gate in their yard. He shot her six times and then two more times in her head, point-blank range. And . . ."

She pours fresh, hot brew into our mugs. "There's . . . oh! The Manson family—they stabbed that musician, Gary What's-His-Name. His house is farther down Old Topanga Canyon Road."

"Wow." Cold sweat now slicks my face. Shaky-handed, I take Margo's gift of coffee, adding to it a spoon of sugar from the small ceramic bowl and a splash of warmed cream from the mini-pitcher.

"Last night, I saw a mountain lion out there—" I point toward the swimming pool. "He caught a raccoon for dinner."

"No!" Margo wails, melting against the breakfast bar as she lifts her face to the ceiling. "Here I am, telling you to leave your door open cuz it's safe, and P-freaking-22 is out there *stalking* you?"

I burst into a laugh. "I wasn't scared of him—I'm in *love* with him. Or her. Whatever. Don't worry. I'm not gonna rush out there to meet a cougar. I'm not *totally* insane."

Margo's smile shows off her perfect teeth. "Phew, again," she says, wiping fake sweat from her forehead.

I take a sip from my mug—wonderful coffee—and ask, "That security guard I met yesterday? How long has he been working here?"

Margo pauses, and a brief flash of "shit" crosses her face. "Umm . . . a while. I don't know how long *exactly*. I don't really pay much attention to the security guards."

"Would you say that he's . . . ?" *A killer? A kidnapper? A stalker? All three?* "That he's . . . a good guy?"

Margo busies herself by swiping sugar from the counter. She's hesitant. Why? "Of course." She peeks at me. "Did he say something to you? Scare you?"

I sip from my coffee. "I've just seen him around. He helped me find the estate yesterday."

Margo sighs, then whispers, "I have to admit—I'm always nervous around him. Don't know why." She holds my gaze, then dusts her hands of sugar. "Changing the subject: Any questions you have for me about the residency?"

I clear my throat, the shakes still quaking around my body. "What time will our days typically start?"

Margo tousles her curls, her good cheer returned. She pulls at a gray hair and peers at it with crossed eyes. "Depends on Jack. Today, though? Nine o'clock."

I glance over at the microwave clock: eight fifteen.

Margo wriggles her nose and pulls her lips into a tight line. "Just so you know . . . Jack has a bleeding heart, okay? And he gives people second chances." She stares at me, doesn't blink. "So if you're a little . . . *nervous* around some staff around here—or the security guards—and you don't know why . . ."

Shit. "Okay," I whisper. "Good to know." And . . . *not.*

Margo lifts her mug. "Here's to South LA and Fontana, bitches."

We clink our coffee mugs, then sip.

Margo takes a plate from the stack arranged by Luann and selects a sesame seed bagel from the tower of assorted bagels. "Things to accomplish for today. Signing contracts. Reading assignments. Jack's gonna walk you around the property. You'll have lunch later out on the deck." Butter knife in hand, she swipes cream cheese across the bottom half of the bagel.

Back in my (*my*) bedroom, my phone chimes, and the sound makes my blood rush through my veins. Cell phone alerts have become my bell, and Apple has become Pavlov. That means that I'm . . . *Apple's bitch.*

After I fill my plate with an everything bagel, pineapple cubes, and a pound of bacon slices, Margo and I settle in the tall chairs at the breakfast bar. Without taking a breath, she tells me that she's worked for the Beckhams for over twenty years. Before that, her parents worked for the Beckhams, her father as a driver and her mother as Big Jack's typist. Margo's been married twice: to a welder named Rogelio and a poet named Elvis.

"Not *the* Elvis," she says. "Just a regular guy whose momma loved Elvis."

She attended USC and majored in communications. "Fight on, Margo," she says, holding her fingers in the victory sign. No kids, no pets, no interest in having either.

"I have a perfect job," she says, "meeting incredible people, traveling all around the world, talking about books and TV and films with an incredibly interesting and sexy man who loves taking care of me—he takes care of everybody, which is good . . . but since we practically grew up together . . . Jack only thinks of me as his little sister. *Ohmigosh*, I'm *such* a tragic rom-com heroine. Ha!"

Margo giggles, waggles her curly head, and snorts. "But that's okay. I'm totally good with that. *Totally*." She laughs, snorts again. *"Not."*

Jack is definitely interesting. Sexy, though? Must be an acquired taste.

Still, I grin at my breakfast companion, my new BFF, my homegirl. Margo Dunn is kinda goofy—and I kinda like that. Being her friend will probably be the *easiest task of all*.

And now, she peers at me, thoughtful. "You're different than our other writers-in-residence."

I cough as a chunk of bagel sticks in my throat. "How?"

She hands me a napkin. "You're cool. Easy to talk to. You're just . . . *more confident*. I guess that's because you've lived a *real* life."

My cheeks burn. "Thank you, Margo." I feel like shit for lying to this nice lady—but that's what PIs do, and I need to get used to that.

Margo takes a last sip of coffee, then dabs her Cupid's-bow lips with a napkin. She stands from the chair, then carries her dishes over to the sink. "Eat. Drink. Get dressed. Then, meet me near the swimming pool at nine."

I raise my coffee cup. "Heard."

"Oh!" She spins around, then points at me with gun fingers. "One last question. Do you smoke? Cigarettes, pipes, anything that uses matches and fire?"

I shake my head. "Don't worry—you won't have to keep my security deposit."

"Ha, it's not *that*," she says, flicking her hand. "*Wait*. Did someone ask you for a security deposit? *Oh*. It's a joke. You're joking. Ha. Funny lady. See?" She snorts, then fixes her face to become Serious Margo.

"Okay. No. I'm asking because of the Great Out There." She points to the world beyond the kitchen and living room windows. "We're in Topanga. Nineteen square miles of forest, forest everywhere and not a drop of rain. Which *means* that everything is dry. Which *means* that our tiny perfect world can go up in flames if you stare at it too long."

She strolls over to the kitchen window and peers out to the golden-green canyon. "The Beckham estate has been here since 1910, surviving nearly thirty earthquakes that registered more than a five on the Richter scale. *And* it's survived countless fires, floods, and riots down in the basin. Let's keep it here for another one hundred years, okay? Sound good? No matches, okay?"

I join her at the window, my worried eyes moving past the glass and to the oaks, pines, and eucalyptus trees. "You all really live up here, holding your breath, hoping that everyone . . . *resists their urge to burn it all down?*"

"Oh, crappity-craps." Margo makes a sad face and pulls me into her arms for a hug. She rubs my back and says, "I didn't mean to worry you. Jack's gonna be so mad that I told you about—"

"No." I ease out of her hug. "Really: I appreciate the warning, and I promise not to say anything to him. About *anything* we've talked about this morning."

Our eyes lock.

Anything: Murdering husbands. Sketchy security guards. Bleeding hearts. Second chances.

I nod. "I think all of this is important information to share with someone from the land of concrete and blacktop. I *like* knowing, so thank you."

Margo pokes out her bottom lip. "We're safe here, Bailey. I promise. And it's May. Still springtime. So really, it's too soon for fire season. The fire captain, Captain Walsh? He'll tell you that himself. He's so brave. Works really hard to keep us all informed. I'm sure you'll eventually talk to him, too."

I say, "Can't wait," then guide her closer to the door.

"I'm gonna let you start your day without me bossing you around." Margo points gun fingers at me again. "Nine o'clock. Poolside."

I make gun fingers and point them back at her. "Got it."

Once she leaves, I lock my door again, then race back to the bedroom. I grab the pen from its charger and my journal from the carpet. Scribble down everything I learned just now from Margo—and I didn't even need to booze her up first.

I return to the kitchen to chomp three more slices of bacon, finish my bagel, sip coffee, and stare at the shadows of butterflies flitting across the wood floor.

Murder. Manson. Mudslides.

Sam disappearing up here . . . yeah, that could happen.

After I wash our dirty dishes, I find my keys in my bag and slip on the cottage's fob. Official now. I grab my phone from the bedroom pillow and tap MESSAGES.

More spam. Nothing from Avery.

I flip through my journal and stop at a page titled "TO DO."

Ask about 11.2.93

Somewhere in my folders, there is a photocopy of a calendar from 1993, and that date—November 2—is circled. I swipe over to Google and for the hundredth time tap in: *What happened on November 2, 1993?*

And Google spits out the same results as before.

It was a Tuesday, Election Day in America.

Giuliani defeated Dinkins to become mayor of New York City.

Actor Roger Moore had his enlarged prostate removed.

I edit my search, adding, *Jack Beckham* after that date.

There's a "Jack Beckham" listed in grave indexes from 1940.

Jack "J. D." Beckham published *Into the Woods*. Closer in relevance than an enlarged prostate and David Dinkins.

Next, I type, *Old Topanga Road SparkNotes*. I've now broken the World Wide Web because the "dead internet" circle spins and spins and spins in the middle of the screen.

One signal bar, that's why.

Unreliable internet in the middle of a state park that is eleven thousand acres wide and cut up by thirty-six miles of trails? No way. Who could've heard of such a thing? *Murder. Manson. Mudslides.*

I still reserve the right to change my mind if I want to leave. This is not 1852, and I'm not living on the Belle Grove Plantation in Louisiana.

I am a free woman, and I will hand over the loaned MacBook and work that cottage key off my ring, and then back my Volvo out of the garage and follow the road south and then . . . *Do not leave this place. But trust your gut.* But if my gut tells me to bounce, then I will bounce forthwith.

But if you leave, you can never come back. It's over.

Which means I may never find Sam.

Which means Avery will then have to take this part on herself.

Which means that I'll lose a chance to broaden my training in these types of undercover investigations.

Which means that I may not pass the licensing test.

Maybe I'm not ready to be a private investigator, not if I'm already thinking about leaving.

Murder. Manson . . .

And brushfires. It *is* California, and like drought, the Santa Ana winds, and earthquake swarms, fire is one of our seasons.

I stare out at those trees and those hillsides covered in sage and chaparral. Can't trust them. Can't trust the sun, either. My lungs fill with ice, making my chest heavy, causing me to sip air like the world around me is already in flames.

Flames licking the sky . . . the undersides of clouds dark gray and dark red . . . the high-pitched whistle of the flames . . . ashes burning my skin and clogging my nose—no. The world beyond this window is all sunshine and puffy clouds against the sapphire-bright sky. Just these trees, their branches trembling in the breeze. Just those hawks drifting and circling and gliding above it all. *This isn't fire season, though.* That's what Margo just told me.

The Beckham estate has withstood more than a century of Southern California weather. She told me that, too. And it will withstand another century of earthquakes, wildfires, and social unrest. Yes, it will. This morning, after my nine-o'clock meeting with Margo, I must find Santa Ynez Falls . . . and I must find Santa Ynez Falls before someone looks too long at the dry hillsides and the world goes up in flames.

7.

There may be people coming into this cottage at any time—some of whom have been given second chances.

Margo said "security guards."

Is she saying that Russell Walker accepted one of those second chances? If so, what did he do wrong before working here? And what about Margo? Beneath the blowsy auburn curls and the Drew Barrymore goofiness, is there a black widow or an angel of death or . . . ?

What the hell did Sam stumble upon during her time here?

I shove all the important-looking files and envelopes that I don't want anyone else to see into the secret zippered section of my suitcase, located beneath my clothes. On top of the luggage handle and over the suitcase's security tumbler, I place a silver three-legged pig charm that lives deep in the folds of my purse, facing my gold trench coat and sitting on the tumbler's "5" between "7" and "2." If someone snoops in my things after leaving behind bacon, bagels, and pineapple chunks, the pig's position will tell me so.

I hope.

I pop two ibuprofen as the sun disappears behind silver morning mist. Fog exists down in South LA, but the glares of car headlights, neon signs, and traffic signals guide us through the haze. The way the fog wraps and hides the trees and hillsides and even the sun here? Beautiful. Worrisome. Can't trust it.

At nine o'clock, I step outside the cottage and into this new world shrouded in silver. My thin puffer jacket protects me from the chill in the air. The pockets sag with a million things, including the now-recording spy pen, the tub of Percocet, and adhesive bandages.

Prepared.

On today's agenda: Santa Ynez Falls. Easy. Learning more about November 2 nearly thirty years ago? Not so easy.

Margo isn't waiting for me by the swimming pool. Jack Beckham is, though, and he's aiming his phone out before him. He lifts his free hand, motioning for me to stop walking.

I stop where I stand.

He places a finger to his lips to shush me, then points to . . .

A mule deer drinking from a large ceramic pot near the swimming pool.

The world is silent except for the doe's tongue lapping at the water. She lifts her tawny-red head to watch Jack and, then, to watch me. She flicks her black-tipped tail and large brown ears and then shifts away from the pool. Her hooves click against the patio tile as she returns to the woods surrounding the house.

Smiling, Jack now aims his phone at brown-and-black-winged butterflies whirling across the gravel walkway. "Mule deer," he says. "I've watched them all my life and it never, *never* gets old."

"Do they come here a lot?" I whisper, my heart jangling in my chest.

"When it starts to dry out, during times of drought, yeah. They're looking for water. I was just standing here, waiting for you and . . ." Light shines in his eyes, and he holds out his hand—*ta-da.*

"In my neighborhood," I say, "we have coyotes, raccoons, skunks, possum . . ." My face burns with embarrassment. "Sounds horrible when I say that aloud."

"Sounds *amazing*," he says, smiling. "All animals bring out another side of humanity, you know? I mean . . . raccoons—they're incredibly smart. Next time you're home and there's a raccoon around? Just watch that little bandit—way more interesting than . . . *deer*."

I dip my head and smile. Anyone who tries to gas up raccoons has to be thoughtful. *Second chances* . . .

I cross over to him, looking back to the woods where the deer retreated. "So," I say, "if deer come here, then, it makes sense that mountain lions come here, too."

"Yeah," he says, "and that can be a little scary, so please be careful. It's a good thing, though, that the lions call these mountains home. Because deer are protected from hunting in the Santa Monica Mountains, they proliferate. While the lions eat the deer for survival, they're also controlling the population."

"Circle of life, right?" I say.

"Yep. I'd rather have the deer go out on nature's plan than being hit by a mom in a minivan filled with Girl Scouts. And we'd rather have mountain lions and ticks here in Topanga than apartments, condos, Targets, and KFCs."

"In my neighborhood," I say again, "we have three Targets within three miles of each other." I wag my finger at him. "And you will *never* hear me complain about that. Now, if they turned into Walmarts . . ."

"Then, give you a picket sign?" he asks.

"Definitely."

He chuckles, shrugs. "Okay, so I'll take a Target over a tick." His tight face colors. "Don't tell *anyone* I said that."

Those brown-and-black-winged butterflies move from the walkway and flutter over to the swimming pool.

"What kind of butterfly are those?" I ask, aiming my phone to record them.

"That's a kaleidoscope of California sisters," he says, still recording the butterflies with his phone's camera. "Welcome to your first morning living in Topanga Canyon. I hope our ambassadors have impressed you."

"Butterflies and deer?" I enthusiastically nod. "Yes, they have. Along with the owl hooting outside my window last night and, oh yeah, the *mountain lion* about to chow down on a raccoon."

"That's awesome for you! We have a pride of three puma—a mother and her cubs—roaming the canyon."

Jack then tells me that Native tribes—the Chumash, Tongva, and Tataviam—consider mountain lions to be relatives and teachers and should be revered. "They deserve space and respect," he says.

"Did you know that LA and Mumbai, India, are the only big cities that are also home to puma?" I ask.

"I did." He holds his heart. "I remember the first time I saw a mountain lion in my backyard. I cried. Not because I was scared of it, but because this big cat was so . . . beautiful and powerful." His face clouds over. "And I cried because I thought my dad would go out and shoot him."

He turns to me, brightening. "But he didn't. He actually loved puma, too. And we'd watch them from up there—" He points to the patio off the main house. "One of the few times we got along."

"Sounds like a special time," I say. "The only cats we had were the ones who'd sneak into our crawl space and fight and then have babies." I wiggle my nose. "Not that profound." But true.

Jack snorts. "Yeah, that's *another* kind of movie."

"When did the fog roll in?" I ask, now watching the pearly soup race across the sky. "I swear I saw the sun this morning."

"You did," he says. "It's just that May gray is thicker up here. It'll burn off the hotter it gets." He takes in my long-sleeved white T-shirt beneath the puffer jacket, light-blue leggings, and black cross-trainers. "Looks like *you're* ready for some adventuring."

"You are, too," I say, appraising him. "We're almost twins."

He's wearing light-gray soccer leggings, a long-sleeved white T-shirt, and similar black cross-trainers. A bead of sweat rolls down his jawline.

"Except it looks like you've worked out already?" I ask.

"Yep. Each day, I roll out of bed at four in the morning. After I get in some writing, I jog four miles. Two going, two coming back. *Then*, I bike a few miles on my Peloton, row for twenty minutes, and end with some yoga."

"Okay," I say, frowning. "I'm exhausted after hearing all of that."

"Gotta stay fit," he says. "I don't want to ever look my age."

Hence the Bro-tox injections. And as I stand this close to him, I notice flaking skin around his nose and mouth. The results from a recent chemical peel, I assume.

"I thought we'd go on a hike together this morning," Jack says now. "You may have hiked the canyon before but not in this context. Today, you're hiking to write about it." He tosses me one of the water bottles set on the chaise longue behind him.

"Sounds good," I say. "I was actually hoping to hike today. My friends told me to do the . . ." I pull out the internet map that I'd printed back in April and show him.

"Santa Ynez Falls," he says, nodding. "Gorgeous hike. Not too hard—three miles round trip. Takes about an hour and a half. I'll join you if you don't mind."

"Of course not," I say, slipping the map back into my jacket pocket. "But I have a nine-o'clock meeting first with Margo."

"That can wait. It gets hot out on the trails, so we should get this hike in."

"You're the boss," I say. "Can I go back for my journal? I'm keeping notes."

He offers me a protein bar. "Don't worry. I won't say anything profound or not easily found on the internet."

Glad I brought my pen, then. I stick the protein bars into my puffer's pocket. "Do we drive to the trailhead or . . . ?"

He heads to the opening in the shrubbery made by the doe. "*Drive*, Bailey? *Seriously?*"

"What?" I say, acting more baffled than I am for his amusement. "There are one hundred seventy thousand trails in these mountains. I don't know which one ends at the waterfall."

"Then, follow me." He tosses me a smile that is a mix of arrogance and innocence, the joy of showing me something exciting combined with the clinical gaze of hanging out with someone new.

"First," Jack says, "you should know that 'Topanga' was the name given by the Tongva tribe. It means 'where the mountain meets the sea.'"

"I've read a lot about the Tongva . . ." I peek at my phone—still at one bar. I shout "Argh!" to the sky.

"No signal?" he asks, looking back at me. "It's like that, sometimes, and it swings between being wonderful and frustrating. 'Sorry, my internet's down' is one of history's greatest excuses to not engage. Up here, though, it's true."

I say, "Ha. So in those times that I can't reach you . . . ?"

"What's that? Sorry, my internet is down."

"Nice."

"Not that it will help much, I'll see if I have an extra booster or whatever," he says. "If not, I'll ask Margo to buy one today. You need the internet for research." He sighs. "We're supposed to have a meeting with someone from the California Public Utilities Commission about holding telecommunications companies accountable for shitty service. Like . . . enforceable *regulations* kind of accountable."

"Until then, I guess . . ." I shove my phone into my jacket pocket.

The sun tries to peek past the pearly fog, but the trees steal that light. The sliver of a path we're on soon meets up with a more distinguished trail. Here, the air smells fresh, earthy, tangy. New dirt, fresh-cut wood, eucalyptus, and sweet flowers.

"Glad you're wearing light-colored leggings instead of shorts," Jack tells me over his shoulder. "Ticks are all over these woods. Rumors say there's Lyme disease in the canyon, but the agencies are disagreeing about whether ticks are the cause or if it's something else."

I say, "Ah," but I'm distracted by the lower right side of my abdomen now tugging beneath the bandages. Feels like the skin around my stitches is either sweating or bleeding.

"Topanga Canyon is one of the largest open-space preserves in the world surrounded by a city." Jack points at a distant field of curved, lilac-colored flowers, their stems and leaves covered in white, woolly hair. "Braunton's milk vetch. Only grows on three mountain ranges in Southern California. Most of it grows here in the Santa Monica Mountains, with more than half in Topanga."

I whisper, "Gorgeous."

"Milk vetch is on the endangered plants list. Between the fires and the bulldozers of Department of Water and Power, this uncelebrated flower is one moment away from going extinct."

We journey on. Has Jack given this hiking tour before? For Skylar Orion? For Sam?

"So," he says, "I have a question for you that I ask every writer who comes here. Your story—about the woman disappearing and the cousin—"

"Sister," I correct.

"Sister starting her own investigation." He tilts his head. "Why *this* story?"

My stomach drops, and I stumble some over my feet. "Umm . . ." *To trick you into thinking that I'm here to write a novel.* "Because . . . I'd like to talk about race and class but in an entertaining way."

"And what led you to writing?" He grins back at me. "Better get used to these kinds of questions. When you're doing interviews, someone *will* ask."

I clamp my lips into a tight line and nod. Then: "I'll have to think . . . I mean, *I* know why I'm writing. Just didn't think I'd have to explain the why out loud."

He lifts a finger. "And that's why you're here. Add that to your list of things to figure out."

Somewhere off the trail, bees buzz together like a congregation before a sermon. Brown-and-white-striped lizards with blue tails skitter across our pathway.

"Those are blue-tailed skink," Jack says.

"Not to be confused by red-tailed skanks," I say, grinning.

He smiles back at me. "No judgments, but a writer must experience *all* that life offers. Including red-tailed skanks."

I say, "I'm experiencing lots of things, don't worry about that. And I've seen more animals this morning than I have all year."

"And?"

"*And* . . . I love it. People have this idea that Los Angeles is all skyscrapers and car chases and reality stars, and I'm . . . I'm people, sometimes. Meaning . . . when I think of LA, some of my first thoughts are police helicopters, the 405, and smog. And yeah, LA can be all of that, but it can also be peaceful hikes and canyons, hills and clean air . . . spaces like this."

Jack waits for me to catch up to him. "Owls and wildflowers and trails filled with people who enjoy a good hike in a forest close to home. Drugs and peace and rock and roll . . . speaking of which . . . fun fact: back in the day, the Beatles visited Topanga. A bunch of locals let the air out of their tires so they couldn't leave."

I laugh. "Stans."

"See those dirt roads across there?" He points to bald patches of dirt scarring the hillsides. "A women-only crew of inmates from Malibu Conservation Camp 13 makes these fire roads."

My skin prickles. "How do you know they're inmates? Do they *look* like—"

"No, no, of course not," he says, then sips water. "I know because my family helped support the program."

Second chances.

"Ah. I thought you were going to say . . ."

"Something terribly racist?"

I wait a beat and then nod. "Because Black and brown people hike, and sometimes they hike in groups that aren't inmates."

"No way."

"True story."

"I've never seen it on TV," he says. "Therefore: no, they don't."

"Behold." I hold out my arms and strike a pose. "I am Black people hiking. Not an inmate."

"I appreciate your honesty," he says, screwing on the cap to his water bottle. "I'm actively learning how to identify my own biases. I'm making every effort to be an ally in more ways than just . . . *saying* it and wearing a mass-produced T-shirt with a watered-down slogan."

"That makes me happy to hear." I sip from my bottled water, adding convicted felons into the mix of people who could've disappeared Sam.

We walk on, and I wonder at fallen acorns and tiger lilies—I've never seen either in the wild.

"I remember taking my first hike," I say, charging into my next lie of the day. "My mother wanted to do something atypical for her, for us as a family. So she broke out the Thomas Guide—"

"Oh, this is ancient history, then?" Jack says with a crooked grin.

"Moses was our block captain," I say. "And Mom opened that sacred book of maps with its pages falling out, and she held up a page that had drifted to her foot. And verily, she pointed to an immeasurable swath of green, and that green patch was . . . ?"

"Topanga State Park?" Jack asked, his voice low, playing along.

"Yes. And so verily—"

"You like that word."

"Verily, I do. And so, we piled into our battered Honda and yea, we drove from South-Central to . . . to . . . I can't remember the name of the trail, but it was off a main street. And that day was November 2, 1993, her birthday."

"Verily?" Jack asks, eyebrow cocked.

"True story," I say.

It is not.

"That was the first and last time Mom hiked," I say. "She called on Jesus the entire time."

"First and last?" His brows furrowed. "What happened?"

I rub my elbows. "Not sure, but it's one of those tentpole moments in my life. Maybe she was sore that day. Maybe being out here scared her. Maybe it was too much, too soon." I shake my head and shrug. "I thought about the day we took that hike, and I wonder if something big, something historical happened that day."

Jack says, "Something historical *did* happen. Her first and last hike."

I shrug. "Maybe." The sweat beneath my arms chills. "Maybe I got hurt that day, and it freaked her out."

"Or . . ." Jack tips his head and assesses fallen trees piled beside the trail. "Maybe it was the Old Topanga Fire. It started that day. Sent a bunch of firefighters to the hospital and killed three people. The majority of those milk vetch plants were destroyed. You guys probably hiked right before it started, and she probably realized how close to danger you were."

He waits a beat, then says, "Why haven't you asked your mother?"

I push out a breath. "She's not around to answer."

He dips his head. "Ah. Sorry."

My eyes burn with tears, strangely affected by my bullshit story.

"You okay?" Jack asks, then sips water.

I nod, try to smile.

"It's okay," he says, nodding. "No need to be brave. My mom's gone, too. And we also had some unresolved bullshit that I think about all the time." He shakes the water bottle, his gaze resting on the hillside. "And *that* drives me to write what I write. Maybe the story you came here to write is related to that."

"Free therapy posing as writing?" I ask.

Jack points at me. "Highly efficient and often lucrative."

Countless fallen trees litter the sides of the trail, the inside rings of their trunks countless because they're that old. The petals of purple blossoms and yellow flowers seem too soft to touch. Birds sing, hidden in the leaves, and sometimes I stop to listen to their songs, wishing that I could sing along.

Forty-five minutes into our hike, I ask, "Why did you choose me for this residency?"

"That's an easy answer," Jack says. "Because you're older. Because you're Black."

His candor makes me jerk my head. "Wow. Can you be more honest than that?"

He snorts. "Why would I dance around it? Why should I be ashamed?"

I hold out my hands. "I'm just . . . surprised by your frankness."

"All throughout my career," he says, "I've written book after book about young white men and young white women. And it's the same thing—in my novels, in crime writing both fiction and nonfiction. Every missing white woman is twenty-six years old and lights up a room, which leads her to become a dead white woman. In a city as wonderfully diverse as Los Angeles, you'd believe that only twentysomething-year-old white girls would give you the shirt off their backs, who don't have enemies, who are kind and sweet and wouldn't hurt a fly.

"And frankly? I'm embarrassed, and I desperately want to change that, starting with the women in my stories. It only helps me grow—as a human being, yes—but also as a writer. I want to learn more about how *you* see the world. Hear what *you* think about car chases and recycling and COVID-19 and marriage and the criminal justice system. Tell me about the cats under your house, and the raccoons and skunks and coyotes that call the middle of a big city their home."

"*I'm* the representative?" I ask, shoulders rigid. "All of middle-aged Black womanhood lives within me?"

"Not *all* of middle-aged Black womanhood," he says, "but enough that I'll have a small glimpse into a world that's a total mystery to me. 'Wearing a bonnet to bed' thing *alone* . . ."

I laugh, remembering my satin bonnet. "Margo saw me wearing it this morning. She thought we'd made the bonnet thing up."

"Why would you make that up?" he asks, his eyebrows scrunched. "That's what *I* said."

He rubs his face—*Oh, Margo*. "I'm at a point in my career where I can open the Beckham tent to bring in more people," he says now. "Help more talented people receive acknowledgment and the space they need to tell interesting stories that rumpled white guys—"

"With names like Skylar Orion?"

"Yeah," Jack says. "Like Skylar Orion."

"Your protégé."

"Yeah." His cheeks burn red hot.

The silence hangs between us.

"I admit," he says, "the past writers-in-residence are not the most diverse." He clasps his hands behind his head and stretches. "I know, Bailey. I'm talking diversity and inclusion, but my last mentee was a white kid who wrote a book that wouldn't have made a difference to anyone other than his family if it got published or not. When I read *Catch* in draft, I didn't clutch the manuscript to my chest and say, 'Skylar Orion saw me, he reflected my life, my culture, my people. I will diminish and go into the west and remain Galadriel.'"

I snort. "And by working with me, I'll help you pass the test?"

Jack shrugs. "Hopefully I'll just do *better* on the test. I mean . . . I'm still working up the courage to change my heroine's race. And then, there are the questions: Why am *I* the one to write this? You and me working together? Gives me validity. I already have a platform. And I can say something one time that you've said a million times, but readers and critics will listen to me because I'm a rich white guy."

"Back to what you were saying earlier," I say. "The whole 'write what you know' thing. Are you saying that I shouldn't?"

Jack shakes his head. "It's impossible. Have you ever solved a murder? Are you an investigator? Hell, do you even have a sister?"

His questions scratch at my skin. Because *yes*, I *am* an investigator. In training. Still . . .

"Doesn't matter," Jack says, sweeping his arm across the sky. "Because what you're *saying* is more important than *who* is saying it." He dips his head. "In my humble opinion."

"Of course," I say, also dipping my head.

As we walk on, Jack points to more plants and flowers. I aim my phone every time to take pictures.

"You know, Bailey?" he says, gazing at me. "It's awesome to have people on the property again. COVID made me—*made us*—scale back a lot. Before the pandemic, I'd gained the reputation of being a Howard Hughes–crazy recluse. But I see myself as more of a J. D. Salinger than a Thomas Pynchon."

"But you've published more than one bestseller," I point out. "And you're working, not cackling like a madman in a dark room."

"True." He squints as he thinks. "Cormac McCarthy said, 'If you're writing a book, you probably shouldn't be talking about it. You should be doing it.' And so, I *am* doing it. But it's taking me longer—I've really been through a lot over the last few years. Since my last book, which I barely eked out, writing has become *hard* for me."

He rolls his eyes, flicks his hand. "Says the rich white guy. But it's been tough, and shit's just worn me out, and so I reverted to my naturally introverted ways." Jack's chest swells as he takes a deep breath. "But I'm ready to rejoin society. It may be the death of me but . . ." He makes a clipped nod. "I'm ready to do this thing, Bailey, and I'm so glad that you're here. We'll all be careful in our cozy, COVID-free bubble. But if you feel sick, just let Margo and me know."

"Will do," I say. "And I'm glad that I'm here, too, Jack. Thank you for inviting me."

And we walk.

Up ahead, I spot the ruins of a homestead. The gray-and-pink-boulder chimney is the only part of the structure that remains. The chimney's opening is sizable enough to shelter two grade-schoolers. "What was this?" I ask.

Jack takes a long glug of water from his bottle. "A cabin once upon a time." His body heat rolls off him like a sunbaked highway.

"No shit," I say. "Give me more than *that*. Did weird cult murders happen here? Animal sacrifices or . . . ?"

He shrugs again and runs his hand along the old stone.

"We can make this a site in the novel," I suggest, noting his quiet reverence for this space.

"I agree," he says. "It's always felt . . . *heavy* here."

"And it does now." Like my knees and neck are covered with thick syrup. A tattered MISSING PERSON flyer is duct-taped to one of the cabin's stones. Jack taps the picture of the missing young woman featured on there. "Poor thing."

"Do you know her?" I ask.

"Nope. But she's somebody's daughter, right?" He tsks, runs his hand over his mouth. "I helped in the initial search, and I donated to the reward. No luck." He uses his forearm to swipe at the sweat beading across his forehead. "People have forgotten about her, I fear, and this flyer has become just another *thing* in the forest."

I snap a photo of him standing beside the mysterious fireplace. I don't want Sam to be forgotten, to be just another *thing* anywhere. But now, I fear that I'm too late. We haven't posted any MISSING PERSON bulletins. We haven't launched grid searches. No one's offered a reward. Hell, I didn't even *know* Sam was missing. How can I fault others for not paying attention?

"Onward." He beckons me to follow him. "Almost there."

Sunshine blinks off shiny green leaves and shiny green grass and the pink things and purple things. The world is a sequined ball gown.

We navigate a creek busy with caramel-colored amphibians—

"California newts," Jack tells me.

We reach a tall brown sign with yellow letters: WATERFALL. Another MISSING PERSON flyer has been duct-taped beneath the words. Now I take more time to read it.

KADENCE HATFIELD hasn't been seen since 2015.

She was last spotted in Topanga Canyon.

"It's like I've seen this flyer before," I say.

"Yeah, back at the old cabin ruins," Jack says.

"Not that time, but before. I can't place it, though."

"Remember," Jack says, "you're writing about the worst thing that could happen to someone, happen to a family. You're writing about violence and psychopaths, and try as you may, it *will* affect you. Faces will blur, and then you'll see murder everywhere, and you'll always question their motives. All that to say: you *didn't* see this flyer before—it's just affecting your memory."

Maybe.

"Should I be worried, though?" I ask Jack, my stomach jittery, my mind flitting to Russell Walker out creeping in the dark canyon. "I know about Manson and the husband-wife gate murder and so . . ."

"Is this canyon safe?" he says. "True story: small-town Ohio. Church potluck. People eat. Thirty-six hours later, folks are experiencing drooping eyelids, weak muscles. Twenty people, sick from botulism. One dead from potato salad or whatever it is they ate."

"Damn," I say.

"Another true story: two planes collide in the skies above Cerritos. *Boom.* Almost seventy people die. Planes fall from the sky, and debris rains down into the neighborhood, sets sixteen houses on fire. Three people in one of those houses die."

My throat closes, and I whisper, "I remember that."

He pulls at his ear. "Sometimes, Bailey, you don't need the devil."

"Bad shit can happen anywhere, in any town," I say, nodding.

"To answer your question about being safe here," Jack says. "First, Kadence disappeared six years ago. Second, this forest has wildlife, sudden drops, bees . . . *those.*" He points to the forest floor.

Mushrooms—white hairy ones, pink flaky ones, dome-shaped ones that grow in clumps. The clicking rasp of rattlesnakes, heard but not seen. Trickling water . . .

"Sometimes, you don't need the devil," I say, eyebrow arched.

We plow ahead until he stops and spreads his arms. "Here we are."

I blink at the shallow creek and the dry rock slabs and . . . "Where's . . . ?"

"The water?" Jack asks.

My eyes skip to ropes that have been fixed to the boulders by climbers. "The water that . . . *falls* at Santa Ynez *Falls*?"

"Drought."

"Oh. Yeah." Disappointment twines around me, and I want to cry just standing here. I bite my lip and force myself to take pictures of the scene.

"It's not Niagara Falls, even after the rain," Jack says. "Still: when there *is* rain, it's incredibly . . ." He glides into silence.

"It's incredibly . . . *what*?" I ask.

He's watching something behind me.

"What's wrong?" I ask, alert now. "A snake? A mountain lion?"

"No, it's . . ."

I about-face.

Way, way over there, thin black smoke rises from the tops of distant trees.

I gasp. "Oh no."

A man hiking from the opposite direction says, "Just some dipshit's campfire that got out of control."

My eyes flare. "Should we call 9-1-1?"

Jack places his hand on my shoulder. "It's okay. Relax."

The hiker twirls his walking stick, then swipes at the sweat on his forehead. "Somebody already called. The fire trucks pulled up a few minutes ago. It's all good in the neighborhood." He tosses us a wave and journeys on the path we'd just taken.

"All good?" I ask, gooseflesh all over my body. "Will they put it out before it spreads?"

Jack points to the way, way over there. "See for yourself."

The black smoke has now grayed. As we stand and watch from our spot near the trickle of a drought-affected waterfall, that smoke lightens from gray to white.

"See?" Jack says. "All good in the neighborhood." He taps my shoulder and points north. "Topanga Canyon Boulevard connects to the 101 that way"—he points to the south—"and Pacific Coast Highway that way. Cuts right through the Santa Monica Mountains."

I point in every direction. "Got it."

"Ready to head back?" he asks.

I wring my hands, crack my knuckles. "Yeah . . ."

After one last worried look back, I turn away from that dying pillar of smoke.

Never turn your back on the ocean.

Is there similar wisdom for fire?

Item Number: 1507336
Item Description: paper receipt (1)
Victim: Doe, Jane
Offenses: Death Investigation
County of Offense: Los Angeles
Offense Date: November 2, 1993

Comments:

One (1) paper receipt collected from Santa Ynez Falls—Topanga State Park, 20828 Entrada Road, Topanga, CA 90290 near cabin ruins. Receipt from CY'S LIQUOR EMPORIUM at 9099 W. Pico Blvd., Los Angeles, CA 90036.

(1) bottle of Moet & Chandon Imperial Brut, 750 ML
(2) bags of Doritos, nacho cheese flavor
(1) pack of 18-piece Hubba Bubba, strawberry watermelon
(1) pack of Trident, spearmint

Other Information or Requests:

I talked with Martin Lebowitz of Cy's Liquor Emporium who rang up these purchases for the victim. He recalls (and the attached receipt confirms) that she paid in cash. Victim was alone on this trip and did not seem distressed. Please see the attached sheets for transcript of interview, map, and collection photos.

If you have any questions, please contact Detective Kimball. Thank you!

8.

The sun hangs white-hot above Topanga Canyon—the marine layer that brought chilly fog has burned off, and now brown and golden sun-drenched hills fade beneath the vibrant living thrills of wildflowers and tall grass. And now, craggy and curvy sandstone boulders and slot canyons glimmer and hunker and twist across the face of the earth. And now, brown, white, and yellow signs—No Bikes on Trails, Poison Oak, Waterfall, Trail Unmaintained—can be seen and ignored by groups of hikers wearing flannels, leggings, cargo shorts, and T-shirts. Way, way back over there, the smoke from that campfire thins, barely deserving a second thought.

"Told you," Jack says, giving me a thumbs-up. "That fire was nothing to worry about. I'd never put you in harm's way or downplay an emergency. Trust me, Bailey."

As soon as Jack and I step back onto his property, my phone vibrates. Jack's phone dings over and over again like the end of a typewriter carriage. We both hold off from checking our messages, though, and instead check each other for ticks.

"The western black-legged tick has eight legs, is reddish black or brownish black, flat when they haven't eaten, and they freak me the fuck out." Jack slowly turns me around as he scans my body. "Aah. Here." He points to a spot on my inner thigh that's the size of a poppy seed, its top half black and its bottom half reddish brown.

"Oh, wow. Look at *that*." With my phone, I zoom in on the creature, curiosity jolting through me. "How do you know it's full of Lyme disease?"

"I *don't* know," he says. "Let her bite you, and we'll see if your face collapses. Ask me how I know about *that*."

"Oh no! You . . . ?"

"Yep. Never looked the same after that happened."

Maybe *that's* the reason for all the cosmetic procedures.

I waggle my thigh at Jack. "I'm done with discovery, and now . . . get it off, get it off. Seriously, it's creeping me the fuck out."

Jack laughs, pulls tweezers from his leggings pocket, then plucks off the parasite. He holds the tick up to the sunlight—such sleek engineering—and then he crushes it between the prongs of the tweezer. "Your turn."

He has strong, lean legs beneath his light-gray leggings. Strong, lean arms beneath his long-sleeved T-shirt. He has the physique of a ballet dancer, like the blond Russian guy who played the terrorist in *Die Hard*.

"No ticks," I say, patting him on the shoulder. "It's like they know not to hitch a ride on the guy who will end their world between effing tweezers."

"Do not fuck with that Jack Beckham. That bitch is crazy." Smiling, he strides toward the house. "Let's eat."

I pluck at my sweaty shirt. "Seriously? I need to shower—"

"Yes, you're filthy and you stink and blah blah blah," he says, "but I have a meeting in an hour, and one more after that, and I won't be able to chat with you until later, but I'd understand if you don't wanna do that." He disappears into the main house.

Crap. Panic bubbles in my gut—I'm here to investigate, not take showers.

I take a quick peek at my recording pen snug in my pocket. Still blue. Still recording. I swipe at my phone's screen to check messages.

"Bailey," Jack calls. "Are we eating together or not?" He stands at the top of the deck, holding a wedge of pineapple.

"Yes. Coming." I slip the phone back into my pocket—I can check later.

Seeing the features of the main house in full daylight . . . I'm speechless. Astounded. Agog. Beams hug the ceiling, and skylights bring in natural light. Everything glows. The white oak hardwood floors spring beneath my shoes. Stainless steel kitchen. Wood furniture. Desert tans and browns. Even with its sleekness, this place gives off "just a simple hacienda" vibes.

"Lunch is out on the patio." Standing at the kitchen sink, Luann, Jack's chef, wipes her strong hands on a dish towel. She's a tall, older woman with a full bosom beneath that orange University of Texas sweatshirt. Short, curly bob and wide face, overplucked eyebrows and hooded eyes. A small gold crucifix on a delicate chain completes the modern Texas grandma cosplay. She's smiling, encouraging me to move along, to come eat lunch.

I hold my hands, prayer-style. "Thank you for breakfast this morning. The bacon was perfect."

"You're welcome, hon," she says, grinning, her eyes now raisins in her face. "And I hope you don't mind, but I closed your door this morning. Didn't wanna wake you."

"That was *you*?"

"Yes, that was me," she says, giggling. "How did you think it closed?"

"Ghosts."

She chortles and flaps her hands at me—*Oh, go on, now.*

I release the breath I've been holding since this morning.

The cook points to french doors that lead back outside. "Don't keep him waiting, hon. He gets cranky when he's hungry."

Jack stands at the patio sideboard, ignoring the golden butterflies, the soaring hawks, the stunning view of Topanga State Park, his backyard.

Lunch . . . once again, I'm speechless. Astonished. Agog.

Fresh-cut fruit and baby salad greens with goat cheese and beets.

Lemon tarts.

Roast beef and fried chicken.

Homemade potato chips.

Four different kinds of bread.

"And Luann's famous fruit punch." Jack pours pinkish-orange liquid into two ice-filled glasses. "It's the only nonalcoholic drink I'll consume that isn't water or coffee."

"I'll need to hike twice a day if I'm eating like this," I say, filling my plate.

This fruit looks too perfect and vibrant to eat. That cheese board with figs and olives looks too perfect to destroy.

I settle across from Jack at the patio table.

Fruit and undressed salad are the only foods on his plate.

"Vegan," he says, reading my mind. "And an under-two-thousand-calorie diet." His iceberg-gray eyes sparkle, his body lacks fat, he isn't breathing heavy after hiking, and he jogs to the equator twice a day. His strict regimen is working. "Other than seeing smoke from that small brushfire," he says now, "you have a good time this morning?"

I pop another grape into my mouth. "Other than the small brushfire?" I nod. "I had an *awesome* time this morning. You're a wonderful tour guide."

"Glad that you got something out of it," he says. "And do you need anything other than better internet in the cottage?"

"No," I say. "It's perfect. Thank you."

We scroll through the pictures he and I both took during our hike.

Those are my fingers holding a small fuchsia flower.

There I am, resting in a cave, appearing pensive.

Here are two strangers, Jack and Bailey, a newly formed writing team, standing in front of a chimney in a cabin that no longer stands, smiling like they've known each other forever. Future collaborators. Future friends. One a liar.

Jack bites into a golden beet chunk.

I chomp potato chips.

Hawks cry out as they glide over the canyon. Wind whistles through the trees. Birds sing.

"How long has your family lived here?" I ask between bites of roast beef.

Jack wipes his mouth with a cloth napkin. "My great-grandfather bought lots of land back in 1910. Since then, Beckham men have always occupied this piece of Topanga Canyon. My father only modernized the estate to keep my mother happy."

"Your mother," I say. "Her name is . . . ?"

"Liliana, and she left Dad and me in 2003, two days after my twentieth birthday."

"'Left' as in 'died'?" I ask. "Or 'left' as in . . . ?"

He pops an olive into his mouth. "Left as in . . . she joined a cult and moved to Montana."

"Damn," I say. "I'm sorry."

Jack traces a bead of condensation on his glass of punch. "We tried to convince her to return but . . . she didn't. I don't know if she's still upright and walking the earth or if she's met the comet in the sky or spaceship or whatever it was she believed in and chose over me.

"I try to rationalize her leaving—she and Dad had me when they were absurdly young. Only nineteen years old. She didn't know who she was, then."

"I'm forty," I say, "and I don't even know who *I* am sometimes or who I'm supposed to be by now." This is true.

"Same," he says. "She was *my* age when she left, not even forty yet. Dad . . . the older he got, the surlier he became." Jack stares at the potato chips on my plate. "People around the canyon say that I look just like him when *he* was almost forty. The eyes. Jawline. Nose."

He eats the rest of his beet. "I'm a better version, though. Definitely healthier. More balanced. Respectful of my body. Disciplined."

I nibble a cube of smoked Gouda. "Did your dad remain a widower, or did he remarry?"

Jack jabs at another beet chunk with his fork. "I had a lot of almost-moms, but he never proposed to any of them. They disappeared without saying goodbye, too. I stopped trying to connect or engage."

"Because what would be the point?"

He points at me with his fork. "Exactly. And they could *never* replace my mother."

"And so . . . ?"

"And *so*, nothing. He wrote about his exes, cast them in his novels, exorcised his anger by killing them off in his stories. One of his girl-friends disappeared, and the cops even questioned him. She turned up, alive, living at some commune up in Idyllwild. He drove her away just like he drove my mother away. Not *entirely* illegal—being an abusive asshole—but definitely fucked up . . . and for me, embarrassing that he'd earned this reputation of being . . . *problematic*." Jack pops the beet in his mouth. "But women kept finding him dangerous in that *sexy* way, you know?"

Filled with sincere sorrow, I touch my heart. "I know it doesn't help any, but I'm so sorry."

He leans over to the credenza and grabs the bowl of potato chips. He shakes more into my diminishing pile. He doesn't eat a single chip, not even a small, broken one. What human can resist potato chips?

"Big Jack died years ago," Jack says, "and not from anything long and painful like cancer or heart attack. He went like his favorite writer."

Virginia Woolf filled her pockets with rocks and tottered into the river.

David Foster Wallace hanged himself on the patio of his home.

"The Heming-way," Jack says, answering my unasked question. "Shotgun in his mouth. He wrote a single-spaced two-page note. I found him at the casita."

My eyes goggle, and I bolt upright in my chair.

"Oh!" Jack says, his eyes also wide. "Not in *this* casita. I mean the one my family always rents in Belize. Two years after my mother disap-peared, he joined me on my backpacking trip through Central America.

I was working on my MFA—the oral histories of indigenous cultures and their influences on the stories we tell.

"And my father didn't do it inside the casita. No—he sat outside on the other side of the bedroom window so that he could face the rising sun." Jack clucks his tongue, then adds, "That blast echoed all around the jungle. I hopped out of bed and found him . . . up until that moment, I'd been the happiest I'd been since my mother's departure. But then, he took that away from me, too."

His gray eyes glaze as they stare into the distance, and his face loses color. "In a way, I was grateful for that tick biting me and changing my face—I didn't have to see him in my reflection anymore. But then, I couldn't see my mother, either. Except for my eyes. Hers were gray, too."

"That's awful, Jack," I say.

He regards me with sadness and exhaustion. "Are you strong enough to write this story?"

I open my mouth and pop it closed.

"Writers dredge up our own issues and wrestle them into a structure, and then into words. Writing and tapping into your trauma, calling back ghosts . . . it can and will be painful, even if you think you're okay."

He pauses, then asks, "Do you think people who had happy childhoods can write good murder stories?"

I pick a chip from the pile, but I don't eat it. "You said that you don't have to write what you know, so . . . yes?"

"That's not what I'm asking. Can they write *good* murder stories? Stories that tear at your heart because they've torn at the writer's heart?"

"I don't know . . ." I eat the potato chip, but I can't taste it. "You said that your father wrote a note. Did his reasons for ending his life make sense to you? Not that any explanation would make sense—I don't mean to imply that."

Jack swats my apology away. "I won't share all that he wrote in that note, but . . . *I get it?* And so, I moved back to Topanga and continued the legacy of the Beckhams living off Old Topanga Canyon Road. I got my MFA *finally*, about six years ago."

He pops an olive, then says, "I had mixed emotions coming back here. Parts of me froze. Other parts begged me not to. But I came back, and all the memories associated with Topanga rushed over me, the good *and* the bad. The incredible hikes but the explosive arguments. The book parties but my mother's depression. The peace of the forest but the sound of her weeping."

I sigh, and say, "Yeah. That's . . . wow."

"What about you?" he asks. "Did you go back to your parents' home after Stanford?"

Shit. What's my cover story for that? What have I told him so far?

My cheeks burn as I think. "It was just my mom and me," I say, "and . . ." I swallow the soggy chip I'd just popped in my mouth. "She tried hard to make our pocket-size duplex comfortable and safe. I didn't hear weeping or arguing with anyone—my dad was long gone. But I *did* hear her gun clicking—she was always cleaning it. She taught me to shoot, too. And now, every time I visit my old neighborhood, I smell fried-bologna sandwiches and white bread and gun oil, and I remember how her stomach ached every time she drank one of those SlimFast shakes."

Jack chuckles. "Whose mother *didn't* drink SlimFast shakes? Even mine, the lady of Topanga, drank those. And then, she complained about the gas they gave her."

"Your parents lived here through all those big fires, right?" I ask, then sip from my glass of fruit punch.

"And yet, the fires didn't kill them," Jack says. "Nor did fire ever burn down our house. I have pictures—and I'll show them to you later. Pictures of my father with a cigar clenched between his teeth, up there on the rooftop"—he points up—"wetting everything down with a garden hose. Every fire captain Topanga's ever had hated him for never evacuating. Dad would always say"—Jack squares his shoulders and lowers his chin to his chest—"they can go to hell. I'm my own rescuer. I'm not leaving my home, I'm prepared to live or die."

I smile. "A manly man, huh?"

Jack rolls his eyes. "I haven't shown it to you yet, but he had this elaborate fire bunker built, just in case we got trapped up here."

"A fire bunker?" I nibble a piece of roast beef. *Interesting.*

"Remember that Topanga fire back in 1993?" he asks. "I mentioned it on our hike."

"Oh, yeah." I rub my eyes, then slump some in the chair.

"There I was, a ten-year-old kid with a forest fire bearing down on us, and I'm trying to convince my father to evacuate. I was convinced that we'd all die if we stayed here."

"He didn't listen to you," I say.

"Nope. He didn't listen to my mother, either. He told us—" He drops his chin again. "'This house hasn't burned down in eighty-three years, and it won't burn down for another eighty.' And what sucks is . . . that massive fire in '93 skipped right over our house—just like previous fires had also skipped over our house. It's like . . . like there's some kind of wizard's protective ward shielding it or something."

"Did you and your mother ever evacuate without him, then?" I ask. "To save yourselves?"

Jack shakes his head. "She couldn't leave him, and she resented him for putting my life and hers in danger. No wonder she left him, right? I mean . . . the canyon on fire resembles every depiction of hell you've ever seen. Forty-foot-long flames. No sun. Black sky in the day. Orange sky at night. Wicked wind. Cherry-colored fire retardant dropping from planes. Fireballs . . . Three days—that's how long that fire burned."

He rubs his face, then gazes out to the hillsides rolling around us. "My mother really wasn't a religious woman back then. More of a Christmas, Easter, Mother's Day churchgoer. But then, she lived through that fire and . . . she needed to heal in a lot of ways, from a lot of things. Me too."

"I didn't know my father," I say. "Mom never talked about him. Every time I go into spaces with lots of people, I scan the crowd, looking for my nose, my eyes, but on a man. Never found him." I scrunch my eyebrows, hating that I'm sharing this true story.

Jack sighs, then whispers, "I'd do anything to bring her back. I have so many questions, the simplest being . . . *Why?* I loved her. Wasn't that enough?"

I tear apart another slice of roast beef. "Is love ever strong enough to keep someone in a place they're desperate to leave? To stay in a place that's slowly killing you?" I cock my head and nod at my surroundings. "Yes, it's beautiful here . . . for your mother, though, a beautiful prison is still . . . a prison."

Jack rubs his eyes. "The saying goes, 'Don't change Topanga—let Topanga change *you.*' And it sure as hell did. I channeled all that hate and dread and fear into every book that I wrote afterward. *Old Topanga Road* eventually came after my first two novels, and it was a relief. And now, sometimes, people confuse me with my character, Axel Fletcher. And sometimes, I *think* that I am, I've been writing him so long. Now it's . . . Where do I end and Axel begins? This is what writers do. This is *our* church and religion, right?"

I offer him a small smile. "Guess that's why people love your novels. Your memories and life experience make your stories authentic. In this case, you're writing what you know: loss, fear, love . . ."

He holds up his glass of fruit punch. "And you'll do the same. Piece of advice: don't force or stage situations in the drama you create. Let it happen as it would in real life."

Avery, in a way, told me the same thing in that email she sent back on Wednesday.

My damp leggings cling to my skin. I'm starting to itch all over—arms, neck, and face—and even on the inside, I flare with heat.

Jack's eyes narrow into slits. "Did you fuck around in the poison oak?"

My itchy eyes grow big. "You're seeing what I'm feeling right now?"

Like I'm covered with welts and fire.

"You have any food allergies?" he asks, sitting up in his chair.

"Umm . . ." I scan my plate—roast beef, beets, potato chips. Regular food. Nothing provocative.

Jack shouts, "Luann," then says to me, "Hold on."

Luann ambles out to the deck. "Everything okay?"

"Maybe not," he says. "You have Miss Meadows's food restrictions?"

"Margo sent them over to me this morning." She pulls her phone from her back pocket, then scrolls . . . swipes up . . . swipes up . . . "Here it is."

As I wait, flames sweep across my skin. My throat and tongue swell.

Jack comes to stoop beside me. He places his hand atop mine—his touch is ice. "It's okay," he whispers.

Luann zooms in on something on her screen. "Says here . . . *coconut*."

Our eyes skip around the platters on the sideboard, and then they land on the pitcher of fruit punch.

Luann gulps, then covers her mouth with a hand. "I used coconut water."

"She's allergic," Jack snaps.

Luann holds her hand to her neck. "Oh no."

"EpiPen," Jack tells her.

Luann scurries back into the house.

"No worries," he whispers to me. "I got you. You'll be fine. I keep EpiPens stocked since we host lots of guests with different . . ." His eyes go soft and blurry. "I'm so sorry, Bailey. I should've triple-checked—"

I nod and nod. Nervous. Scared. Throat closing. Fire everywhere.

Luann returns to the patio with two elephantine tubes ending in an orange tip.

Jack takes one tube, removes the blue safety cap. "Ready?" Before I can answer, he jabs the orange tip into my thigh.

I cry out. "Ow!"

The sharp needle breaks past my leggings and punctures my skin.

I whisper, "Ohmigod."

Jack holds the pen in my thigh for three seconds. "Go call Torrance," he tells Luann. To me, he says, "Dr. Torrance lives down the road. I wasn't planning to introduce you two so soon, but . . ."

My heartbeat careens, and all of me feels thin and shaky. My thigh aches. The sting ebbs. My throat opens. The itching eases . . .

Jack takes my hand. "It's working, okay? It's working."

Luann returns to the patio, her eyes red rimmed and her cheeks wet with tears. "I just left a message with Dr. Torrance's answering service."

I wilt in my chair and croak, "I should've paid more attention."

"I'm so sorry, Miss Meadows," Luann says, her voice shaky. "I didn't think. I—I . . . we'll be extremely careful from now on." She takes the pitcher of danger juice from the sideboard.

Jack sinks to the floor. "*That* was terrifying."

I try to smile. "If you don't want me here, just tell me. You don't have to poison me to death."

Jack tries to chuckle. "If you don't wanna be here, just leave. You don't have to drink poisoned juice to void your contract."

"I'm good," I squeak.

I didn't know that eating lunch at the Beckham estate could kill me.

What if there hadn't been any EpiPens around? How long would I have lasted without that shot? I don't wanna know. I'm not ready to leave this world, not yet. But I know that decision, ultimately, isn't mine to make.

Fruit punch this time. A coconut-oiled doorknob the next? Or maybe, just maybe, a plane falling from the sky and on top of my bedroom.

Sometimes, you don't need the devil.

9.

Dr. Torrance from down the road is over in Malibu, visiting with his granddaughter—he can't examine my welt-covered skin at the moment.

"I can drive you to the ER," Jack says. "I don't care about my meeting."

I tell him no, that I'm fine with waiting for Dr. Torrance to return to the canyon. "I'm too tired to zigzag all the way down to PCH and wait three hours in an ER full of COVID-19 only for a doctor to say 'all good.'"

"You sure?" he asks, his skin pale, his eyes full of concern. "I don't mind."

My head dips. "I just wanna rest."

Jack escorts me back to the cottage. Tense, his shoulders now ride his earlobes, and the muscles in his temples and jaw twitch.

And now, the trees aren't so beautifully ancient to me, and that disk of light in the sky feels like hell on my face. And now that I've met death—it tastes like coconuts, berries, and orange juice—these twisty roads that keep the world away keep doctors and emergency rooms away, too. So many nasty things can happen beneath this daunting blue sky, a daunting blue sky free of rescue helicopters that could stop and land and save your life if you wave a white towel frantically enough.

"Really," he says, "I'm serious. I'll cancel my meetings—"

I touch his arm. "No, keep it. Go to your meeting. I'm good. I'm gonna take a nap."

How has this—putting my body at risk over and over again—become part of the job? How is constant danger and injury a part of the journey to expose the lies, expose the truth?

Since forever. Girl Reporter Nellie Bly acted insane to be committed to an insane asylum to see firsthand patients assaulted and faced with sexual violence, forced into ice-cold baths, compelled to eat rotten meat and drink contaminated water . . . if she could last for ten days at Bellevue Hospital, I can come close to asphyxiation after sipping a little coconut water.

I stand before the bathroom mirror, watching my reflection vanish behind the steam from the shower, my second in less than twenty-four hours. A woman sways there with bloodshot eyes, crusty nostrils, and dry lips. There's a hole in her thigh made by an EpiPen, and on her leggings, there's a splotch of blood memorializing the violence done to her thigh. Her ponytail is tangled, and the wisps of hair around her forehead run wild as the chaparral growing across these hillsides.

Raggedy—that's how I feel. As puffy as a water balloon or a packet of spoiled ketchup. I want to unwrap my bandages—fortunately, there are no new bright-red posies on the gauze—but I *won't* unwrap those bandages. Right now, I'm not ready for any new reveals even though I feel solid inside, all of me fused together by epinephrine and gumption. This solidity—a false sensation. I'm actually too wobbly to write all of this down in my journal. I won't forget this day, though, the day I experienced Topanga Canyon using all five of my senses.

Or . . .

Maybe I *will* forget this day. Maybe this day will fade into my memory like the other near misses we all experience: first knee scrape, first broken finger, first near choking, almost drowning . . .

Yeah, maybe I'll forget. It's only a matter of time.

◆　◆　◆

I am allergic to coconut.

Who uses coconut water in fruit punch?

Luann had access to my food allergies—and yet, she prepared something with coconut anyway. Was this truly an accident? Did she do that on purpose? How could this happen?

Maybe I'm doing that thing Jack mentioned earlier. Questioning everything, including people's motives.

At the same time: Why am I moving about the world as though it will look out for me? I should've asked Luann for the ingredients of the fruit punch. I know better than this. Blame Topanga Canyon's "leave the door unlocked" kind of living.

I'm still thinking about this after showering, and I'm still thinking about this as I stare at the silver three-legged pig charm facing the gold trench coat. The charm hasn't moved from the suitcase tumbler, on the "5," right between the "7" and the "2." Either no one has gone through my things, or they noticed my trap and placed the pig in the right position.

After grabbing my laptop from the suitcase's hidden compartment (I have yet to log on to Jack's MacBook), I huddle in bed beneath the comforter.

All that buzzing from my phone post-hike and pre-lunch? Texts from the phone company, Spyscribe, and DoorDash.

Nothing from Avery.

I text her anyway.

Scary moment today

I drank fruit punch at lunch

But there was COCONUT in the punch

WTF??!!

Got caught up and forgot that I'm allergic

Each message whooshes into the ether. DELIVERED.

I may forget today, and I'm not okay with that. I retrieve my journal and document my day so far—from watching the mule deer and the California sisters at the swimming pool to hiking with Jack and reaching the ruins of the old cabin to reaching the trickle of a creek at Santa Ynez Falls. Jack's father dying by his own hand, a fire occurring on November 2, 1993, and Big Jack staying and fighting the fire with a water hose. I capture as much as I can, using strong adjectives and active verbs—*pinching, shuffling, evasive, quivering, unshakable sense that something is wrong.* I've muted some of the urgency, but I'll fine-tune later. Just like I'll fine-tune the stabbing in Oakland, being followed in Las Vegas, and . . . and . . .

I text Avery again.

Haven't learned much about her

Will keep digging though

I'll keep going until I find something definite that proves whether or not she came to Topanga Canyon and to this house!

No response.

No DELIVERED stamp this time.

Limbo.

Odd. Or . . . is this simply the canyon being the canyon, blocking and dropping signals every thirty minutes?

The phone rings in my hands, and I startle some—that debunks *that* theory of a dropped signal. Caller ID shows a number that I don't know. I stare at it, wondering if it's Quincy or what's-her-face from La Quinta Inn or someone altogether new. I tap ANSWER. "Hello?"

Dead air, just like last night.

"Hello?" I repeat.

Dead, dead, dead.

My spine stiffens. I don't like this. I tap END CALL.

A second or two passes and the phone rings again.

I tap ANSWER again.

Dead air again.

"Who's calling?" I ask, annoyed.

In the world on the other side of this call, there is heavy silence, there are bursts of sound: traffic and talking, heavy silence again, someone's faraway voice, and finally, complete silence.

My phone beeps three times and then . . . nothing.

END CALL.

The phone doesn't ring again, and in my heart I know it's Avery calling, probably concerned after reading about my near-death-by-coconut experience.

Whoever it is will call back—they always do.

As I wait, I flip back to older entries in my journal.

Wednesday, May 12—Attended Skylar Orion's book launch party and met Margo and Jack. Rumpled and smug. Drives an orange Saab. They still have car parts for Saabs?? House is amazing. The cottage, incredible. All moved in—

Tuesday, May 11—I've packed enough for two weeks, and remembered to include those envelopes and expanding files and fully loaded Shirley the Glock. Filled the car with—

Monday, May 10—Picked up my prescriptions from CVS. Fruitvale Ave. Feeling better now that I'm medicated. Percocet. This shit's good—

Friday, May 7—Still trying to figure out the panic button situation. If this doesn't work, how the hell will I let Avery know something's gone wrong?

Does the coconut thing count as "gone wrong"? If I'd had that panic button, would I have pressed it, hating that I had, since I've recovered?

I scroll back, back, back—*researched Topanga Canyon, sent Eddie Skinner TC address, picked up gun from Guns & Gals on Washington*—

There's a cute Danish bakery with tasteless sweets down the block from Guns & Gals.

Thurs., 4.29.21—We accepted the offer! I'll start the residency in May. Avery is remarkable—I still can't believe we did it. Deep undercover shit. I'm scared and excited as FUCK. So close to figuring out what the hell happened to her. The truth is out there! And I will learn the truth and the truth will set us free!!

This was the first entry in this journal. Less than a month ago feels like a lifetime ago. I tap the phone icon beside Avery's name, tired of waiting for her to call.

But the line rings . . . and rings . . . and rings . . . there's a click, and there's dead air, and then:

"The person you have reached is not available—"

I tap "7," fast-forwarding to leave a voicemail message. "Hey, Avery. It's Bailey. I think you just called—the reception up here isn't great. Just wanted you to know that I'm feeling a little loopy and tired, but I'm good. I can keep going. Onward. Talk soon."

I end the call, pick up the journal again, and add to today's entry:

I asked him about his father. Suicide in Central America, Belize, specifically. Mom Liliana left to join a cult in Montana. Jack uses Bro-tox and chemical peels to look young. Lyme disease victim. Fitness addict.

My head pounds across the bridge of my nose. I will take the next dosage of pain pills, but I need to work first. I peek at my phone: ohmigod, four bars of internet reception! Before I even complete this thought, I lose a bar. Yeah, I need to do some things before the internet dies again.

I resume my search on "Samantha Morris," drilling past the scientists and jocks and turn-of-the-century widows buried in the Midwest and—*oh!*

Samantha Morris, African American, thirty-three years old, MFA student. Born in San Diego. Writer. She peers at me from the web page with soft brown eyes and tawny skin.

Even though I haven't seen her in person, I know that this woman isn't *my* Sam Morris. She wasn't born in San Diego—she was born in Los Angeles.

I'll figure it out, Sam. Don't worry.

Two bars.

I find a website that provides plot summaries and chapter-by-chapter analyses of novels, including *Old Topanga Road.* Twenty dollars for a yearlong subscription. I pluck one of the Visa gift cards from my handbag. The "purchase completed" circle spins and spins and spins . . .

Crap.

One bar.

Spinning . . . spinning . . . spinning . . .

How much is left on this gift card? I don't wanna waste good internet to find out. I close my eyes and pray for a burst of reception and—

Two bars! My phone purchase completed.

A voicemail banner blinks onto my phone screen. The person who called minutes ago has left a message.

"Are you good now?" a man asks. *"You keep calling, and it's frustrating me. Do you wanna just stop and end this? Your decision. Just . . . don't ignore me, okay?"*

My eyes bug. Is this a breakup call? Can't be for me—I'm not dating anyone. Haven't danced or canoodled or anything since . . . since . . .

that long. What will the person who this call is *actually* for decide? End it? Try again?

I need that booster to strengthen my internet connection. But I feel like I've taken so much from Jack already, and I don't want to agitate him. I don't want him to shut himself off from me because I'm being too needy. Weird—his cook nearly kills me, and *I'm* the one who feels awful.

While I have two bars, I tap *Jack Beckham, Sr. City of Exile* into the search bar.

The circle spins and spins and spins.

NO SERVICE AVAILABLE.

Of course.

I kick off the comforter and wince—my thigh muscle still aches from the EpiPen and the adrenaline forced through my system. I slog to the kitchen for water to wash down the pills I'm about to pop.

At the end of the hallway, though, I stop walking.

Someone has come in again without my knowledge.

A stapled packet of legal-size papers and a black ink pen are sitting on the small dining table. A yellow sticky note is fixed on the top sheet of the packet.

I creep over to the table and read the handwritten note:

Hey, Bailey!

This is the contract for the Beckham Writer-in-Residence program. Congrats (again!) and welcome (again)! I've highlighted places for you to initial and sign. This contract was due to our lawyers early this morning but Jack insisted on taking that hike with you. A courier is coming at 3 to pick it up.

XOXO,

Margo

I glance over at the clock on the microwave oven.

Two fifty.

Shit.

The sour-milk taste of panic floods my mouth. I flip through the contract—there's no time for me to read and analyze everything—

Outside the cottage, a woman laughs.

I peek out the window.

It's Margo, and she's talking on the phone, tromping in my direction.

I read the first few sentences of the cover letter and then scan it. *Attest . . . missing sister . . . untitled work . . .*

Shitshitshit.

I flip the page.

Social Security number—what is it?

Shitshitshit.

I leave that space blank.

NONDISCLOSURE AGREEMENT

> Dear Bailey,
> We are thrilled to work with you on the next Jack Beckham bestseller—

I flip to the next page. My eyes cross at "hereunder" and "paragraph 3(a)(ii)" and "applicable copyright law."

If I sign this contract, will it stand up in court? I'm signing this, but the Bailey Meadows I am *now* is not the Bailey Meadows I will be after I leave Topanga Canyon. So . . . am I the *real* Bailey Meadows, beholden to these attestations?

Margo, still holding the phone to her ear—"Uh-huh, that's nuts . . . Did you tell her that?"—knocks on the door.

Shitshitshit.

With my pulse booming around my body, I rush over to let her in, then rush back to the contract on the dining table.

Margo rolls her eyes and says to the person on the phone, "Yes . . . yes . . . she's signing them now . . ." To me, Margo pantomimes writing with a pen, then mouths, "Hurry."

I initial the highlights here, here, here, and there. On the last page, I sign my name on the line above the typewritten BAILEY R. MEADOWS and write the date: May 13, 2021. Jack has already signed—one oversize "J" and one oversize "B." I drop the pen back onto the table, then take a big step back.

Margo gathers the contract, leaves the pen, and says to the person on the phone, "Got 'em in my hot little hands . . . I'm walking to the front right now."

"Do you need my ID?" I whisper to her. "The W-9?"

She shakes her head, gives me the "okay" thumbs-up, then whispers to me, "I know who you are."

But you don't. Not at all.

Margo marches back out the front door, and I'm left with remorse for lying to her. I'll make it up to her. In the book, I'll cast her as a supportive, lovely person. And that is true.

Oh! I remember my fake Social Security number now . . . or is that number ending in 6719 my *real* Social Security number? I need to write it down over and over once I determine what's real and what's fake. I need to repeat it like a mantra so that it flows like the rest of my story. But something worse than my forgetting this number has happened.

"What did I just sign?" I whisper, watching Margo disappear into the glare of the sun.

Doesn't matter. You signed the damned thing. You're in the army now.

◆ ◆ ◆

The light in the living room is a golden halo. Shadows of butterflies and creaky tree branches darken the pale hardwood floor.

Although my skin still hurts, I postpone drugging myself. Instead, I self-medicate with a bottle of Bordeaux from the kitchen wine rack as well as a package of thin, crispy toffee chocolate chip cookies from the pantry. The ingredients: everything except coconut.

I settle on the couch with *Old Topanga Road* and my laptop opened to the plot summary: *Mystery/thriller tale . . . the Hiker, a kidnapper and murderer . . . women off a popular trail in Topanga Canyon . . . killer has a taste for brunettes . . . known for leaving his victims with a backpack over their heads . . . connection between the Hiker and a serial killer known as the Canyon Creeper . . . Both killers are now collaborating and competing . . . washed-up private investigator Axel "Ax" Fletcher . . . before it's too late.*

Since I've already read the first chapter, I flip to chapter two.

◆ ◆ ◆

Axel watched the LAPD black-and-white helicopter race across the twilight sky. He drained the glass of scotch, racing now to the bottom before the bird disappeared into the night—

He stood in the dark now, only because he had to—he'd forgotten to pay the light bill. That had been Natalie's job—

◆ ◆ ◆

Two demented, blood-hungry villains.

One devoted, sad drunk hero.

The novel before this one, *Fire Road Loop*—*homicide detective Axel "Ax" Fletcher . . . finally found love . . . Evelin Adams, a behavioralist with the FBI . . . work together to stop an arsonist committed to creating the fire of the century . . .*

How much of Jack is in either story? Did he drink a lot of scotch? Did he date a behavioralist once upon a time? Did he consult with an arsonist to write realistically about the madman he's named "the Match"?

And the novel before *this* one—*Mayhem . . . singer/songwriter Grace Stanley . . . voices in her head led to commercial success, but now they are telling her to commit murder . . . who are these people to Grace? Will she listen to the voices . . . boyfriend Ethan Kane is on the list . . .*

For our novel . . .

How about . . . ?

Someone has killed the killer.

Yeah.

Everyone loves a cat-and-mouse game.

◆　◆　◆

November 2, 1993
Baldwin Village

Theresa and Sammi Morris chose to eat breakfast at IHOP that morning. Wearing khaki shorts and a *Raiders of the Lost Ark* T-shirt, Terri looked like she'd jump an unsuspecting high school student after AV club, then take the Air Jordans off his feet. If she wore a silk shirt and trousers instead, she would've looked like that actress—no, the other one—the young woman who'd wowed audiences in that movie, that actress in the perfume commercial—she's running through the City of Lights in a skirt made of pink tulle and silver dreams, yeah, that one.

On the second morning in November, though, in those Timberland boots and short-shorts, Terri existed somewhere between butch and femme. Bone-straight hair parted in the middle. Neck tattoo. Prison muscles. Gold stud in her delicate nose.

To celebrate her twenty-ninth birthday, Terri ordered the Rooty Tooty Fresh 'N Fruity pancakes. Sammi, her daughter and twin at twelve years old, ordered an omelet with bacon, mushrooms, and onions.

"Mom," Sammi said, giggling, "you're gonna lose a foot after eating all that sugar."

Terri rolled her eyes. "*Please.* I've been taking mini-hikes during my lunch break. So my blood pressure's down, and so are my prediabetes levels. I eat some apples every day, and this lady who works with me at the Visitors Center brings shit like flax cookies and quinoa nuggets for snacks."

"Ew. Flax? Quinoa? How is that fun?" Sammi asked.

"Right?" Terri grabbed the small pitcher of maple syrup and poured it over her stack of loaded pancakes. "That shit tastes like slavery and depression, but hey! At least I'm not constipated no more. Anyway, we're about to hike one hundred fifty thousand miles all over God's creation, so leave me alone and let me enjoy my strawberry compote and whipped cream."

The two studied Terri's Thomas Guide as they ate, deciding that the Santa Ynez Trail—a three-mile hike—had the most to see: a waterfall and grotto, a creek and stream crossings. Only an hour and a half hiking time.

"Yeah, cuz if we're doing all that," Sammi said, sucking her teeth, "at least gimme a waterfall at the end."

Terri cackled, lifted her coffee cup to clink against Sammi's juice glass. "You ain't lied *yet*, baby." She had picked up her daughter from Miss Nancy's house to celebrate her birthday. The old lady had swerved her neck, crossed her arms, and scowled as Terri had flitted around her daughter. *You're almost taller than me!* and *This time, I'm gonna do it!* and *There's this apartment!* and *I love this job!*

Back in their burgundy Honda Civic, Sammi cracked open her biology textbook to stay ahead in class. Terri sang along to Earth, Wind & Fire's "Fantasy" and followed the 10 west to Pacific Coast Highway. Thirty minutes later, once the air softened and smelled of salt, Sammi pushed away her biology textbook. The Pacific Ocean glimmered over there. The sandstone bluffs and multimillion-dollar beach homes towered over the world up there. Porsches and Ferraris raced north and south on PCH, slipping from one lane to the next. Surfers loaded and unloaded longboards and boogie boards from Subarus and VW buses parked on the side of the road.

Children with floaties on their arms held their moms' hands. Dads grasped dog leashes and Igloo coolers. Seventy-seven degrees—a perfect day in LA.

Terri, now singing "Reasons," lifted her knockoff Ray-Bans and grinned at her daughter. "This is gonna be a perfect day. Thank you for . . . you know . . . ditchin' school—I know you like school. I thought I was gon' spend it eating Apple Jacks from a bag, wipin' tears away, and watchin' Mister pull Celie away from Nettie and shit for the fifth time."

Sammi kissed her mother's hand. "You're kinda special to me, Mom."

Terri sucked her teeth. "Whatchu mean, *kinda*?" She snorted, then dropped her sunglasses back over her eyes. "I'm the most special person you'll *ever* know. And wait till you see me at Thanksgiving. After all my lunchtime hiking and eating that flax shit, I'ma be *at least* five pounds lighter."

"Okay, Jane Fonda. Calm down."

Happiness buzzed through that burgundy Honda as it raced down Pacific Coast Highway, making that right turn at a red barn and zooming onto Topanga Canyon Road. That was when the world shifted from gold to green, and trees and grass and brush reclaimed space stolen by a city made of concrete. No billboards on the side of these roads. No skyscrapers or Mickey D's or El Pollo Locos. Only oaks and pines and other trees here that both Morris women had only read about in books. These trees' leaves filtered the sunshine, making the twisty road ahead mimic stained-glass windows.

"Damn, Sammi," Terri said, "we ain't in the Jungles anymore." She gripped the steering wheel with both hands. Her jaw tightened as she navigated one curve after another. "Ain't no curves like this in *our* part of LA."

Sammi paid no attention—she was too busy gaping at the golden canyon rocks and at boulders as large as houses. "How did they cut through these mountains to make these roads? Mom, what kind of tree is that? What are those—"

"Are you paying attention to the map, Brainiac?" Terri snapped. *"Damn."*

A stone pressed against Sammi's windpipe—"Brainiac" had never been a compliment coming from her mother. She hoped now that the excitement and adventure would quell Terri's temper before it caught on fire and burned down their day.

"I've never been back here," Sammi said now. "Some of the kids at school—their parents have houses in Topanga Canyon, but I didn't know this place was like . . . the *wood* woods."

Terri pulled to the side of the road to let faster cars pass. She snatched the Thomas Guide from her daughter's hand. "You gon' get us killed up in these *wood* woods."

"Sorry," Sammi said.

"Ugh." Theresa flipped to the dog-eared pages that gridded out Topanga Canyon. "We so fuckin' lost." She tossed the guide in the back seat. "We'll stop at a liquor store or a gas station or whatever to ask for directions. I should *know* this shit."

Convicted for drug-dealing and the possession of a Social Security card not her own, Terri had been sentenced to two years in prison. Instead of spending that time in a cell at the Frontera women's prison, she chose hard labor: firefighting with Malibu's Fire Camp 13. Before today, she'd already lost twenty pounds—from daily runs and hikes through the Santa Monica Mountains, from clearing brush and cutting fire lines, gaining calluses and filling up with self-determination. After doing her time, Terri applied for a job as a park ranger but needed two years, *at least*, of coursework. She immediately enrolled in classes at Cal State LA and took a job—she came highly recommended by the fire camp's commander—at the Topanga Canyon Visitors Center. To further strengthen her future application as a ranger, Lieutenant Fenton suggested that she complete all the hikes the canyon had to offer. This hike with Sammi would be her first.

"So, you never been to a slumber party or whatever back here?" Terri asked her daughter now.

Sammi's eyes burned with tears. "Ain't been invited. They kinda ignore me most of the time. They call me 'Scholarship' and 'AA.'"

Terri clenched the steering wheel tighter. "AA? What does that stand for?"

"Affirmative Action."

Terri's knuckles hardened. "You kiss one of those rich boys yet?"

Sammi chuckled, then threw her tearful gaze out the car window.

Terri knew—*that's a no.* She took her daughter's hand and kissed it. "You need to get that eighties action-movie heart, Boo. Blow some muthafuckas up—either with your smarts or with your beauty. I say both. Them bitches always gon' say something to slap you down. But if you be like Ripley from *Aliens* or Sarah Connor from *Terminator*?"

She sucked her teeth. "You gon' save the world while them fools are getting sucked into space and splashed with acid and snapped in half by T-1000s. You feelin' me?"

Sammi sniffled back her tears and swiped at her runny nose. "I feel you."

"And you got into that school," Terri said, "not because your daddy own the Lakers. But because you smart as fuck. Them teachers know that, and they grateful that you there. No lie."

Sammi said, "Okay."

"Now," Terri said, "use them brains to find us a goddamned gas station."

There were no gas stations on the roadside to stop and ask for directions, but there *was* a store that had been dunked into a third grader's toy box. Sparkling letters that spelled HIDDEN TREASURES hung beneath the eaves. A stuffed pirate stood behind a giant teal helm on the widow's walk. Inside the store, vintage clothing hung from racks. A disco ball and a miniature airplane hung from the ceiling. A deep-sea diving suit was strung with big-bulbed Christmas lights. A gilded seafoam chair and matching ottoman—Marie Antoinette's chair if she lived in Los Angeles—sat between the racks of long coats and dresses.

Terri gaped at . . . *everything* and muttered, "What the *fuck*?"

"We're lost," Sammi told the woman behind the cash register. "Can you help us, please?"

The salesclerk had long silver hair and a wrist laden with jeweled and beaded bracelets. "Let me see what you have," she asked, taking the Thomas Guide from Sammi's hand. "Hmm. Maps were never my strong suit. I hope that I can—"

"Where are you trying to go?" The man's voice sounded deep and warm, like s'mores and cashmere. "I can take you there. Anything for two pretty ladies."

TAKE ON ME

10.

The orange flame starts as a flicker—like a thought as small as "water is wet." But this flicker of flame spits across dry sage and rips into chaparral and spreads across brush until the hillside pulses with wildfire.

At the bottom of the hill, I watch this fiery ocean, wide eyed, frozen in a world that has become an inferno. *Trapped.* At the top of the hill, a woman with my brown eyes and my brown skin stands still even as that blaze races toward her. She's crying, the veins in her face popping hard against her skin. She finally marches down the hill, heading my way, closer . . . closer . . . and right as she reaches out to me, fire consumes her arms, and her skin bubbles and melts. In pain, the woman snaps her head back, and her mouth opens impossibly wide, and she screams.

Down here, at the bottom of the hill, my own arms ache, and my skin also bubbles and blisters. A light glows throughout my bones, and that glow becomes fire, and I open my mouth to scream and flames burst from—

◆ ◆ ◆

My eyes pop open. Pulse racing, I stare at the wooden beams running parallel like train tracks along the cottage's ceiling. I'm already holding my breath even though I'd been . . .

Dreaming.

About . . .

Fire.

Being trapped in a place with a woman who resembled . . .

Me.

Or *was* she me?

Chirp.

What was that?

Muted sunlight dapples across the window—it's dark enough to be tomorrow but light enough to be today.

Confused, I search for my phone and find it twisted inside the comforter with my laptop and *Old Topanga Road.*

It's still Thursday, May 13, but it's almost six o'clock.

How have I slept for nearly three hours?

Fruit punch allergy scare.

Ah. Yes. I nearly died today. Almost dying would certainly exhaust a girl.

My punctured thigh hurts more than the wound in my side. At this rate, I'll be nothing but a composition of holes and two ears (which, *technically*, are also holes). More than that, I'll never find Sam.

Outside the bedroom, wood creaks—either from a floorboard or from the eaves of the cottage, from weight or from wind.

"Hello?" I call out, in case it's the weight of a man.

No answer.

Someone coughs—but that cough sounds far away, farther away than the creaking. An echo of a cough.

"Anyone there?" I ask.

No response.

Is that good? Or bad?

I kick away the comforter and force myself out of the bed. The world sways, then settles into a mild wobble. Wicks of pain pop around my legs and torso. I peek out the canyon-facing window and—

Russell Walker! Not even ten feet away, skulking from my window! Oh *shit.*

My skin turns cold and sweaty, my mind spins and spins, and *oh shit,* was he watching me sleep? Did that cough come from him? The creaking?

The old man makes his way across the hillside, now not walking like an old man, not really. He climbs down and across, down and across, and, breathless, I watch him as he disappears into the tall grass, and I stand there at the window long after he's gone.

How many times has he come to my window?

Chirp.

That sound . . . that chirp of a dying battery in a smoke detector . . . it pulls my focus from the tall grass and back to this cottage.

I look one last time out the window—no one's there—and move back to the bed.

My T-shirt and leggings are drenched in sweat. I pop three ibuprofen dry and then grab a fresh sweatshirt and another pair of leggings from my suitcase. *I should probably do a quick load of laundry*—a rather domestic, everyday thought despite the extraordinary day I've had. As I sort through my bags to grab more dirty clothes, my hand finds a thick book with a spiral-bound spine. *Thomas Guide for Los Angeles County—1989 Updated Edition.*

No MapQuest or Google Maps back then in those ancient times.

My hands shake—I haven't even opened the book, but I already smell basement and peppermint. There's a name written in thick black marker on the inside of the tan- and cranberry-colored cover: *Theresa Morris.* This book of maps belonged to Sam's mother—and Sam's kept it all this time. And now, *I'm* holding it, a reminder of my mission, a clue to Sam's possible route throughout Southern California.

Theresa Morris . . . seeing the name of the woman Sam came here to find . . .

My mouth tastes like spoons now, and I swipe my hand across my lips to keep from vomiting.

Did Sam find Theresa? Did mother and daughter reunite before they disappeared together? *Are* they together?

Are they alive?

I take a deep breath, then flip past the table of contents to yellowing pages, battered pages taped together, and coffee- and grease-stained pages that are no longer spiral-bound and can drift free to the floor like napkins. There are handwritten notes, tight words that slant left, in the margins of some pages—*try here, June 6, no longer open.* At one dog-eared page, the grid squares are highlighted in yellow: 590, 591, 630, 631. *Topanga State Park.*

The names of other trails have been written into the green squares.

Santa Ynez (waterfall)

Rock Loop (caves)

Temescal Canyon (close—Sunset)

Parker Mesa (hard at first)

Paseo Miramar (no parking on Sat/Sun)

Is the plan really for me to hike each of these trails?

There are highlights and notes on this map that *aren't* trails but are street names:

Webb Trail (open area behind house)

Medley Lane (open area behind house)

Paradise Lane (open area left of house)

Open area . . . open area . . .

Ah. Theresa—during her time at Frontera prison, she'd worked on the all-female fire crew that Jack mentioned this morning. How long did she cut through brush to make fire roads? Were the "open areas" in the Thomas Guide the same highlighted areas designated for brush clearing? Or . . . were these escape routes? *Open area behind house. Open area left of house.* Or was she planning to hit homes that were easy to access? If so, was she caught and maybe shot by the prison deputies who killed her and then covered up her death? Are these notes simply innocent markings of a map?

Blood rushes in my ears as my mind conjures all possible scenarios. *Dangerous* scenarios. Because what if Sam found out something she shouldn't have and now . . . ?

Chirp.

So, I *did* hear that. I'd probably imagined the cough and the creaks, but this chirp . . . I *know* this chirp. I've heard this chirp in almost every home I've visited in South LA. No one has fresh nine-volt batteries needed for a smoke detector just sitting in hallway junk drawers. I'll tell Margo or Luann the next time I see them.

Back to laundry.

I untangle my pink bra from around my flip-flops and shove my feet into the cheap sandals. I gather the small load of dirty clothes into my arms and start my search for a washing machine.

Chirp.

I grab a trash bag from the box beneath the kitchen sink and fill it with my dirty laundry.

There's no washer-dryer in the kitchen.

There's no washer-dryer tucked in a hallway closet.

But there *is* a note left on the breakfast bar along with an EpiPen and a bouquet of yellow roses.

Hey, Bailey.

Heard about today. I AM so SORRY. Don't know how Luann missed that—she's usually incredibly thoughtful. We all feel horrible. Jack said that Dr. Torrance came to examine you, but you were sleeping so heavily, they didn't want to wake you. But from the quick exam Dr. Torrance gave, he pronounced you ALIVE!! Hooray!! Take a moment and relax for the rest of the day. Dinner's at six thirty. Luann will knock first. Don't want you to accidentally shoot the cook LOL! Jack may join you. I'll see you later!

Margo

P.S. You skipped a line in the contract. Social Security number. No worries. We'll handle everything tomorrow.

I sniff the roses—*lovely*—and sling the makeshift laundry bag over my shoulder and head out the front door.

The world smells of fresh-cut sage, chopped wood, and garlic. The trees drip with silks—cicadas and spiders drifting like paragliders from trunk to stem. Sunlight glimmers on the swimming pool, and California sisters have returned to flutter over the water. I want to smile, but there's a sadness bubbling in my core. I swallow the saltiness of that pool of tears and hold my breath to keep from crying.

You're okay, it's okay, this is a lot, stop acting weird.

I *am* okay. I *will* be okay. The bushes to my left rustle.

Has that doe returned?

Or last night's mountain lion?

Or this afternoon's Russell Walker?

Maybe I should retrieve my gun—for what reason, though? Because I feel unsafe and vulnerable?

You're trying to become a licensed investigator, Bailey. Get used to it. Stop acting weird.

I don't want to make any sudden moves—but I don't want to encourage a lion or a stalker to come any farther by standing in place. I remain still and scan the patio for a makeshift weapon.

The brush crunches and swishes.

There's a patio chair, a side table, nothing sharp, nothing portable.

I peek over to the crunching and swishing.

A pair of brown eyes is watching the swimming pool . . . and those eyes *don't belong to a deer or a mountain lion.* These hooded, sunken brown eyes sit like stones beneath scraggly gray bangs and a pale sunburned fore-head. The old woman creeps from out of the wilderness and steps onto the patio's flagstones. She's tall but stooped. She's wearing crusty hiking boots, dirty jeans, and a torn blue T-shirt. Despite the sunburn, her face is gray, like she's been trapped in a vault without citrus since 2008.

And now, she's creeping closer toward the pool.

"Excuse me," I shout, my voice an octave lower.

The woman startles and spins around. Her eyes bug and her jaw hangs open.

I take a step toward her. "You need to get out of here."

The woman gapes at me, frightened but fascinated.

"Go," I bark. *"Now."*

"You . . . you're . . ."

"Leave before I call the police."

The trespasser takes a step back. Her mouth moves, but she can't speak. Her head snaps toward the main house, then back to me. "The tall grass," she whispers. "She's in the tall grass."

"What?"

"Somewhere in the canyon." The old woman points at something behind me. "Go there. Right now."

I'm not falling for this trick—I'm supposed to turn away, and that's when she stabs me with a rusty butcher knife. That's why I have this wound in my side. A man fell in front of me on the sidewalk. I reached down to help him. He jabbed a knife at my side. Fortunately, my wool coat took most of the knife's energy. The blade still found my side, though, and the mugger stole my travel wallet filled with a motel key card and ten bucks.

Yeah, I learned that lesson and survived, only to experience the ruse again, now by this woman from the woods.

She backs away from me, slowly . . . slowly . . . until she's immersed in the wild grass again, rustling and swishing, backing away slowly . . . slowly . . . until there's only the cry of songbirds and the wind whistling through the canyon.

She's in the tall grass.

What the hell is she talking about?

Which tall grass? The entire canyon is nothing *but* trees, rocks, and tall grass. And who is "she"? And why am I trying to make sense of anything that this wild woman just sputtered?

Now that I'm here, she can no longer wander out of the canyons to swim or steal or whatever the hell she's used to doing here in the quiet of the day. She'll get an ass full of lead if she dares to enter my (*my!*) cottage without permission.

I stomp to the main house to report the trespasser to Margo, Jack, or Luann.

But the patio door that leads from the deck to the kitchen is locked.

I peek into the kitchen window to see spotless, gleaming counters and appliances. An empty sink. Apples and oranges perfectly arranged in a bowl on the breakfast nook's table.

I knock on the glass. "Anybody there?" Am I alone?

Where did everybody go?

I drop the laundry bag onto the deck, then march around the side of the house to reach the front.

The garage doors are down. No cars are parked in the driveway.

I pop onto the front porch and ring the doorbell just in case Jack's asleep or Luann's in the bathroom. The *bing-bong* from the doorbell is followed by a few seconds of silence until the doorbell intercom speaker squawks.

"Bailey?" That's Jack.

I look up to search for the camera. "How do you know it's me?"

"The camera's on the doorbell."

"Oh." The small circle beneath the doorbell button glows hot blue. "Hey. Hi. Sorry about all that at lunch," I say. "I should've remembered that I'm allergic to coconut."

"I'm just glad we had pens," he says.

"You make your afternoon meetings?"

"I made the second one," Jack says. "And he understood—his daughter has peanut allergies. They had a scare just last week after a soccer game." Jack pauses, then says, "What are you doing out front?"

"I was hoping to do laundry, but I can't find a washing machine in the cottage, so I came to the main house, and I knocked on the doors off the deck, but no one's answering." I take a breath and smile. "That's probably TMI."

"Ha. You're funny," he says. "I stepped away for a moment. Margo's gone for the day, and Luann's out doing errands before dinner. But one of us will be there soon. You feeling better? You're not locked out of the cottage, are you?"

"Yes, I'm good, thanks, and no, I'm not locked out." I give him a thumbs-up.

"I really do hope that you'll forgive us," Jack says. "It was an honest mistake. I trust Luann with my life."

I nod. "I know . . . hey. Everything's content, right?"

He chuckles. "Everything is content. Just . . . don't hold this against us. I promise to make it up to you."

I blush. "Thanks, Jack. I appreciate your kindness."

This is weird, talking to a doorbell.

I think of telling him about Russell Walker and the wild woman from the woods, but the doorbell speaker squawks.

He's gone.

No matter—behind me, rolling tires crunch against the gravel. Dust trails behind a dark-blue sedan now cruising toward the house. A leviathan of a man hunches over the wheel of the car, his eyes hidden behind a pair of mirrored aviator sunglasses.

He looks like a cop. The kind of cop with tats of his secret police gang on his arms and back and his nostrils crusty with someone else's cocaine.

Shit.

Is Jack onto me and sent this guy to break my face?

Does this mountain of a man know that I'm here to do something other than write a bestselling novel with a legendary author?

Am I about to be outed?

Or is this like Las Vegas, and the random thug who followed me down Fremont Street? I *still* don't know why he was following me, but

I found a club bouncer bigger and thicker than him to face him down. After that encounter, I wrote a fevered entry in my journal that captured all the fear and uncertainty I faced that night, the *risk* of it all. And now, here I am again, with another mountain of a man bearing down on me.

Am I strong enough?

Numbness sweeps over my body, and I can no longer feel my feet. Rigid and stupefied, I watch the man park the dark Lincoln sedan in the driveway and climb out of the car.

He's tall and broad, built like a pro wrestler. His gray sports coat strains against his arms and torso. Pockmarks pepper his olive-toned forehead. He doesn't have a lot of hair, but the hair he *does* have is shorn low on the sides and the top gelled to form a small fin. "How you doing today?" he asks, his voice croupy and deep. He stops a few feet away from me, giving us both space to move, if needed, and rests his hands on his hips to show me his holstered gun without being too braggy.

My tongue feels like cold clay, but I manage to say, "Hello."

Say as little as possible.

Nervous, I whisper, "Zero-five-zero-six-one-one-three-six-three"—my Social Security number—over and over again.

"You're a new face here," he says in that gravelly voice.

I don't respond—he didn't ask a question.

He grins and shows off dazzling white tiles for teeth. Red chewing gum is wedged between his molars. Cherry flavored, not cinnamon—I can smell the gum from here. He nods at the house behind me. "Jack home?"

I shrug. *Zero-five-zero-six-one-one-three-six-three . . . Zero-five-zero—*

He says, "You speak English?"

I say, "I speak English. *Je parle anglaise. Hablo ingles. jIQaD.*"

"What was that last language?"

"Klingon."

He chuckles. "A Trekkie, huh? Then, you're smart enough to know."

"Smart enough to know *what?*"

"That you shouldn't be wandering around the forest."

"Who's wandering?" I ask. "I'm simply standing here."

"Just sayin'. It's dangerous out there, and I'm not just talking lions, tigers, and bears, you dig? I'm only telling you this cuz you didn't grow up around here—"

"Who says I didn't?" I ask, chin high.

He chuckles again. "The way you talk. The fear in your eyes. You're shaking and don't even know it."

I glare at him. How long can I keep doing this?

The man toes the driveway gravel with his boot. "Okay, so . . ." He reaches into his sports coat pocket and pulls out a smaller steno pad and small golf pencil. "I didn't catch your name."

"I didn't throw it," I say.

He pauses in his writing, then scrutinizes me. "May I have your name, please?"

"Bailey."

"Hi, Bailey. I'm Ro Patrick. I need to talk to Luann. Is she here?"

"No."

Who the hell is this new person?

"It's important," he says. "She coming back today?"

"Don't know."

He sighs. "It's not easy tryin' to get up here. You know what time she left?"

"No."

A thought bursts in my mind.

Did Dr. Torrance report my allergy crisis to, like, Social Services or something? Was Jack pissed off enough to call the cops on his personal chef? Luann *did* have access to my allergy restrictions, but somehow she still managed to send me into anaphylactic shock.

Ro Patrick is now scribbling in his notepad with that gun on his hip.

Heghlu'meH QaQ jajvam.

No. Today is *not* a good day to die.

"Everything is fine now," I say, lightheaded. "I'm feeling good. Really, I should've been more careful. I'm a grown-up, and I . . . I . . .

no need to . . ." I wave at his notepad. "I'm not trying to get anyone in trouble—*oh!* That's not true."

Saying too much, I'm saying too much.

I point to the side of the house behind me. "There was an old woman—possibly homeless—who left the forest and came onto the property just a few minutes ago."

Nervous babbling.

Ro Patrick's eyebrows lift. "Oh, really?"

"A white woman with graying hair . . ." I continue to describe the woman from the woods.

"She look familiar to you?" he asks.

I shake my head. "Never seen her before."

"Anything else strange happening around here?" he asks.

"Not that I know of."

"And what's your last name, Bailey?"

I pause, then say, "Meadows."

"Lovely name." He drops the notepad and pencil back into his coat pocket. His eyes drift down to my T-shirt.

I also peer down to see that dull-red posy on the T-shirt's fabric. "Oh, that." I tap the spot there. "That's just old blood. War wound. Not Baghdad. Oakland. I'm doing laundry right now."

Shit. I'm still talking. Oakland. The old lady. A vulnerable old lady now on this man's radar.

Zero-five-zero-six-one-one-three-six-three . . . zero-five-zero—

"Okay." Ro Patrick holds my gaze for a moment until his eyes dip back to that bloodstain. "Well, this has been a waste of time, no offense. I'll come back when Luann's here. But please tell her to call me. We need to talk, like, *immediately.*"

I say, "Okay."

"See you later, Bailey. That's 'goodbye, Bailey' in English." He laughs, then turns on his heels and plods back to the sedan.

The dust kicks up again as the Lincoln retreats back up the driveway.

I stay in my spot, and my mind spins and spins and spins.

11.

The trash bag filled with my dirty laundry waits at my feet. I need to pull off my bloodstained T-shirt and shove it in the bag, too—it's causing conversations I don't want to have. But I don't move to act. Instead, I roost on the cottage's living room couch, cell phone in hand, trying to will the internet to tell me who "Ro Patrick" is.

Spinning circle.

You should know. That's what Ro Patrick said. *Dangerous out there . . . lions, tigers, and . . .* And . . . *what?* Homeless people? No big deal. Unhoused people are everywhere. Mountain lions? They don't want me, even if I *do* have the ass of a mule deer. Ticks—okay, *they* want me for my delicious blood. Other than that . . .

Anything look strange? Ro Patrick had asked. Honestly, *I'm* the only strange thing here in Topanga Canyon, the Black girl with her bandaged torso and coconut allergy and satin hair bonnet. *You don't belong here*—that's what he told me. How did he know? Did I say "ax" instead of "ask"? "Am*b*alance" instead of "am*bu*lance"? Did I say either word? Is it because I don't smell of patchouli or because I'm not wearing hemp shorts or . . . ? And I'm *always* careful. I've *never* wandered off alone in the woods.

Should I warn Jack that a man came calling and specifically asked for Luann?

No—I'm not here to "make something happen." If anyone asks, I'll offer an answer.

I'm in limbo right now, except that I'm not supposed to be just sitting and doing nothing. I'm *supposed* to be reading *Old Topanga Road*. I'm *supposed* to be searching for evidence that suggests that this house in the woods and the owner or a worker or someone nearby played a role—big or small—in the disappearance of Sam Morris.

The woman from the woods told me that "she" is in the tall grass . . .

Could she be talking about Sam?

Or do I give all this weight to someone who lives in the forest, someone obviously unwell?

But there's something about that woman from the woods . . . something familiar . . .

I open my cell phone's CONTACTS app and scroll down an abbreviated phone list.

Payton Wiggins, WPC Accounting

My talk with Payton lasted six minutes on October 3, 2020. A woman can be named "Payton."

Javion May, Realtor

My conversation with Javion lasted an hour on October 10, 2020. Javion—that's not an older white woman's name.

Madelynn Stafford, LA County Records—Norwalk

I chatted with Madelynn on October 3, 2020, for ten minutes. Now, *that* name . . .

Could she go from an office job with the county to being an unhoused woman living in the wilds of Topanga Canyon?

Of course she could—we're all one paycheck away from homelessness.

But I don't think the woman in the woods is Madelynn Stafford.

There are other calls in the phone history, but none of those numbers have names labeled to them. Just random phone numbers that used to mean something to me but now mean nothing at all. Numbers with 541, 702, 323, 424, and 458 area codes. The 702 area code—that's Las Vegas. I visited Las Vegas last October. That's where the guy who now reminds me of Ro Patrick followed me up and down Fremont Street. Eventually I left Las Vegas with a voucher for thirty-eight cents from the MGM.

Two other messages remain in my voicemail inbox, one of which I've already listened to. I tap the old one.

Not Madelynn. A man with a smoky voice. *"Hey, it's me. Got an update. Gimme a call ASAP. Bye."*

A new message was left this morning, and I tap it now to listen.

"What's going on? If you need to talk, I'm here. This shit's hard, but we're gonna make it, all right? You really did mean it when you said that you'd do anything."

Not Madelynn.

It's the same smoky-voiced man who has now called six times before leaving this message.

Message 2: *"It's Zeus. Are you in Hades now?"*

Do people name their children "Zeus" in today's America?

Message 3: *"Are we doing this or not?"*

Message 4: *"What's happening?"*

Message 5: *"It's Zeus. Are you in Hades now?"*

Message 6: *"Pick up . . . pick up . . . You there?"* I tap the phone number, curious now.

Silence . . . and then, the *beep-beep-beep* of a failed call. A common sound of failed calls thanks to crappy cell reception in the canyon.

Avery warned me—*don't rely on technology.* Seemed easy to do back when I was in the city. But now? How can I move forward if I can't even make a phone call?

My arms and ears tingle. Tears threaten to roll down my cheeks—but it's still not time yet to cry. Instead, I take a deep breath, close my eyes, and think.

Could the guy who left these messages be a confidential informant? Someone who knows something?

Who is *Zeus*? Why is he asking if I'm in hell?

We're in a pandemic right now. Aren't we *all* in hell?

I swipe over to the digital photo album and the recent shots I took this morning on the hike. Those pink flowers. That blue-tailed skink. The waterfall . . . the smoke in the sky . . . passing through time—the party, the parked cars, that view of Los Angeles . . . back, back, back to . . . a late-model gray Ford pickup truck parked at a dusty pink hotel. The Royal Hawaiian neon sign.

In the distance, a highway sign. BAKER. Off Highway 15 to Las Vegas. Home of the world's tallest thermometer.

Swipe back to a picture of . . .

A hot-pink flyer.

MISSING PERSON—Kadence Hatfield, 27 years old.

My breath snags in my chest. I knew I'd seen this flyer before. It's a copy of the flyer posted around the woods!

Kadence Hatfield . . .

Missing since 2015. Last seen in Topanga Canyon.

Contact LAPD at . . .

That number to the police department . . . I scroll through my calls. That number isn't in my phone.

Who loved Kadence? Who continues to hurt every day since she disappeared? Was she a daddy's girl? Have her people moved on? It's been six years. Her loved ones have not forgotten her, no, never that, but have they stopped setting a place for her at Thanksgiving? Have they stopped writing her name on Christmas lists and vacation itineraries?

What do they pray for each night: for her to be lost and missing, or found but dead? Hope or certainty—those are the only choices.

I find the journal entry made on the day I visited the Royal Hawaiian off Highway 15.

Talked to Lara. Says so many women come in and out of this place. True. Just as I'm sitting here, six women have shuffled into hotel rooms and five men have dropped into their cars. She showed me tape from security cams. Can't tell who the woman is. FUCK MY LIFE!!! Can you tell I'm frustrated? Another lead just poofs away!

And now, my mind whirls, leaves caught in a dust devil as I stare at these shots and zoom in on the gray truck's license plate and scrutinize the hotel and its neon sign. As though any of this will shake loose a clue that I haven't found before.

Nothing gives, and so I keep swiping pictures from the past until . . .

AFTER-VISIT SUMMARY FOR SAM MORRIS

You saw Maren Blackburn on Thursday, November 5, 2020. The following issues were discussed: primary hypertension, prediabetes, and stress . . .

Test results . . .

Basic metabolites. Sam's potassium levels were down. A banana a day keeps hypokalemia away.

Lipid panel. She had good cholesterol numbers.

Cranial MRI with contrast. Normal, no sign of brain injury or any neurological damage, according to Dr. Blackburn.

Did someone suggest that Sam was mentally vulnerable? I *do* have that sheath of papers discussing dissociative fugues, so . . .

I swipe back to the MISSING flyer for Kadence Hatfield.

Gone since 2015.

What were the circumstances around Kadence's disappearance?

Did she leave due to stress and trauma?

Did Sam know about Kadence? She *did* work to find missing women. Was she searching for Kadence while also searching for her mother?

12.

She's a pretty one. Been to this trail before, sometimes with friends. Lately, though, alone. Headphones on. Yoga pants clinging to her curviest spots. Not paying attention to anyone or to her surroundings . . .

At least, pretending *not* to pay attention.

He's caught her glancing at him on the last two hikes he's taken here. She's even smiled at Biscuit, the Australian shepherd he brings on these trips. That day, her hazel eyes flicked at him and lingered for just a second.

Of course they did. He's perfect in every way. And now, as she winds her way down the trail, he puts on a new mask: glistening eyes filled with worry, quivering jaw, furrowed brow, and the coup de grâce, a leash without a dog.

Worried pet dad.

Right as she rounds the corner . . .

"Biscuit," he shouts. "Come here, boy!"

Here she comes, headphones around her neck this time, turquoise yoga pants that end midcalf. She smiles seeing him, but that joy quickly diminishes.

"Biscuit! Come on, boy!" He turns to her with great sadness. "Have you seen an Australian shepherd? Brown-and-white coat? Has those gorgeous icicle-blue eyes?"

She gasps, "Oh, no," and shakes her head. "Is he lost?"

He covers his mouth with his leashless hand, then says, "I let him off, and he just . . . *bolted*. I'm about to lose my mind." He pauses, then wanders away from her, eyes on the brush. "Biscuit!" He whispers, "This is un-fuck-ing-believable." He turns back to her. "Sorry for cursing."

She holds up her hands. "Your baby is lost. I'd curse, too." She looks at her phone, then sighs. Then, she studies him—he can feel her eyes landing on his strong arms, lingering on his Rolex, noting his strong clenched jaw—a perfect specimen—and she decides . . . "I can help you look for a minute. Not too long, though. I have class—I go to UCLA."

He holds his hands together, prayer-style. "Bless you. Thanks so much. I'm Scott." He holds out his hand.

She takes his hand and pumps once. "Kinsey."

"I saw him go down there somewhere," Scott says, pointing farther down the trail now overgrown with shrubs and chaparral.

Together, they call out "Biscuit," who doesn't hear these calls. Because Biscuit—

My phone vibrates from the couch cushion.

I yelp and the novel tumbles from my hands. I peek at the phone's screen.

UNKNOWN.

I watch the device, trying to decide if I should even try to answer. I hit the green ANSWER button. "Hello?"

Dead air.

Of course.

I disconnect.

The phone rings again.

Someone knocks on the cottage's front door.

I yelp again and nearly tumble off the couch. I leave the vibrating phone and hustle over to the door. Maybe reading a novel about a serial killer who prowls the very forest right outside my door isn't the best thing to do alone as I search for a woman who went missing *for real* for real in, once again, this very forest.

Luann's at the door, smiling and standing behind a serving cart packed with silver cloches.

Breathless, I hold open the door and say, "Hey." I exhale loudly and pull at my sweaty top. "Been reading *Old Topanga Road* and got freaked out."

Luann chuckles. "Jack's books will do that to ya."

Together, we lift the cart up the single step and carry it into the cottage.

"Sorry for bringing dinner so late, hon." The cook scrunches her face. "Whew! It's hotter than a two-dollar pistol in here."

"I like it a bit warm." I close the door behind us. "I wasn't sure how dinner tonight was supposed to work."

Luann rolls the cart over to the kitchen. "Jack asked me to bring it all back since you're still recovering and he's running a bit late." She washes her hands in the kitchen sink and grabs a dish towel to dry them. "He's so busy, you'd think he was twins. You get some rest?"

"I did, thank you. But then, I started reading the book, and any calm I achieved quickly went bye-bye. Other than that . . ."

Should I tell her about Ro Patrick's visit? That he came looking for her?

My tongue flops in my mouth, refusing to work. Silence hangs in the air like a naked man stuck on a swing.

The cook waits . . . she crinkles her eyes. "Something wrong, hon?"

The warnings roar in my throat. *Tell her about Ro. No, keep your mouth shut. Warn her, but what if she runs away—*

Chirp.

"That," I say, pointing to the ceiling, relieved. *Say as little as possible.*

"Smoke detector battery's on the blink." Hands on her hips, Luann scrutinizes the disk on the kitchen ceiling. "Thought Azealia replaced them batteries. I'll tell her she missed one."

"Also," I say, "where can I do laundry?"

"Good question. Come on." Luann beckons me to follow her to a small pantry area off the kitchen. She opens a tall door, then points at a stackable washer-dryer. "Easy as pie."

I wince. "I'm so stupid—it's right here. I thought I searched everywhere. Obviously, I didn't. Thank you."

"No problem, hon." She marches back through the kitchen and over to the dining cart. "No coconut was used in the making of this meal. I will never ever *ever* forget that again, Miss Bailey. This time, coconut's not even in the same zip code of this food."

She lifts the silver domes. "Roasted carrots, roasted chicken, a pear-and-burrata salad, and for dessert . . . apple pie à la mode. I'll put the ice cream in the freezer."

I smile until my cheeks ache. "It looks delicious. Thank you. And I didn't know that I was craving roasted carrots until you whipped off that cover."

She chuckles as she leaves a small silver dish covered with plastic wrap on a freezer shelf. "Jack loves my carrots. But then, I can make that man eat anything. Rutabaga, once. He never forgave me for that one, heh." She moves the plates of food from the cart to the small dining table.

"You cook for the Beckhams for long?" I ask.

Her chin dips to her chest. "I have, but only for Jack, and I'll always be grateful for that chance. He is *the* best boss in the world, and this is *the* best *job* in the world."

"Where did you work before?" I ask.

Her cheeks pinken, and she throws me a glance. "Dr. Lane Murray Unit." She pauses, adds, "That's a women's prison—Texas Department of Criminal Justice, off Highway 36 in Gainesville." She waits a beat, then: "And before you ask, I didn't *work* there, per se. I was a trustee there. An inmate."

I open my mouth, but I can only make a strangled "Oh."

Jack gives people second chances.

"Killed my boyfriend," Luann says, folding a linen napkin. "Self-defense. He'd been whalin' on me for almost a year, and I let him cuz I was so young and so stupid, I could fall up a tree. I had the nerve to ask him about another woman—had that whiskey courage. I'm the jealous type anyway, and then, when I'm drunk? But I come from a small town, and back then, Gary was my ticket out. And this bitch was threatening that, and so . . ." She shrugs, then shakes her head.

"That last time he punched me, I just snapped. I had to protect myself. And I was successful in that. But the jury saw how tall and strong I was—my people were farmers from the old country—and how drunk I was that night, and they didn't view me as a battered woman. Especially since I'd done some . . . *other* things which—"

Luann wags her head. "But that was just being a dumb kid. Anyway, I got to know the Texas correctional system real good. Jack was visiting cuz he was on the board of directors for this writing organization, and they'd created a writers in prison program and . . ."

She laughs and her bosom quivers. "I joined the program faster than a scalded cat, and, boy, was I an awful writer. Like trying to bag flies, me and words. But Jack was so kind to me and to all the other women. I told him that my dream was to cook, and he told me to find him after I was released, and his kindness made me as soft as a two-minute egg.

"Ten years later, Texas released me and . . ." Luann spreads her arms. *Ta-da!* "First, Jack sent me to cooking school, and then he hired me on. And that's why you're now taking a gander at food that's going cold."

She removes the already-opened wine bottle from the bottom shelf of the cart, then surveys the spread. "Hope you don't hold me goin' to prison and all that against me."

"Of course not," I say. "Leave the past where it is—behind you."

"Jack believes the same," Luann says, "and if I'm anything, I'm his number-one fan. When it comes to J. D. Beckham, I can get as crazy as a bullbat. And now, he lets me read his drafts, even before he sends 'em to his agent. He asks for my opinions—for plots, for characters. I always tell him to crank up the creepiness. I send him true-crime articles almost every day. And I give him inside information about being a victim on one day and a convicted murderer the next."

She lifts her chin, sticks out her chest. "He says that I'm an indispensable part of his creative process." She laughs and flicks her hand. "That man is the prince of second chances."

"I heard Margo say that," I share, nodding. "But I think she was talking about that old security guard, Russell?" My face burns from this lie, but hey: maybe he shouldn't be so creepy.

"An ex-con?" Luann asks. "Wouldn't be surprised. He's always lurking around. To be honest? I don't think he is who he says he is." She pokes my arm. "You be careful around here, understand?"

"Yes, ma'am."

She winks at me. "There I go. Hon, you can't let me just ramble. I'll talk the ears off a mule when you bring up J. D. Beckham."

We laugh.

"I'm gonna let you eat before the food gets cold and greasy," she says, pushing the cart back toward the front door. "But if you see an Australian shepherd named 'Biscuit,' run for the hills."

"Ha. Right?"

"Biscuit was *my* idea," Luann says. "Anyway, I'll come back to get the plates and such. Enjoy!"

Standing at the threshold, I watch the cook march up the dark pathway to the main house, which now glows in the night.

Luann seems lovely but . . .

Do I really believe that—leave the past behind you? Because right now, I can't—I'm searching for someone who disappeared while searching for someone who disappeared. If that's not the past, then what is?

As for Luann's past . . .

Why was Ro Patrick asking about her?

Is she still on parole?

Is there another dead boyfriend?

Wait.

When did Luann arrive to Topanga?

Is it possible that Luann and Sam's mother, Theresa, were . . . *friends*? Two ex-cons finding each other and hanging out in Topanga Canyon, a place so different from their hometowns?

What if . . . ? Theresa and Luann and a third person . . . love triangle? And Luann became threatened by Theresa . . . Would she kill again out of jealousy or "self-defense"?

She just said it moments ago. *I'm the jealous type.*

And what were those "other things" Luann did as a young, stupid kid?

Stomach rumbling and mouth watering, I gaze at the roast chicken and apple pie.

Luann had promised that there was no coconut in these dishes. What if she lied about that?

Why would there be coconut, though? Why would she try to poison me? She'd need a motive—and she doesn't have one. As for coconut . . . Where could she hide it? The pie!

My stomach drops. Not the pie—I need to eat the pie.

I grab *Old Topanga Road* from the couch, then settle at the small dining table. I keep the extra EpiPen left by Margo above my plate as I gobble the carrots and delicate pears. The wine, a Napa Pinot Noir, tastes like bright berries, and all of this food makes me lightheaded, makes my eyelids flutter. I don't recall eating a home-cooked meal that's given me the vapors.

So Biscuit was the lure for poor Kinsey. In *Silence of the Lambs*, the senator's daughter helped Buffalo Bill load carpet into the back of the van. In real life, Ted Bundy wore a cast on his arm and had asked women for help. Rodney Alcala, the *Dating Game* contestant, posed as a photographer and offered to take pictures.

Sam—would she see through a ruse? Would she unwittingly help a woman who was working with a bad guy—or bad gal? The cook who prepared this meal, for starters. Monsters have preyed on the goodwill of women since the beginning of time. Smart women, experienced women, women not prone to falling for bullshit—they can all become ensnared.

Sam was a smart one, a tough one, and now she's gone.

After eating dinner and dessert, I carry the empty plates to the kitchen. No leftovers—and I'm relieved to be breathing free and clear, and I'm thrilled that my skin hasn't broken out in welts. I wash the dishes, placing them in the drying rack. I pop my dirty clothes into the washing machine, pull on a T-shirt and boxers, and then grab my journal. I update the floor plan to include the stackable washer-dryer in the pantry. Then, I document the last few hours of my life here in the TC.

A visit from Dr. Torrance but not meeting him. The woman in the woods. Ro Patrick. Roasted carrots.

I trace my fingers over this new entry—the paper and ink razz against my skin. There are answers between these leather covers. How much time do I have before Sam's lost forever?

Over at the thermostat, I tap the arrow button until the numbers reach seventy-four degrees—hotter than *two* scalded cats. Then, I grab *Old Topanga Road* again along with my laptop and—

A hard thump on the roof.

I duck my head and my heart shudders in my chest.

What was that?

Sounded like a dropped brick . . .

My eyes watch the ceiling.

Silence. And then . . .

Huh-HOO. Huh-HOO.

That lonely owl.

I creep over to the window and peek outside.

The swimming pool glows with light while the world around it hides in the night—

Shit.

At the edge of the patio, behind the brush and tall grass . . .

A bouncing beam of a flashlight . . .

BAM!

Another hard thump on the roof.

I drop to my knees. *What the—*

BAM!

Like something is testing the strength of this—

BAM!

I watch the ceiling, bug-eyed, winded, then dare to peek out the window again.

The bouncing light in the grass . . . *gone.*

BAM!

Something knocks on the wall . . .

Knocks again . . .

Then . . .

Bambambambambambam.

I crawl to the front door—it's locked.

Bambambambambambam . . .

Something clicks.

Whoosh.

The cottage's overhead vents vibrate. Hot air spills over me, and the pages of *Old Topanga Road* flutter.

Jeez, Bailey.

I'm freaking out over an HVAC and a furnace that probably hasn't been used in a while.

Feeling stupid, I shake out my arms and rub my face.

A knock on the front door.

I look over to the microwave clock.

Almost nine thirty.

Relax. Take a breath. Chill the hell out.

I do none of these things as I creep over to the door and peer through the peephole.

Jack Beckham stands on the porch, wearing a sports coat and a gray sweater over a white T-shirt. His hair is tousled.

I open the door.

Jack smiles. "It's late—sorry for that. And apologies for disappearing earlier in the day."

I push out a breath. "No need to apologize. Come in?"

He hesitates. "Another time—you're dressed for bed."

"Huh?" I drop my gaze—I'm wearing a T-shirt and boxers. "Ah. Yeah." I clear my throat—can the pen hear this conversation way over here? "Did your appointment go well?"

I take a quick sniff.

Jack doesn't have BO . . . but he definitely smells like vitamins. He shoves his hands into his jeans pockets. "Not really. I was a little distracted. The producer was a little peeved, but he's also an asshole."

Heat sweeps across my neck. "I'm *so* sorry."

"C'mon, Bailey. Who would've thought the afternoon would unfold in such a *dramatic* fashion?" He smiles. "Anyway, I just wanted to check in before it got too late. I saw the lights on and saw you standing in the living room, so I figured . . ."

"Just relaxing. Reading. Had an incredible dinner—no coconut— and . . . yeah." I gnaw the inside of my cheek, then say, "Oh! A detective stopped by just after I talked to you on the porch. I'm assuming he's a detective, actually."

"Really?" he says. "A detective? What happened? What did he ask about?"

"Luann mostly," I say. "I didn't mention anything about lunch—I know that was a *total* freak accident."

His eyes linger on a spot behind me. *Does he see something suspicious that I left on the coffee table?* "Did this detective leave a card?"

I shake my head. "But his name is Ro Patrick."

"Huh. I haven't told anyone about lunch."

"Maybe Dr. Torrance did," I say. "He *is* a mandatory reporter, right?"

Jack grunts, not a yes and not a no.

I also tell Jack about the homeless woman who'd snuck onto his property.

He now snaps out of his fog. "Older. Graying hair?"

I chew my lower lip. "Should I be worried?"

He clenches his teeth, offers me a strained smile. "Can't say. We're in the middle of a crime spree up here. Bling rings and home invasions, mostly. Drugs driving people to do desperate things . . . I'll have the security company do a walk-around. Because she's not the only one out there. People camp all around the canyon, and sometimes they wander up here. Sorry about that. Anything else I can do?"

My cheeks burn—I sound like a ninny. "No. You've done a lot already."

Jack swings out his arm to eyeball his watch, a heavy silver thing that costs more than my life. "Even though I'm giving you a few days to read," he says now, "we'll do a master class on the Beckham Writing Way, maybe tomorrow afternoon. My dad taught me, and now I'll teach you. Sound good?"

"Sounds great."

He nods.

"Oh," I say. "I talked a bit with Luann. She told me how you basically saved her life."

His blush spreads to his neck, and he runs his hand through his thinning hair. "I wouldn't use the word 'save.' She's a good woman. She's *very* talented. She's *very* kind. She simply needed another chance. My mother would've wanted me to extend a hand, not out of charity, but . . . I don't know . . . the word 'humanity' keeps popping into my head. Anyway, I should let you get back to—"

"One more thing," I say. "She also mentioned that the smoke detector needs another battery."

He tilts his head. "Azealia *just* replaced them."

"That's what Luann said, but it's still chirping."

He tilts his head, actively listening now. "I haven't heard any chirping since I've been standing here."

I smirk. "Give it time."

We stand there in the silence, waiting . . . waiting . . . waiting . . .

As we wait, I sneak peeks at his hair . . . thinning, yes, but now, in this light, I also see there are darker strands of hair and no split ends. And tonight, he smells like . . . *vitamins*. Sweet-sour-bitter. Weird.

I laugh. "I promise you there was chirping. Even Luann heard it."

He grins. "If you say so." He claps his hands once, then says, "So. Here's hoping for a more productive day tomorrow. How about reading, writing, and then a trip to the village?"

"Sounds like a plan," I say. "But if you have other obligations, though, don't feel pressured to entertain me. I can drive around and find things."

Find all the highlighted places in Theresa Morris's Thomas Guide. Visit that store, Hidden Treasures, where (according to Avery) Sam also visited before disappearing.

Jack snorts and his eyes shine with mischief. "No girlfriends, no obligations."

I snort. "No girlfriends? Okay. Sure." I roll my eyes. Then again, if he's approached women smelling like vitamin B, then . . .

But the angles of his face soften—he believes my compliment, and his shiny eyes are now brilliant as the sun. "What? I don't have anyone. No lie."

"Why not?"

"I guess it's because . . ." As he thinks, his eyebrows lift, then drop. His mouth pooches, then relaxes. "I guess it's because I'm boring. I work a lot. I travel a lot. I surround myself with books and trees. I'm very particular about what I eat, how I look when I don't work out. What sane woman wants to put up with *that*?"

I gape at him. "But you're an incredible storyteller—right now, I'm totally scared reading *Old Topanga Road*, and I hope, in this master class, that I learn how to write like that."

Which Bailey hopes for this? Both, maybe?

He throws back his head and laughs. "Thanks for that. I needed a pep talk after today." He exhales, then takes a walloping step away from me, then another . . . and another . . . until he's standing on the gravel walkway. "It's late—I'll let you sleep."

"Thanks for checking in on me." I point at him. "I'm going back to the book. If you hear me scream, that just means that I'm at chapter ten."

He gives me a thumbs-up as he retreats down the pathway. He looks back over his shoulder and shouts, "Close the door now. I don't want P-22 coming after you for a midnight snack."

I clutch the neck of my T-shirt. "No mountain lions inside the cottage. *Check.* Closing the door now."

"See you tomorrow," he shouts, farther away now.

"See you tomorrow," I shout back, then close the door.

Over on the couch cushion, my phone vibrates.

A text message from . . . *Avery!* Finally.

Have you asked Jack about his dead wife?

Chirp.

Item Number: 150776C
Item Description: Red Fanny Pack (1)
Victim: Doe, Jane
Offense: Death Investigation
Offense Date: November 2, 1993

Comments:

One (1) red fanny pack collected from Santa Ynez Falls-Topanga State Park, 20828 Entrada Road, Topanga, CA 90290 in fireplace of the cabin ruins.

(20) scratcher lottery tickets
keys (including 1 Honda key and 1 Ford key)
Lipstick (1)
ChapStick lip balm (1)
Sunscreen
Photocopy of map of Santa Ynez Falls

Other Information or Requests:

The photocopy of the Santa Ynez Falls Trail came from the Thomas Guide and was highlighted in yellow. There is also a handwritten note in blue ink on the map. Other handwritten notes on the following page in T. Guide. "Great meeting you. Think about doing this one. It's not difficult." Distinctive letters *Y* and *G*. Will send to handwriting analysis. Haven't found a Honda or a Ford to match these keys.

By the way, two of the scratchers are worth $100 each. Jane Doe was lucky in every way except this. See attached photos.

If you have any questions, please contact Detective Kimball. Thank you!

13.

The fire spills like waves over the forest floor. A woman who looks like me ducks and dodges falling fiery branches—but the fire doesn't touch her. A naked man with wild hair and flat black eyes bursts from a ball of flames and chases her through the woods. Fire coats his skin, but he doesn't burn. He pursues her around the trunk of a massive sequoia that still offers shade and protection even as the forest around it burns. She slows with every trip she takes around the sequoia's trunk. She slows . . . slows . . . until he reaches out with blazing hands and grabs her hair. She screams—

Chirp.

My eyes pop open. My mouth feels saltine-cracker dry.

Above me, a shaft of amber sunlight falls perfectly across the cottage's dark wood ceiling beams. Shadows of birds, bees, and trees move against the walls. Topanga Canyon is slowly opening her eyes.

I've been dreaming about . . . about . . . don't know. The nightmare starts to melt the more I try to remember. No images stick except for a giant tree standing in the middle of nowhere.

Last night, the smoke alarm continued to chirp, but not enough for me to leave my warm bed, hunt it down, and kill it. I flashed in and out of sleep because of that brief, high-pitched *chirp*, one time imagining that Russell was standing at my canyon-facing window. I froze in bed, praying that he couldn't see me in the dark. Was I frozen for real, or was I frozen in my dream? Either way, I closed my eyes and fell back to sleep.

I massage my temples, recalling the message from Avery:

Have you asked Jack about his dead wife?

During my time here, neither Jack nor Margo has mentioned Finley Beckham. I've seen no pictures around the estate of the lovely brunette climbing the canyon walls or seated in a meadow surrounded by golden poppies during the spring super bloom. I've seen no selfies of manic Finley and courageous Jack moments before they hop out of a skydiving plane or as they feed each other slices of wedding cake. I sense no woman at all living here on this estate, past or present.

But then again, I've only stood in the main house's library, sat off the sunroom with Margo for a few minutes on Wednesday night, and then ate lunch on the patio yesterday.

Chirp.

I grab my fully charged iPhone from the nightstand and read that text from Avery again. My blood burbles—she didn't even ask me how I'm doing, how's it going, just . . . *Have you asked Jack about his dead wife?* The room's atmosphere feels heavy but frigid, rebelling against the sun's warmth and the cottage's furnace, and my body's own heat. I stay in bed, beneath the comforter, not ready to poke anything except my head and one hand out into the stubborn chill.

I have files in my suitcase, but I don't want to leave this warmth. I tap *Jack Beckham wife* into the search bar, hoping to review some of what I already know. But the search engine circle spins and spins . . . spins until the pixel-art dinosaur pops onto my screen. No internet. Try checking the network cables, modem—

I should've reminded Jack about the wireless booster-router-modem thing . . .

How will I weave Finley into today's conversation? She grew up in one of the canyons—Laurel or Runyon. Rich family. Attended private school all of her life. Kidnapped with her family one time in the forests outside Cancun—but it was a prank played on them by a rich family friend. And then, she married Jack and years later disappeared.

I'm gonna have to get out of the bed. I finally have time to read more background information—the specter of Kadence Hatfield and the concept of dissociative fugue diagnoses and Finley Beckham's last day in Costa Rica. I can't waste this time all because *I'm cold.*

I scoot over to the closet, grab every folder from my suitcase, and then rush back to bed.

The red folder holds the least amount of paper. Just a blank "Contract of Retainer" form and a blank "Incident Report" form. It's ready for more—that's *my* job.

The yellow accordion folder is stuffed with all kinds of research. I pull out a few articles printed off the *LA Times* website. Highlights and handwritten notes in the margins.

LAPD Seeks Missing South Bay Woman

December 12, 2019—Elsa Good, 20, was last seen late afternoon in Topanga State Park. Search teams are currently conducting a ground and air search in the park, paying close attention to Red Rock Canyon Park, a popular hiking destination, to find Good, whose car was located not far from those trails.

A current student at Loyola Marymount University, Good has not been seen or heard from since Friday. The family is offering a $25,000 reward for information that leads to the discovery of Elsa.

Anyone with information about Elsa should call the Los Angeles Police Department.

My handwritten notes:

- *Interview w/boyfriend on 3/6/20*

- *Related to . . . ?*

- *Vehicle of interest, late 90s–early 2000s model, possibly Toyota Tercel*

- *No police records*

- *Phone tower??*

I'd bookmarked this article to serve as background for Sam's case. The history of missing women in Southern California, specifically this canyon. The resources used to unsuccessfully find Elsa Good. The reward. Why did she get an article but Sam did not?

They both disappeared in Topanga.

Both were young-ish—Sam was in her midthirties.

Neither had a police record prior to their disappearance.

Neither woman has been found, dead or alive.

So many obvious instances of disparity in media attention and police support, and I sit with my burning gut for a moment—I've used this seething anger as a source of energy to keep going. The contents of this accordion folder also include a photocopy of telephone records, a receipt from a CVS drugstore, photographs, handwritten notes on hotel stationery, a clump of sticky notes, a flattened drinking straw in a plastic baggie, another plastic baggie holding a flattened, half-eaten Twix candy bar, a receipt from Home Depot, and a KCAL News article dated January 6, 2016.

Bestselling Writer's Wife, Finley Beckham, Missing in Costa Rica

Two days have passed and no one has seen Finley Beckham, wife of bestselling novelist Jack Beckham. She was visiting the Four Seasons Resort Costa Rica with her husband. She left her villa on Wednesday morning and never returned.

The Los Angeles County Sheriff's Department, the US State Department, and the Embassy in Costa Rica have all confirmed that a missing person report has been filed.

Beckham said that Costa Rican authorities immediately launched an investigation. "I don't know what to think right now. I'm so confused," Beckham told CBS affiliate KCAL.

Beckham spoke to KCAL by phone on Wednesday.

"Finley loves the ocean and she loves morning swims. I pray that someone may have seen her in distress and plucked her out of the ocean in their fishing boat. I'm hoping for the best ending."

Was Finley here in Topanga during one of Sam's canyon searches? My friend has been missing for a while—Avery only realized it months ago. Maybe Sam's and Finley's paths crossed way back in 2015 before either woman disappeared.

As I'd pried apart Finley's life, I'd learned that, unlike Sam, Finley's digital footprint remained active. Instead of being featured in articles from the *Los Angeles* magazine or *LA Weekly*, instead of red-carpet and stop-and-repeat pictures from Getty, Finley shows up as "Bring Finley Home" and "Have You Seen Finley?" Every birthday for the last five years, friends and family leave birthday wishes on her social media pages. Same thing happens on the anniversary of her disappearance.

We miss you, Fin-Fin!

I hope you've found peace where you are.

We'll find you, Fin!

Jack leaves a beautifully written tribute to his wife on these occasions. The last one:

> The sun doesn't shine as bright. Kettle corn doesn't taste as good as it did every time we shared bags of it at farmers markets. My life is not rich and vibrant with you gone. You were my lifeline, my better self, my ambassador to a world that's taken so much from me—and so publicly. Please come back to me, babe. I will never hog the covers or the remote control or those perfect salty-sweet kernels of kettle corn again. I promise. Love you, FB. Eternally yours.

If the world can't find beautiful, rich, white Finley, what hope is there in finding the rest of us?

14.

The town of Topanga is home to about eight thousand people, with the median household income of $121,000. Famous and former residents include Lisa Bonet, Jason Momoa, Robin Williams, Mick Fleetwood, and, of course, the Beckham family. Known for its bohemian nature, Topanga hosts countless music festivals, sponsors Earth Day each year, and has its own nudist club. There are no hotels, gas stations, or Targets in this part of LA County.

Yes, I knew that last one—especially since we mentioned the lack of Targets before our hike yesterday—but I won't interrupt as Jack tells me all of this from behind the steering wheel of his Porsche. I capture it in my notepad and my recording pen as we zoom along Topanga Canyon Road in a two-seater sports car that makes me feel like I'm riding the wind. Makes me feel like I'm Beyoncé and Diahann Carroll and Truman Capote—breathtaking, gleaming, glamorous, unbothered, and sneaky as hell.

A Jeep Wagoneer is in the oncoming lane.

Jack toots the Porsche's horn and waves at the driver.

Russell Walker–Security Guard sits behind the wheel of the Wagoneer.

I toss a wave, too. Creepy old man skulking through the nighttime canyon. And why is he the only Privatas security guard I've seen up here? Can't neighborhood watch afford at least two more?

Jack's blond hair is flying everywhere. He's relaxed as he speeds past hillside homes, as we drop in and out of canyon shadows, curve after curve after curve. His eyes smile behind his aviator sunglasses. Crow's-feet crinkle against his taut golden skin—

Her! The woman who'd crept from the woods and onto the Beckham property. On the side of the road! Still wearing that filthy blue T-shirt. She holds my gaze for the few seconds that we breathe the same air.

I can't tear my eyes away from her even as she melts back into the chaparral.

"See something?" Jack glances over at me, then peeps the rearview mirror. "Everything okay?"

"I thought . . ." My mind is racing. Bile burns up my throat.

Maybe it wasn't her.

She's in the tall grass.

"Just a bit nervous," I say, ready to lead this horse to water. "One of my ex-boyfriends drove a Porsche. Nothing as nice as this. Like the starter Porsche. One time, he got a little cocky with me in the car, and he . . . he . . ." My stomach twists and tightens.

"He crashed it?" Jack asks softly.

Air from holding my breath squeezes my chest, and I force it out with a cough. "I survived the accident. *Obviously.* Escaped with just a broken arm and a concussion from the airbag. But he . . . he never walked again." I wipe my sweaty hands on my jeans.

Jack slows the Porsche now and grips the steering wheel with both hands.

I wince. "Oh no. I'm sorry—I didn't mean for you to . . . I just keep . . . ugh." *Ugh* because I'm experiencing liar's block. Did Capote sweat and hyperventilate as much as I'm doing right now?

"It's okay, Bailey," Jack says, picking up speed again. "That's a horrific story. I'm glad you came out of all that. Thank you for telling me. I'm here to support you. Remember that. And if I'm driving too fast, grab hold to the side of the door—my mother did anytime I drove her *anywhere.*"

I say, "Ha, mine too," as I focus on the road ahead of me—literally and figuratively. I ignore the weight of my lies, but celebrate the seed being planted. Just need more bullshit to get a bud to blossom.

That won't happen right now—his mouth is tight, and his jaw is flexing, and the veins in his temple are poking his tight skin. Maybe he's wrestling with telling me about his beloved Finley, but something in him refuses to share.

I'll wait.

We reach Cafe on 27, a mountain lodge–looking restaurant nestled in the trees. Inside, the restaurant boasts restored VW bugs and buses over there and over there, lots of sunshine, and canyon views of puffy white clouds and soaring hawks.

"Feels like I'm eating in a tree house," I say.

Jack and I slip on face masks, then settle on a patio that overlooks a sea of trees. The masked server brings us menus, but it's hard for me to tear my eyes away from the mysterious shadows playing above us on the canvas canopies or the mandarin-colored blossoms disrupting that sea of trees.

"This is so beautiful," I say. "Our heroine should definitely meet the bad guy here."

"Yeah." Jack chuckles. The laugh sounds hollow.

Uh-oh. Did I go too far? Did I let something slip? My gut is telling me that all is not well.

I order french toast.

He orders the vegan club sandwich.

We order Americanos—cream and sugar for me, black for him.

Even Jack's voice has changed—slight, flat, quiet.

Shit shit shit.

Neither of us speaks once the server leaves us, and I pretend to show interest in the grasshopper resting on a nearby rock.

"Success," a man shouts. His voice sounds familiar.

I turn in my seat to see Russell Walker–Security Guard tottering over to our table. He's holding a vibrant red silk scarf.

Jack smiles. "Russell! How's it going, man?" He sounds normal again.

The old guy claps Jack on the shoulder and dips his head at me. He grins widely—he's not wearing a mask. "Oh, I'm good, Mr. Beckham. Just great. When you drove past, I was saying to myself, 'Doggonit,' cuz I was actually heading your way. I was hoping that you was coming here cuz . . ."

He waves the scarf in his hand. "I think I found something that belongs to our lovely guest here."

My eyebrows lift in surprise. "Me?"

Russell Walker presents me with the silk scarf. "I believe this is yours? Found it where you were parked back on Wednesday evening. You wore such vibrant colors that night, so I knew it *had* to be yours."

My mouth opens, then shuts.

Jack looks at me. "Not yours?"

I shake my head. "Lovely scarf, though. That color *is* so rich and brilliant. I'm sure that whoever owns it must be bummed." I glimpse his badge number beneath his name: 73916.

The old man rolls up the scarf, his face still bright. "Just wanted to be sure." He pauses, then asks, "You doing okay up here, Miss Meadows? Finding Topanga agreeable?"

Seven-three-nine-one-six . . . seven-three-nine-one-six . . .

I nod, annoyed now by his interruption. "I am. Thank you again for helping me find—"

"The driveway?" Jack asks, smiling.

"Yep," I say. "I was pretty lost that day."

"No problem, Miss Meadows," Russell says, tipping his baseball cap. "Just doing my job. I'll let you two finish your meal in peace. Good seeing you, Mr. Beckham, Miss Meadows."

Jack and I watch the old man totter back out of the restaurant. I grab my journal and scribble "73916" on a page. Is this number true, or is it as fake as the person it belongs to?

"What do you know about him?" I ask.

Jack scrunches his face. "Come again?"

I grin. "You told me that everything is content, so I've started collecting characters, including Mr. Walker. How did he come to work as a guard from another part of town and is now working nearly forty miles away? Like . . . did he always dream of patrolling the forest? Was he a cop once upon a time? Is he an ex-con?"

Jack tilts his head, thinking. "I've never really talked to him beyond the usual chitchat."

"Do you have to undergo a background check to become a guard?"

Jack nods. "Probably. Don't know for sure."

I drop my journal back into my purse. "Can someone *lie* about that? Like . . . how people use their friends' clean urine report to pass drug tests?"

Jack thinks, the cucumber he was about to eat held inches from his mouth. A slow smile spreads across his face. "I like where you're going with this." He chomps the cucumber. "But may I ask? Where is this 'casting the security guard as a villain' scenario coming from?"

I shrug and pull my fork through the syrup pooling around my french toast. *Shit.*

"You're worried about something," Jack says.

I clear my throat, all of a sudden not wanting to tell on the only Black man in Topanga Canyon. "It's just . . . I've just . . . I've been seeing random people roaming the canyon. And then, you told me about all the crime . . . and maybe the people who are supposed to be protecting us . . . you know."

"Yeah. Sure." He pushes back from his plate. "Not too long ago, someone stole a safe with more than one million in cash and jewelry in it. The house had a security system, and a random thief wouldn't have found that safe—it was in some closet in some random part of the house. Well, the maid knew about that part of the house—she and her son had stolen the safe. They were actually a part of some eastside gang responsible for a lot of burglaries around here. And then, there was . . ."

He wipes his mouth with a napkin. "Someone robbed another café down the road. *While the workers were still there, cleaning up.*" He points at me. "It was the security guard, and he'd used his brother's fingerprints and clean security check to land the job. He came up here, got the job at the café. Worked there for a month or two, getting to know the routines, and then *bam!* I think he shot and killed someone—"

I throw my napkin on the table. "You're not supposed to be *scaring* me."

He points at me again and smiles. "*You* started it with Russell being the head of a bling ring *maybe*. Russell is a great guy. Honest."

I nod, remembering him not walking so bowlegged and old in the nighttime canyon.

We return to our meals and sip our coffees.

I dab my mouth with a napkin and then clear my throat. "So, what was it about my application that Margo and the selection committee liked about me?"

"Selection committee?" Jack pops an olive into his mouth and chews. "*I* went through every application—Margo simply weeded out the weirdos and the stalkers. She sent me your writing sample, and there was one line that made me   *shiver.* It was . . . 'Inside us there is something that has no name, that something is what we are.'" Jack shakes his head in wonder. "I knew right then . . . what a gift you have."

I blush, impressed by my own writing.

"Margo also knows Avery," Jack adds. "I think they went to school together or something. So *maybe* there was some bias? But it was definitely a fair selection process. And like I told you, I wanted a new face with a new point of view. Someone who's lived a life different from my friends and me."

I lean forward in my seat. "Whenever anyone says that LA is too big to make connections, I always assume they're being East Coast and Midwest snobs. Avery and Margo seem totally different, personality-wise, and yet somehow they're good friends."

Jack takes a quick sip of coffee, then says, "Margo is bubbly and kinda goofy—"

"And Avery is no-nonsense, get it done yesterday."

"Avery is a *beast*."

I pause, then say, "You've met Avery?"

He smiles. "I have."

Ice pops in my chest and spills through my veins.

"You . . . seem surprised," he says.

"Avery didn't tell me that she knew you like that." I try to sound dismissive about this discovery—*Does it really matter?*—but it snags in my mind.

He smirks. "Avery's keeping secrets from you?"

I drop my eyes to the tabletop. "I guess we don't know *everything* about someone we think we know."

"Hmm," he says. "That sounds familiar. Like something a wise man—me, for instance—would say."

I try to chuckle—he *did* say that. But this nugget of knowledge—Avery and Jack knowing each other—bothers me. Like . . . why didn't she mention that to me?

Jack waves his hand in front of my face. "It's nothing to be worried about, Bailey. You just said how small the world is. Well, the world of writing, especially crime fiction, is even smaller. Everyone knows someone you know."

I shrug and smile. "I guess. Oh, how cute! How am I just noticing these now?" I take pictures of the ceramic squirrel salt and pepper shakers. "Cute." And then, I snap pictures of the Turkish pottery placed on the café's shelves, of those orange lilies in the sea of trees, the tiny yellow Inspector Clouseau VW inside the café, and a patron's cute Lab wearing a tie-dyed bandanna. Then, I aim the camera at Jack. "Smile, Mr. Beckham."

He smiles, but his eyes have turned flat and frosty. The muscles that lift his cheeks and eyes don't move.

I lower my phone. "You okay?"

"Yep." He pokes at the watercress spilling from the sandwich he's bitten into only once.

"Don't like your sandwich?" I ask.

He stabs at a tomato. "You got me thinking about something."

I nibble a strawberry. "I did?"

"Yeah." He watches a hawk now drifting over the forest. "Not sure if you know this, but I was married before."

I lick the syrupy fork. "I *did* know that, but you hadn't brought it up. And since I didn't see any pictures of her around . . ."

"That's because we went on vacation in Costa Rica, and she disappeared." Shadows settle over his face. "Well, *she* was vacationing. I was writing, and to her, that was the problem." His eyes dart to mine. "Cone of trust," he says, leaning forward.

"Of course," I say, also leaning forward, my legs numb.

"She'd planned to get pregnant on that trip," he shares. "I was totally on board with that. Finally open to the idea. But Fin was spoiled—she grew up over in Laurel Canyon—even before we met. I only added to it—we were both orphans, and I overcompensated. Her family died in a car crash right after we married. Anyway, she pouted a lot to get her way—she *constantly* wanted attention. There I was, though, in beautiful Costa Rica, taking care of her, wanting to make sure we'd be okay financially before kids, and there *she* was, demanding center stage, always expecting to be the main character in our lives."

"How did she feel about the writing residency here?" I ask.

"Hated it," Jack says. "I was, once again, paying attention to something and someone other than her. And if the resident was a woman . . ." He blows out a huge breath and lets his head fall back. "Fin could be a fuckin' *gremlin* sometimes."

"How many residents were women?" I try to keep my voice as steady as possible.

"That's the kicker. One—Patricia—was a late-in-life poet, like older than *you*. Patty was, what? Seventy years old? The other—Sienna—wrote lesbian noir. She was an ex-cop and *a lesbian*. Like, Finley, what the *fuck*?"

"That happens sometimes. I've been insecure over totally irrational things." I swallow, then say, "I was actually jealous of one of my friends. Her name is Sam, and she took one of your extension writing classes over at UCLA. She told me that she landed a spot at this residency. But you've only had *how* many women?"

"Two." Jack cocks his head. "Maybe she *applied* to the program? She probably was a student in that course—that's where most students find out about the residency. Hmm . . . maybe Margo encouraged her to reapply? I mean . . . I've only had seven writers total here, Patty and Sienna, but none named Sam. Three women, including you."

I tap my heart. "Okay—I feel better about that. You're right. She probably applied and pretended that she got accepted—how would I check that, right?"

"Anyway . . ." Jack rubs his face, then drains his coffee cup. "Finley brought this ovulation kit to Costa Rica, and she monitored it the entire time we were there. She became *obsessed* . . ." He stares at the tabletop.

"We argued one night," he says, "and we did something we promised each other that we'd never do: we went to bed angry with each other. She got up early the next morning and left our villa—I don't remember if the sun was even up yet. She wrote me a note. 'Went for a swim.' She did that here, too. Went out to surf before the sun cracked the horizon. Came back and made smoothies . . ."

He shakes his head. "This time, though, in Costa Rica, she never came back. If she wanted my attention before, she got it that day and every day since."

A cloud slips across the sun, and the temperature dips, and now we're the only people in the woods, people who found this tree house with a table set for two.

"What happened after she disappeared?" I ask.

Jack's eyes shine. "What you'd expect. They questioned me—I'm the husband. It's—"

"Always the husband," we say, together.

"And my father's history of domestic abuse didn't help. Like father, like son, right?" He rolls his eyes and shakes his head. "But I had alibis of where I'd been for most of the day. With closed-circuit security footage backing me up. I was being interviewed for a *Vanity Fair* piece most of the day. Went out to lunch. Went to the spa. Had a drink at the bar . . . eventually, the cops moved past me and actually started to focus on Finley."

My eyes widen. "Come again?"

His lips slant into a sneer. "My beloved wife had secrets—we all do. But Finley . . . she had a history of pulling disappearing acts all of her life. She sleepwalked as a child, so her parents constantly lost her overnight. When she turned sixteen, she ran off to Coachella without permission or warning.

"In college, Fin drove down to Tijuana and Rosarito Beach, just to—as she explained—'feel free.' Sometimes, she was gone for just a few days. Sometimes, a few weeks. Once, I called the police and felt like a fool when she showed up two days later, with a tan and new tattoo of a manta ray. Like it was no big deal. So her disappearing when she didn't get her way? Standard operating procedure."

"You weren't alarmed that she was gone at first," I whisper.

His smile now feels strained. "Some days, I don't believe that she abandoned me just like my mother had. That was another promise Fin made me, that she'd never leave me. Some days, I feel like she actually drowned off the coast of Costa Rica and *has* been dead all this time. The other side of me, the *creative* side, the skeptic, knows that I was duped into believing she wanted to be with me. That she successfully got one over on me, Jack Beckham, bestselling author of twisty, unputdownable books, who didn't see it coming.

"My ego bristles at that. Who wants to believe and admit that, because you were so in love, you couldn't see the truth? That she pretended to like my books and read them? That she pretended that she loved me? That she was always planning to take off for good one day?

"Deep inside, I knew she wasn't always going surfing. There was one time she claimed she was headed to Pacific Palisades. By then, I had a detective following her—the one who I consulted with for my novels. And he followed her one morning down the hill where she turned into a driveway . . ." He chuckles and shrugs. "Another man. No big reveal. It was right there all along, a burr in a bag of cotton balls."

My stomach churns—burrs live there, too.

Also: he's dining right now with another burr.

"It's been five years since she left that morning," Jack continues, "and not a day ends that I don't think about her. She disappeared while I was writing the sequel to *Old Topanga Road*, and I couldn't finish it, nor could I write anything else. And I'm *still* suffering with the worst kind of writer's block."

I try to swallow the burning brick caught in my throat—but it refuses to budge. "Whatever happened with that *Vanity Fair* article?" I choke out.

Jack picks up his water glass, takes a sip. "Never published. The editor couldn't run a story—at least a *favorable* story—about a man who may have disappeared his wife even if, ultimately, he *didn't* disappear his wife and was cleared by the police. I mean . . ." He sips more water. "It sucked, but I understood. But if Finley *is* alive and well . . . ?"

He slips down in his chair and rubs his face. His skin flushes, his eyes sag, and his smile is now weary and overworked. "Guess it still hurts to talk about." He clears his throat, then adjusts the collar of his shirt. "Today, I choose to believe that a rogue wave swept her out to sea. Tomorrow? Who knows."

His eyes move over me, and he watches the forest behind me, back to thinking again. "Tomorrow, I'll go back to wondering if she's in the forest behind us right now. Watching me and laughing her ass off."

I gasp. "She's not that—"

"Cruel?" He snorts. "She could be *incredibly* cruel, and there were a lot of people who couldn't figure out why I chose *her*, why I chose someone as pathological as my father." His eyes flick at me. "But you said it best. I also collect characters. Broken people, especially. Fin was broken and money couldn't fix her. Her parents couldn't fix her. I couldn't.

"Maybe one day," he continues, "I'll put pictures of us back up on those 'my love died at sea' days. For now, though . . ." He chuckles. "On her good days, she wanted me to be happy. But if she's still alive, she's happy seeing me languish. That was her favorite word: *languish.* I wish her peace, and I hope she finds what she's searched for all her life. 'Drop in, pull in, kick out'—that's what surfer Fin always said. That's some bullshit."

Jack slaps the tabletop, and the rest of his vegan club sandwich topples over to become an uneaten salad. "I'm kicking out. I'm done *languishing,* and now, I'm ready to be back on the bestseller lists again. *All* of the bestselling lists. And then, *you* will land a seven-figure book deal and become the new voice of crime fiction. We'll go on the road together—my readers will become *your* readers."

I press my cheeks with my hands. "Promise?"

"Cross my heart." His frosty eyes have now warmed, and they sparkle, and the crow's-feet scratch against his skin again. "I know what I want our story to be, but I won't tell you—don't want to influence your creativity. But I feel a hit coming on. Something new and dangerous. Something—"

"Unputdownable?" I say.

"Unputdownable and transcends the genre." He lifts his water glass. "No guts, no glory, right?"

15.

Fire Department Station 69 is south of Cafe on 27.

The Smokey Bear sign posted on the curb offers this reassuring forecast:

TODAY'S FIRE DANGER IS **HIGH**

"Be thankful it's not 'very high' or 'extreme,'" fire captain Mark Walsh tells me.

Captain Walsh, a giant man in blue khakis, is now leading Jack and me around the station. Right here, two red fire engines glisten in their parking spaces. Over there, TOPANGA 69 has been nailed above two crossed fire axes. That over there is a wooden four-leaf clover affixed to a wall beside a skeleton holding a "Penalty Box" pennant.

"This station started out as a volunteer company back in 1929," Captain Walsh shares, "and back then, firefighters with lousy attitudes got sent here to work."

"Not now," Jack says, clapping the captain on his back.

"I paid him to say that," Captain Walsh says.

We laugh.

"The Beckhams have been invaluable boosters since the very beginning," the fireman continues. "They were one of the first families in the canyon, and they made sure we had all the equipment and all the resources that the county couldn't provide. As a matter of fact, Jack still sponsors blood drives—"

"A Beckham man always sticks out his arm for the first jab," Jack boasts.

Captain Walsh tosses me a station T-shirt he grabbed from a box of them. "Charity softball games, summer concerts. You name it, the Beckhams did it, keeping us up to date and ready to roll, and with COVID, not so many activities over the last year. But one day soon, we'll be back to normal." He jostles Jack this way and that. "Guess the Beckham tradition will be sunsetting anyway. No Beckham babies, right, Jack?"

Jack shrugs. "Hey, I tried."

Yeah. Him, Finley, and that ovulation kit in Costa Rica. He's the last of his family—just like Sam. I'm no different. Other than my mother, I have no one else. Well . . . I have Avery.

"We all flew down to Central America to help look for Fin," Captain Walsh says. "Since authorities down there didn't seem to care if she was found or not. She was a rich white lady—who cares about them?"

Only the rest of the world.

"This guy," Jack says, pointing at the fireman, "got some kind of disease on that trip—"

"Dengue fever," Walsh says. "Fucking mosquitoes, man. But we wanted to go since we have a lot of experience searching for lost hikers in the forests and canyons."

"So you think she may have made it back to land?" I ask.

Walsh nods. "But not close enough to the tourist areas. She came out, and the forest was right there. We had hope she'd survive, because she grew up in a similar biome."

I tilt my head. "That's a background question I have. How do you *not* get lost when hiking? What should I carry?"

Wear bright clothes—orange, red, yellow. Helps you get spotted easier.

Wear the proper shoes. No flip-flops.

Don't count on your cell phone. "If you haven't noticed," the captain says, "we hardly get any reception even in the developed areas. Imagine being deep off in the woods."

Bring a satellite messaging device that sends rescuers an SOS with your exact location.

Water.

Protein bars.

There's no evidence that Sam carried *any* of that on her trip here. And if she wore civilian, everyday clothes . . . *anything* could've happened to her—and those possibilities include flash floods, freezing at night, overheating in the day, thirst . . .

Jack softly pounds his fist on the fireman's shoulder. "I'll be forever grateful, Mark. Wish I could've given you more little Beckhams raising holy hell up here."

"There's always hope," I say now. "Men can have babies until they're six hundred years old."

"You're right about that, Miss Meadows," Walsh says, nodding his big bear head. "What would Topanga be without the Beckhams?"

I twitch my nose at Jack. "You better get crackin', sir. Drop in, pull out—well, no, you shouldn't do that, not if you want kids."

Walsh roars with a cannon laugh. "I *like* her!"

Jack appeals to the ceiling, all *These two.* "Walsh, got a new joke for you," he says. "A firefighter and a cop fall off the side of a boat, and you could only save the firefighter . . ."

We laugh.

Walsh dabs at his eyes, tearing up from laughing. "Miss Meadows," he says, "did Jack tell you that his father made the captain back then help build that fire bunker not far from the guesthouse?"

"I *did* tell her that Big Jack was a stubborn bastard," Jack says.

"And since Cap knew Big Jack was never gonna leave his property," Walsh continues, "he thought, 'Well, at least I'll help the stubborn bastard live to see another miserable day hunkered down in this cinder block hotel in hell.'"

"Can a fire bunker really keep you safe, though?" I ask.

"If it's built underground, sure," Walsh says. "You stay in there until the flames have passed. That's about thirty minutes or so. If that fire doesn't swing back—which it can—you're good. But it's gotta be airtight and well insulated with enough oxygen for everyone sheltering—that's *most* important."

"Do you know of any cases where the bunker failed and people died?" I ask.

"I heard that Australia was having a problem with one company," he says. "They were selling shelters that weren't accredited. Folks suffocated from lack of oxygen. Not airtight, those shelters.

"Then, there are people buying do-it-yourself bunkers . . . a total mess. Knowing that, the fire captain and the manufacturers used Big Jack as a kind of study."

Jack snorts. "And he used it once, right? The '93 fire?"

"Yup," Captain Walsh agrees.

"And it held?" I ask.

"Yup," the fireman says. "And after that, we could never get him to evacuate."

"Does it get hot in a bunker?" I ask.

"Heck yeah, it can get hot in there," the captain says, nodding eagerly. "Humans can tolerate between two hundred fifty to three hundred degrees, especially if there's some water around."

"Our shelter is the best that could be built for private citizens," Jack says. "Reinforced concrete, a three-hour fire door, a roll cage to keep debris from blocking the exit. Completely airtight."

I pretend to wipe sweat from my brow. "That's reassuring."

"Jack tells me you're helping him write a book?" the captain says.

Heat climbs up my neck and roosts in my cheeks—which could be interpreted as embarrassed emerging writer syndrome. "I still can't believe it, but yes, I am. So, all of this is helpful information. I'm from South Los Angeles, so fire moves differently down there than it does up here. I mean . . . I've seen car fires, house fires, office buildings on fire . . ."

"Fire fuel is different where you live," Captain Walsh says. "In the canyons and green places, fuel includes fallen leaves and twigs that become kindling. The Santa Ana winds we get every year? They help fire spread in the forest parts but also in urban areas, from building to building. Synthetic products found in every home—couches, rugs, curtains instead of trees and dry grass. More people are building homes in fire-prone areas.

"You think, 'Oh, there's a Target and a bunch of fast-food restaurants and traffic,'" Captain Walsh continues, "and you think you're in the city. No, you're still in wildland areas. And then, on top of *that*, climate change, and that affects *everyone*. Cities, rural areas, suburbs."

Because of hot, dry weather caused by *us*, fires are now starting in high mountain areas that used to be thought of as too wet to burn. Not anymore.

Captain Walsh holds up his hand. "I'm about to rant, so I'm gonna shut up now." He runs his forearm across his nose, clearly affected by what he's witnessing.

"What should I know about *this* area?" I ask. "And if I'm asking too many—"

"No, no, no," the fireman says. "I *like* talking about this stuff. Just get a little frustrated sometimes." He clears his throat, then starts. "You should know that this district is one of the most challenging districts in the country, if not the *most*. We get a *lot* of fire in this state. By June of last year, we were over six hundred fifty thousand acres burned. Next month, we're acquiring a specially built Chinook CH-47 helicopter made to fight large fires. Holds about a thousand gallons in her belly. She'll be up and running in time for fire season."

"Damn," Jack says. "A thousand *gallons*?"

"And," the fire captain continues, "we've upgraded our helistop up the mountain. We got four eight-thousand-gallon metal water tanks up there to refill the birds." He wags his head. "But then, you flip it, fire season ends and the rains come. Flash floods. Mudslides. Land that's changed because—"

"Of the fires," I say.

The captain points a scarred finger at me. "Correct."

I learn so much about fire and Topanga Canyon, listening to this big man speak. Like:

Although there is a "fire season" in California, climate change makes that fire season year-round.

And:

It takes only ninety minutes for a fire to burn from the Topanga Overlook to the Pacific Ocean—and it would take seven hours to evacuate every resident, since there is only one main road in and one main road out.

Captain Walsh points behind me. "And that road is Topanga Canyon Road. If you're ever trapped by fire while you're in your car? Get out. That thing will blow up before you know it."

Even though my pen has been recording nonstop since leaving the Beckham estate, I'm scribbling all this down in my journal. "Since we're writing a crime novel," I say, "have you ever found a deceased person who actually did not die from the fire but by someone's hand? In other words, the killer had hoped to hide that murder with the fire."

Captain Walsh scratches the whiskers on his chin as he thinks. Then: "Up in NorCal, a woman went on a date with this guy, and he killed her and started the Markley Fire. Six people died. About fifteen hundred homes destroyed."

Also:

"Down here in SoCal," Walsh says, "triple homicide. The suspects had started a house fire to hide those three bodies and to destroy evidence. It's no longer surprising to see this."

"A lot of times," Jack adds, "victims have to be identified with dental records because they're so badly burned."

My phone vibrates in my pocket again and again.

Is that . . . ?

A signal?

I shuffle from foot to foot, holding my breath, wondering if this conversation will be ending soon, because I want to take advantage of the cellular network. I can barely hear Captain Walsh now because my heart is pounding so hard.

"There were seven hundred seventy-six incidents involving fire in LA County last year," the fireman is now saying. "About five percent were classified as arson. That number probably includes fire used post-mortem to conceal the homicide, get rid of the body, keep us from identifying the victim."

"Are there ways to tell if a person died before a fire?" I ask.

"Despite their portrayal on TV and in movies," Captain Walsh says, "criminals are stupid. Sure, fire burns away a lot of evidence. But not bones. Not teeth. Yeah, heat from fire changes the cranium in certain ways—but those ways typically aren't shaped like bullet holes. Sometimes, investigators can analyze blood samples from the victim and see if carbon monoxide levels are high enough to indicate that the victim was alive when they burned. They also look for soot particles in the victim's airways from breathing in—because lungs tell the story, too."

He pauses, then dips his chin to his chest. "You don't have to be a firefighter to know . . . dead folks don't inhale."

16.

The talk of fire—from "burned people smell like roast beef" to "steam explosion in the head shatters the skull"—makes my throat prickly and tight. I jot down incredibly useful nuggets from Captain Walsh ("There are two types of lightning: hot and cold" and "The UN predicts a fifty percent increase of global wildfires by 2100" and "Large wildfires can create their own weather" and "Most animals can escape wildfires with some beetles actually thriving in the scorched trees") even as my mind remains on investigators looking at the size of skulls and smoke in lungs. And now, I also worry about Sam being a Jane Doe in some coroner's office, burned beyond recognition. Avery has checked "Jane Does" down here in Los Angeles. But what about Oakland? Or Las Vegas? Or wherever they take the dead in Baker, California?

My vibrating cell phone isn't helping—I want to review my messages, but I can't review my messages. That would be rude, first of all, and second, I don't know what my face will do if I read something completely off the wall.

And also now, another fireman with arms like tree trunks and brown hair with an exact side part joins our group. He has something to add, and as he winds up to tell us that time he—

Can't breathe. Can't focus. I feel as though I placed my finger in a socket and electricity has replaced my blood. All the shiny things hurt my eyes—the red fire engines, the buffed gray floor, the perfect blue sky. Air hurts my lungs as though soot and poison are my new oxygen.

Why am I freaking out hearing all of this? I've never been trapped in a fire. Maybe because fire is unpredictable or . . . or . . .

Jack doesn't notice my distress. He crosses his arms and narrows his eyes as Walsh and the brown-haired engineer tell us about the piece of walking garbage who threw gasoline on a sleeping homeless guy, then lit a match. "This *dumbass* didn't realize that the vapors from the gasoline would catch," the engineer says, "and so he caught on fire, too. Burned down his *own* tent. Dumbass."

I touch Jack's elbow with a shaky hand, and say, "I'm gonna head to the car. Move some of the stuff from my brain and onto paper."

Jack winks at me, then hands me the keys to the Porsche. "I'll be out in a minute."

I thank Captain Walsh and the brown-haired engineer for their time and rush out to the parking lot.

Right now, cars are zooming up and down Topanga Canyon Road. *One way in, one way out.* Couples wearing sunglasses and shorts walk their dogs. With earbuds in, joggers and fast walkers scuttle across sun-stippled sidewalks in the middle of the forest.

I slip into the passenger seat of Jack's car.

It's nearly three o'clock—Jack and I have been out for a while now. There are four strong bars of cellular reception—the cause of my phone exploding in my pocket. My hands are shaking so much, though, that my finger keeps missing the icon to check voicemail. And because I keep missing the icon, my breathing becomes more frantic since I don't have a lot of time to get my shit together. I take a moment to breathe . . . breathe . . . gain the control I had before all the fire talk started. I have to—Jack will return, and we'll drive away, and those four bars will become no bars.

Calmer now, I tap the icon into MESSAGES.

The texts here . . . are all from me, with each text I've sent annotated with a red exclamation point. None of my messages have gone through.

Over at the firehouse, Jack and the firemen haven't moved from their spots beneath the crossed axes.

I hit each red exclamation point to resend those texts, *swoop swoop swoop*.

Each message lands successfully in Avery's phone. DELIVERED.

I add one last text:

Why didn't you tell me that you *knew* knew Jack?

WTF?

What else aren't you telling me?

The results from my last search—*Samantha Morris*—still sit in one of fifteen tabs.

Hold on . . . What if "Sam" isn't short for "Samantha"?

What if "Sam" is the nickname for Samuela, Sameera, Samaira, Samanvitha, Samaya . . . one hundred variations of names, and my "Sam" could have adopted any of them.

What kind of private detective am I? How can I not know her full first name?

Next, I tap the tab with the search results for *Jack Beckham wife*.

There are 105 million results.

Finley Crawford Beckham, 1984–2016. A picture of her and Jack posing in front of a step-and-repeat at some movie premiere. She resembles Angelina Jolie in her *Mr. & Mrs. Smith* vamp-girl era. Wavy dark hair, sultry lips, smoky-blue eyes that almost match Liz Taylor's lavender.

A link to a short Wikipedia blurb: "He lives in Topanga, California, with his wife, Finley Crawford, whom he married in May 2010."

Over at the firehouse, the brown-haired engineer is gone. Jack and Captain Walsh are edging closer to the parking lot.

The next link related to Finley is new. An article from KCAL News:

Bestselling Author Cleared of Wife's Death

On the morning his wife of five years went for a swim off the coast of Costa Rica, Jack Beckham was sitting at a desk in their Four Seasons villa, being interviewed by a reporter writing a feature for *Vanity Fair*. Finley Crawford Beckham exchanged greetings with that reporter before departing the casita. "Going out to get my surf on," Crawford Beckham shared. According to Jack Beckham, and witnessed by reporter Peyton Ruiz, Crawford Beckham kissed the top of Jack's head, waved goodbye, grabbed her beach bag, and walked out the door. He never saw Finley alive again.

According to this new article, the interview between Jack and Peyton Ruiz lasted three hours—and proved that he'd been in the villa while Finley had been swimming off the peninsula.

But didn't he say that she left at the crack of dawn? Or was he referring to surfing here in Los Angeles?

I tap another question into the search bar:

Is there surfing off Costa Rica Four Seasons?

The answer loads in less than a second.

"Within a fifteen-minute boat ride . . . Peninsula Papagayo . . . two surf breaks offer waves 365 days . . ."

There must be a record of Finley boarding a boat. Investigators must've checked the passenger manifests. What did they find—and how can I get a copy?

Next, I search for the number for Privatas Security and tap the link of the phone number. My fingers turn to ice as the line rings . . . rings . . .

"Privatas Security," a woman announces. "How may I direct your call?"

"Hi," I say, "I need to leave a message for one of your security guards. I'd like to give him some information—my family and I will be going out of town, and I forgot to tell him a few things."

"Certainly," the woman chirps. "Who would you like to leave that message for?"

"Russell Walker. He patrols Topanga Canyon. His badge number is seven-three-nine-one-six."

"One moment, please." Her fingers *tap-tap-tap* against the keyboard and then stop. "May I place you on a brief hold?"

"Sure." My underarms flood with flop sweat.

The hold music—"I'm So Excited" by the Pointer Sisters.

"Ma'am?" the woman says.

"I'm here," I say.

"I'm sorry, but we don't have a 'Russell Walker' in our database. Maybe he's with Allied or Kasper Security?"

My mind goes boom and—

"Sorry about that—" Jack plops behind the steering wheel.

I fumble my cell phone, and it slips between the passenger-side door and my seat.

Shit. For many reasons, Russell Walker doesn't work at Privatas. The receptionist is saying "Hello?" and "Are you there?" to my ankles.

"Didn't mean to freak you out with all that fire talk," Jack says.

I shove my shaky hand into the gap and feel around for my fallen phone. "I *did* get a little freaked out. I'm not used to talking about all that. Fire scares me."

Ah! Here it—

This . . . is not my phone. Yes, this is an iPhone, but the glass on the upper right corner is cracked. My phone has no cracks.

"How . . . ?" I swallow, then start again. "How do you handle that? Any little blaze can become a historic blaze. And the one way in, one way out . . ."

Who lost *this* phone?

Don't know, but I wrap the courtesy T-shirt from Captain Walsh around it and then shove the bundle into my purse. I dip my hand back between the seat and door again.

"Everything okay?" Jack looks at me with concern. "You seem rattled."

I chuckle. "That's because I *am* rattled. So much so that I dropped my stupid phone."

"If fire doesn't scare you, nothing will," Jack says, nodding. "Nothing scarier."

A serial killer—*that's* scarier than fire.

My fingers brush against another mysterious rectangular-shaped device. "Success! Here"—I hold my breath and hope for the best—"it is." I hold up an iPhone. *My* iPhone.

On cue, the phone vibrates in my hand, the banner on the screen a text message.

"One more stop and we're done," he says, pulling out of the parking lot.

"I've learned so much today," I say, "but I still have a few questions. Like . . . which trees burn quicker? Where does it all go? The ashes and all that? Basically, are we breathing Pompeii's ashes like we're breathing Caesar's last breath? How do they take DNA from a burned-beyond-recognition body?"

I have Jack's DNA—that flattened Twix bar came from him. But now that I know him and have seen him eat . . . Was the chocolate bar a rare cheat from his strict diet?

◆ ◆ ◆

The Spiral Staircase is located beside the restaurant Inn at the Seventh Ray. With its ivy-covered facade, this bookstore feels more "Narnia meets 1969 Hippie Los Angeles" than "2021 Barnes & Noble at the Grove." Wind chimes strung to hanging potted plants tinkle as we pass, and the store smells of eucalyptus and sandstone incense. Narrow aisles are crammed with shelves of crystals, candles, canvas tote bags, and books. My ass comes close to knocking over a display of tarot cards and Buddha boards.

"This store has been here for years," Jack says. "It's a little New Agey, a little witchy and woo-woo, but the staff are very lovely people. And there's a *fantastic* organic wine section."

Jack leads me to the rear of the store and to a table with a small stack of books. The placard says, "The Beckhams of Topanga." His eyes lighten as he traces the spine of *City of Exile*. "My first book," he says.

I scrunch my eyebrows. "I thought *The Overlook*—"

Jack glances at the novel he's caressing and snatches his hand back as though the book stung him. "He'd kill me if he saw me trying to claim that as mine, accident or not." He places his hand on the book next to it, *The Overlook*. "Anyway . . . What was the point I was trying . . . ? Yes. I was saying that this store has been one of my favorite places since I was a kid."

He bends toward me and whispers, "I felt safe here. For an hour, I was in a kingdom of books, a fairyland that hid me from the ogre of Topanga."

I pick up a hardcover of Jack's *The Lost Canyon*. "Your father sounds terrifying."

Jack pales. "Let's just say . . . there were a lot of dry eyes at his memorial . . . and my eyes were probably the driest." He pokes the spine of Big Jack's *City of Exile*. He mutters, "Fucker."

"Excuse us . . ."

We turn toward the woman's voice.

Her lower face hides beneath a mask, and the rest of her straddles the space between Wavy Gravy and St. John, grunge-hippie trust-fund kid all grown up and married to IBM. Her two girlfriends have their own vibes: athleisure wear for the blonde, and mom capris for the brunette. Neither wear their face masks over their mouths and noses. But they all clutch copies of *Old Topanga Road*.

Wavy Gravy eyes me, then says, "So sorry for interrupting." To Jack: "We were *just* having lunch—we came over earlier to buy your books, and now here you are! Would you mind signing our copies? We're huge fans."

Jack's joy drills all the way down to his spleen. "I would absolutely love to." He takes Wavy Gravy's copy of *Old Topanga Road*. "Bailey here will be cowriting the sequel to this," he shares, holding up the book he just signed.

The women fall silent and consider me with new eyes.

"You must be incredibly talented for Jack to pick you," Mom Capris says, her head cocked. "I must say, and I'm sure you will agree: this man right here is *so* generous. Did he tell you that he always, *always* makes sure we make goal for our little TC fundraisers."

"He donates silent auction items," Wavy Gravy adds. "And gives—" She whispers, "Money."

"Sometimes, he only needs to be just a face in the room," Mom Capris says. "Why, yes, he *is* the perfect man, why do you ask?"

All the ladies giggle.

Jack blushes, smiles, and drops his head.

Yoga Pants says, "I'm all for you writing—*Bailey, was it?*—as long as you don't change anything that makes Jack's work so special."

"In other words," Mom Capris whispers, "we don't like politics with our entertainment. Can't let the bookstore staff hear me say that. They'll ban me from the store." She and Yoga Pants giggle.

"Well, then," Jack says. "Let me tell Irene over there what you just said." He's smiling, but there's also a glint in his eyes.

"Have you written a novel before?" Wavy Gravy asks me. "Anything we would know?"

I shake my head. "A few pieces. I'm just starting out—"

"Bailey is the new Beckham writer-in-residence," Jack explains.

I say, "I'm learning, and the pieces I've written are nothing comparable to Jack's work. I'm glad he's giving me an opportunity to collaborate and come up with new—"

"None of that woke stuff," Yoga Pants says, shaking her finger at Jack. "Just some good ol' fashioned murder mystery."

"'Woke.' Do you even know what that word means?" The glint in Jack's eyes has become scalpel sharp.

Yoga Pants giggles. "Of *course* I do—I watch that sitcom, the one about the Black family. Diana Ross's daughter is in it. And my Pilates instructor? She's from South-Central LA, and the music she plays . . ." Yoga Pants rolls her eyes to the ceiling.

Jack folds his arms, his squint hard. He flexes his jaw, then says, "We were leaving—"

"I like your books so much more than your father's," Mom Capris tells Jack, her chin down, her gaze coquettish.

"Me too!" the other women add.

"Don't get me wrong," Mom Capris continues. "Big Jack's stuff was good."

"But they got too . . . *campy*," Wavy Gravy adds. "The plots became . . . *unbelievable*."

"And kinda . . . *irrelevant*," Yoga Pants says. "Provocative but not . . . *organically*."

"His novels jumped the shark after he wrote that one about the two spies and the military making zombies, and there was a lost dog—"

"What was the thing with the lost dog—"

"None of it made sense—"

"I threw it across the room—"

"He'd throw *you* across the room—"

"And not in the good way—"

"Okay, ladies," Jack says, his mouth hard. "No zombies or spies or dogs. Got it." He turns to me. "Usually, you don't get fans who hurt your feelings like this *to* your face."

Wavy Gravy gasps. "Did we go too far?"

Yoga Pants covers her face. "We meant no disrespect."

Jack says, "You sure about that?"

Another reader joins us in the cramped space, and I'm jostled to the edge of the crowd. All of Jack's fans fall into one of the three categories of the original trio. All of them are white. Some have plumper-filled lips and Botoxed cheeks and foreheads, and chemically erased smooth faces now partially hidden beneath partially worn protective masks. They—*including Jack*—must share the same plastic surgeon. No wonder he's bored.

How will they react once they discover that *they* aren't the main character of the new book, that the next Beckham heroine will look like . . . *me?*

No woke stuff. Just good ol' fashioned murder mystery.

Because murder—especially the murders of women—is *never* political.

The impromptu signing takes close to an hour. In that time I learn that Yoga Pants is a casting director. Mom Capris found her meaning after undertaking her own *Eat, Pray, Love* journey around the world. Wavy Gravy is a former supermodel who now hosts tea services beneath the big oak tree in her backyard. After flinging a few more apologies at us, they wave as we exit the bookstore to retrieve the car from the valet.

"An interesting group," I say to Jack as he speeds out onto the road. "Talk about die-hard fans."

I'm holding a bag of fragrant goodies, gifts from Jack: two candles, a bag of wax cubes for the wax warmers in the cottage, a bag of handmade spiced tea blend, one book about "racialized trauma," and the other book, a modern bestiary.

"I got to see 'Famous Jack' just now," I say. "So different than 'Chill Jack.'"

"I'm one and the same," he says with a small shrug.

"How must that be for those ladies," I say, shaking my head, "to feel safe enough that they can say all that to me? To *you?*"

"Don't know," he says, shaking his head. "My question is: How are you not mad all the time? What's that James Baldwin quote? To be Black in this country—"

"Is to be in a state of rage almost all the time," I finish.

Jack drops his aviators onto his nose. "'No woke stuff,' and 'are you worthy' and 'good ol' fashioned murder mystery'?"

"I was speechless."

"You know, they're the biggest consumers of mystery," he shares.

I shoot him a look. "I guess my writing career will be short-lived."

He laughs. "Don't say that. Yeah, it sucks, but I don't know, build a safe room for yourself, and when they start talking, just go there and wait that shit out."

"In other words: fake it."

"We all do," he says. "If you're a writer—*hell*, if you're an *artist*—there's the genuine-creator you and the 'I give a fuck with every asinine comment you make, dear reader' impostor you."

My stomach churns, but I go for it.

"My writer friend?" I say. "Sam? She told me something similar when she came up here to write. She rented an Airbnb from a woman who said shit like we just heard. I think they were in the same critique group or something. I think that made Sam crack, taking it in and not responding. Not having that safe room you just mentioned."

"What's Sam's last name?" Jack asks.

"Morris."

He narrows his eyes, then shakes his head. "Yeah, I don't know that name. Which house did she rent? If she lived anywhere near me, I'd know the owners."

"I'll ask her," I say. "But there she was, trying to create, and her writing partners are tearing her down, discounting her life experience. She had a nervous breakdown. She didn't know *what* to write because she had to be too many versions of herself."

"The creative mind, especially, is a fascinating place," Jack says, taking each curve in the road slow and steady.

"What do you mean?" I ask.

"For instance: there's something called 'malleable identity,'" he shares. "You pointed out that I'd acted totally different around those women in the bookstore."

"Chill Jack versus Famous Jack and Angry-as-Hell Woke Jack."

He snorts. "That's a new one. Everyone does that, you know. Have versions of themselves. I'm pretty sure you act and talk different around your family, around your friends, around other Black people."

"Code-switching," I say.

"Exactly. Who you are depends on *where* you are and who you're having drinks with—or meeting at a bookstore. One reason I isolated myself from the world was partly because of people like those women. They were telling me what to write, what not to write. Don't write about that, skip writing about that. Not too this, not too that. Your dad's stuff sucks. Your stuff is better. Not that much different from what happened to your friend."

Jack sucks in his cheeks, then scowls. "People feel too . . . *comfortable* saying shit like that to you, like they own pieces of you just because they bought your books. Like you're not even human anymore, and that you're not supposed to snap back anytime they insult you and your family. I mean . . . I know Big Jack was a complete monster, but I don't want to hear strangers telling me just how bad he was."

The cords in his neck stiffen. "So I said, 'Fuck it, fuck this.' Between Finley disappearing and readers telling me what to do, my head just . . ." He makes explosion sounds and squints at the road before us. "I remember waking up one morning and standing before the mirror, and I looked like I'd aged twenty years. No lie. I didn't even *recognize* myself anymore.

"And it wasn't just how I *looked*. My entire creative process was *shit* because I had way too many critics rattling around in here"—he taps his temple—"telling me what to do and what not to do. You can't make meaningful art hearing shit like, 'Only three percent of the population has green eyes, so she can't have green eyes,' and 'It doesn't rain in LA, so why do you have rain in your books?'"

A gurgle springs from my throat. "No way."

"Yes way. As scary and shocking and sad as it is . . ." He tightens his lips and pushes air out of his nose. "I hate to say it, but I'm gonna say it: this pandemic has given me a chance to be alone, a chance to think about my next act, about the types of stories I want to tell, who I'd like to collaborate with. And because of the pandemic, I could do all this in isolation without people thinking I was some weird recluse. I mean . . . we're *all* weird recluses right now. We've *all* aged prematurely."

I nod. "True. All of it."

"But I snapped out of it," Jack says, "and weaned myself from all self-destructive behavior. Binge eating, staying up late, not sleeping, not exercising, stressing out over what others say . . . I worked with a nutritionist on my diet, which meant Luann needed to learn how to cook vegan and vegetarian meals.

"And then, I hired a personal trainer to develop a workout plan. New sleep routine—blackout curtains, temperature-controlled mattress, supplements, lots of supplements. Stress and depression—brought on by my father—only worsened after Fin's disappearance. And so my hair was falling out and turning gray . . . Now, though? I'm at my optimal health, and I'm ready to write again."

"That's . . . *a lot*," I say.

"Sure, but I'm rejuvenated and . . ." He glances over at me. "And now, I don't even look my age."

I smile, and ask, "And how old *are* you?"

"Timeless," he says. "Old enough to know how incredible it will be to see you fully realized." He pauses, then adds, "I'll be hanging out with Famous Bailey at Murder by the Book in Houston in the near future. Can't wait to meet her. Hope she's fun."

I lift my eyebrows and say, "I hear she's a hoot. But sometimes she puts too much woke shit in her stories. Why can't she just write books about talking cats who watch over cupcakeries until one day she finds a dead body in a vat of buttercream frosting? But make it funny. Oh, and make her white. Or Black but, you know, *normal*. Not *Black* Black."

Jack snorts. "We can always kill what's-her-face in the book. If writers are anything, we're petty as fuck."

17.

Who am I when I'm not me?

Like . . . during those times when I've had too much to drink? Or when I'm dunked into twilight sleep to have my wisdom teeth removed?

Am I a mean drunk or a flirty drunk? Do I sink into the quiet and let controlled substances work as balms to soothe my wounds or drown my depression?

Will I ever meet that other me?

And if I do meet the other me—by some weird coincidence or providence from God—would I even recognize her and know that she is me?

Is meeting that other me even possible?

Who does Avery think I am? A brilliant researcher? A promising investigator? Someone thorough and reliable? Does she believe that only because she needs me to be?

She could ask me the same question. *Who do you, Bailey, think I am?* Definitely someone who doesn't share *everything*—she never told me that she knew Jack. That information? That's shit I need to know. And now, I think that I *don't* know her.

Jack is late to yet another meeting in Santa Monica. He parks in the driveway of his estate and races inside the big house. "Reservations for dinner tonight are for seven," he shouts at me.

Heading toward the side gate to reach the cottage, I give him a thumbs-up. "I'll be ready." But I need wine *now*, not at seven o'clock.

Nothing in the guesthouse has changed since my departure this morning. No new platters of food have been placed on the dining table. My wineglass and mug are still sitting in the drying rack. I grab the bottle of Pinot Noir from the fridge and pluck the wineglass from the rack, almost dropping it. The mouth of the bottle *ting-ting-tings* against the rim of the glass, an SOS.

Guess I'm still shaky from fire talk and the lying and the women in the bookstore. I need to capture all of this in my journal, but I need to settle down first.

After missing and sloshing wine onto the countertop a few times, I finally manage to spill wine into the glass. I take one big gulp and slide down to the kitchen floor.

Russell Walker does not work for Privatas. So who *does* he work for? Who *is* he? How long has he been pretending? How can I find out more?

I take another gulp of wine and then another. I fish out my phone from my bag and tap questions that I need to solve into my Notes app.

Does Russell have fingerprints on file? How long has he "worked" here? How did he obtain a Privatas truck? Is that a real Privatas truck?

I drain the wineglass and stare at the oven door. I see me, just a reflection in the glass, not quite there, and past that ghost, there's nothing but darkness.

I need more wine—I'm so tired and scared and frustrated, and I just want to sleep and say, "I tried, six thousand hours is too much . . ."

Bah. I pull myself from the tile floor, then trudge down the hallway to the bedroom. There, in the closet, the three-legged silver pig remains positioned on the "5" between the "7" and "2." The comforter remains hastily made and the pillows stacked and plumped.

I shed my jeans and sweater and change into pink leggings and a long-sleeved T-shirt. I dump the contents from my reusable bookstore bag onto the bed—the wax blocks, books, tea, and brown sugar–scented candles. Then, I unwrap the mystery phone I found beneath Jack's passenger seat from the firehouse T-shirt.

I press the power button.

The screen stays dark.

Dead.

I connect the phone to my charger, then shove the device between the mattress and box spring.

Chirp.

I glare at the smoke detector above the door and snarl, "Don't you start with me."

The last thing I wanna hear right now is a stupid piece of plastic crying out for a new battery.

The stupid piece of plastic heard my threat—no more chirps. Silence hangs over the room.

Chirp.

I grab the chair from the writing desk in the corner of the room and place it in the doorway. Tall enough to reach now, I twist off the cover of the detector, snatch the dying batteries, and toss them into the waste can.

I try the same with the smoke detector in the living room, but the cover won't come off.

Chirp.

I grab a bottled water from the fridge and *Old Topanga Road* from the couch, then head out to the chaise longue beside the swimming pool. I carry my phone, even though there is no service here. I accept that now . . . but not enough to still want to believe.

The sky has turned silver, with fading sunlight behind a smear of flat clouds. A breeze makes ripples across the surface of the pool.

My eyes flick to the empty spaces between the brush, spaces big enough for a man to hide and watch me. There are too many trees here. Neighbors and houses are too far apart. No one can hear you scream.

Also: fire, mud, mountain lions, and criminals.

"Y'all are out of your minds living up here," I mutter.

Gaze still roving the grounds, I settle into a poolside chaise longue and open *Old Topanga Road*.

◆ ◆ ◆

"Why didn't you tell me?" Axel shouted.

Natalie shrank—divorced now for three years, she had forgotten about Axel's outbursts and how she folded in on herself anytime he lost control. "Because I didn't think it was a big deal," she shouted back. "She was texting me and keeping me in the loop and . . . and . . ."

Axel's anger was volcanic because none of this was new. Natalie had always been the permissive parent, the "we're best friends" mother, the Cool Mom. As a result, Kinsey ran all over LA without rules. Sleeping over at friends' houses—male and female—whenever she wanted. Throwing pool parties that sometimes swelled to one hundred people.

Natalie just went along with it.

And now, *this*.

"Two days, Natalie?" Axel shouted. "You haven't looked Kinsey in the eyes for forty-eight hours? Are you kidding me?" He paced the front yard with his eyes squeezed shut.

Yelling at his ex-wife wouldn't bring their daughter back.

A gray Crown Vic turned onto their street.

Axel muttered, "All I need," and watched the unmarked sedan pull behind Axel's Mustang.

Chief Frank Coleman climbed out of the car— he still wore his uniform, pressed and lint-free. Neat salt-and-pepper hair with the perfect part. Clean fingernails. Coleman hadn't been out in the streets for nearly three years now.

"They got a bird in the sky right now," Coleman told Axel. "Search teams are combing the trails at this very minute."

"I'm going out there." Axel started to his car, but Coleman stepped in front of him.

"Let them handle this, Ax," his former partner said. "No one wants a hotheaded detective tromping all over the Santa Monica Mountains. We don't wanna piss off the search teams, okay?"

"Because now we know she was last seen near the trailhead near the Overlook. That's where we found her car—"

Axel points north, to the mountain range now lost in the haze. "Kinsey's out there, Frank—"

"And we're gonna find her. I promise." Chief Coleman touched Axel's shoulder, and that touch burned. "This is your friend talking, not your boss."

Axel wanted to cry.

Because he already knew his future. Prison, maybe a life sentence. Because once he found Kinsey, he'd find the monster who stole her and put a bullet through his head—

Branches crackle over to my left.

I sit up in the chair.

What's that?

Snapping twigs . . .

Every hair on my body stands straight as I wait . . . and wait . . .

Should've brought a knife or a hammer or—

Her! The woman from the woods! She doesn't see me, but I see her, and she's creeping now toward the main house, still wearing that ratty blue T-shirt. This time, she's holding something in her right hand.

I shout, "Hey!"

The woman whirls around, her eyes big with surprise. "Here," she hisses, then throws something at me.

The object sails toward my head. I duck before it hits me, and it smacks against a potted plant beside the cottage's front door.

"What the hell?" Anger sparks through my muscles. I drop my book, knocking over my bottled water, and launch out of my chair, heading straight toward her.

The woman races back into the woods.

I follow her, and it feels so good to move. My blood feels light, and every bit of anxiety is jostled out of me as I chase this bitch into the forest. My cross-trainers work fine on the established trail made by the Beckhams over the last one hundred years, but these sneakers can't keep me from skidding down a thready path that cuts through the brush. My ankles twist as I follow the wiry, gray-haired trespasser—but they don't twist enough to stop. The woman moves like a deer through the forest, her home. I lumber like a woozy bear just awakening from hibernation—but I'm not woozy enough to stop. Branches scrape my cheeks and hands—but I keep going. It feels good to move this fast, to chase someone, action-movie-hero style.

Down there! A small, ratty blue tent with a clothesline strung between a bush and tree.

I skid to a stop.

Does this tent belong to the old woman, or does someone else live here?

The forest floor is home to empty water bottles, candy wrappers, potato chip bags, and paperback novels, including *Old Topanga Road.*

"Anyone here?" I ask, my voice lower, my eyes closed to listen better. I place my hands on my hips and slow my breathing. "I'm not going away."

Just the wind and the rustling leaves.

I peek into the tent.

There's no one hiding inside the filthy sleeping bag. There are pictures scattered around the tent, all shots of a woman with dark hair and dark eyes. That's Kadence Hatfield, the missing hiker. In these pictures, there's Kadence in a floppy hat. Kadence kneeling beneath a waterfall. Kadence making a funny face.

Could this be Russell Walker's tent? His staging area before he pretends to be a Privatas security guard.

Wait.

What if the old woman is the lure? What if she's the bait to get me . . . *here*? Did I just fall for another trick?

Twigs snap behind me.

I duck back out of the tent.

A doe stands nearby in the brush.

Relieved, I exhale and say, "Hi."

The doe flicks her ear, then steps past the tent to head deeper into the forest.

The shakes I'd chased away with red wine have returned, and now my legs and arms vibrate.

Branches crack behind me.

I turn in that direction.

No woman in the woods.

No Russell Walker.

No curious doe.

My mouth tastes like sawdust, and I run my tongue along my dry lips. Thirsty. My bottled water is back at the house, which is right up . . .

Where?

There are no trail markers here. There are no trails at all.

And all the trees look the same. And all the dirt and green things smell the same.

I blink at the tent, at the clothesline, at the vast green canopy of forest, and I feel so . . . *lost.*

Crap.

There is no sound except for thick quiet and buzzing bees and the far-off roar of empty space. The sky beyond the trees is dimming. Darkness will soon come.

I stare at the tent. When I ran down the hill, was I facing the flap or was I facing the rear? I meander toward the woods opposite the tent flap and stare at those trees, waiting for a memory to spring from my mind's ground like a flower or weeds—either will do. No memory comes.

I return to the tent and pop my head in again, and I stare at those pictures of Missing Person Kadence Hatfield, and I wonder . . .

And I wonder . . .

And I . . .

I . . .

. . .

. . .

The world around me . . .

I swipe my face—my skin has lost sensation, and it prickles beneath my touch.

My mind is filled with cobwebs and fog.

How long have I been standing here?

What time is it?

My phone . . . is up at the house with the book and the bottled water.

I take a deep breath to steady a heart that's revving in my chest.

"Gotta move," I say.

What if I waited until the old woman returns?

What if this isn't her tent?

What if it is, but I scared her, and she won't come back?

"Are you out there?" I shout to the woods. "Could you please help me? I'm not here to hurt you. I'm a little lost."

The echoes of men yowling bounce all around me.

One man shouts, "She's lost. She's not here to hurt you." He cackles, and others laugh with him.

And now, the woods smell like weed and burning plastic and chemicals. The woods have come alive.

I don't know this kind of living.

No, I can't stay here and wait for the woman.

"Lost girl, lost girl," another man sings.

"Here, kitty-kitty."

"Lost girl, lost girl."

Trembling, I grab a sharp, thick stick from the forest floor and march in the direction I *think* I came.

But those yellow puffball plants right there don't look familiar. Neither does the rock outcropping over there. All the browns and greens have stumped my recall.

Why did I chase her?

Why didn't I just stay in the *freaking* cottage and burn my sugary-smelling candle and drink some of that special-blend tea and just be basic?

"Why you quiet?"

"Aww, baby! Don't be that way!"

The men sound close. *Too* close.

Go. *Now.*

Up the trail I go, passing trees shaped like vampires, passing rocks covered with green moss, passing gorges hidden by fallen oaks and grass almost as tall as me, and I pass a lot more even though everything has now smeared together.

A fluorescent-green MISSING PERSON flyer—Kadence Hatfield's flyer—has been stapled to the trunk of a tree. Without thinking, I snatch it off the trunk and immediately regret doing that. That bright paper could've served as a landmark, a sign that I'd passed this place before. And now, this oak resembles the thousands of oaks in Topanga State Park.

"Lovely lady," a man calls out somewhere behind me.

I shove the flyer into my pocket and press on.

Tree roots tug at my ankles, demanding that I sit and stay awhile. But this forest is not my home. Topanga Canyon in the domesticated part with a swimming pool and a stackable washer-dryer—that isn't my home, either. I belong in a concrete forest with Astro Burger and pastrami burritos, hair-supply stores, smoke shops, and people selling Kobe Bryant T-shirts from gas station parking lots.

I hurry deeper into the forest, and then I hurry to the edges of the forest. The air feels hot behind me, and I'm being hunted by those ghouls who'd taunted me from their nook in the woods. I go as quickly as I can, escaping the twisted vampire trees, tangled vines, and high grasses trying to close in on me. All the birds are gone. Branches and twigs snap, and the hunters' feet pound the ground as they chase me, and their breath burns the back of my neck. I'm just a reach away. One of them will catch me, I know they will, and—

Fuck this investigation.

This very thing happened to Sam—I know this like I know my name.

I don't like this feeling. I don't want to search for her anymore. I don't want to be a private investigator anymore. This isn't what I imagined. In my version, I'm not scared. In my version, the world is not this dangerous.

The men in this forest aren't *pretending* to be off the grid, *pretending* to cook meth and urinate wherever the hell they want. These smells and these dark woods weren't created by writers and artists. This shit is real life. This shit is *authentic.* This fear powering me all around the

Cars!

I hear cars! That means there are drivers—*people*—nearby!

The men of the forest howl.

"Lovely lady!"

"Where did you go?"

"I got something you should see!"

They sound even closer than before.

Tears burn in my eyes, and I berate myself for being so impulsive. Yeah. I *deserve* to be in this situation. Why would I chase a stranger through the woods? When did I become the star of fucking . . . *Magnum, P.I.?*

As the forest thins, the louder the sound of cars becomes. The dirt beneath my feet turns ordered—others have tromped here. There's a plastic water bottle! There's a protein bar wrapper! Others have escaped the forest using this very path.

Up I go, toward the sound of cars racing up and down a road.

There, right there! *Light!*

Fueled now with adrenaline, my legs push me . . . I keep going, going, going until I burst from the forest and into an empty parking lot. "Thank you," I gasp. "Thank you."

But the light of this world is almost gone.

I press my sweaty cheeks between my sweaty hands to keep from falling apart.

Because I'm still lost. And behind me, someone is breathing hard, their shoes scuffing against dirt.

"Lovely lady," the man calls out. "You can't leave without saying goodbye."

Ohmigod.

A white man with blond dreadlocks steps out of the forest. He isn't wearing a shirt, but all the ink on his chest and arms keeps him warm.

I didn't imagine him.

He leers at me. "You sexy," he says. "I like dark meat."

Is this how I will end?

The world around me brightens, and millions of gnats dance in that light.

Headlights! Moving in my direction! Those headlights—from a car or from a UFO, I don't care—grow brighter and bigger the closer they come.

I step out onto the highway and wave my arms and yell, "Please stop."

The SUV slows. The orange security lights swirl. *Danger.* The Jeep Wagoneer rolls past me. A Privatas Security Patrol decal shines on the door. The driver's-side window rolls down.

Russell Walker–Security Guard smiles at me from the Wagoneer's dark cabin. "Well, if it ain't my damsel in distress."

18.

The Wagoneer's warm cabin smells of cigarette smoke and tuna salad. The passenger seats hold jackets, rope, pliers, an ax . . . A Platters song—"The Great Pretender"—plays on the stereo. The old man's gold badge gleams in the twilight. There is no wedding band on his ring finger, but that doesn't mean that there isn't a Mrs. Russell Walker waiting at home with a new pack of Kools and more tuna salad in a plastic tub.

I've prayed three times now. Did I make the right choice? Please show me a sign.

Both choices sucked—stay in the forest with the white guy or climb into the Wagoneer with the old Black man who doesn't actually work for Privatas and may be a serial killer?

I want to cry, but I can't cry, I can't show weakness. At the right time, once I'm in civilization—hopefully near the bookstore or the fire station—I will hop out of the car. He doesn't even need to stop or slow down—I'm gonna hop the fuck out.

And now that I'm here, sitting this close to the old Black man . . .

His gray hair . . . is not true. A bead of milky sweat is rolling down his right temple. He's not as old as he seems.

The white guy in the forest—his eyes were vacant and yet still . . . desperate, still . . . predatory. What would've happened to me if I'd stayed? What other types of meat does he like, and did those women ever see skyscrapers again? Will I?

"You actin' like you don't know who I am," Russell Walker says now, scrunching his eyebrows. His mouth and nose are hidden by a black face mask.

"You're Mr. Walker, the security guard."

"And?"

"And . . . a very helpful person." My voice wavers.

He blinks at me, then turns his attention back to the road.

Wrong answer.

That milky bead of sweat soaks into his mask.

Who is he?

"Anyway, that's how I came to work in Topanga," he continues. "Sheer stupidity. I've seen more lunatics and dope fiends up in these woods than I've ever seen at that bank down on Crenshaw." He peeks over at me, expecting a response.

That badge isn't real. The old-man affectation . . . not real, either.

I say, "Um-hmm," but I barely hear the great pretender speaking because of my banging pulse. My heart hasn't stopped racing, and I'm clutching the side of the door as though he's driving 100 miles per hour toward hell—and he may be.

Being lost has made me woozy, and my internal compass wobbles in my head like a broken toy. Welts and scratches cover my hands and my neck, and dirt muddies the beds of my fingernails. I'm a mess, inside and out.

The pretender notices my failure to relax. "You okay?" By the way his eyebrows furrow, he wants me to say, *Yes, I'm fine. Thank you for rescuing me.*

So, that's what I say. "Yes, I'm fine. Thank you for rescuing me."

He's creepy as fuck. For two nights now, he's snuck through the nighttime canyon and has watched me sleep.

"My head hurts," I say, pressing the bridge of my nose. This is true.

"Maybe you should see a doctor," he says, tapping the steering wheel. "You look . . . shaky."

"That's because I am."

He waggles a thick finger at me. "Didn't I tell you? You can't be going off in the woods like that. Bad things happen to young ladies going off by themselves in these woods."

"I know," I say, agreeing. "But wandering off wasn't my intention. Someone snuck onto the property, and I just reacted and chased her down."

"Oh, yeah?" he asks, chuckling. "You tryna do my job?"

No, I'm not—cuz this ain't your job.

"The woman I'm talking about"—the bait—"looks like she's been living in a tent down from the house. This was the second time she's come up to the house." I pause, then add, "I've told Jack and the cook. They're probably looking for me right now." In other words: I will be missed.

The pretender clucks his tongue. "She needs to watch her back, too. Them meth-heads and rapists and Charlie Manson hoo-haws like the one that was harassing you, they're always lookin' for trouble, always looking to make a name for themselves."

I say, "Yeah." Yeah, I'm gonna hop out and yeah, I'm gonna survive. Yeah, escaping is possible.

That woman escaped from Ted Bundy . . .

That other woman escaped the Grim Sleeper . . .

"Back in 2018," Russell Walker says, "this couple found the body of a young woman near a hiking trail. They say she died from sunstroke."

"But she didn't."

"Nope. And then, there was the young Black woman who was having a manic spell—remember her? Didn't pay her bill at that fancy restaurant in Malibu and got arrested? Cops let her go in the middle of the night, in the middle of nowhere, and she disappeared. They found her, dead on the other side—" He points west.

"Did they find the murderer for either case?"

He sighs. "No, but he's around. He knows these hills and canyons, too. Ain't scared of them, either."

Leave some DNA. If something happens to me, pieces of me can be found in this Wagoneer. Cops and forensic investigators will know that I was in this car with him.

I turn my head and fake a sneeze. Disgusting, but I spray my spit all over the passenger-side door. Then, I shift in my seat and touch the seat-adjuster switch—my fingerprints. If I could somehow leave blood . . .

Russell Walker is now telling another murder story about the Sunset Strip Killers, and how they murdered eight people and dropped one of their victims down an embankment in Topanga Canyon.

I tear at the dry skin on my lower lip until I taste blood. I tap my pinkie against my lip and then touch the space behind the door handle.

But I'm gonna make it out of here . . . alive.

Just be cool.

Russell Walker nods at my hand. "What's that you holding on to for dear life?"

I say, "Huh?" and then look down to my hand: the crumpled MISS-ING PERSON flyer for Kadence Hatfield. I open the ball and say, "I've seen this flyer all over the trails, stapled to trees and signs. Did they ever find her?"

The pretender's eyes flick down to the fluorescent-green flyer, and then his eyes meet mine. "Nah. She's still missing. Some people believe that she's alive. I don't."

"And how do you know?"

"It's my job to know."

But this ain't your job.

"Lotta caves in these mountains," he says. "Lotta gutted, abandoned houses, just sitting, decaying." He drums the steering wheel. "And then, you got Mrs. Beckham." He squints at the road ahead. "But that didn't happen out in the woods. Nope. That happened at the house."

The house? But Finley Beckham disappeared off Papagayo . . . ?

"Wait," I say. "What happened to Mrs. Beckham at the house? I don't know this story."

He flicks his hand. "Okay, so that don't count. Ignore that example." He pauses, then says, "You seem really curious. If I didn't know better, I'd think you was a reporter."

"I'm not." True.

"People up here get suspicious. They up here cuz they like their privacy. You need to—"

The old man's flip phone rings from the cup holder. "Lemme get this." He plucks the phone from its holder. "Good evenin', Russell Walker speaking . . ."

I need to hop out of this SUV. Or I need to stab him in the neck with . . . with . . . there's nothing sharp or dangerous in the cup holders.

The pretender keeps peeking over at me as he talks on the phone. Is he talking to his partner, the woman in the woods?

Outside the SUV, the hillsides flicker by, one tree, sixty trees, all one big tree in the dark. The Jeep rambles down the road with Russell Walker still talking to someone he calls "sweetie." He's still sweating milky sweat down his temple until it either soaks into the mask or beads at his jawline. His dark face swings from tender amusement to pointed annoyance and finally to wide-eyed exasperation as he turns left into a driveway.

Jack's driveway! There's the house!

As soon as he rolls to a stop, I open the door and whisper, "Thank you," then hop out of the Jeep. With tears in my eyes—I survived!—I take deep gulps of air. I'm shaky, my legs are weak . . . I will never forget this fear.

The pretender waves at me, then slowly rolls back up the driveway. And now, I am alone.

The porch lights of the Beckham house are the only lights shining, and the house waits in the darkness. Cicadas *retch-retch-retch* and the crickets *chirp-chirp-chirp*. Birds—no, those are bats—make no sound as they swoop across the last band of sunlight flickering over the hill.

I totter along the side of the house and to the chaise longue. I grab my phone from the cushion, where I'd left it to chase a woman into the forest.

It's almost six o'clock.

Four bars of reception. Then, three bars.

I hurry back to the driveway, forcing my core to be stronger now before the wireless connection dies with the sun.

Four bars again.

I text Avery.

I may have found the killer/kidnapper!!!

2 possibilities to check out

CALL ME RIGHT NOW!!!

The message goes *schwoop*. DELIVERED.

I tap into the internet. There are eight tabs open. The most recent tab: one of the last articles I'd read.

Wife of Popular Novelist Still Missing in Costa Rica

No, not this one.

And then you got Mrs. Beckham, Russell Walker said.

I'd bookmarked an article about the other Mrs. Beckham days ago and tap on it now.

Mystery Still Surrounds the Disappearance of Bestselling Novelist's Wife

December 15, 2018—On December 12, 2003, Jack "Big Jack" Beckham, Sr., reported his wife, Liliana, missing from their home in Topanga Canyon, California.

Fifteen years later, Liliana still has not come home—or been found. Beckham, the author of bestselling thrillers and domestic suspense, reported his wife missing after she failed to come home after a church meeting with Congregation of Sacred Harmony.

"If I'd written this story," Beckham Senior was reported saying to police, "my editor would've said 'delete that—too unbelievable.'"

Liliana is the mother of the Beckhams' only child, Jack, Junior, also a bestselling novelist. Jack is the husband of Finley Crawford, daughter of the late Esme and Douglas Crawford, who revolutionized vegan food products.

Detectives found a typewritten note written by Liliana Beckham that shared her intentions to join the Congregation of Sacred Harmony. Jewel Genesis, founder of the organization many consider a cult, claims that Liliana left the group's meeting on the night of December 10, 2003, and never—

"Bailey, everything okay?"

I fumble and drop my phone—the woman's voice brings me back to Topanga Canyon.

Luann, wearing blue jeans and an orange UTA sweatshirt, grabs two paper shopping bags from the back seat of her Prius, now parked in the driveway. An electric car—no wonder I didn't hear her coming.

"Everything's good," I say, trying to smile. "Just taking advantage of the strong internet connection—mine is pretty weak back in the cottage." With a shaky hand, I snatch my phone from the gravel. "Need help carrying the groceries?"

"Sure do. Thanks, hon." She fills my arms with two paper bags. "Glad you're out here. I'm exhausted."

"Long day?" I ask.

Luann grabs the last bag from the trunk. "Just too much stuff goin' on." She heads to the porch.

My cell phone rings in my hand, which is also holding a grocery bag. *What if that's Avery calling?*

Luann digs in her purse for her keys.

My phone keeps ringing.

I try to shift the bag to see the caller. Just as I start to put the bag down on the porch, Luann opens the door, not with keys, but by placing her finger on a smart-lock touch pad. The door opens, and cool air rolls over me.

The phone keeps ringing.

On shaky legs, I follow Luann into the house, rushing ahead to the kitchen.

The phone keeps ringing.

I place the bags on the breakfast counter, then tap ANSWER. "Hello?"

"Hey," a woman says, and then . . .

Silence.

My heart stops.

Three beeps. Dropped call.

"So what have you been up to today?" Luann looks over at me as she unloads the bags. "You sound like you've been crying up a storm, and you look like you've walked across the state of California."

True. Dirty T-shirt, grimy pink leggings, pollen dust and burrs and pine needles and tree resin—all of these ingredients working to keep me together.

"I got a little lost for an hour or two," I say. "So you're hearing *that* in my voice."

Luann gasps. "Really?"

"Mr. Walker, the security guard? He found me, thank goodness. That woman from the woods I told you about? She *threw* something at me, and just like that—" I snap my fingers. "I started chasing her through the forest. I know: stupid. I found her tent but then . . . I lost myself. And there was a man in the woods who started chasing me, and ohmigod, I've never been that scared. And it sounds like I'm rambling, sorry about that."

Luann evaluates me with surprised eyes. "That's quite a story, Miss Meadows."

I shake my head. "Those trails get pretty scary—"

The thought slams into my brain like an asteroid. *What if . . . ?* What if Luann and the pretender . . . What if *she's* his partner? She's an ex-con. He's a liar and probably . . . an ex-con. The two of them could be working together to abduct women lost in the woods.

"You tell Russell all of this?" Luann asks. "It's his job to make it safe around here."

"He says that he'll check it out."

She unloads tubs of ice cream, meat wrapped in white butcher paper, a box of steel-cut oats, and a jar of applesauce. "And next time I see him, I'll warn him that *I* will let Jack know if he doesn't do something about this gal. He's used to city folk cuttin' up, but he don't know a bit from a butt sometimes when it comes to Topanga. Good guy, but there are moments I wonder about him."

"Quick question," I say. "I thought Finley went missing in Costa Rica? Russell said Mrs. Beckham died *here*."

Luann pauses in her step, then continues putting away food. "He's talking about Jack's momma, Liliana. And she wasn't missing like kidnapped or nothin'." Her face pales, then flushes. "She willfully disappeared, is how they put it. And no one says that she's *dead*. I don't talk about that stuff with Jack. It's none of my business."

"Yeah, especially with all that happened with his dad . . ." I'm pushing it—I know I am because Luann blinks at me.

One more nudge. "Heartbreaking, really. Both his parents are gone, and then Finley's disappearance."

"Lil could start a fight in an empty house," Luann says, smiling. "Big Jack was so patient with her. Any other man would've slapped her silly—"

Didn't he, though?

"But he knew who he was dealing with," Luann continues. "Once the spell passed, she was sweet as pie."

"Spell?" I say.

"She was . . ." Luann makes a circle at her temple.

I say, "Ah."

And Big Jack was . . . *what?*

Instead, I say, "She and Finley sound like they were nice ladies."

"You ever meet Finley?" Luann asks, spurs in her voice.

My scalp crawls. "No."

Luann angles her head. "Then, how do you know that she's a nice lady?"

"Just . . . just . . . from what . . . from what I read." I clear my throat. "Like all the donations she made to the Boys & Girls Club and the women's shelters and that program that teaches inner-city kids how to surf."

"I'm not sayin' that she wasn't generous," Luann says, a hand on her hip. "I'm just saying . . . that gal could strut sittin' down. Always acting like she's done something important in her life besides spending Jack's money." She chuckles, then shakes her head. "Ain't you a writer?"

I nod.

The cook grabs an apron from a peg behind the pantry door. "Then you of all people should know: don't believe everything you read."

19.

The woman in the woods didn't throw a *rock* at me. No, she threw a note stuffed inside a balled-up sock at me. The tall-lettered words have been written with purple felt-tip marker.

Check the high grass.

She's somewhere in the high grass.

I scope my surroundings—the main house, swimming pool, and cottage. No one's watching as I read the note. My eyes then skip over to all the high grass beyond this property.

Topanga is nothing *but* high grass.

And . . . that's where *who* is? Who is *she*?

Bad things happen to young ladies going off by themselves in these woods.

That's what Russell Walker–Security Guard told me.

A warning. A prophecy.

The wind sweeps over the patio. I shiver from the chill and listen to my stomach growl. I grab my left-behind water bottle and *Old Topanga Road,* and then I trudge into the cottage a changed woman. A sore, sticky, shaky, and famished woman who *may* be out of her league now. I want to take a Perc to sleep and sleep until it's time for me to leave this place. But I can't go. I can't stop caring.

Back in the bedroom, I drop one of the wax blocks into the warmer, then push out a breath. I rest my head against the dresser, stealing all the chill in the wood.

Liliana—I haven't found much on her. She grew up in the canyons, too. Benedict Canyon, which is more curvy roads in the city than trees, boulders, and big sky. According to one newspaper article I found, Liliana's father was a businessman with holdings in Las Vegas and Reno. Land. Hotels. A vibe of organized crime. She met Big Jack in college—they both attended Stanford, fell in love, married. She dabbled in acting, clothes design, rich girl–rich lady jobs, but . . . *not*. But as much as Big Jack was loathed, she was loved. Her and Jack's names were always listed in donor honor rolls for homeless shelters, civil rights organizations, hospitals, and their alma mater. Liliana volunteered, joined boards of directors, smiled . . . she was sunshine. And then, she was gone.

I've read nothing that closes the loop—that she was found, dead or alive.

And then, there's the second Beckham woman, Finley Beckham. Another rich girl raised in the canyon. This time, Daddy created a burger out of vegetables, beans, and seasonings, and this time the meatless patty tasted *good*. After a few years, and after he'd made a fortune, he sold his share and spent his money on a private plane, a yacht, a home in Vail—

What if Finley's *there*, in Colorado? Or what if she's living on that yacht? What if she's flying here, there, and everywhere except Los Angeles on her family's private plane?

According to Luann, no one will miss Finley—she can stay wherever the hell she is, that's what Luann said but didn't say.

Before hopping in the shower, I grab my journal. I close my eyes to recall all that happened since the moment I sat in the patio chair this afternoon—the ratty tent, the photos of Kadence, getting lost, the man with the dreads, Russell Walker, and then my mind spins and spins and spins . . .

Empty.

I try to return the call of the number from just a few minutes ago. No luck. No signal.

I turn back to my journal, searching for anything—a bare mention, one sentence—that says "Russell Walker" or "security guard." Have we overlooked the obvious? The sketchy security guard who *isn't* a security guard?

I pop two ibuprofen tablets, then grab the yellow accordion file from my suitcase. Still searching for Russell Walker, I flip past articles and notes I've already read, stopping once I reach . . .

CHRONOLOGICAL RECORD

1400—Pierson/Kline were contacted by Vacero. Vacero stated that they spoke to the witness who reported the possible sighting of the MP at Red Rock. Was not the MP. The person sighted did not match the MP's physical description (see entry from Vacero).
1500—Pierson/Kline went to the location where MP was last seen and spoke with witness. I/Os showed the recent driver's license photograph of the MP to the witness. This person stated that it could very well be the same person they saw that evening. I/Os surveyed the location.
I/Os drove Topanga Canyon Road looking for signs where the MP could have been with negative results.
1545—I/Os went to an additional location where previously the search-and-rescue dog led sheriff's investigators to and surveyed the location also.
Pierson/Kline showed the driver's license photograph to Margarita Duran and groundskeeper in the area. She had seen a similar person depicted in the photograph 2–3 months ago but not recently.

Red Rock: that's where I'd hoped to visit before Jack decided that we'd go into town.

The statement from Margarita Duran and the groundskeeper—that's what convinced Avery that Sam came here to this estate.

This photocopied chronological record has no date—ironic. "MP" stands for missing person—that's Sam. "I/O" stands for the investigating officers, Kline and Pierson, the gatekeepers, the ones who won't return our calls.

Avery begged her niece, an LAPD detective, to access these records—no luck.

I search the yellow accordion folder for related chronological records, finding only another copy of this same report but with the handwritten note:

The investigator in charge discussed future searches with the sheriff's dept

With no family around to badger the police, there *were* no future searches.

The room fills with the waxy scent of lavender. The smell makes me nauseated, and I click off the wax warmer.

Disgustingly sticky and clammy, I peel out of my stained, sweaty clothes, then wrap my torso again with Saran Wrap. Luann was right—I *do* look like I've walked through all of California. With my stitches protected, I pad to the bathroom and turn the shower knobs.

The hot water is such a relief that I start trembling again.

What led the gray-haired woman to live in a tent—the blue one I found or some other one—on the edges of a state park? Did she have a mental break because of drugs or genetics? How has she survived with all those predators everywhere? Does she suffer from dementia? Schizophrenia? Does she have a home, which would mean that she isn't homeless, but because of her brain chemistry, she no longer functions properly in that space?

Sam's mental state came from a mix of both—her mother's side had people in mental health facilities, jailed people diagnosed with depression, ADHD, or obsessive-compulsive disorder. Sam boxed with depression. Saw a therapist for it. Took meds, too. Did she skip both of these interventions? Is she in a random forest near Boise, Idaho? Is someone interacting with her, wondering about her origins just like I'm wondering about the woman I chased today, a woman who may have wandered long enough to somehow land . . . *here*?

I close my eyes again and let the dirty soap and water rinse off my body. Grateful that I have a shower and soap, sad that the woman in the woods does not.

What is in the high grass?
Who is "she"?

◆ ◆ ◆

I'd like to ask Jack these questions as we drive to dinner. But Jack wants to rail against the article he read today. Some white-guy action-thriller bestseller was interviewed to promote his new book. "And he had the *nerve*," Jack says, "to utter bullshit. He claimed that white authors were having a hard time landing publishing deals. That authors of color were taking these opportunities from him."

I say "wow" and "ridiculous" in the right places—I'm not interested in what white men say. No—I'm interested in what some man in the woods may have done.

We reach the restaurant, with Jack promising, "I'm gonna say this and shut up. Equality for some of us is the same thing as oppression. He's fucking complaining about not being seen . . . while being interviewed in the fucking *New York Times*."

Me? I'm not surprised.

We climb out of the Porsche and step into the fantastical beauty of Inn at the Seventh Ray. Located next to the Spiral Staircase bookstore, the restaurant is wrapped in thousands of fairy lights and clouds of incense. A way station in the darkness.

Jack's mood improves—he's wearing his jacket-sweater-T-shirt combo, and tonight he smells of citrus and sweet tobacco and not vitamins. "You look great," he says as we wait to be led to our table.

I pluck at the strap of my soft pink dress. "This old thing? Me. Not the dress. The dress is new. Ha."

We're seated at a table for two beside a dry creek bed. Those speckles of fairy lights and the glowing cherub fountain and the trees are all so beautiful.

"Before I forget," I say, holding up a finger, "I need your number or Margo's. I realized today that I can't reach either of you in an emergency."

"Ah. True. Sorry about that." He rattles off his number.

I tap it into the phone, then save that number as "Jack."

"Now, put that thing away," he instructs.

I slip my phone into my purse, making sure the spy pen is recording before I close my bag. Blue light on. Cool. I pick up the menu. "This is the most enchanting restaurant I've ever visited. We are *literally* eating in the middle of the forest."

"And seated more than six feet away from the next table," Jack adds. "Little did the owners know back in '75 when the restaurant opened that we'd be in a pandemic."

"What's the seventh ray referencing?" I ask.

Jack spreads his arms. "Some metaphysical thing that came out of the Foursquare Church combined with other stuff about light spectrums and healing and *whatever*. What I do know? The truffle risotto here is one of the best truffle risottos I've ever eaten—that's what I know, and I miss it terribly."

"Not in the diet plan?"

"All those carbs? All that cream?" He snickers. "Absolutely not."

"This spot *must* go into the new story," I say, browsing the menu.

"Definitely. No question. I mention it in every novel, and I write about the risotto, too." He sighs, looks around. "I pray that a wildfire never burns this place down."

"Maybe that seventh ray is protecting it," I suggest.

And maybe God is looking after me, too. I could've died six times today. And because I didn't, I close my eyes and whisper, "Thank you."

Time to eat.

Risotto and potato-leek soup. Striped bass, scallops, and short ribs. Mixed berry galette and triple-chocolate cake. Over shrimp cakes and truffle risotto for me and crispy half cauliflower for him, and glasses filled with an organic Bordeaux ("My one little cheat," he confesses), Jack catches me up on his day after our trip to the fire station and after he dropped me back home. He signed stock at a bookstore in Silver Lake. Took a meeting over in Santa Monica. Picked up prescriptions from the drugstore. "I've been in my car a *lot* today," he says. "Which explains . . ." He lifts the glass of wine.

My meal was made by angels. With this setting, and this food, I'm in heaven, and I don't ever want to eat another Big Mac in the car again. The energy here . . . the Foursquare-Church-metaphysical-healing genetics . . . it feels like cool silk and fresh oxygen.

I dab my lips with a napkin. "Obviously, your father's not one of your favorite people. But putting all that aside . . . Is he your favorite *writer?*"

Jack furrows his eyebrows. "He's *a* favorite. *The* favorite: Hunter S. Thompson. I've read *Fear and Loathing in Las Vegas* at least ten times. I own a signed first edition in my library. What I love about him, though . . ." He places his fork down and leans forward. "Gonzo journalism."

That's when the reporter is personally involved in the story. The reader tags along with the writer, is privy to how they feel and what they think as the reporter tells that story. Totally subjective writing—personal opinions and experiences instead of the detached objectivity of traditional journalism.

"Not necessarily the drugs and alcohol and bad behavior," Jack says, flicking his hand, "but the 'doing it' while 'writing it.' It's different for fiction, of course, but I see it in the same way. Submerging yourself in whatever you're writing—"

"Write what you know because you've either done it or you're learning it and experiencing it?"

"Exactly." He sits back in his chair and cocks his head.

"Truthfulness. Accuracy. It's possible to do that in fiction," he says. "I'm gonna do it. Maybe drop acid and drink up all the whiskey in the house and buy a gun and find some Hells Angels and hang out."

I lift my wineglass. "I'll pass but thank you anyway."

Jack laughs, folds his arms, and watches me eat whipped potatoes from a cast-iron bowl.

"Luann tells me that you asked about my mother."

Just like that, those whipped potatoes cement my tongue. I swallow the paste, then choke out, "I didn't mean to pry . . ."

Jack holds up a hand. "It's okay—really. It's not like she's some kind of big secret. A lot of people who live up here were around when all of that went on." He lifts his wineglass but doesn't drink. "I told you that my parents were young when they got married, nineteen years old. Didn't know who the hell they were as *people* before they became parents. They couldn't relate to each other, and so they fought *a lot*. My father . . . sometimes with his hands.

"He was still this little kid but with an uncontrollable imagination," Jack continues. "He was a bully, not because he was tall or big, but because he wanted to see the person's reaction. People who didn't know us always thought that we were brothers—he competed against me like he was."

He swirls the wine in his glass. "This is a guy who loved going to Central America for a nip there, a tuck here. Recovering peacefully while writing books about men who were gruff and grizzled. Detectives, mercenaries, guns, booze, women, while being incredibly vain and self-conscious.

"He didn't drink, but he smoked one cigar a month and hiked nearly every day. I didn't understand that weird Puritan thing—it wasn't like any of that made him happier. Yeah, here I am with my crazy eating, fitness-nut, and diet shit. The difference between him and me, though? I'm happier than I've ever been."

Jack shakes his head as he remembers his father. "He and Mom had been arguing one night—they'd gone to see a show at the Pantages. They got home. He said something—I still don't know what it was, but she slapped him, and he slapped her back. She ran to the bedroom. He retreated to the cottage."

He watches the flickering candle in the middle of the table. "Next morning, he comes back to the house to apologize, but she's gone. She left a note saying that she went to go find herself with this cult . . . and I never saw her again."

According to the news story I'd read, Liliana Beckham disappeared on December 10. Big Jack reported her missing on December 12. Why the two-day wait?

"He looked for her until he . . ." Jack takes a breath. "He came with me to Belize one summer after she'd left. Said he wanted to do some weird chemical peel that he'd read about, that some doctor in Belize did it or whatever, and that he'd start his next book while recovering. But the procedure didn't go right, fucked up his face, and he just . . ."

Jack takes a deeper breath this time and slowly releases it. "Next thing I know . . . the sun is just rising over the horizon when, *bam!* A .45 goes off outside my bedroom window. That morning, I started my day an orphan."

I shiver from the cold nip of the forest. From the story of a famous writer's ending.

Oh. *Wait.* That ending wasn't done with a shotgun? I thought . . .

Jack runs his hands over his hair. "My mother was always searching for *more.* My father was, too, in his own way. My parents . . . I don't know why they got married. She was pregnant, but so what? Two totally different personalities—and his personality demanded more space. And it *kept* demanding more space until Mom wasn't even a consideration for him."

He frowns, then chuckles. "She ate at this restaurant all the time. I come here to feel . . . *closer* to her. I thought of going to Montana— that's where the cult relocated, but . . ."

Montana! I'd been looking at flights from LAX to Montana—and a theory had formed. *What if Sam joined a cult?* If I survive my time here in Topanga Canyon, I'm flying to Montana next.

He drums his fingers against the table. "My mother chose them, and not me, and my father chose death over me. Finley's gone. I should hide out in that stupid bunker and let whatever happens happen. Survive on nothing but Top Ramen, smoked herring, and Tang."

I frown, disgusted. "Do better than *that*."

He laughs.

"I'm sorry," I say. "I didn't mean for my question to make you sad."

"Hey, Bailey? Guess what? I'm always sad." He rubs his temples. "I just hide it behind dazzling hair and straight teeth, but I carry it here—" He knocks at the space over his heart. "Writing helps."

"Wait a minute." I gasp and my eyes bug. "Your mother . . . she's *Natalie*! Axel Fletcher's ex-wife in *Old Topanga Road*."

He nods. Rubs the rim of the glass against his lip.

"When was the last time you went into your family's bunker?" I ask.

He snorts. "*Family's* bunker? That's *his* bunker. And I've *never* gone into that bunker. Luann goes in every year to check expiration dates on the food and medication . . . no, that thing creeps me out. If and when a fire gets that close, I'm *evacuating*, not hiding in some concrete bullshit built by my crazy-ass father that may or may not still work in real-life scenarios. My mother agreed." He pokes his tongue against his cheek. "I miss her."

"Well . . ." I hold up my wineglass. "Gone from our sight, but never from our hearts."

"That's lovely," he says, tapping his glass to mine. "Still loved, still missed."

We finish our dinner with butterscotch bread pudding—well, *I* finish. Jack sips a cup of decaf, black, no sugar.

"Can anyone access that bunker?" I ask. "Since you haven't been down there, what if someone's living in that space?"

Like Sam or Kadence?

"Nah." Jack sips his coffee, then says, "It's locked. I'm the only one with the key."

Back in the car, Jack taps on the radio. The satellite station plays soft Brazilian jazz. The chanteuse whisper-sings over a sexy syncopation of guitars, snare drums, and piano. The Porsche's headlamps illuminate the curves, and falcon-size moths flutter ahead of us. The glasses of organic Bordeaux have washed away any apprehension I've had about traveling this twisty canyon road.

Back at the estate, Jack parks in the driveway. "You good?"

I nod, my head sloshing with wine. "I'm *great*." After having such a crappy afternoon, yeah, I'm *fabulous*.

Jack parks, and we walk into the house.

The only light in the foyer is the moon's glow streaming through the windows. The walls feel close.

I make my way toward the patio door. "Thank you so much for dinner. I can see why you love—"

His phone rings from his jacket pocket. He plucks it out, frowns some. "Hold that thought, Bailey."

Shit. I just wanna go to bed. It's been the longest day in the history of days.

He answers. "Hey, Luann. What's up?"

I wander over to the windows looking out to the backyard—I can see the cottage from here. Where is the bunker? If I asked, would Jack give me a tour?

"Shit," Jack says. "What else did they say?"

The worry in his voice makes me wander back over to the foyer.

He stays on the phone as he marches up the stairs—with me following him—and rushes to the window at the end of the hallway.

"Okay, good," he says to Luann. "No . . . well, if Walsh doesn't think we should worry, then . . . okay . . . okay. Keep in touch." He ends the call, then runs his hand through his hair as he stares out that window.

My heart pounds in my throat. "What's wrong?"

He takes a deep breath, then says, "Someone set a fire over in Palisades."

I cover my mouth with my hands. "That's just west of here."

He waves away my concern and tries to smile. "Yeah. It's way on the edge of the park, seven miles away. But it's small. Nothing to worry about."

I exhale, then glance out the window to the dark forest surrounding the estate. "If you say so."

"I say so." He waits a beat, then says, "Wanna see it?"

Item Number: 150743L
Item Description: gray backpack (1)
Victim: Doe, Jane
Offenses: Death Investigation
County of Offense: Los Angeles
Offense Date: November 2, 1993

Comments:

One (1) gray backpack collected from Santa Ynez Falls—Topanga State Park, 20828 Entrada Road, Topanga, CA 90290 in fireplace of the cabin ruins.

various alcohol bottles
loose change
plastic zip ties
Polaroid instant camera
various loose pills
pair of latex gloves (4)
hammer with black/red handle

Other Information or Requests:

The chimney may have protected the backpack from the intensity of the fire. This would explain its near-pristine condition. Dried brown substance covers the hammerhead. Holds dark-colored strands of hair. Will send it out for DNA testing. Not sure the pills ID. Will also send for testing. See attached photos.

If you have any questions, please contact Detective Kimball. Thank you!

20.

Jack runs back down the hallway, with me still trailing behind him. He jams down the stairs, to the kitchen, out that door, shooting down the flagstones that lead to the now-dark cottage. "C'mon!" he shouts back to me.

Wearing princess flats and a wispy cocktail dress, I'm having a hard time keeping up.

At the cottage's front door, he taps a smart-lock touch pad.

There's touch recognition on this lock, too? I didn't notice that until now . . .

Why didn't I know that? Before I can ask that question or *Where are we going? Is it safe there? Will we be trapped here?* he's switched on all the lights and is sprinting to the bedroom.

I pace and wait for Jack's return, then pray and try to remember whether I left any files on the bed or any bloody bandages or Saran Wrap on the bathroom counter. The living room is frigid and cold as though I'd opened every window and door before leaving for dinner. The air still smells like my powdery vanilla body lotion—better than smelling like dirt, sweat, and pine trees.

Jack dashes back to the living room, holding the binoculars that live on the shelf above my bed.

Why does he have—

He runs past me and out the door. "We gotta hurry."

"Where are we going?"

"To see the fire."

"Let's not and say we did."

We're outside again and racing back up those flagstones.

"I thought you wanted to know all the things?" he asks, looking back at me.

"In principle," I say, breathless.

In the nighttime, the estate resembles a small town with its cupolas and red-clay tile roof, and bursts of lights to guide weary travelers to safety.

We charge inside and back to the living room. He opens another door off the foyer—a three-car garage.

There's my Volvo!

Jack hits a button, and the garage door rolls up, up, up.

Dinner rumbles in my belly. "Jeez, Jack. Just . . . Can we . . . ?"

"There's nothing to worry about," he says. "Remember: the canyons are my backyard. Every kid knows their backyard."

He dashes over to the maroon Honda and beckons me to the passenger side. Once I'm seated, he hands me the binoculars. He slips behind the steering wheel and backs out of the garage. And we're off! "This is so fucking cool," he says, speeding up the driveway. "This is gonna help your writing. All the visceral and descriptive shit you'll need to pull from . . . there's nothing like seeing a fire in real life. And if you're gonna write about it, you should see it, smell it, hear it."

I shake my head. "But I'm *not* writing about fire."

He glances over at me, his eyes shimmering with excitement. "If you're cowriting with me, you are. And so, you must. Because Topanga *is* fire." He pauses, then adds, "You gotta push beyond your fears, Bailey. You gotta just . . . *go for it.*"

Jack pulls back onto slithery Topanga Canyon Road, now dark as the darkest night. The Honda's cabin blooms with white light from the dashboard and white and blue light from the radio. A shiny and speckled cowrie shell on a string hangs from the car's rearview mirror.

I tap the shell and watch it sway back and forth.

Jack smiles, then stops its motion. "I found that on the beach during vacation in the Seychelles. It was the last trip we took as a family. Did you know? In African culture, people consider these shells to be symbols of fertility and wealth."

And now, he taps the shell, pushing it back into motion. "I think of this shell as proof that we used to be a family. That I used to belong to two people who loved me in their own damaged ways."

I notice a black stain on the tan leather seat between my knees. "Uh-oh. What happened here?"

He rolls his eyes. "I drove a girl home this one time, and her pen burst and . . . she was so apologetic. I stayed pissed for a while . . . made her feel totally guilty." He laughs, then says, "We dated for a year after that."

That's kinda jacked up. But I fake a chuckle for my host's sake.

"When I was a kid," he continues, "I would hike up to the Overlook with those binoculars in your lap, and I'd watch the beginning of fires. Then, afterward, I'd write awkward and angsty poems and prose, usually about a girl or about my father. One time I described fire as . . ." He clears his throat, then says, "Famished fiends as bright as galaxies ripping apart, a crackling symphony of sound."

I wince. "Behold young Jack using metaphors heavier than a thousand tons of granite."

"Call me Updike." He focuses on the road for a moment, then says, "We'll be fine, Bailey."

"This *is* your backyard," I say. "Oh, the door to the cottage. I just noticed it has touch recognition. Margo only gave me a key fob."

"Yep," Jack says. "Every entry door on the estate has both technologies—a regular remote kind of key and a touch pad."

"Should you have my prints? So that I can enter via touch? Not have to carry around—and probably lose—that remote fob?"

He throws me a quick look. "I didn't want you to be creeped out with the tech."

"It's kinda weird, but . . ." I shrug. "Better safe than sorry, right?"

He swipes to the app in his phone. "Add new user and follow the instructions."

I do as Jack instructs, and then the app takes over.

I tap BAILEY MEADOWS into a box and lay my index finger on the screen.

The app scans my print and saves it.

"Done," I say.

A thought flares in my mind. *Did I just fuck myself? He can now find out who I really am.*

Relax. Because who am I? My socials are curated, and my fingerprint isn't connected anywhere else that's tech related—not a PI yet. I have no police record or judgments against me. Crime-wise, I'm clean.

Jack makes a left onto a road only residents would know exists. The forest now shines white from the Honda's headlamps, the ancient trees absorbing this new light in their thick trunks.

I roll down the window. I can't *see* anything, but I can smell the sharp tangs of chaparral and oak, new dirt, and dying sage. This thin road is rutted, and the Honda sways and buckles, not wanting to be here.

Neither do I, Honda, neither do I.

I hold on to the handle above the window. Dinner's whipped potatoes are now petrifying in my gut. "You're not gonna break an axle, right?"

"Nope," Jack says, patting the dashboard. "She's come up this road before—she's used to violence."

I roll the window back up. "How does a rich and famous bestselling author and philanthropist come to drive a Honda?"

"I bought her with my own money. I was a junior lifeguard every summer and winter break, and I'd save my checks until I finally had enough to buy a used car. By then, I was a senior in high school. I went away to college, and so Josie just sat."

"Josie. As in—"

"The Pussycats. It felt good to own something that Big Jack didn't buy."

The road continues to buck and sway beneath the car.

Jack pulls to a line of trees, then comes to a stop. He plucks the binoculars from my lap. "Let's go!"

A Toyota Corolla and a Range Rover are also parked in the middle of Any Forest, USA. My skin goose bumps from the cold, dry air. Gusts of wind blow at my dress but aren't strong enough to do more than flirt with the hem. Above us hangs an immense sky of clouds—made from water vapor or from volatile gases, I can't tell which.

Jack and I walk and walk, going up and up some more. My leg muscles cramp—these flats already aren't the best shoes for walking. For hiking? Hell no.

"Are we there yet?" I ask, half kidding, just a sweaty city chick struggle-hiking in ballet flats.

"Almost," Jack says, eyes ahead.

What if we get jumped or robbed? Sure, I'm with him now and not alone, but one desperate person can have the strength of twenty.

Jack and I aren't the only fire viewers tonight—and that comforts me some. The others stand on a massive concrete slab covered in colorful graffiti, motionless, like meerkats on a savanna. As they stare out to the canyons, some spectators point in amazement while others hug themselves and shake their heads. Both worriers and wow-ers in this collection of seven.

"Welcome to the Overlook," Jack says to me.

"And what am I overlooking right now?" I ask, trying to catch my breath.

"Down below is Red Rock Canyon Park," Jack says. "Where we're standing? Used to be a fire observation tower. On a clear day, you can see the valley, Malibu, Calabasas . . . even Catalina Island."

And now, I perk up a bit. The Overlook was also on my list of sites to visit. And Red Rock, too. I'll still need to come back because right now I can't see anything. I'm trying to take all of this in, but there's darkness everywhere. Stinks of weed and body odor.

Jack uses the binoculars to scan the black sea before us. "There it is." He looks a moment more, then hands me the glasses, pointing southwest toward blackness and blacker blackness.

With knots in my throat, I peep through the goggles. Yes! There it is, way on the other side of the canyon, an orange-rose glow suspended in the darkness, except that darkness is forest. The fire looks so small it can fit in my hand—that's how far away we are.

"That's incredible." I hand Jack the glasses. "But it doesn't look . . ."

"Doesn't look . . . *what*?" Jack lifts the glasses to his face again, twisting the focus knob and a smaller knob, studying, watching, breathless.

The fire sounds like a coming storm, echoes of cracks and claps rolling across a sky that isn't glowing with danger, not yet. Just clouds, moon, stars . . .

My muted fear tumbles in my heart, and I wrap my hands around my elbows like the other worriers on the slab. This is one of the spots Sam was last seen, according to witnesses. I don't want to right now, but I lift my phone to take pictures. These shots will probably be nothing but dark blurs because it's that dim and I'm *that* nervous. Because the gusts of wind, those smoky clouds, the weird cold . . . something awesome and terrible is headed in our direction, and there's nothing to do except wait.

"It doesn't look *containable*," I say. "I mean . . . How will the firefighters . . . *get* there, in the middle of nowhere?"

"Fire roads have been cut all throughout the forest," Jack says, watching that distant glow. "That female-inmate fire crew I told you about yesterday? They helped make those breaks. Anyway, it's not hot or windy enough for it to get totally bonkers—it's not really fire weather right now."

"Dude . . . ," one of the other fire watchers says. He pulls his long hair into a man bun, then grins at us. "Every day is fire weather in the canyon."

Jack squeezes my shoulder. "Which *means* you shouldn't worry, because it's everyday and commonplace and the budget is plump enough to buy equipment and . . ." He peers down at me, his eyes tender. "You okay?" He sees that I'm shaking, that I'm nervous.

Tears burn in my throat and the rims of my eyes. "I want to go," I whisper. "I want to go *now. Please.*"

"Bailey." Jack takes both of my hands. "Calm down. I'd never put you in danger. The fire seems close, but it's way over there." He cocks his head and squints at me and sees that I'm not buying what he's selling. "Okay. We'll go."

I whisper, "Thank you."

He squeezes my hands, then turns back one last time to the fire, a dry-land siren not wanting to release him.

My throat stays tight, and a teardrop spills down my cheek. I'm not willing to burn to death for this investigation—that's affirmed by the gongs banging in my gut. Maybe I'll work in a pet store or . . .

Jack and I hike the mile back down the hill to the Honda.

Soon I only hear our feet tapping against the stony, dirt-packed trail. And now, the cord around my neck loosens. My head stops banging and throbbing. My thoughts make sense, and a feeling of calm finds me the farther we move away from that concrete slab.

I settle again in the passenger seat, taking the binoculars once more from Jack. As he rounds the car, my phone vibrates in my hand.

A text message.

From UNKNOWN.

It's Zeus. Are you in Hades now?

21.

I'm racing through an overgrown forest choked by countless ancient oak trees with countless tangled branches, with ferns that snare and curl, and dirt that cries out with every step I take. Every beat of my heart knocks louder than the last and hits sharper . . . sharper still against my chest. Chasing me: a wolf taller than a mastodon with gleaming red eyes and sharp teeth that drip with flames. I'm screaming as I run, but the trees and the ferns muffle my cries. I see a clearing up ahead and I run . . . faster . . .

To a long carpet that glows white-hot, radioactive, and stretches into forever.

I have two choices: remain in the forest—the place I know—or take that carpet with the nuclear glow and mysterious end.

Behind me, the wolf stops sprinting and starts to lope, smiling like he knows something I don't.

I keep running—and choose that carpet. As I run, my feet swell, and the skin on my arms peels away.

The wolf throws his head back and laughs, turning back to the forest—

◆ ◆ ◆

My eyes snap open to a ceiling that blooms with apricot light. My chest constricts like a mastodon-size wolf—*the laughing wolf in the forest*—is now resting on my neck. I force myself to breathe and force myself to push the wolf off me, imaginary or not.

Yes, a dream.

That carpet . . . Where did it end?

Tat-tat-tat.

What's . . . ?

I sit up in bed, knocking my journal to the carpet. Guess I fell asleep writing about all that happened—

Tat-tat-tat.

That tapping . . . sounds like a bird's beak hitting the window.

Did *that* sound pull me out of my dream, or . . .

Chirp.

That sound?

The batteries of every smoke detector in this cottage are now in the trash. What the hell is still—

Tat-tat-tat.

The air in the bedroom smells smoky, and the color of the sunlight shining in . . . a weird orange . . . like there's a campfire on the other side of the sky.

I slip over to the canyon-facing window.

Tat-tat . . . tat . . . tattattat . . .

Grit—that's what's hitting the windows.

Tat-tat . . . tat . . . tat tattattattattat . . .

The sun is caramel-colored, and the sky crème brûlée—and neither of those colors is correct. I've lived here in the canyon for three days, and since then the morning sky has never—

Shit.

The fire.

Jack assured me, though, that all would be fine—Captain Walsh and his crew and those fire breaks and the Smokey Bear sign only indicating that the fire danger was "high," which is less than "extreme" . . . and . . .

What's that noise?

Not tats—nothing light like that but deeper . . . like . . .

I close my eyes to hear better.

Thunder, but not . . . cannon fire, but not . . .

As the sound rumbles louder, I open my eyes in time to see . . .

Large helicopters—not traffic or police copters—but big-ass birds that carry thousands of people or millions of gallons of water from one safe place to a less dangerous and burning place. I grab my phone from the twisted comforter. The last text that I sent to Avery before falling asleep—I think I should leave—has been tagged with a red exclamation point. The message didn't go through. Neither did WRONG NUMBER— my response to "Zeus."

Tat-tat . . . tat-tat-tat . . .

Just grit, that's all it is. From the wind, nothing more.

My finger swipes over to email—I'd also reached out to that *Vanity Fair* reporter who wrote the piece on Jack. No response from her yet. That's probably because "Bailey Meadows" is a no one. Maybe LinkedIn can help. Maybe a friend of a friend . . .

That raggedy blue tent in the forest—it's related to Sam somehow. Those pictures of Kadence Hatfield on the tent's floor tell me so. I wish that I had taken my phone—I would've had pictures of that to include in the files. Maybe I can take Avery with me next time. Make her bring along her niece, the LAPD detective. Or maybe I'll go again, taking my gun and water with me this time.

Who *is* that woman in the woods?

I need her to return, and this time communicate like a regular person instead of a prowler throwing a balled-up sock—

That sock.

I scramble over to the closet and find the sock behind my suitcase. I read that note again.

Check the high grass.

She's somewhere in the high grass.

But *all* of Topanga is covered in high grass.

I grab the thickest accordion file from my suitcase to search for anything I've pulled that may be related to Kadence. Starting at the beginning of the file, I ignore documents I've touched so many times, the paper is now limp and stained. I find one half sheet of yellow notebook paper speckled with my handwriting.

Leesa Hatfield—mother, single woman, six kids, mostly drugs, RV life. Former drug user

Kadence—youngest, Laughlin, NV worked as dancer no boyfriend/pimp no police record clean? No contact AT ALL

Undated.

I need to be better about that.

How did Kadence move from Laughlin to Topanga? That Royal Hawaiian Hotel—someone out there reported seeing her. And so I traveled to Baker and checked it out. Where are *those* notes? Where's the sheet with letters and arrows and bubbles that make connections between the letters and arrows, between Sam and Kadence? I may suck at dating documents, but I *do* write everything down.

And so I keep searching—all that I need has to be in these . . . my fingers slow—not true. I left documents at home that I didn't consider necessary for this specific assignment. Which would include anything I'd found on Kadence Hatfield.

Great.

I grab the yellow accordion file.

Here's another brochure about The Way Home, and this one is clipped to a photocopied article from the *Los Angeles Times*. The picture with the article is that of a young Black woman, Shynisha Alexander, who (according to the caption) had been missing for nearly ten years. Missing since 2011, Shynisha Alexander was found alive with the help of TWH.

A callout box shares Shynisha's story. The twelve-year-old had been last seen on the night of August 22, 2011, at her home in Compton. She'd written a message to her mother on the back of a church bulletin.

You dont love me no more and I hat u.

Angela St. Clair, Shynisha's mother, found the note on the refrigerator and saw that the kitchen door was unlocked. St. Clair raced through the house, hoping that Shynisha was playing a practical joke.

Five years passed with no sign of the girl. There would be no movement—authorities had hit a wall and the case went cold. The article:

> Sam Morris isn't afraid to go into places other young women dare not tread. Morris, 35, has been chased by gang members and threatened by angry husbands and boyfriends, and has traipsed dark alleys in search of those who have disappeared. She doesn't like to share her origin story and what drove her to partner with Cheyanne Carroll to establish The Way Home.
>
> "It's not about me," Morris says. "It's about the missing person and my job to find them."

I've read this article several times, and I always return to that one sentence:

Sam Morris isn't afraid to go into places other young women dare not tread.

Including Topanga Canyon.

And that's why I'm here, still.

Because she came to Topanga, probably searching for her mother *and* Kadence Hatfield, and a bad guy found out and he . . . and he . . .

I rub my face, frustrated, tired, and alone.

What do I do now? Where do I go? Home? If I leave, I can never return. Should I try to do one more thing like . . . search Jack's office? And look for . . . *what? Anything.* Maybe he exchanged postcards or wrote a check to The Way Home or . . .

How do I stay in his office long enough to search it?

Maybe I can lie to him (some more) and say that I'd like to take pictures of his office as reference for my book. I've never been in the workspace of a rich person. A bestselling writer? Give me a break. (All of this is true.) Maybe he'll leave me alone for a moment as I take pictures. Maybe he'll go take a call. Use the restroom. Fetch us glasses of wine.

Yeah, I'll suggest a cocktail, and once he leaves, I'll poke around.

Will that be enough time?

It'll have to be.

Now that I have a plan, my stomach settles some, and I finally let myself look up.

That weird, caramel-colored light is spreading across the walls of the bedroom.

The *tat-tat-tat* of grit hitting the windows sounds heavier, insistent.

I grab my phone and stand at the canyon-facing window. I tap RECORD to capture the sounds of the helicopters, the delicate sounds of that tapping grit, the color of that sky. "This is kinda scary," I say, adding an editorial comment to the recording. "This feels like the beginning of a disaster movie."

One day I'll look back on this, and I'll be glad that I'd experienced fire in the canyon. Gonzo, but fiction, as Jack said. I retreat to the bathroom and stand before the mirror as I take off my tank top. My slender, knobby shoulders as brown as tree bark. My breasts the size of small, softened melons. A bandage stained with dried blood . . .

I pull away the first layer of gauze, exhaling through pursed lips like I'm blowing smoke from a cigarette. Nothing's hurting, not yet, but for how long? My brain is crunching, and my hands are trembling as I peel away another layer of gauze, this one more stubborn and stained than the last . . . one more layer . . . right above my right hip bone, there's a row of black stitches holding me together.

The man had come out of the shadows, and he'd held out his hand, asking for money, except that it wasn't an ask. He was holding a knife, and I didn't realize that until it was too late, and I tried to twist away . . . and the space above my hip bone started to burn . . . my hands were wet with thick blood . . . I watched his gauzy shadow hang above me, and felt him rifling through my pockets and . . . and . . . there'd been a white sign with red letters—CAFÉ ERITREA D'AFRIQUE . . . and then . . . people in scrubs were asking my name, asking for the man's description, asking if I had loved ones to call . . . I'd stared at a man's shirt and the patch on his shoulder—Oakland Police in yellow thread against blue and . . . and . . .

And now, here in Topanga Canyon, the world tilts and sways, and I'm dizzy and breathless again, just like I was in Oakland. I grasp the bathroom counter and wait for the spell to pass. I wait . . . and I wait . . . keeping my forehead pressed against the cold porcelain, waiting . . . waiting . . . until my legs regain their strength.

Steady again, I stand up straight. Alive. *Here.* I step into the shower, and a tapioca-colored glow spreads across the shower tile. That color reflecting in the bottle of shower gel worries me more than these seven stitches above my hip bone. Because I know what *these* are—thick thread sewn through my skin to close a wound. Beyond these windows? I have no clue.

After showering, I pull on cargo pants with many pockets and a hoodie that has a front pocket. I detach my spy pen from its charger, unsure of what this new day will deliver. I reach into my tote and dig around until I feel the soft, cold polymer of the Glock 9. The gun slips into my hoodie pocket.

Because something's wrong, something more than just the growing fire. It's a feeling, like an invisible mosquito buzzing against the nape of my neck.

Time to start the day.

My stomach growls, ready for breakfast—but there are no plates of bagels, fruit, or bacon on the breakfast bar.

Am I eating in the big house this morning?

I open the front door, and the smell of burning things slaps me—trees and grass and wood, yes, but also plastic and . . . and . . . my stomach drops, and my mouth goes dry. My eyes burn from all the grime swirling in the air.

Push through it. This is just one more thing.

Smoke creeps across the sky, and ashes drift and settle on the flagstone pathway and float on the surface of the cool waters of the swimming pool. Those helicopters are not above the house, but their blades still hammer the sky.

Luann is here—her head is bobbing around the kitchen.

And now, my sense of dread slackens a bit. I'm not alone.

The closer I get, the stronger the aroma of bacon becomes.

I tap on the kitchen window. "Good morning!"

Luann glowers over her shoulder but sees me standing there. A rigid smile finds her lips, and she hustles over to the kitchen door to let me in.

"What's going on out there?" I ask, heading to the breakfast bar.

She shakes her hands like they're on fire and says, "Sorry for not getting back there this morning."

"I'm guessing the fire's not out yet?"

There's a platter filled with bacon, sourdough toast, and strawberries. She's set out a pot of fresh-brewed coffee along with tiny pots of sugar and creamer.

"Yep, fire's still raging," she says, "but don't *you* worry too much about it."

I chomp a piece of bacon. "Even though *you* look *very* worried?"

Sweat bubbles along the older woman's hairline, and I think about that dyed sweat of Russell Walker, the pretender. Is Luann also hiding something like he is? Is she really who she is, or is she someone else? And now, she tries on that "Topanga Canyon living is heavenly" smile, but it lands on "Fuck this shit." Her face colors until it's the shade of blush wine.

"I'm still not used to fire season," she admits. "Give me Texas tornadoes any day. I know, I know. Two different types of natural disasters, two different buckets of possums. But I am *not* a fan."

"I'm not, either, and I grew up here." Then, I tell her about my freak-out last night at the Overlook.

She nods, understanding. "Jack shouldn't have done that. He knows better."

"Margo—have you seen her?" I ask.

Luann frowns. "That girl's got some snap in her garter. She was smart enough to call in sick yesterday." She wrings her reddened hands, then sets them on her hips. "I told Jack I'm gonna stay with my cousin over in Bellflower until this fire's out. That's where I always go when the canyons start burning. Bellflower is as exciting as a mashed potato sandwich, but at least it ain't burning down. And they got a Golden Corral so . . ." She shrugs.

"Should I leave, too?" I ask, anxious now that she isn't sticking around.

Luann tries to smile. "You'll be fine, Lord willin' and the creek don't rise."

I chuckle.

She chuckles.

Two bad actresses.

"Seriously?" she says. "If you don't see Jack in ten minutes? I'd get out of here. Ask for forgiveness later."

"What about the bunker?" I ask. "If we have to, we can take cover there and wait it out . . . Right?"

"That's true."

"Where is it? In case I reach minute eleven and Jack's not around, and it's too late for me to drive down?"

Luann bites her lower lip, tosses a glance out the window. "If you start walking to the cottage but instead of going inside, you turn left and keep walking . . . it's there on the edge of the property. Right beneath your feet. The door is hidden beneath the grass."

"Jack says that it's locked."

She nods. "The key is in his desk drawer. But I don't think you should chance it." She's inching toward her purse, now hanging on the back of the stool beside me.

I nod and hold her gaze. "Thanks, Luann. I won't stick around too much longer."

"Nine minutes, darlin'," Luann says, slipping her purse over her shoulder. "I know he's down at the fire station right now, getting updates directly from Captain Walsh. Just . . . don't get to freakin' out. No one thinks right, thinks *smart* when they're scared to death."

I hug myself. "Too late."

"Go get your stuff and get out of here, then." She swipes at her forehead. "I'll see you when this is all over. I'll even bake us a big cake to celebrate being together again. What's your favorite flavor?"

"7UP."

Luann smiles. "Your people must come from the South." She gives me another long look before saying, "I'm outa here." She hustles out of the kitchen. Moments later, the front door opens and closes.

She's right: it's time to go.

But the key to the bunker . . . I want that key, just in case. And if I can't find it, I'll grab my things—the files and folders most importantly—get in my Volvo, and scram. And as I rush up the staircase, my phone vibrates with a text message . . . from UNKNOWN.

Get your stuff and GO!!!

22.

The key—I need that key to the bunker.

Because what if I'm trapped on the road—*one way in, one way out*—and need to double back? At least I'll have another option—hiding out in the bunker.

Or do I stick it out here, pray that the fire doesn't come this way . . . ?

But there's no way to predict the path the blaze will take. It only takes one good ember landing . . .

I need that key. And if I can't find it, then I'll take my chances on the road.

I pull the recording pen from my cargo-pants pocket—my phone would be too obvious, and if Jack saw it, he'd probably wonder what else I've been recording. I hold it before me and creep down the hallway lined with family photographs. Weird golden light falls from the windows of the bedrooms' open doors and coats the hallway. Up ahead, there's one closed door and two open doors—the one on the left opens to the library.

Which is Jack's office?

I choose the last right door.

Good choice.

I shiver as I step across the threshold.

The rough-hewn wood and sleek leather decor of this large space matches the furniture in every room of the parts of the house I've visited. The expansive Moroccan floor rug is worth more than . . .

me. The large windows look out over the swimming pool to the cottage and an overgrown lawn of tall grass that must be hiding the bunker door.

Framed book covers fill the wall, and writing awards fill the shelves. On the desk, there's a polished-nickel pharmacy-style lamp with a heavy rectangular base. There are cups of pens and pencils, paper clips, and sticky notes. Three notepads in three different sizes sit on the corner of the desk along with a picture of a willowy blonde performing a tree pose on the Overlook's concrete pad. She isn't Jack's wife—Finley's brunette and curvy. Is this Liliana, his mother?

"Please, please, please let me find it," I whisper, crouched now at the desk.

There are thin drawers and wide drawers, side drawers, and drawers only big enough to house a hummingbird's heart.

Which drawer did Luann say the key . . . ?

She didn't say.

I open the top desk drawer: writing supplies, chewing gum, thumb drives. The tiny drawer—big enough for a key—holds a thumb drive. In the larger bottom drawer, there's a bulky expanding folder—and I can't help but peek in the file.

Medical Certificate of Causes of Death

Issued by the Belizean government for Jackson Beckham, Sr., who'd been forty-one years old on the day he'd died. Occupation: writer. Cause of death: self-inflicted gunshot wound to the head.

My face burns—even though snooping has been my primary goal, I'm supposed to be looking for the bunker key and . . . and right now, reading this feels . . . *wrong.* Still, I take a picture of the death certificate, then flip past that document to find . . .

CONTRACT
This agreement is made on February 3, 2021, between Jack Beckham,

Jr. (client) and Rowan Patrick of Patrick Greer Associates, to conduct investigative activities consisting of:

Surveillance of Avery Turner for the purpose of attempting to document stalking activities, to include relevant photographs and relevant documentary evidence.

Frost crackles up my spine.

What?

Stalking activities?

Ro Patrick isn't investigating Luann. Ro Patrick is investigating . . . *Avery?* And on Jack's behalf?

That frost snaps up my neck and freezes my face.

Jack knows that Avery has been following him, so much so that he hired a private investigator to track a private investigator.

Does that mean Jack knows that I'm a PI in training under Avery's license?

Does that mean Ro Patrick knows that I'm Avery's baby detective?

My fingers turn frigid as I keep flipping through reports sent by Ro Patrick, all bundled together with a large butterfly clip. In one report, Patrick includes pictures of two cars.

VEHICLE INFORMATION

Subject is known to operate a green Acura Integra bearing license plate 3SRU972. Additional known vehicle is a white Toyota 4runner, license plate 7DOP564.

SURVEILLANCE REPORT

Day 1, Thursday, February 11, 2021

6318 Green Valley Circle, Culver City, CA

5:30 AM: Our minvestigator arrived at the provided address. Upon arrival, the Integra was observed parked at the office park. Surveillance was initiated with a direct view of the subject's office.

7:35 AM: The subject was observed exiting the building. Video was initiated as she departed area as the sole occupant of the Integra.

According to the investigator, Avery drives the Acura to Topanga Canyon for the rest of February, March, and the beginning of April. The 4Runner doesn't move at all from its spot in the office parking lot. Avery isn't spotted in the canyon again until April 12, 2021.

12:16 PM: Subject exited the vehicle and took pictures of the driveway at 61147 Old Topanga Road.

April 12, 2021.
That was a month ago!
There's a thank-you card clipped to this April 2021 report:

Dear Jack,

We wouldn't have been able to cover all those costs without your financial help. Macie and I will be forever grateful Ella will grow up knowing who helped heal her heart. There are not enough ways to thank you for that. Anything you need, just ask.

Forever grateful,

Ro

Jack paid for medical procedures for Ro's kid?
Way to nurture loyalty.

I slowly move the spy pen over the rest of the documents, then use my phone to take pictures of the surveillance reports, investigation recommendations ("performing a social media investigation of Avery Turner to help us gain a better understanding of who she is . . ."), a claims document ("Los Angeles County Superior Court indices reflect one civil and one judgment file under the name AVERY D. TURNER . . .)."

Is my cover about to be blown? Or was it already blown the moment I attended the party for Skylar Orion? Can we be sued?

But what we're doing . . . it isn't *illegal*. Avery didn't set foot on Jack's land—as beautiful and twisty as it is, Topanga Canyon Road is a public street. From what I've read in these reports, Avery has yet to make contact, to come face-to-face with Jack. He didn't say that he's breathed the same air as Avery, just that he *knows* her. Avery didn't tell me she knew Jack, because she *didn't*. Not like how *I* thought. As for the recording-everything part—Avery already told me that we could secretly record if there's some type of crime happening. And the abduction of Sam Morris in this area? The same Sam Morris that Jack's maid, Margarita Duran, and the groundskeeper spotted?

Because my hands are shaking, I have to type Avery's name six times to start a text.

Did you know that Jack has a detective following you??

Icy pellets whiz though my belly as I attach to the message the picture of the investigation retainer. Then, I stare at my phone, anxiously awaiting my boss's response.

Find the key! Read this later!

I grab the top sheet of Avery's mental health evaluation, fold it into a tight square, then shove it deep into one of the many pockets on this pair of cargo pants.

My phone rings.

I don't know the number, but I still answer.

Static.

I hang up.

The phone rings again.

I answer again.

"Bailey—" The man's voice cuts in and out of the static. "—come get you!"

He sounds like Russell Walker.

"You hear me?" he shouts.

Silence. No more static.

Biting back hysteria, I hit END CALL.
He's coming for me.
This would be the best time for the pretender to "disappear" me.
But he wouldn't have my cell phone number . . .
Unless Jack gave this man—
"What are you doing in here?"

CALL ME

23.

The man's voice is raspy and deep, filled with wonder. He gives me no time to answer his question—*What are you doing here?*—before grabbing my arm from behind.

With my free hand, I grab the desk lamp, somehow tearing the plug from the outlet and swooping the lamp behind my shoulder.

BAM!

The desk lamp smacks him in the face.

The man howls but tightens his grip on my arm.

Explosions of pain and panic give me the strength I need to yank out of his grip and swing the lamp again.

BAM!

The desk lamp hits the side of his face, and parts of it break in my hand.

I donkey-kick him off me, then grab from the desktop a red leather weighted bookmark. I scramble over the desk, knocking over files and reports, pen cups, and cubes of multicolored sticky notes. I turn to see . . .

Bull-necked Ro Patrick, the private investigator that Jack has hired to follow Avery, the same man I met in the driveway back on Thursday evening. He now clutches his bloody nose and mouth, and sputters, "You crazy *bitch*!"

I hold up the limp penis–like bookmark and shout, "Stay away from me."

"Will you just—" He reaches for the small of his back.

I can't give him enough time to pull his gun, and I don't have enough to pull *my* gun, so I throw the weighted bookmark at his head.

He shouts, "What the—"

Fwap.

The bookmark hits him in the ear.

I reach behind me and grab from the bookshelf a ceramic bust painted white, black, and blue and shaped like Edgar Allan Poe's head.

Ro Patrick lunges for me.

I slam Edgar Allan Poe against Ro Patrick's chin.

Bwak.

And I swing again.

BWAK!

The PI doesn't cry out—the only sounds are the *bwaks* of Edgar Allan Poe breaking against the dick's face. Ro Patrick stumbles back, crumples to his knees, then falls onto his left side, and in front of Jack's desk. Blood and sticky notes foul the teakwood floor beyond the rug.

I drop the base of the broken statuette and race out of the office, past those framed pictures of foggy canyons and pretty white people wearing pretty white clothes, back down the hallway and to the door off the foyer that leads to the garage. My heart is rocketing in my chest, and my mind is roaring—*I just killed a man* and *Did I kill him?* and *What do I do now?* My Volvo is parked beside Josie, Jack's maroon Honda. I run to the driver's side of the Volvo and pull at the door handle.

Locked. The key is in my purse.

My purse is in the cottage.

Shit shit shit.

With a heart of glass, I peer inside my car, just in case I left those keys on the seat. I'd bust a window, if I did . . . nope, of course not. In South Los Angeles, we don't *intentionally* leave keys in the car.

In the Volvo window's reflection, my eyes look big and bleary, mad-cow crazy. Maybe because I *am* mad-cow crazy.

But not too far gone to understand that one key—car key or bunker key—will determine if I live or die on this day. I step away from the

Volvo and creep back to the door that leads into the house. My weak fingers wrap around the knob and slowly . . . slowly . . . turn . . .

Not much turning before the knob stops.

Locked.

The lights of the garage flicker off.

Dunked into sudden darkness, I try to ignore the fear clawing at my throat like a trapped cat. I contain the urge to scream and instead wave my arms in the air.

The motion sensor tracks me, and the garage lights flicker back on.

Hoping that I was doing it wrong before, I twist the doorknob again. No give.

Shit shit shit.

Stop. Focus. Breathe.

I can't call for help—Ro Patrick will find me if I do. If I lift the garage door, Ro Patrick will find me. And if I lift the door, what then do I do? *Run down the hill until I reach Pacific Coast Highway.* What if I stay here in this garage? The climate is nice, thanks to the $140,000 German piece of art that lives here. And Jack—he'll be home soon with news from the fire captain. He'll see me camping out in the Porsche's empty space . . . unless he parks in the driveway.

Shit shit shit.

I pace and try to think, but my mind spins . . . spins . . .

Is Ro Patrick still in the office? Is he alive and pissed off?

I try to hear past my own breathing—yet I can't hear anything *but* my own breathing.

Tat-tat . . . tat-tat-tat . . .

Grit from the wind and far-off fire strikes the garage door.

Right—I can't stay in this garage forever. There's a fire burning out there. I need to evacuate, but I need my car keys to do that. Fuck the bunker key.

I shove my hands into my hoodie and startle. *My gun!* I'm armed. More confident now, I grab the doorknob again with my free hand. The body of the gun feels frosty beneath my palm. This feels so familiar—it's the most natural thing I've done today. I lay my cheek and ear against the door to the house. The wood is also cold and vibrates against my face like the planks are filled with bugs.

One more try—if this door doesn't open, then I'll open the garage door.

One . . . two . . . three . . .

I turn the doorknob slowly . . . slowly . . . until I can't turn it anymore.

Click.

Unlocked.

Happy tears spring to my eyes until I remember that moments ago I fought a man the size of a brown bear, and because of that, I'm now gripping a semiautomatic pistol.

There's nothing to be happy about right now.

Silence and darkness greet me as I sneak back into the house. In the foyer, I pause in my step, cocking my head to listen . . .

No stirring. No scraping. No moaning.

I reach to grab my phone from my back pocket to call Avery or 9-1-1 or . . .

No phone in this pocket. Or that pocket. Or any . . .

No phone.

Where's my—

On the desk in the office.

I'll have to go back for my phone.

I pop out the Glock's magazine. Nothing's changed since my last ammo check on Wednesday evening before leaving the car to attend the publication party. The gun still has bullets, lots of bullets. I push out a shaky breath, pointing the gun at the floor. My stomach burbles as I creep down the hallway with my shoulders against the wall. Slowly . . . slower . . . the floorboard before the office doorway creaks beneath my sneaker.

No no no . . .

I wait, the grip of the gun becoming tackier with my sweat the longer I wait. The less-than-two-pound weapon continues to gain mass the longer I stand here.

What if I already killed that man?

Self-defense.

Who aims to actively kill someone with a desk lamp and an award shaped like Edgar Allan Poe's head?

True. *Still . . .*

I wait and listen . . .

No labored breathing. No groaning. No cursing.

Dead men don't groan, nor do they curse.

My skin feels too tight for my body, but I *gotta do this.* I have to check—I need my phone. There's a fire out there, and I'll need to call for help.

One . . . two . . .

Please don't be waiting for me.

I take a deep breath and push away from the wall. Arms up and gun out, I spin into the doorway and immediately crouch.

The broken desk lamp parts are littered across the carpet. Loose pages are scattered all over the floor like confetti. That red leather page weight sits flaccid by the small waste can. Drops of blood stain the rug and the teakwood floor.

Ro Patrick isn't lying in front of Jack's desk.

That's where he was when I ran out of the room.

My soul thuds to my feet. My mind races, and I blink to make sure that I'm not seeing what I'm supposed to see . . .

A man with a head injury splayed before Jack's desk.

My eyes skip around the office. There aren't many places to hide in this room, especially for a man the size of a brown bear. There's a closet. There's a bathroom.

I tiptoe over to the closet door and reach for the doorknob with my gun-free hand.

One . . . two . . .

I yank open the door.

Jackets, banker's boxes, boxes of books, reams of paper . . .

No Ro Patrick.

I swipe the rolling beads of sweat on my forehead with the back of my wrist. I roll my head around my neck, then roll my shoulders. Every bone in my upper torso cracks and pops. I pivot to the bathroom.

The door is already open.

Breath hot in my chest, I creep over . . .

One . . . two . . .

I pounce into the bathroom.

Intricate Spanish-style floor tile. A double-mirrored medicine cabinet. A spa tub, no dirt ring. Clear-door shower. No colossal, bear-necked private eye hiding behind the towel rack.

I search the floor tile for any obvious signs of injury. Blood drops—none. Bloody shoeprints—there aren't any.

That!

There's a bloody fingerprint on the top sheet of the toilet paper roll.

My phone—I came here for my phone. I back out of the bathroom and return to the office. Jack's desk is still in shambles. The high-backed desk chair is toppled over, and the teakwood floor is still spattered with the disappeared man's blood.

My phone isn't on the desk. My phone isn't on the floor. My phone isn't in the top drawer.

I left my phone here—I *know* I did.

I pat my pockets again just in case . . .

No phone.

Outside the office window, the sky matches the color of the hillsides: brown and orange and sickening green. The sun hides somewhere up there, its light unable to push past this melting-Popsicle sky.

Where is Jack?

Why isn't he home yet?

Why haven't we evacuated—

Oh no.

What if Jack is waiting at a safe shelter and sent Ro Patrick to pull me out of here? What if I just injured my knight in shining armor? What if, after the PI gained consciousness, he said, "Fuck this," and left me here to burn?

Oh no.

Ohmigod.

No no no no no no.

My phone. I need my phone.

Is there a landline telephone?

There's no old-fashioned phone on the desk.

Maybe I left my stupid, untethered phone on the breakfast bar.

Yes, as you watched Luann prepare to leave! Possibility lights in my chest and head—that makes some sense . . . but no, it doesn't. I took pictures of the surveillance reports.

With my phone? Or with the pen?

No no no.

The breakfast bar, my phone has to be on the . . .

I shake the nerves out of my arms and legs, and then I creep back down the hallway.

The Glock is pointing to the floor, ready to fire. I reach the staircase.

No one lingers in the living room or stands in the foyer.

My pulse revs less than it did minutes ago, but it still has the power to work the Hoover Dam.

Onward . . .

I slink to the kitchen, the light there now copper colored instead of lemony white.

There, on the breakfast bar alongside the plates of strawberries and cold, greasy bacon strips . . .

My phone!

I let out a breath that's closer to a sob than a sigh and race over to—

Cracks run across the glass on the phone screen, spidering from the top of the device to the bottom.

I press the phone's side power button.

The screen stays dark.

No no no no no.

I force back my fear—hysteria can't help me now. I return the gun to my hoodie pocket—hysteria will thrive the longer I grip the Glock.

Try again try again try again.

With both hands now dedicated to this task, I press the phone's power button again, longer this time . . . dead.

◆ ◆ ◆

November 2, 1993
Topanga Canyon

Theresa Morris glanced over her shoulder and smiled up at the tanned man in the shabby denim work shirt and frayed cargo shorts. The faded blue Vans on his feet looked like they'd hiked the Appalachian Trail and now begged to be burned and buried. Golden-haired and gray-eyed, he smelled of sunscreen and leather. He could have come only from Southern California.

Joy ballooned in Sammi's chest, and she giggled to herself—her mom was gawking and blushing. Her mother *never* gawked or blushed.

"Where are you trying to go?" Golden Boy asked.

"The Santa Ynez Trail," Terri said.

"This your first time in Topanga?"

Sparks in her eyes, Terri squared her shoulders and squinted at him. "No, it's *not* my first time in Topanga. I work at the Visitors Center, but I just started a month ago. So I don't know every rock and tree around here yet."

Golden Boy smiled. *Sure.* "Got it. Just so you know: Santa Ynez Trail isn't really marked well."

"Really?" Terri asked. "A friend of mine said she loved it and had no problem."

A friend. Baby Boo, recently incarcerated for her strong-armed robbery of Nix Check Cashing down on King Boulevard, just a stone's throw from USC.

"Your friend probably *did* love it," Golden Boy said, "but it can still be a bit . . ." He winced. "Two different things can be true at the same time, ya know."

"No shit?" Terri asked.

"No shit," he said.

"He should know," the salesclerk said. "Mr. Beckham's family has lived here for a hundred years. They cut many of the trails through the forest."

"Beckham?" Terri asked, turning back to the man. "You not related to Jack Beckham the writer, are you?"

Golden Boy's face lit, and his cheeks burned bright pink. "I *am* Jack Beckham the writer."

Sammi's eyes bugged.

"Ohmigosh," Terri exploded, her eyes also huge. "We're huge fans," she said, motioning frantically between Sammi and her. "I've read every book you wrote *twice*." She'd had a lot of time on her hands.

Beckham's eyes flicked at Sammi but returned to the stony beauty of her mother and those golden almond eyes and cheekbones that went on forever. Even with a few pounds at her gut and around her thighs, she still had those generous, smirking lips and an ass that women in this part of the world would pay thousands of dollars for.

"I didn't catch your name," Beckham said, hand out.

"I didn't throw it," Terri said, that eyebrow high, shaking his hand.

Ha! Sammi's favorite line. She'd practiced saying, "I didn't throw it," almost as much as she practiced Spanish.

"I'm Terri," her mother said. "And this is my daughter, Sam."

This time, Jack Beckham met Sammi's eyes. "Nice to meet you, Sam. You in middle school?"

Sammi grinned and nodded. "I attend Harvard-Westlake."

Beckham blinked and blinked, hearing "Harvard-Westlake." His mind refused to believe, though, that this girl, the daughter of a thug (even with those cheekbones and that ass, he saw those tats rippling across Terri's wrists) was attending a private school that cost more than some college tuitions. Movie stars and basketball stars sent their kids to Harvard-Westlake. Owners of Big Things and Everything sent their kids to Harvard-Westlake.

"My son is in fifth grade," Beckham said, "but he'll go there, too. I went there. So did my father. All Beckham men are Harvard-Westlake men." He paused, then added, "Jack Junior hates it already."

"Sammi loves it." Terri waggled her daughter's arm. "She's shooting for UC Berkeley and majoring in history. Wants to sign up with the FBI, which could happen or . . . *not*." Terri flushed, then dropped her head, knowing that her conviction could possibly scuttle her daughter's dream . . . again.

Beckham whistled and peered at Sammi. "So, you're a smart one, then?"

Sammi blushed. "I am."

"Straight-A student." Terri lifted her chin, proud of her girl, a success despite her jailbird parents. "Anyway, she's ditching school cuz she's spending the day with me. We came up here as part of my birthday celebration—"

"Birthday?" Beckham patted Terri's shoulder. "Happy birthday! Hey! If you're not busy later, I'd love to treat you and Samantha to a late lunch—"

"Sam doesn't stand for 'Samantha,'" Terri said. "They're her initials all smashed together. Simone Alaina Morris. S-A-M."

The writer thought that over and said, "Ah. Got it. So, I'd love to treat you and Simone to a late lunch."

The salesclerk clapped and her bracelets clanked. "How special!"

"Oh, we can't do that," Terri said.

"You *can* do that," Beckham said. "I insist. After your hike—"

"We'd be all sweaty and gross," Terri said.

"Inn at the Seventh Ray," Jack said.

"I heard about that place," Terri said.

"And everything you've heard is true." Beckham positioned the Thomas Guide so that he could read it and plucked a pen from the cashier's cup. "Here's what you're gonna do . . ." He marked the map, showing the Morris women where they were *now* and where they needed to go next.

Sammi followed his finger as it dragged across the map. "So curvy and confusing."

"How about this?" Beckham said. "You follow me up there—"

"Oh, no. I can't let you—" Terri shook her head.

"And you park, and I continue on with my errands," he said. "Then around four, I'll meet you and *Simone* at your car, and you follow me down to the restaurant. We'll have dinner alongside the creek. That way, no one will see you being dirty and gross."

Terri turned to Sammi. "You were going to cook dinner."

"Cook," Sammi said, making air quotes with her fingers. "Hamburgers, frozen french fries, and a grocery-store birthday cake. Let's do better, Mom."

The writer laughed, and the crow's-feet at the corners of his eyes crinkled.

The salesclerk nodded at Terri. *Go. Do it.*

Eyes glossy, Terri gazed at the helpful stranger.

Beckham held her gaze and Sammi saw something . . . *adult* . . . pass between them. There was another invitation bubbling beneath "dinner."

Terri said, "Okay. Deal. Wow. This is incredible. Thank you."

Sammi and Terri thanked the clerk for being so worthless in her efforts that a handsome rich stranger whose books sat in their library—at home, in prison—and whose videocassettes of his adapted novels sat next to their VCRs—at home, in prison—had rescued them and offered to be their personal tour guide.

Minutes later, Terri slipped back behind the Honda's steering wheel. "What the *fuck*, Sammi?"

"Right?" Sammi said, laughing. "Happy birthday to *you!*"

Terri wiggled her nose, then checked her reflection in the mirror. "He wouldn't like someone like me . . . would he?"

Sammi rolled her eyes and threw up her hands. "He invited you to dinner. If he was the delivery guy back at home and invited you to dinner, you'd be all—" Sammi swerved her head and smirked, and in her best sexy-thug Terri voice said, "And he *better* not look at me funny when I order the lobster, cuz I will kick his fine ass to the curb."

Terri blushed, covered her face with her hands, squealed, then peeked over at her daughter. "You sounded just like me. Like for real."

Sammi threw her one more sexy-sneer eye roll and then sighed. "That's cuz I study everything you do. I wanna be you when I grow up. Not the going-to-jail-again you but like . . . the *other* strong you. The 'I'm the shit and the most beautiful bitch up in this place' you."

Terri snorted. "Do you see me right now? All nervous and shit? Over a *boy*?"

"But you know the truth," Sammi said. "He *is* just a boy but with a bank account. He wouldn't have invited you—"

"*Us.*"

"*You* to dinner if he didn't like what he saw." Sammi flicked at her mother's ear. "You got it like that, Theresa Monalisa Morris, even at twenty-nine years old."

Terri pointed at her. "But if he turns out to be one of them weirdos, we bouncing. No arguing. Got it?"

"Got it." Sammi's heart cartwheeled in her chest. Maybe she'd get to meet Jack Junior at dinner. Maybe he'd take her on a hike. Maybe he'd become . . . *her stepbrother!*

Terri clasped her hands together, prayer-style. "Lord, I have seen what you've done for others. Gimme some of that. Just a little. That's all I'm—"

"Ready?" Jack Beckham shouted from his convertible black Porsche.

"Always ready," Terri shouted back, lifting the pair of binoculars that Sammi bought her as a birthday gift. "I'm ready to see something new."

24.

"Bailey, what's going on?"

Jack's velvety voice—so calm and hypnotic even with the fire racing across the canyons—pulls me out of my shock.

Phone in hand, I whirl around to face him, hysteria tugging at my face and neck, grimacing, crumpling, smiling, frowning.

The aroma of smoke wafts from his clothes. The sour-sweet aroma of vitamins wafts from his skin. The sleeves of his gray sweatshirt are rolled up to his elbows. His trainers and Adidas soccer shoes have come straight off a department store mannequin in the soccer section, and now he's ready for round three of the FIFA World Cup.

He points at my dead iPhone. "What happened to your phone?"

"I—I . . . you-you . . . I . . . I . . ." I take a deep breath to stop my stuttering, then shout, "Where were you?"

Annoyed, Jack turns red, and his eyes darken to mop-water gray. "I was getting evacuation information from Captain Walsh. Why are you screaming at me?"

"I'm sorry." I take a step back, then rub my face. "Ro Patrick, the detective you hired? He attacked me in your office."

"What?" He squints at me. "*Who* attacked you?"

I squint back at him and shake my head. "Don't play dumb. I know everything. Why are you having him follow Avery?"

"Where'd you hear that?" He pauses, then looks back at the hallway. "Ah. I see. You were in my office, and you were snooping in my files." Jack stares at me, a smile playing on the edges of his lips.

I hold out my hands. "I wasn't trespassing or lurking or whatever. Luann gave me permission to find the key to the bunker—"

"Excuse me?" he interrupts.

"And she said the key was in one of the drawers, and so I opened your drawers—"

"For the key to my family's bunker, and not Luann's." He studies me as though wings are slowly sprouting from my back. Right now, he's more amused than annoyed.

"And as I was looking for the key," I continue, doubt now spiking my words, "I saw the reports from Ro Patrick." I ignore the growing smirk on his face and press on. "You're having Avery Turner watched, and the man you hired just attacked me in your office. I had to defend myself . . . I broke your desk lamp and Poe head. Sorry."

Jack blinks at me, then blinks at the ceiling, runs his tongue across his lips. "Is Ro Patrick back there right now?"

I shake my head. "No."

"The Edgar is ceramic and has a stone base," he says. "It's sort of heavy."

"Yeah."

He's smiling now. "Did you kill him?"

"You think I'm lying about this?" I ask.

Jack pivots and marches to the hallway.

"But he's not there anymore," I shout, following behind him. "He's gone."

Jack regards me over his shoulder. "You just told me that you hit Ro Patrick over the head with a desk lamp and a statuette, but he's now disappeared?"

"Yes?"

Jack gives me the "okay" signal and continues down the hallway.

I squeeze shut my eyes, walking blindly, but needing more to push against the fraying edges of my brain. And the light . . . it may now be amber colored and muted, but that glow from the windows feels sharp and dazzling, new pennies against my eyes.

"He's not here," Jack shouts from the office door.

I open my eyes. "I know—I just said that."

"You also said that you broke my desk lamp?"

"Yes," I say. "And I'll pay—"

"But the desk lamp isn't broken," he says, bisected by that office door. "And my Edgar is right there on the bookshelf. It looks clean. No blood, no gunk."

"What?" I race down the hallway and push past him to enter the office.

An immaculate, ordered space with stacks of paper and file folders on the desk. Stacks of sticky notes in the metal organizer. An unbroken, pharmacy-style desk lamp of brushed silver, and a picture of a blonde woman performing the tree pose at the Overlook. The red leather weighted bookmark sits on the desk, and the Edgar Allan Poe bust sits on the bookshelf. Jack is right—clean. No blood. No gunk. It's like I never snuck into this room. Like I was never here at all.

But I'm here now, standing in the middle of this immaculate, ordered space, blinking at the order, confusion bobbing around my achy head. "I—I . . . don't know what to say."

Jack says, "Neither do I."

"Come look," I say. "There's a bloody fingerprint on the toilet paper—" I march to the bathroom.

There's no fingerprint on that top sheet of toilet paper.

I spin back into the office and send my eyes across the room in search of something, in search of anything . . .

With his head tipped and arms folded, Jack watches me in silence for a few seconds, then says, "Maybe . . . you should stop taking the Percocet."

Rage explodes in me, and I shout, "Excuse me? How the hell do you know—"

Jack holds out his hands. "Unlike what you're doing to me, I'm not snooping on you. Dr. Torrance mentioned it when he visited after your allergic reaction. He has access to your digital health records, remember?"

"But he can't be—he's not supposed to be discussing my medical status with you."

Jack nods. "You're exactly right, but this . . . you didn't put down phone numbers for any family members. Avery—I called her, but her line just rang and rang." He shrugs. "Dr. Torrance saw that I was the only person in your life at that moment, and so he discussed your aftercare with me. And he hated doing that—I practically forced him to, Bailey."

Black spots spin before me, and my mind is in tatters, and I don't know what to say.

"I know Percocet, and it's some good shit," Jack says. "I went to WebMD, though, looking for side effects: drowsy, dizzy . . . ringing in ears and . . ."

I press my palms against my cheeks—my face is burning. This office—it's too hot, too stuffy . . .

"The ringing in your ears," Jack says. "That's probably the chirping that you keep hearing."

My face numbs now, and I pinch my cheeks just to feel something. "But Luann," I say. "She heard it, too."

Jack takes one of my hands and rubs his thumb across my knuckles. "Luann probably felt awful for nearly killing you with her fruit punch."

Oh. That's possible. My ire dims some.

"And to answer your question," Jack continues, dropping my hands. "Avery Turner may be your writing instructor, but she is dangerous, at least to me. She's been stalking me for years, Bailey. She started out as a fan, and then she became a superfan, and then she transformed into one of those fanatical, obsessed—"

I take a step away from him and cross my arms. "That's . . . no. She's not a stalker. She would've told me."

"Told you?" Jack snorts. "That she's trespassed onto my property twice? That she's left unhinged notes on my doorstep? That she's followed me on hiking trails and around the village? I tried to have her arrested, but my lawyer told me that I didn't have sufficient evidence to make any charge stick." He waits a beat. "This is the same person who didn't tell you that we knew each other."

I crane my neck up to him. "Then why did Margo say she was a friend?"

Jack also cranes his neck down to me. "Because Avery *was* a friend. We even went out once, romantically. But after I said that I didn't want to pursue anything further with her, she lost her shit."

I purse my lips, speechless, all follow-up retorts dust on my tongue.

Jack's face softens. "Avery disappeared after her last bit of stalking, but then she resurfaced to tell me that she was gonna kill me. But cops wouldn't do anything about threats, so I hired Ro Patrick to keep an eye on her, and to collect evidence anytime she did something that couldn't be brushed away with an innocent explanation."

He rubs his face. "I didn't want to penalize someone as gifted and as promising as you because of her. I mean . . . my dad was a complete bastard, and to this day I always hope that the people who hated Big Jack Beckham give me a fair chance to prove that I'm nothing like him."

Jack pauses, then adds, "You know some fans go too far. You met a few at the bookstore yesterday. Avery—she was going too far, and I feared she would kill me."

Mark David Chapman killed John Lennon. Andrew Cunanan killed Gianni Versace. Yolanda Saldivar murdered Selena.

Each celebrity died at the hands of a superfan.

So Avery sent me here to spy on her favorite writer? Not to investigate Sam's disappearance? Did she launch this investigation with me because she needed to do something to advance her true desire and knew that I needed six thousand hours of work as a PI for my license?

Am I Avery's stalker by proxy? My shoulders slump, and I pinch my bottom lip and squeeze the bridge of my nose. The urge to tell Jack everything, every bit of the truth, swells inside of me.

Jack lifts my chin. "It's okay, Bailey. And I forgive you for snooping in my office."

My vision smears from the tears in my eyes. "I'm so sorry."

He tries to smile. "I didn't want to say anything about any of this to you. Neither did Margo. And I really hate to admit this because it's so . . . contradictory but . . . I find Avery fascinating. Her mind trips me out. How she can be so smart and so normal on one day, and then . . ."

He snaps his fingers. "I'm thinking of basing a character after her."

I sink into the low-slung sofa across from Jack's desk. My head throbs like it's caught in a vise. "I know she's been awful to you, but isn't that a little cruel? Like . . . keeping a bug in a glass?"

"But she isn't a bug in a glass," he says, settling beside me on the couch. "I haven't trapped her. I'm just watching and observing her. Like how researchers put monitors on dolphins. I'm simply recording everything she does to me and around my home."

He shakes my knee. "Listen. To write the Beckham way—and any way—you have to mine your life, and the people in your life. Everything is content, including stalkers and weirdos, like Avery. Good writers keep an open mind in order to learn things, to write as truthfully about what can be considered impossible."

I swallow, but my throat feels tight. "But it feels . . . wrong."

"We must become other people sometimes," Jack continues, "and if you want to write with me, to write like me, you must be willing to do that. You have to be all in. Everything, except killing a dog, is fair game."

He stands and offers me his hand. "I hope you appreciate all of this, Bailey. That I'm willing to give you a chance despite Avery Turner."

I take his hand, squeeze it, and nod. "I do appreciate everything, Jack. Thank you." Embarrassed, my gaze drops to the Moroccan floor rug.

There! In the low strands of the carpet. A tiny sliver of white ceramic, a tiny sliver of black ceramic, and a tiny sliver of blue ceramic.

I try to blink, but my eyes are now too dry. Am I seeing . . . ? Is that . . . ?

Pieces too small to notice during a quick cleanup of a busted-up ceramic Edgar Allan Poe head . . . but the head on the shelf right now doesn't look like it's been hastily glued back together. So what are these slivers in the rug from?

I feel sick—relief and disbelief are not a good mix.

Jack and I slip back down the hallway in silence and return to the kitchen.

"Luann left," I tell him. "She's driving to Bellflower to stay with her cousin until the fire's out. She sounded scared."

"The big bad Texan ain't a fan of our wildfires." He flashes me a smile and plucks a strip of cold bacon from the plate left on the breakfast bar.

When did he start eating meat? Pork, especially? Is bacon, the most perfect preparation of meat ever, his only exception?

He opens the kitchen door, and together we step outside and into a world that resembles any painting of the biblical last days. Brown smoke and dirty sky. The overwhelming stink of burning wood and burning leaves, burning animals and softening metal. Hot and wet air that feels thick and electric. Sirens and car horns and the thunder of those roving helicopters—but not the thunder from a giant Chinook that can hold Lake Michigan in her belly and will be delivered next month, right in time for fire season.

This . . . all of it. How will I ever forget about this sky, these sounds, how my eyes burn? My damp legs and spidery heart, the need to cry, the push to run? I'm freaking out—all the pinching and squirming and prickling around my body is warning me. I'm terrified—that everything

I've done is a farce, that I've been betrayed, that I'm living right now in the path of many fires, and not only the fire making this sky.

"When are we evacuating?" I ask now, nearly whispering.

Jack searches the last-days sky, no fear on his face. No fear wearing down his shoulders. "We're okay for now. Today, I regret not having the lawns and trees trimmed and maintained. I wanted cover from the Averys of the world."

I understand.

"I'm gonna water the rooftops now and wait for Captain Walsh to call me back on our sat phone. Everyone can't leave at the same time—you heard him say that yourself yesterday."

"One road in, one road out," I say, my voice shaky, my stomach roiling.

Jack is now headed to the cottage.

Keep it together.

Something vibrates in the leg pocket of my cargo pants.

My heart leaps—my phone has come back from the dead.

Who tried to destroy it in the first place?

The only person around at that time: Ro Patrick.

The water in the swimming pool is now gray and ashy. The flagstone walkway is also dusty-ashy gray, and the stones feel soft beneath my feet. The colors of Topanga Canyon are dotty, a Seurat painting.

At the cottage door, Jack touches his thumb to the smart-lock pad. *Click.*

He pushes open the door. "Start packing," he instructs. "Only your most-important stuff. Be ready to get out of here when it's time. It'll be quick when the call comes. You won't have the time to pull everything you brought to a fire truck."

"Okay." My mouth tastes gritty.

The cottage is still cool, but the smell of smoke is wafting through the now-open door. Ashes swirl across the tile of the small foyer. The dark screen of the television bolted to the living room wall reflects the last-days sky outside.

"You good?" Jack asks me, both hands on my shoulders.

"I'm good."

He cocks his head. "You are not good, and that's okay, okay?"

"I'm scared," I admit. "I'm not used to this."

He pulls me into a hug. "It'll be okay. I swear. I hate that this . . . I hate this . . . damn it."

I hold my breath as we embrace. I bend my knees some so that he doesn't feel the gun weighing down my hoodie pocket. Distrust—of him, of his intent of Ro and Avery—rises and falls. Those shards of broken ceramic left in the floor rug. That Edgar Allan Poe on the shelf, unbroken and unspoiled.

I need to take something. Drink something. Hell, even smoke something. Just to calm my nerves, to slow my heart, to clear my head. But the only remedies I have—Percocet and wine—could incapacitate me. I could fall asleep and never wake up due to carbon monoxide poisoning.

After this, yeah, after this, I may need therapy. It's become too much.

Are you strong enough?

No, I'm not.

"I'll start packing," I say, pulling out of his embrace. He smells of sweat and vitamins and smoke—I want to gag. "About Ro," I say. "I didn't imagine hitting him."

Jack stares at me for a moment before shifting his gaze back to the main house. His brow crinkles for just a second—he doesn't know what to believe. Back to me: "Whatever happened, it was simple miscommunication. There's no reason for Ro to hurt you, Bailey. He's a good guy. I promise you that."

I stick my hands in my hoodie's front pocket, curl my fingers around the Glock. "If you say so."

Jack nods once—he says so. "Stay sober, okay? Because if there's anything to fear . . ." He points toward the main house. "It's the bad guy on the other side of that hill."

25.

Jack jogs back to the big house and grabs a garden hose coiled around a reel cart. The hot-and-dry sky above him swirls with ashes from a world that has finally met its end.

I taste dead earth—warm and moist, a memory of what was before the fire came. The cool air of the cottage kisses my skin, but that won't last much longer—the filters of the HVAC system will soon clot with soot and will be forced to stop.

The worry of waiting here as the fire consumes more and more of the canyon twists my gut. Captain Walsh, though, is the expert, and we move when he says to move because there is only one way out, and that bear of a man controls that way. Some Topanga residents won't listen—the roads are probably jammed right now with cars driven by women like the ones I met at the bookstore, the ones who told me to skip writing that woke shit in Jack's next book.

I hope their tea gardens and PEACE flags burn—but not the oak tree, the "dog" in this instance.

I rush back to the bedroom and bathroom and start throwing my things into the duffel bag and red purse, starting first with both laptops and my bag of tea. I pluck the three-legged pig off the suitcase lock, yank my mustard-colored trench coat off the hanger, and thread it through the suitcase handle. On the shelf above the bed, Jack's binoculars catch my eye. I take those, too.

I'll be back, my heart says.

No, you won't, my mind corrects.

You leave, you can never come back, Avery had warned me.

While crouching in the closet, I take the gun from the hoodie pocket and stare at its angular perfection—should it stay on me, or should I keep it in my purse? Cold and black, its body shines from my sweat and body oil. I run my fingers over the grooves and valleys, then rest my index finger against the trigger.

I don't ever want to pull this trigger. Once I shoot, I can't take it back. "Please don't let me have to shoot someone," I pray.

Keeping the Glock in my hoodie pocket, I rush to the living room to find anything left behind. My eyes rove the living room, pausing at the television that I never watched, pausing at the armchair I hadn't sat in yet. The fireplace that stayed dark and cold. The stove I never used, although I *did* wash dishes in that sink and wash my clothes in the—

"*Oh!*" I hurry to the laundry nook and open the dryer to find my clothes waiting to be folded. The blood has come out of the top of my skirt set, the sweatshirt, and tank top. I carry the small load back to my suitcase in the bedroom.

Since I must wait, I grab my journal and add to the floor plan: the garage, Jack's office, and downstairs bathroom off that office. The same office where I left Ro Patrick . . . before he disappeared. As I flip past filled pages to find a clean page toward the end of the journal, I can track my emotional state through my handwriting—ordered and textbook printing (ordered mind) to slanting cursive (hurried yet still . . . *controlled*) to at this moment a mix of both cursive and print words, abbreviations, and cross-outs, from illegible to readable one word to the next. Since the journal is small enough, I shove it in the bottom leg pocket of my cargo pants—don't want it separated from me. I'm two pounds heavier now from the gun and Moleskine.

My upper left arm still burns from Ro Patrick's manhandling—he probably left a welt across my biceps. I probably knocked him the fuck out with a desk lamp and ceramic Poe head. Guess we're probably even.

I tap my struggling iPhone.

There are four bars of Wi-Fi! A Christmas miracle in May. As I tap into Google, though, the phone dies. I plug it into the charger and enlarge one of the pictures I took of Ro Patrick's surveillance reports to Jack regarding Avery.

Monday, November 9, 2020

10:37 am: Subject is seeing a therapist, Dr. Emilia Pham, who specializes in trauma and post-traumatic stress disorder. Dr. Pham will not confirm that subject is a patient.

Friday, November 13, 2020

7:47 pm: Makena Gould, the personal assistant of Dr. Pham, met with me on the outside patio at Café Vida. "She's nutso." That is her assessment of subject, that she is now thinking unclearly and is uneasy around her coworkers. Gould says patient has been holding back her emotions all this time, that anything can happen with patient any time now, including a psychotic break or even a dissociative fugue. A psychotic break occurs when someone loses touch with reality as their mental state declines. Gould shared that fugues involve retrograde amnesia triggered by a traumatic event. Subject will maintain "procedural memory," which are skills learned over time (riding a bike, swallowing pills), but will have no recollection of their autobiographical memory and personal identity. They are unaware that they're in a fugue, and so they fill in memory gaps by creating family, friends, and facts about their new lives—not even knowing they've created that memory. This is called "confabulation." Psychotic breaks are triggered by trauma and by drugs, both illicit and prescribed. Dr. Pham wants subject to continue therapy to avoid either fugue or break. Both would be "disastrous."

Monday, November 16, 2020

10:08 am: Subject did not attend weekly session.

Monday, November 23, 2020

10:15 am: Subject did not attend weekly session.

Tuesday, November 24, 2020

3:16 pm: According to Makena Gould, subject has probably left Los Angeles. "She probably is experiencing what we talked about."

My heartbeat bangs once and steals my breath.

Avery isn't "nutso." She's experienced *trauma*. That's . . . Avery *trying to survive*. A former cop, she'd worked the streets of South Los Angeles and then ascended the ranks to detective, confronting the worst people in the world, placing herself in danger over and over again. Yeah, she's probably suffering from PTSD—after being jumped, chased, and threatened. I'm not surprised that her mental health rests on a needle.

I swipe back to my digital album and tap the picture of Kadence Hatfield's bulletin.

MISSING PERSON AT RISK

Female, White, 24 years old

5'4", 120 lbs. Long brown hair, brown eyes

SUFFERS FROM DEPRESSION

Detectives from the Baker City Police Department are seeking assistance in locating the above missing person.

Kadence Hatfield was last contacted on December 22, 2015, at 9:00 pm when she flew from Nebraska to Ontario, CA, and drove to Baker, CA, where she checked into the Royal Hawaiian Motel in Baker, CA. She is driving a dark-red 1997 Toyota Corolla. The missing person suffers from depression and the family is concerned for her well-being.

Why wasn't there a bulletin created for someone as important as Sam? *Because maybe she isn't missing. Because maybe Avery sent you up here to spy on Jack Beckham.* Why would she go through such extremes just to do that, though? *Her mental health rests on a needle.*

But Kadence—she *is* missing. This flyer tells me so. This hotel—*the Royal Hawaiian*—it's the hotel in the picture I've stowed in my files, the hotel with the gray Ford pickup truck parked out front. As for the dark-red Toyota Corolla, in that chronological police report (one of the few) witnesses saw a dark-red Corolla parked at Red Rock.

I keep coming back to this connection between Kadence and Sam . . . *Kadence* is missing. Maybe Sam was searching for Kadence through her work with The Way Home. Maybe Avery knew Sam had come to Topanga Canyon, following a lead, and saw the opportunity to send a mole into Beckham's world, a mole to gather information on her icon that she'd use for . . . blackmail? *Love me or I'll tell the world that you . . . that you . . .* What?

But what would've led Kadence to come to Topanga Canyon?

Some things are unknowable.

But not this thing.

Because the truth is out there.

And so is Sam.

26.

I've learned something about myself.

I don't like waiting for someone else to tell me when I can move. This waiting for Jack, who's waiting for Captain Walsh, is *killing* me. *Hold on. Soon. Hold on.* I keep telling this to myself, but every step I make that is *not* toward a rescue vehicle pulls tighter and tighter on my sanity.

I grab the tub of Percocet from my purse and then toss the bottle back into my purse. *No.* Even though this waiting is like counting down until the needle jams into your skin, like waiting for the dentist to pull your tooth.

My mouth tastes like pepper—ashes from outside coat my tongue. I retreat into the bedroom and throw a worried glance out the canyon-facing window. I can't even *see* the canyon anymore. Nothing is visible behind that smoke and the dull orange light from the smothered sun.

Is that a flicker of a flame way over . . . ?

I pull the binoculars from my duffel bag and peek out . . . not a flame, just a reflection. I push out a breath, then step back from the window. Instead of searching for fire, I peer at the yellow-inked inscription on the hard plastic of the binoculars' left barrel.

To Mom on her birthday.

Jack gave them to his mother, Liliana, on her birthday, paying for them himself like he'd paid for the Honda. Now that Liliana is most likely dead, he doesn't want them lost and keeps them in this bedroom as a memorial. He'll be grateful that I thought to grab these.

I return the binoculars to my duffel bag and run my tongue along my teeth. Everything tastes like pepper *and* sand now. When was the last time I drank water? I take one last look out the bedroom windows and at smoke winding through the oaks, laurels, and pines. Back on Wednesday, I didn't think this would be my life.

Water—I need water.

I shuffle to the kitchen and reach for the refrigerator door—

What the—

There, on the refrigerator door, beneath the Peace, Love, Topanga magnet . . . there's a Polaroid picture of me, standing in the forest beside that blue tent, my face racked with fear. There I am, lost Bailey clutching her elbows with terror bright in her eyes. I smell her fear—sweat and sagebrush—and I remember the taste of salt from her unfallen tears, and I remember hearing those buzzing bees and the taunts of the forest folk, and I remember the coming dark and thinking that I'd remain lost in those woods and never be found again.

Someone was watching me.

Who took this picture?

Ro Patrick?

Russell Walker, the great pretender?

How would either man get into the cottage . . . ? Maybe Jack let Ro in—the PI *was* following Avery. Maybe he was also following me.

I can't see the Polaroid picture—or *anything*. The tears in my eyes have blinded me.

Outside, the roar of helicopters grows louder, and even in this cottage, the weight of their steel bodies makes the air feel heavier. The distant cries of fire truck sirens grow louder . . . louder . . . like they're right outside the cottage.

Has Captain Walsh arrived to personally escort us to the evacuation zone?

I pluck the Polaroid from the fridge-door magnet, stick it into another pants pocket, and then quickstep over to the living room window. The sirens sound so close, like the bright-red trucks are parked in the driveway up front.

A radio bursts with static.

I hear the faraway shouts of men.

The firefighters *are* here!

I run back to grab my phone from the nightstand and the handles of my duffel bag and suitcase. I drag all of my stuff to the front door and reach to turn the doorknob.

The doorknob doesn't twist. No give at all.

Just like the garage door, I now can't open *this* door.

I wipe my sweaty hands on my hoodie, and then deliberately turn the knob.

The knob doesn't turn.

Still no give.

Dazed, I stare at that silver doorknob before grasping it again and letting its metal warm in my hold. I count to ten, and then, with great patience and deliberation, I turn the knob again.

The knob will not turn.

You're fucking kidding me.

Outside, more static bursts from nearby emergency radios. Men are speaking and shouting and updating and commanding, their voices deep and filled with urgency.

Fear snakes from my hands to my brain as I bang on that stuck front door and shout, "Help! I'm stuck! Hey! I'm in here!"

A fireman dressed in full gear—he's the same brown-haired engineer I met during that meet-and-greet with Captain Walsh—lumbers toward the swimming pool. He's wearing a dirty yellow coat and pants, hard hat, and tanks of oxygen on his back. He holds up a cell phone and takes video of the pool, the cottage, and all that overgrown brush spreading across the north-facing sections of the estate.

I keep banging on the door. "Hey! Help me! I'm stuck!"

The engineer peers at the inky sky, squints at the helicopter cutting through the drifting smoke and flying ashes.

I kick the door, but the thundering bird drowns out my noise.

The brown-haired firefighter turns and heads back to the main house.

Climb out the window! Go!

I run over to the living room windows—there's no latch to slide open the windowpanes.

I run back to the kitchen—there's no latch to open these windows, either.

Back in the bedroom—these windows don't open, ohmigod.

I'm a prisoner.

Cell phone out—and full bars still—I tap the phone number Jack gave me last night—he can't forget that I'm still back here. *Trapped* here.

The line rings. Calling . . . calling . . . connecting . . .

"Jack," I shout.

"Welcome to Callin' Oates," a recorded voice says, "your emergency Hall & Oates helpline. To hear 'One on One'—"

"What?" I end the call and redial.

Calling . . . connecting . . .

I say, "Hello?"

"Welcome to Callin' Oates—"

Did I enter the number wrong last night?

Doesn't matter right now, cuz bitch? You trapped.

I race to the kitchen and rummage through the cutlery drawers until I find . . .

A meat tenderizer!

I hustle back to the living room.

Someone's now banging on the front door.

It's the woman from the woods, and her wide eyes are bloodshot from the smoke. "You gotta get out of there!" she shouts, now twisting the knob from the other side of the door.

"It's stuck," I shout even though I know that she can't hear me. "Stand back—I'm gonna break the glass!"

She peeks through the window. "Are you in there?"

"I'm right here!" I shout. I'm standing right in front of her.

But she keeps squinting into the cottage—she doesn't see me *standing there right in front of her*. She doesn't hear my shouts or cries.

I can't give up, though. I shout, "I'm breaking the window," then slam the meat tenderizer against the windowpane.

Thwap!

Wide eyed, the woman hops back—she felt that hit.

The wooden handle of the meat tenderizer bounces in my hands.

The glass doesn't break. The glass doesn't even *crack*.

I swing the meat tenderizer again.

Thwap!

The window stays whole and immaculate, unbreakable.

The woman from the woods pulls a knife from her hiking boot.

My stomach drops to my knees. "No no no no no!"

The woman slides the knife against the fleshy part of her upper arm.

Vivid red blood pebbles bright against her grimy skin. Tears now tumble down her cheeks as she dips her index finger into that bright blood now slipping down her biceps. She writes on the window, and the bloody letters appear backward to me here on the other side of the glass.

I dash to the bathroom, grab the hand mirror from the sink counter, and return to the living room.

But the woman from the woods is gone. At the end of her ensanguined message: a crinkled white flyer stuck to the window, glued there by a glob of blood.

I hold up the hand mirror to first read the backward message.

RUN DANGER

And then, I read that flyer . . .

COME MEET TWH FOUNDER

SIMONE "SAM" MORRIS

APRIL 26, 2019—7 PM

MOUNT BETHEL AME CHURCH

And beneath those words, there's a picture of . . . me.

Los Angeles County Sheriff's Department

911 Call From #13-39741211
Legend:
OP = 911 operator
CA = Caller
Location of Call: 691337 Santa Ynez Trailhead
Date of Call: Wednesday, November 10, 1993
(The following may contain unintelligible or misunderstood words due to recording quality.)
OP: 911. What is your emergency?
CA: I'm up at the Santa Ynez Trail in Topanga, at one of the emergency phone stations off [unintelligible] Vereda De La Montura and um, you need to send somebody up here. There's a dead person laying right off the trail.
OP: Okay. Stay on the line.
CA: —looks like [unintelligible]—
OP: Hold on, sir.
CA: Yeah. Sorry about that. Just a little freaked out.
OP: You're doing good. Okay.
CA: —come up here all the time and wow.
OP: Repeat the address for me one more time.
CA: I'm in the parking lot at Santa Ynez, you know, where the waterfall is? The trail is about a mile away. We're standing where the fire burned last week.
OP: Okay, they're on their way. Tell me what happened.
CA: My girlfriend and I were just walking our dog Cher and let her off-leash. I know we're not supposed to. There are rattlesnakes up here. But we did. And Cher got stuck in the brush, and when we went to pull her free, we thought she'd got tangled up in old ropes or something, but it was, like, a skeleton.
OP: Okay. All right. Stay on the line with me, sir. Okay?
CA: Yeah. My girlfriend is pretty shaken up.
OP: And you're not on the trail—
CA: [unintelligible]
OP: Would you know how to get back to the trail to show the emergency team?
CA: Oh, definitely. Like I said, we come to this trail all the time. First time

since the fire. Maybe that's what happened. Whoever it is got trapped and, you know, died there?

OP: Can you describe [unintelligible]? Where you [unintelligible]?

CA: At the place with the chimney or fireplace and nothing else? The bones and all that stuff are inside.

OP: Inside the chimney.

CA: Like where the logs go to burn? There.

OP: Very good, sir. The team will be there shortly, but please stay on the line with me.

CA: [unintelligible] —wanted to know if we're gonna be fined for having our dog off-leash?

OP: Well, thank goodness he was.

CA: She. Her name is Cher, like the diva?

OP: Just stay on the line.

CA: How much longer?

OP: The fire department is almost there. Fortunately, they were training near—

CA: I see a fire truck. The firemen are—[unintelligible]

OP: Okay, sir. You can go ahead and hang up.

CA: Thank you. Bye.

OP: You're welcome. Bye.

27.

RUN DANGER

Run?

Where?

I can't even see the big house anymore, which means I can't see anything coming from that direction. And, physically, I'm stuck to my spot because I'm still staring at a picture of myself on this wild woman's lecture invitation.

> As the founder of The Way Home, Sam Morris knows firsthand about the horrors of a loved one going missing—and the trauma that occurs afterward. In this seminar, she will share ways to manage the case-work during your beloved's investigation while also offering resources that will heal your heart and foster the strength you'll need throughout the search—and recovery—of your loved one.

> Connect with law enforcement agencies, private investigation firms, clergy, and social workers to help you navigate this journey with purpose and understanding.

This picture makes no sense, because I am not the founder of anything. I'm just a rookie private investigator in search of a missing woman, *the* Sam Morris. Also, I am not Sam Morris, because my official California driver's license tells me who I am: Bailey Rose Meadows. We decided to keep *that* real. Yes, I *do* live on the 4500 block of . . . maybe the graphic designer of this flyer somehow mixed *my* photo with Sam's. That *has* to be what happened.

My stomach spasms the longer I stare at my picture. The blood used as glue darkens and dries on the windowpane, and the wind pulls at the edges of the flyer until it tears away from the glass, swoops and loops into the air, and lands in the ash-filled swimming pool. All that's left to see are those smeared, bloody words, the blackening sky . . . and Jack emerging from the smoky nowhere to bang on the cottage's front door.

"What the *fuck*, Bailey?" he's shouting.

My heart jumps in my throat, and I blink—*How long has he been standing . . . ?*

"What are you waiting for?" Sweat pours down his dusty face. While his gray eyes aren't manic or rolling in his head like a frightened stallion's, he's definitely on the road.

"The door won't open," I shout back, knowing that he can't hear or see me—no one else could.

Before he enters, I quickly slip the gun from my hoodie pocket and shove it into the only empty pocket of my cargo pants.

Outside, Jack places his thumb against the smart-lock touch pad. *Click.*

The door opens as easily as any door in modern Los Angeles.

"Bailey," Jack says, his arms out.

I throw myself at him, relieved to touch *someone*, thankful to have that door open again. "I've been stuck in here all this time," I say.

"Stuck?" He places his hands on my shoulders.

"The door wouldn't open." I move over to the windows. "And none of the windows would open or break—I tried. I was trapped."

Jack shakes his head. "The windows don't break, but they *do* open. It's not some unpermitted backyard bootleg apartment—they're *required* to open." He strides over to the window, then lifts the pane from the bottom. "And the door," he continues.

He swipes his wrist across his sweaty temples. "Well, the smart lock *will* freak out sometimes, and with the power and Wi-Fi going in and out . . ."

Smoky air from the outside billows through the window screen and fills the living room.

My face burns with embarrassment. "I thought they slid left and right. I'm a little panicky right now, and I'm not thinking clearly."

He points at the dried blood on the window, now tinged brown and filled with ash and grit. "What happened there? Did a bird freak out? They fly into the windows all the time, especially when there's fire."

"Yeah," I say. "Probably couldn't see past the smoke. It just . . . *Bam.* Right into the *unbreakable* glass."

"Walsh and his fire crew stopped by," Jack says. "Told me that it's almost time to go. The fire is just a few miles away from the driveway, and it's bigger than anyone thought it would be." His eyes flick around the living room. "Make sure you take everything. We won't be coming back here for a long time. Get your phone chargers, medicines, all of it."

The phone between the mattress!

He rubs his temples and pulls at the already-pulled skin there. "I wanted to give you the Topanga Canyon experience, but not this kind."

Did you have that picture taken of me frightened in the woods? Cuz that *was the worst part of this experience.* Instead, I say, "What a page-turner this will be."

"Is this what you're wearing?" he asks. "You won't have time to change."

I pluck at my hoodie, then say, "Yep. I'm good." A teardrop rolls down my cheek—I refuse to let another escape. *Right now.*

He clips his head, shakes it, then sighs. "I'm so sorry."

I try to smile. "It's okay."

"Do one last check around the house, then meet me at the swimming pool. Keep the doors and windows closed, though, to keep out the smoke. I've switched off the HVAC. And I'll turn off the routers to keep all the smart tech dead. You won't have internet."

"I never really . . ." I swallow the rest. *You were supposed to bring a router-whatever back here.*

"Did you find Ro?" I say.

Jack flicks his hand. "I don't have time to worry about him—he's an adult. He can figure out his own shit." He points to me. "I'm responsible for *you*, though. So be ready in ten minutes." Then, he runs up the gravel walkway and disappears into the ashy gray.

"Jack," I shout. "What's your phone number again?"

Too late—he's gone. My eyes burn the longer I stand in this open door.

After plucking the Polaroid picture of terrified Bailey from my pocket, I slip that picture over the dead bolt to keep it from "freaking out" and locking me in again. Heart quaking, I close the door and pray that Jack will remember to disarm the smart tech.

My phone vibrates in my pocket.

A text message from Avery!

DON'T BELIEVE HIS LIES!

My hands shake, and I feel sick to my stomach. I want to say so much to her—*Where have you been? What mess am I in? Why have you been stalking him? What aren't you telling me?*—but I take a breath to force myself to stay calm in the chaos. Once my hands stop shaking, I clutch the phone tighter and tap:

Forest fire!

COME GET ME!!

AM I MISSING???!!

Ellipses bubble—she's replying.

I rush back to the bedroom, jam my hand between the box spring and mattress, and grab the cracked cell phone I found in Jack's car.

The HVAC thumps off—the air no longer moves, nor is it chilled.

Back to the found phone . . .

The shattered screen blinks to life—power! The lock screen picture is a frosty wineglass of rosé.

I swipe up, hoping that the phone isn't protected by a passcode or face recognition.

The desktop!

I tap into the photo album and swipe through the pictures . . .

A basket of perfect, dew-kissed grapes.

A goat wearing a blue kerchief around its neck.

Three pairs of hands—brown, browner, pink, holding clear-glass tumblers of wine the color of sunsets.

There's a picture of a woman with brown, wavy, shoulder-length hair. She's sitting with Margo and . . . *me*. We're captured in mid sip with rolling hills of grapevines twisting behind us. There's a roaring firepit and a sky of coming night. Face masks are left crumpled and neglected on the table.

Whose phone *is* this?

Every muscle in my back tenses as I swipe to SETTINGS.

Margarita Duran . . . but there's a picture of cutesy Margo Dunn, Jack's manager, in the circle.

Margo's Latina? More than that . . . We've hung out before? And who is the third woman? And when did this wine-time happen?

Wait.

Margarita Duran . . . that name shows up in the police's chronological record.

. . . photograph to Margarita Duran and groundskeeper in the area. She has seen a similar person depicted in the photograph 2–3 months ago but not recently.

So, yes, the police *have* come to the estate. And yes—Margo knows more than what she's shared. I peer closer at the woman I don't know . . . except maybe . . . those sad, tired eyes don't meet the smile on her face. I know her . . . this woman holding that tumbler of wine . . . wash the dirt off the woman in the woods, and she'd be my wine-time friend. She just told me to . . .

RUN DANGER.

When was this picture taken?

I tap on the circled "I" for information.

Sunday, October 4, 2020.

How do I know the woman in the woods? Because we *do* know each other. That must be why she came back to warn me. In this picture, her arm is draped around my shoulders. We're being winos together— behold those hundreds of empty wineglasses on the table.

That flyer that she stuck to the windowpane with her blood . . . the caption beneath that picture of me . . .

Something clicks and rattles in my head, but I leave it alone so that it can become *more.*

I check back to see if Avery sent her reply text.

No ellipses.

That's because there are no signal bars—

What's that?

What's that sound beneath the heavy silence that comes once the heating and air conditioner dies?

Whirring . . .

Coming from behind me . . . barely there but insistent, like that mosquito buzzing in your ear at nighttime, buzzing you wouldn't normally hear over the roar of the HVAC or the low hum of a refrigerator motor or the crackling ice maker.

I tilt my head and close my eyes.

Yeah. That's whirring . . .

Like a video camera zooming in . . .

Silence again.

My eyes skip around—from the mattress and dresser to the futon and desk, and then up to the corner near the closet. I fix my gaze on the dresser . . . and the wax warmer.

The warmer is faux bronze and the face etched with an oak tree. The rest of the lavender-scented wax that I burned yesterday has hardened in the warming disk.

The whirring stops.

I remove the warming disk and peer inside.

There's nothing there except a small light bulb.

I yank the warmer's plug out of the outlet. Then, I go out in the hallway, to the small table set in the nook . . . I unplug that wax warmer, too, and hurry to the living room. There's a wax warmer on the coffee table. I unplug that one.

Over in the kitchen . . . there's one near the toaster. Why would *that* space need a wax warmer?

I unplug the kitchen warmer, then throw it to the ground.

The plastic body breaks, and the wax block skids across the tile floor.

I pick up those broken pieces and study the guts of the warmer . . . plastic pieces except for . . .

A camera the size of a USB plug.

There are tiny black words on the back of that tiny camera: SpyOnU.

Shit.

I'm being watched.

28.

Nothing on me—my heart, lungs, fingers . . . nothing feels real. All of me . . . I'm light as air. Because maybe I've died. And maybe I died because I'm now holding five hidden spy cams in my trembling hand. I know these cameras. While shopping for my pen, these SpyOnU hidden cameras were in the "Customers Also Purchased" carousel. Avery and I went back and forth on them, arguing to place or not to place hidden cameras all over the estate. "But what if they're found?" I asked then.

Just like I found these?

Who's behind these cameras?

Jack, of course.

Why does he have them?

Outside, Jack is kneeling beside the swimming pool. He dunks a plastic bucket into the water and carries it someplace beyond my line of sight.

How much has he seen me do?

Does he know that I have files in my suitcase filled with information about missing women? Does he know that I'm carrying a gun? That I shoved Margo's cracked iPhone between the bedroom's box spring and mattress? That my pen has captured almost all audio and some video of nearly all that's happened to me since my arrival on Wednesday night?

I stomp out of the cottage and into brutally hot, smoky air, into a world screaming with sirens and roaring, roving helicopters. My eyes sting from all the debris swirling in the air. My feet kick mounds of ashes as I rush to follow Jack northeast, past the potted trees and the overgrown lawn and into the crackling and shrieking wind and the echoes of sirens somewhere in the distance.

Where is he going?

What's way out here?

Where is *here*?

I stop, disoriented.

Where . . . ?

I peer down at the LA snow in search of his footsteps.

"Why are you just standing here?" Jack pops up to my left, the plastic pail in his hands now empty. "Are you ready to go?" He hustles back to the swimming pool.

I keep my head and eyes focused on where he's come from—the high grass in the distance.

I finally pry my gaze away and follow behind him. "Actually, I'm pissed off right now."

"*What?*" Irritated, he throws me a look. "You gotta speak up." He points to the shadow of a red-and-white, big-bladed, big-ass fire helicopter zipping low across the broiling sky—the sound of its rotors keeps me from hearing my own thoughts.

I shout, "I'm pissed off right—"

Jack starts walking again, and we reach the swimming pool.

"I *said*, I found *these*." I hold out my hand to show him the small spy cams.

He dunks the pail into the pool. As it fills with water, he looks back to see my outstretched hand. "Okay, so you broke up my shit? That's the only way those cameras can be in your possession right now."

I blink at the cameras, and then I blink at Jack. "Why were they *there*?"

Bucket filled, he stands from the tile. "Are you seriously asking me why I have a security system in my seven-million-dollar estate in the middle of a state park that is home to cougars, bears, meth-heads, and bling rings? You're *really* asking me that question right now?" He carries the bucket to a ladder set against the side of the main house.

"Are you spying on me?" I shout.

"Seriously?" he asks, gaping back at me.

I cross my arms. "Seriously."

"Yeah," he says, foot on the first rung of the ladder. "Because I didn't know you back on Wednesday. You're here because *Avery* recommended you. Avery, the woman who has trespassed on my property, who has stalked me all around the city, the woman who needs psychiatric treatment cuz she's *fucked* in the head. So, yeah, I watched you. To make sure you were who you claimed to be. Margo assured me, told me to trust you, but she also has a soft spot for that lunatic bitch you call a teacher."

"Wow," I say, shaking my head. "You're saying *all* the wrong things right now."

"But I *stopped* spying on you after we took our hike on Thursday morning." He carries the bucket up the ladder. "I wanted to give you a fair chance, Bailey, even after everything Avery's done to me. Like I said—"

He throws the water across the red clay tiles and then climbs back down the ladder. "The water hose has a giant leak, so I have to—" Breathing heavy, he reaches the bottom rung. "Wet everything by hand." With the sweaty soot on his face, he resembles a chimney sweep, or one of the men doing meth in the woods behind his house. He glares at me with watery, bloodshot eyes, then throws the bucket into the haze.

"You're frustrated," I say, "and I'm sorry for that. I'm sorry for piling on, but this?" I hold up the cameras. "This is something your father would do."

His fingers claw through his hair. "Do you know how *tired* I am of people comparing me to that man? I've worked my ass off to *not* be compared, good or bad, and I'm proud to say that Jack Junior is more interesting than him. A better thinker than him. Not cruel or violent like he was. My father would do *worse* than putting some cameras around his own property.

"And when I met you, Bailey, I knew that I'd finally become the man I wanted and needed to be, and I knew almost immediately that you were nothing like Avery, and for you to stand here and say that I'm acting like *him*?"

He takes a deep breath, squeezes his eyes closed as he holds in that breath before pushing it back out. Calmer now, he holds out his hand. "May I have my very expensive tech back, please?"

I drop the cameras into his palm.

He chucks the cameras into the swimming pool. "Satisfied? Would Big Jack do *that*, since you know him so well?" When I don't answer, he says this: "I guess I need to remind you of the contract you signed."

"Contract?"

"I emailed you a copy. It informs you that there are security cameras all around this property and that you acknowledge and grant permission to being recorded. It's the law—I needed to notify you." He cocks his head. "And you signed the waiver back on Thursday."

I start to shake my head no, but I stop. Because I remember:

Yes, I *did* sign that contract, right after waking up from nearly dying of coconut poisoning. The contract had been left on the dining table. Margo had rushed me, and I'd scribbled my initials and written my signature there—*under penalty of, I attest, more and more*—there and there without reading the terms.

My skin chills, and I whisper, "I know."

Jack offers me a frosty smile, then says, "It's almost time to go."

My numb feet push me past the pool as Jack's glare burns the space between my shoulder blades. This impossible sky of thick brown clouds will smother me. This ground—dirt and flagstone—is disappearing beneath growing piles of black and gray snow that will never melt or refresh, that will never be shaped into balls or magical men with carrots for noses and coal for eyes. This forest is now perdition.

The door of the guesthouse is still unlocked. I leave it cracked as I take a final walk-through of the rooms. I tap my pockets—journal and pen there, Glock here. The way Jack just went off on me . . . he's become unpredictable in his stress. Irrational in his despair. But then, so have I, now the Angry Black Woman with hands on her hips, breaking shit, demanding answers. But I'm justified in my anger. I can no longer "go along to get along." Now, with this threat of fire, I must survive. Which means that I need to be *real* Bailey.

DON'T BELIEVE HIS LIES!

Is Jack looking at a similar text message about me?

DON'T BELIEVE HER LIES!

I want to grab my shit and race the hell out of here. But if I leave, all of this will have been a waste. Something's not right, though. Either Avery is playing me, or Jack is. Maybe both are. The truth is out there—I can't leave when I'm so close to discovering it.

Never get desperate to complete an investigation. Whoever said that must not have ever been close to a big breakthrough.

I've grabbed all of my belongings from the bathroom. I quickly peek beneath the bed—there's my treaded sock and one of my flip-flops.

"Hey, Bailey, are you still here?"

I know that Valley girl vocal fry, and I poke my head up over the bed like a gopher. *"Margo?"* My surprise eclipses my anxiety.

Margo's face hides beneath a black Dodgers baseball cap and the rest of her beneath a black sweatsuit. "Where is he?" she whispers, peering over to the dresser.

I join her at the bedroom door. "The cameras are gone," I say, reading her mind, pissed that she *knew*. "I found them a few minutes ago. And Jack's throwing buckets of pool water on the rooftops because the water hose—"

"Is busted," she says, nodding. "I cut it." She blushes beneath that cap—even her hands flush pink. "Bailey, I'm so sorry for everything."

"We met before I came here, didn't we?" I say, tamping down my anger to get answers.

"Yes. It took me a long time to come to this decision, but I finally agreed to help. It hasn't been easy, you know? Jack's been my boss, like, *forever*. But I knew when my parents quit, not a lot of time would pass before I'd quit, too. They couldn't stand it anymore. Ma kept saying, 'Too much evil here,' and Dad had started carrying his pistol. So they left and became caretakers of a winery up in Napa. That's where you and the team met me."

Margo grabs my hand, slips a small plastic card in my palm, and pulls me into the hallway.

"What are you giving—" I snatch my hand back.

"You need to go with me *right now*," she says. "You're not safe here."

"Are you talking about the coconut or the fire or—"

"Ohmigod, the coconut," she says. "They told me not to worry because they had a million EpiPens and . . . and . . . they knew that you were allergic. And he told Luann to give it to you anyway. To see what would happen. That's when I had enough—"

"*What?*" I shriek. "You knew about that, *too*? How did they explain all of this to Dr. Torrance?"

"Bailey . . ." Margo places her hands, prayer-style, against her lips. "Dr. Torrance has been on a medical mission to Paraguay since 2019."

We stare at each other, neither of us wanting to say the lie aloud.

"If I'd had Wi-Fi," I say, "I would've found that out—"

"But Jack didn't *want* you to have Wi-Fi," Margo says. "Yeah, this place is in the boonies, but when you're rich, it's not as isolated as it truly is. He has the best in everything, including technology, and he's been controlling your Wi-Fi since Wednesday."

"What the fuck is happening?" I ask, squeezing my eyes shut. "Why is this . . . ? I don't understand."

"There's so much to explain right now," Margo says. "But that's why I'm gonna participate in the investigation." Her eyes now glisten with tears. "He tried to stop me, to keep me here, but I jumped out of the Porsche—"

"Your iPhone," I say.

"I lost it."

"I found it . . . *Margarita.*"

She covers her mouth with a shaky hand. Then, she exhales, relieved that the lie is off her chest. Teardrops tumble down her cheeks, and yet she still tries on her "it's all gonna work out in the end" smile.

But *I'm* not relieved. There's so much that I don't know. It's *not* gonna work out in the end. Not with fire and lies and . . . and . . .

"This—" Margo holds out her arms. "This is all a setup. I took that picture of you in the woods. You were terrified out of your mind. That's when I quit this job. My conscience couldn't take any more of this shit. I couldn't watch you—"

BAM!

A single gunshot makes me shudder, drop the sock and flip-flop, and fall to my knees. There's no pain sparking around my body—I wasn't hit.

Margo, though, crumples to the hardwood floor. Her Dodgers baseball cap has been blown off, and her red hair is now a tangle of blood and brains.

I have no air in my gut to scream—my lungs have twisted into paper balls. I can only gape at Margarita Duran, now sprawled beside me, and I can only stare at the space where her head had once been, a space now filled with microdroplets of blood, a gleaming silver gun as big as the world, and the thick, calloused hand holding it.

29.

But I'm still here and I'm still breathing. Still no pain. No parts of me have been torn apart by a bullet. I tear my eyes from that meaty hand and to the person attached to it.

Luann holds that silver gun like she's slept with it beneath her pillow for the last million days, like she's named it and vowed to die with it by her side. Her eyes—brown and flecked with gold—show no emotion, even after just killing someone. *Murder*—she's done that before. Those blowsy curls in her dark hair and that tiny gold crucifix . . . yeah, Luann was the hot one back in the day, her vim still uncontainable beneath age and a shapeless orange UTA sweatshirt.

Her lips are moving now, but I can't hear anything past the echoing boom of that .357. Once the personal chef from Texas aims the gun at my head, though, my senses snap and sharpen—I can now hear an owl sigh.

"You didn't have to do that," I say, my voice sounding weary and remarkably calm, like I'm talking to a toddler who just dumped her bag of Cheerios in the church pew.

"You tellin' me *what* now?" Luann asks, almost smiling. "While you're lying there as dumb as a prairie dog?"

I dip my eyes. Blood—Margo's blood, not mine—colors the wrinkles of my knuckles and the veiny skin stretched across the top of my hand. I swipe that hand against my cargo pants, leaving red smears on the cotton. I'm still holding the card Margo handed me, and I slip it into my sleeve.

"Time to tell the truth and shame the devil," Luann says. "Who *are* you?" She takes a step closer to me, gun still aimed at my heart. Droplets of Margo's blood also mix with the freckles on her gun hand and the cuff and forearm of Luann's sleeve.

"You ain't Bailey Meadows," she says. "According to *my* research, 'Bailey Meadows' is either a comedienne living in Seattle, a fundraiser in Memphis, or a cricketer in New Zealand. Not a fortysomething-year-old Black gal who drives a Volvo and enrolled in some stupid extension writing class at UCLA and goes into anaphylactic shock after one glass of fruit punch. Guess we'll find out soon enough when your fingerprints come back."

"Fingerprints?" I say. "I never gave anyone my—"

You gave one print of your index finger to use the smart-lock touch pad for the front door. You freely offered that print to Jack.

That one print will tell an employer if I've robbed a bank or assaulted a stranger, if I've been busted for a DUI or used a notary public to sign mortgage papers. That single fingerprint is the most dangerous print in my life at this very moment.

My tongue freezes to the roof of my mouth. The vessels behind my eyes pulse, and my vision blurs with tears. "I—I *am* Ba-Bailey Meadows," I stutter.

"Bullshit." Luann cocks the revolver. Waves of her body heat roll over me.

I close my eyes as the warm end of the gun barrel taps my forehead. A teardrop tumbles down my cheek and slips into the corner of my mouth. Salt and sweat hit my tongue, adding to my growing nausea. "I—I—I'm nothing," I stutter. "I'm no one. I'm just . . . a . . . a . . ." *A devoted friend. A PI in training. I'm not Magnum, P.I. I'm not even Nancy Drew or . . .*

The metal leaves my forehead. The gun clicks. The heat of Luann's body breaks off.

I open my eyes.

Luann studies me as swaths of firelight break through the living room windows. Beyond that unbreakable glass, the world grows smokier and windier, and pebbles hit every surface like raindrops and hail. Color no longer exists beyond that unbreakable glass. Up and down no longer exist, either. Who will survive out there? And who will survive in here, inside this cottage, with guns and cons and a woman already dead in the hallway?

If I ever see the sun again, if I ever see one of those famous blood-orange skies made by simple smog and not fire . . .

"Who do you think you are?" Luann asks. "And that's one of them rhetorical questions, because . . . *girl.* You tried to trick Jack into believing that you're a *writer* writer, first of all. I warned him about that. So, he ran your writing samples through some fancy software program, and seventy-five percent of it was written by other people. 'Inside us there is something that has no name, that something is what we are.' You didn't write that. José Sara-somebody, the one who won the Nobel Prize—*he* wrote that. And then, on top of *that,* the part I find more ridiculous than you plagiarizing? You thought you were some kind of temptress."

"Temptress?" I say, shaking my head. "To who? I've never once *flirted* with Jack—"

"Don't lie to me," she says, "You flirted—I seen it with my own eyes—and he totally rejected you." She chuckles. "As Jack's number-one fan, I can safely say on behalf of his readers all around the world: *nobody* wants to read that."

The older woman gives me the up-and-down. "He needed to try something new, to write a book that's never been written before, but he can be such a . . . a . . . *man* sometimes. He actually thought you could be his next leading lady cuz you're pretty, and sometimes you say interesting things. Well, plot twist, darlin'. This ain't BET. Not interested."

"Luann, I've never hurt anyone," I say, sadness filling my core. "I've never—"

"Girl, you're slicker than a boiled onion." Luann snorts. "But you know what? We're glad you're here. Jack needed a bestseller—he got bills to pay, darlin'—and you're helping him do that."

She holds out her free hand and waves it around the room. "Welcome to the Beckham living laboratory. You're our first guest. Don't worry: no one can see past these windows and into this little house. Which means no one can see our pint-size black rat—our *anonymous* rat—selected for this new and innovative workshop. Jack is doing what his favorite writer was famous for."

But Thompson didn't *do* things to people—he joined them, he smoked that shit, he rode those hogs. Jack has risked nothing—he's watched *me* do it all. *Like Hunter S. Thompson, but fiction . . .* Jack said that, and not once did I think he was talking about *me.*

That feeling that I was being watched, hunted, and haunted wasn't just me being a city girl in the forest. That feeling was real—I *have* been watched and manipulated my entire time here. And now, I have every reason to worry, because down at my feet, Margo's blood is oozing onto the teakwood floor and seeping onto the rubber soles of my sneakers. Her eyes stare at a ceiling now splattered with pieces of her. *This is all a setup,* she'd told me. But not this part. Her sweatpants are darkening as her dying bladder relaxes and releases.

"The only person who knows you're here is Avery," Luann shares.

"Ro Patrick knows that I'm here," I say, chin up, defiant.

Luann guffaws and gapes at me with eyes full of wonder. "Hon . . . Ro Patrick helped me clean up Jack's office after we locked you down in the garage." She tsks, shakes her head. "Ro Patrick *owes* Jack. His daughter would be deader than buzzard bait if it wasn't for Jack. So again, Ro Patrick ain't runnin' to report you being here if *I* say you don't exist."

"Avery—" Her name dies in my throat.

"Avery just got a long-deserved bullet in her brain," Luann says. "That was this one's"—she pokes Margo with her foot—"last job this morning. And Ro saw her do it. He sent me pictures and everything. So, no. Avery ain't comin' to save you, hon.

"No one's gonna rescue you, especially since there's a big-ass fire burning down the world right now. You *will* disappear off this planet, Bailey Rose Meadows, and no one will give a flyin' fuck. But thank you for your service—it'll put Jack back on the bestseller lists again."

"Who's to say he won't do the same to you?" I ask, trying to put some bass in my voice.

"Do *what* to me? Make me the heroine in his novel?" The cords of her neck tighten. "He doesn't see me like that. I'm past my prime. Unfuckable, according to him. I'm not arguing that he's wrong, cuz he *is* wrong, but you know what? That man has taken care of me, and he's helped me get my life right. And he includes me in all his life decisions, including about book stuff, cuz my opinions *matter* to him cuz his *books* matter to women like me. He *sees* me. He can relate to women like me. And when he chose *you?*"

Her lips curl. "What a fucking betrayal. He tried to explain it to me, slow-like, talkin' to me like I'm a piece of bacon that don't sizzle. But once he told me everything?"

Luann's eyes shine, and she grins again. "Let's just say . . . I'm *thrilled* that it's you, not me."

My mind jams from one thought to the next, then—

Pain explodes near my nose, and I cry out as I stumble across the room and fall back against the coffee table. White-hot fire jams my side and takes my breath away. My nose burns, and I taste blood, dirt, and smoke. Something sour and sharp blisters my throat. My hip feels warm and wet. Can't hear anything except for a high-pitched single note. My head pounds and scratches, full of broken glass.

Luann wipes blood off the gun. This time, that blood is mine.

"You're right," I gasp, my ears still ringing. I run my tongue along the inside of my bloody lower lip. "I *don't* know who I am. I *don't* know *where* I am. No one will believe me. *I* don't believe me. So let me go. *Please?* We need to leave this place, Luann. The fire—"

"Did you ever finish reading *Old Topanga Road?*" Luann comes to stand over me.

"I—I didn't get to finish."

"Of course you didn't. Spoiler alert. The girlfriend dies. The book before that? *The Overlook*? Spoiler alert. The girlfriend dies. And the book before that? *Fire Loop Road*? Take a guess. The girlfriend dies.

"But they all die a good death. They were smart, resourceful, witty, fully realized women, but they were the same, one after the other. Jack tried to kill 'em in new ways, but the critics started calling his stories 'unbelievable' and claiming that he knew nothing about true fear, and that he couldn't write women, and that he—Jack Beckham—had now become the master of torture porn. *Porn!* Words matter, hon, and his words ain't porn.

"Girls die in real life all the time. Jack's only writing what he's now seen firsthand and experienced by watchin' you. Like Method actin', you know. He's braver than the first man who ate an oyster."

Luann's jaw hardens, and a muscle beats around her mouth. "His publisher dropped him, can you believe that? After all the money he made them? And *why* did they drop him? Other than calling his work *torture porn*? They lied about him being late turning in a manuscript and about him missing deadlines. But he was dealing with his health, and then Finley, *that* bitch, stole his energy. He told them he was having a hard time. Who can write under all that stress?

"But it just didn't matter to them New York fuckers. It's all about the almighty dollar for them. But wait until they read *this*, though. They're gonna all be *begging* him for it! Oh, yeah, he has a hit on his hands with *this* story. It has to be big if he's gonna keep this place out of foreclosure. He ain't gotta worry, though, because women like me? We're gonna lap this shit up. This book's about to be sweeter than stolen honey, and I can't *wait* to get my hands on some pages."

She crouches beside me.

I scoot away from her and back against the short wall beneath the windows. I swipe my hand across my lips and shudder at the sight of bright blood against my fingers. I grab my knees and tuck in my aching head, making my back the stone shield I need it to be. I swallow more of my blood along with bile and ashes and pray that this magic mixture will numb me.

I want to see the sun again . . . I want to eat another pastrami burrito . . . I want to bitch about traffic . . . I want to take a deep gulp of big-city air and hold it forever in my chest like it's worth all the big-city air in the world . . .

"It's time to evacuate," I shout from my ball. "Captain Walsh—"

"Told us to leave a long time ago," Luann says. "He's not coming back."

No no no no no.

I can't die, not like this. Please, no.

"The bunker," I shout, peeking out at her again. "Are we gonna hide in the—"

"We?" Luann lifts her eyebrows.

Not *we*.

My abdomen flexes with sad laughter. "Of *course*, not *we*. Being kind would be off brand, right?"

Luann smiles. "You don't know *mean*, hon. Big Jack . . . now *that* man was mean. Brought Miss Liliana back from that cult in Montana and made her pay for deserting him. Kept her tied up and left her out there in the high grass. Then, he wrote his biggest, most popular story about it. A bestselling book. A smash hit movie. That's where Jack got inspiration for *this* story."

She shakes her head, and then she stares at the floor. "*My* Jack dispatched her out of kindness and mercy, but he couldn't free her—no key to them cuffs she wore."

Cuffs? Dispatched? As in . . . *kill?*

"He thought his daddy would finally free her when she died," Luann continues. "Bury her body somewhere on the property. But he didn't. Big Jack kept her there until *he* died and . . ."

She runs her tongue over her dry thin lips. "*That* became Jack's first novel—the first Hiker and Canyon Creeper story, and it sold millions of copies because he experienced it firsthand. I read that book in three hours."

Luann's lips relax into a sneer. "You will die, too. *For real.* But it won't be too much of a loss, seeing that you don't *technically* exist, Bailey Rose Meadows."

I *do* exist—the way pressure is building in my head, the way my nerves twang like breaking strings in my arms. This pain means that I'm a real living person.

Luann backs away from me, her eyes flat, emotionless. "Jack really thought you'd be a more interesting character just cuz you're Black." She snorts. "That was his cock talking more than his head, and if that ain't a fact, God's a possum. But he finally agreed with me: you ain't no different than the tragic white girls in his other books."

The back of my throat clicks—no words. I can't speak words, I can't think words.

Luann's gaze picks over poor dead Margo, and she shakes her head. "We're almost done, Bailey Rose Meadows." Her gaze slips back to me, and she wags her finger at me. "Don't squat on your spurs now. We need an ending. Better make it a good one."

ME, MYSELF, AND I

30.

Somewhere in the distance, a dog barks, a voice cries out in pain. Sirens and car horns and car alarms and house alarms all sound so far away that they may as well not exist at all. Yeah—even though Luann didn't shoot me, my head still screams with pain, my stitched-up hip aches, and the rest of my body is an hour away from breaking down completely.

That's better than dead.

I am alone again—and I'll take that over keeping company with Luann.

Although . . .

I'm not *totally* alone. All life continues to leak out of Margo, the help's daughter turned manager and reluctant partner in crime with a heart of gold. Why did she go along with Jack's plans? How could she cash paychecks with ink made of blood? How could she watch him do this to me for a *story* until she finally said, "Enough"?

The heat of my anger against Margo whooshes across my cheeks, and even though I'm enraged at her participation in this scheme, I still grab the comforter from the bed and drape it over her cooling body.

I fish the plastic card she gave me out from my sleeve.

Jack's expired driver's license, issued in August 2000.

Why did she give this to me?

I scan the card. *Address . . . Old Topanga Canyon Road . . . Height: 6'3" . . . Weight: 215 . . . Expiration . . . Date of Birth . . . Eyes: Blue . . .*

What, Margo? What do you want me to see?

I scan the license again but not understanding . . .

Don't have time for puzzles.

I tap EMERGENCY CALL on my iPhone, but there is no cellular signal.

The front door is open—Luann left it open on purpose, to see what the black rat in the maze would do next.

Outside, the world is now a burning hellhole, and the hillsides aflame, and the sky black with smoke.

The end of the world.

I can run into the forest and risk being trapped by walls of fire and smoke.

Or . . .

I can search for the fire bunker, hidden somewhere out there in the tall grass. Reach it before Luann and Jack do, lock them out and wait for the firestorm to pass. But the key—Jack has the key. I grab my red purse and dig my hand around for my set of . . .

Where are my . . . ?

Where are my keys?

Back in the living room, I dump everything in my purse onto the floor—two MAC lipstick tubes, a tub of lip balm, a tissue pack, my wine-colored leather wallet, a roll of twenty-dollar bills, and Visa gift cards . . .

No keys.

Did they steal my keys?

I place my head between my knees—I'm trapped. After taking as many deep breaths as I can, after trying to will away my body's aches and pain and tenderness, and failing, I return to the open front door.

The swimming pool is now thick with ashes, leaves, and tree branches. A safer refuge than the cottage, if needed. There's a problem with that, though. I may not burn up, but I could run out of oxygen and suffocate to death.

This house will be hot soon. Smoke will force its way through every crack and every window.

I close the door.

Luann said that I'd never leave this place.

Oh, but she's wrong.

How do I survive, though—the fire as well as Jack and his cook?

Just days ago, green lacewings and California sisters and mule deer, that mountain lion—all these creatures had served as the canyon's ambassadors. Green hillsides and blue skies, the sun, that owl hooting in the darkest night. And then, the canyons exploded . . .

Do something.

Before I can, I must make the best decisions. And to make the best decisions, I need information. General Patton stayed on the offensive, always moving, formulating plans and backup plans to win the Battle of the Bulge.

Start small to do big things.

First, I'll try to minimize my pain and dry swallow four ibuprofen. Not good for my liver, but what good is a healthy liver if I'm *dead*?

Next, I pull every towel of every size from the bathroom and linen cabinets. I wet each towel, then roll a few against the foot of the front door to keep out smoke. Then, I wince as I push the living room couch and the dining table over to that door to act as a barrier, stopping to rest a few times because my injuries combined with this physical labor are making me lightheaded. But I can't have Luann or Jack sneaking in here again. Over at the living room window, I make sure the window levers are locked.

No one can enter this place without me knowing first.

My soles are blood-sticky as I step over Margo and hurry back to the bathroom. I pull the stopper in the bathtub, then fill it with water. I dump more towels into the filling tub—these towels will block the space under the bathroom door if I'm trapped. Then, I hurry as fast as I can back into the bedroom, wincing all the way. I ease down to the floor on the side of the bed that faces the canyon—don't want anyone watching me from the main house—and I dig into my suitcase for all the file folders I'd brought with me.

I grab the orange file folder and flip to the last few documents toward the back cover.

There's a picture of me with my hair styled as a wavy bob. I'm wearing a badass red pantsuit, shaking hands with a mustachioed white man wearing a police uniform. We both hold a framed certificate. The caption beneath reads . . .

> Simone A. Morris receives from Police Chief Charlie Beck 2018 "Civilian of the Year."

I blink. *But I'm . . . I'm . . .*

> Morris, vice president of The Way Home, a nonprofit committed to bringing missing people home, works in partnership with LAPD's Missing Persons Unit officers. Since its founding in 2000, Morris and The Way Home president, Cheyanne Carroll, have helped to solve more than one hundred missing persons cases.

Blood drains from my face as I stare at that picture, at that caption, at that picture, and I . . .

I . . .

. . .

My shoulders twitch. My cheeks burn. My vision swims.

I'm . . . just lounging on the floor, file folders and contents of file folders spilled all over the carpet. My back is against a bed, and I'm clutching an orange folder in one hand . . . and the autopsy report of a Jane Doe in my other hand.

> Burned body of a young female . . . The body is charred . . . revealed a gunshot entrance wound in the hard palate, a bullet track through the anterior . . . Opinion: this is a fatal injury. A second close-range

gunshot entrance to the neck traversing the trachea . . .
Opinion: this is a fatal injury . . .

I sweep past other documents: evidence reports on items found with Jane Doe at the cabin ruins and fireplace off the Santa Ynez Trail in Topanga Canyon. Case update written by Avery Turner, the detective in charge . . .

I flip past incident reports, interview transcripts, and newspaper clippings until I reach a stapled bundle of reports, starting with a memo dated April 22, 2018.

1993 Jane Doe #78 Murder Victim Identified after 25 Years.

Robbery-Homicide detectives continue to seek more information regarding the 1993 murder investigation of Theresa Morris, also known as Jane Doe #78. On November 10, 1993, the unidentified victim's body was discovered in the brush off the Santa Ynez Trail in Topanga Canyon. She had been burned from the recent Old Topanga Fire, but investigators discovered bullet wounds in the victim's head and neck.

Theresa Morris, born November 2, 1964, died November 2, 1993. She was 29 years old.

The sticky note on the back of this document reads:

Send death certificate to Mom's insurance company

I flip to the next page: a printout of an email string.

Date: September 6, 2020, 10:33 am PST

To: Avery Turner <Avery.Turner@mpulapd.gov>
From: Simone A. Morris <SAM@TWH.org>
Re: Re: Subject: MOM

I know, but you've used CIs before to solve a case. You've relied on drug addicts and drug dealers to go into situations to get you the information you needed. USE ME—I have extra motivation. *This is my mother!*

Date: September 6, 2020, 11:13 am PST

To: Simone A. Morris <SAM@TWH.org>
From: Avery Turner <Avery.Turner@mpulapd.gov>
Re: Re: Re: Subject: Mom

You're right, I have used less reliable people in investigations. But those cases don't involve their loved ones!

We keep doing this, Sam, getting closer and closer to understanding what's happening up there, and then it gets to the end of October, close to the anniversary, and you change your mind and we have to back off. What if you change your mind once you're up there? I can't risk that.

Date: September 6, 2020, 1:27 pm PST

To: Avery Turner <Avery.Turner@mpulapd.gov>
From: Simone A. Morris <SAM@TWH.org>
Re: Re: Re: Re: Subject: Mom

Ouch! As your colleague and friend, my feelings are hurt. I've *always* come through. That stings, being called a flake when I've helped so many families and the LAPD and this city! I'M READY TO DO THIS.

WE ARE SO CLOSE.

And I have a concealed carry permit now—I've completed 3 weeks of weapons instruction and boy, are
my arms tired. ☺ I used all my vacation time to train.
I'm ready, Coach. Put me in the FUCKING GAME!!!
From one motherless kid to a father searching for his
own daughter: let me do this. PLEASE???

IF NOT, I'LL DO IT WITHOUT YOU.

I'm not bluffing.

Date: September 10, 2020, 9:46 pm PST

To: Simone A. Morris <SAM@TWH.org>
From: Avery Turner <Avery.Turner@mpulapd.gov>
Re: Re: Re: Re: Re: Subject: Mom

Let me think about it.

By the way, thanks for the tip on Jane Doe #112. The
family just called. I admit: it's nice to have a civilian
as smart and persuasive as you out in the Wild West.
Gary's fine but he's an old school chauvinist who thinks
this work ain't cut out for "girls," ha ha ha. I'm coming
around.

As for the case. I know JB is hiding even more than we
know, including what happened to you and your mom
and his dad back in '93, and like I told you the day we
met: I will catch that bastard and you will finally be at
ease. There's no such thing as closure, but at least

this chapter of your life will close. See you tomorrow
at Norms. You can buy me a chicken-fried—

Someone somewhere knocks on a door.

I pause.

Another knock, this one more frantic than the last.

Am I supposed to answer that?

I swipe at my cheeks, wet from the tears still falling without me
knowing. I'm soggy with the frigid perspiration pooling in the small of
my back, the scoop of my neck, and under my arms. My abdomen and
lower back throb—did I fall? There's blood on my hoodie. *How . . . ?* My
pants legs feel heavy. My journal is in one pocket, folded papers shoved
in two pockets, Jack Beckham's driver's license in another pocket, and
in the last pants pocket . . .

My gun.

What the fuck?

There's blood drying in the fine lines of my hands. My face aches
like I've been hit. But there's no blood on the carpet around me.
There's no blood on the bed stripped of its comforter. This bed—
whose bed . . . ? This room—where . . . ? My nose hurts, and the skin
beneath my hoodie feels wet. Injuries after being jumped in Oakland
by some dude with a knife.

On wobbly knees, I stand, and then I send my eyes skittering
around this . . .

That bed and that desk and bureau and bathroom, these windows . . .

Where the hell am I?

Nowhere good, not with this blood on my hands, not with this
pain in my head.

I pull my Glock 9mm from my pocket and hold it out before me.
Muscles tense, I creep out of the bedroom.

At the end of the hallway, there's a comforter on the floor, spread
across a lump shaped like a body.

Panic shudders through my arms and hands and to the gun now dipping and swaying in my grasp.

Breathe. Focus. Take your time.

Whoever it is keeps knocking on the front door.

I tiptoe over to the living room window and peek out.

Hallelujah!

My partner in crime.

31.

"Sam, you're still . . ." The man chokes, tears in his eyes. "Are you *here* . . . right now?"

I tilt my head back to look at him—he stands well over six feet, and he's as broad and solid as a dining room table.

Together, we push the couch back against the door.

There's pain still sparking around my head and torso, but it feels dull.

"It's Zeus," he says, reaching out to touch my face. "Are you in Hades now?"

I step away from him, still speechless. Then, I double over, my hands gripping my knees, because just him standing here with me . . . my breath grows thin, and there's squeezing near my stomach, and I want to cry and I want to fight and I want to run out of this . . . this . . . *wherever the hell I am.*

Because I'm *not* okay. I haven't been okay since my mother went to jail for check fraud. And I haven't been okay since we drove to Topanga Canyon in 1993 to hike the trail that ended at a waterfall. Am I *here?* No, I'm not.

Avery's brown face is slick with sweat, his eyes red and puffy. The gray in his hair looks ridiculous—he didn't go to my hairstylist like I'd suggested. The bathroom-sink gray dye is now rolling down the side of his face. He smells as though he's wandered through fire to be here with me—and maybe he has. He's wearing jeans, a Privatas Security baseball cap, and a long-sleeved PRIVATAS SECURITY T-shirt that appears square and bulky underneath. Nothing screams "LAPD," which means Zeus a.k.a. Detective Avery Turner is probably still working undercover as a security guard. The name tag on his shirt reads RUSSELL WALKER.

Confusion coils through me. "Is something on fire?" I ask.

Avery laughs and scratches his right temple. "Yeah. You know, Southern California likes her little fires."

I watch him, sensing sarcasm—the smoky air in this house tells me that the fire is more than "little."

"Are we driving to Beckham's place now?" I ask.

Avery holds my gaze and says, "We *are* at Beckham's place. You've been staying in this guesthouse"—he holds out his arms—"since Wednesday night. You came here straight from the airport."

Oakland. My eyes go big, "Excuse me, what did you say?" big. "And the party for the guy with the overworked name?"

"You attended that party," Avery says, squinting at me. "Skylar Orion was his name. And a few days before you came up here, you flew to Oakland following a lead even though we were supposed to meet and go over what you were gonna do for this residency. You didn't show up to our meeting—we ran out of time—but I knew you'd be here. You're not a flake. You've always kept your word."

My mouth tastes salty. Feels like a heavy block is pressing against my forehead. The same sensation came over me that night before boarding the plane back to Los Angeles on Wednesday morning. I'd slept poorly, and I woke early, nowhere close to feeling refreshed. Like always, I'd been terrified to revisit the place that had taken my mother and had trapped me as fire burned all around the canyon. But then, I'd been excited to finally seek justice for Theresa Morris and even a little justice for me.

Seems like that night at Oakland International Airport was just . . . *last night.* Because that terror still burns in my gut, and I wanna cry, *I change my mind, I don't wanna go, I don't wanna do this investigation after all.*

Too late.

I'm already here.

"I look like a . . ." Avery flicks at his T-shirt and swipes at his filthy jeans. "The last time we stood together, I wore that bad suit from JCPenney. You called it my Mississippi pallbearer's uniform." He chuckles and peers at me. "Please, Sam. Please say something."

I open my mouth, and the hinges of my jaw creak. *"Something."*

He throws back his head and laughs. "It's a weird-ass thing, laughing with all that fire burning on the other side of the hill but . . . damn it, girl." He pats my shoulder.

I don't move, letting him touch me.

Outside, there's complete darkness—is it six in the morning or six in the evening? Somewhere out there, whole swaths of ancient forest are burning from flames that still want more.

Avery steps past me and gapes at the duvet-covered body behind me. "Who's *that*?"

I shrug. "Don't know. I haven't peeked beneath the cover."

Avery blinks at me, frowns, then pulls back the duvet. He mutters, "Margo," then places his fingers against the woman's wrist to check for a pulse.

"What?" I ask, horrified. "She's dead?"

He catches my gaze. "Did you . . . ?"

I shake my head again.

Truthfully, I don't know if I shot her. I don't know what I've been doing since the hospital, after being stabbed and boarding the plane bound for Los Angeles. I don't know how I got here or how Avery found me. I just now learned that I'm standing in the living room of the guesthouse at the Beckham estate with Avery's dead informant on the floor.

"Margo called me on Friday morning," he says. "She'd decided to work with us after all." He pulls the comforter back in its place. "Did Luann do this?"

I hold his gaze—flecks of amber spark in his irritated eyes. "Did who . . . ?"

"The cook. Jack's number-one fan. A dangerous woman."

We stand there in silence until I say, "I . . ."

Avery tells me that Margo had come to the safe house yesterday. That she'd changed her mind and wanted to tell everything she knew about the Beckhams.

"But all she had was a story," Avery says now. "She was coming back *here* to grab evidence, to record conversations, all that. Guess that won't happen now." He squints at me. "You still got that pen?"

"Umm . . ." I pat my pockets and whip out the writing tool from my hoodie—the blue light is no longer bright. "Guess it ran out of juice." I pull my journal from a cargo-pants pocket. The leather cover is bloodstained . . . and so are my pants. I tap my side—I feel undone. But not because of the stitches. Those are still intact.

"Why haven't you evacuated?" he asks.

"No idea," I say. "Isn't there a fire bunker on the property somewhere?"

He nods. "Leesa Hatfield—"

"You talked to her?" I ask.

"Better than that—*you* found her. Or maybe she found *you*. You didn't know this when you told me, but she's been living in that tent down in the woods. She looks a little different—that's why you probably didn't recognize her."

Leesa . . . after she left our office over a year ago, I thought I'd never see her again. I'd never seen her get so angry. We hadn't found her daughter, and all the leads had gone cold. Since she couldn't scream at the police, she screamed at me. Busted a mug and vase on my office credenza.

"I'm *looking*," I told her. "I would *never* lie to you about that. I'll never give up—you know in your heart that I won't."

But then, we lucked out earlier this year. Someone left a comment on the HELP US FIND KADENCE Facebook page: **I saw her on the trail in TC Red Rock. Maybe she's in the forest?**

Topanga Canyon.

Made sense: Kadence and Finley Beckham, Jack's wife, had been college roommates during their first year at UC Santa Barbara.

Leesa wanted to know when I planned to look.

I had no good answer—I'd failed each time I drove there for myself to search for clues related to my mother's murder.

Leesa stopped returning my calls, never giving up her own search. But then, Leesa—a writing professor at UCLA Extension—happened to read an announcement in the work break room about a writer-in-residence program supported by the Beckham Family Foundation.

Together with Avery, we devised a plan that allowed me to look for Kadence while immersing myself in the last place I saw my mother alive: the Beckham estate in Topanga Canyon.

Avery now leans against the couch and crosses his arms. "Before the fire, you were doing pretty good, doing everything you were supposed to do but . . ." He swallows and says, "I think something's . . . wrong. What's happening now . . . this feeling of being lost? I told you it would happen. I *warned* you that you wouldn't know where you'd end and where your made-up self began."

I shake my head. "But I'm good. I'm not lost. I'm here." A lie. A few months before I left for Oakland, I'd been worried after finding myself standing in the parking lot of a grocery store one time or at a pier another time, not knowing how I'd got there or even where the hell I was. Something was happening, something far beyond "Am I Bailey or am I Sam?"

Those brief moments of grocery-store fog had frightened me, so I'd started therapy again with Dr. Pham, going every week, twice a week, if needed. Dr. Pham and I talked about my mother, the father I never knew, and my depression after washing out at Quantico to become an FBI agent. And then, we discussed my mother's identification—she was no longer a Jane Doe.

The conversations after that . . . I'd needed Valium after one session. After another session, I stayed in my car and sobbed for hours. Too much—talking about it hurt me down to my first atom. She prescribed an antidepressant to help me deal with my trauma. But coming back to talk week after week . . . to drill down to my core . . . "No, ma'am," I remember telling Dr. Pham on that last appointment. "I know there's the other side where I come out, but what pieces of me will I lose? How much of me will be left?" And that was that. I never saw Dr. Pham again.

"On the day you were supposed to interview with Jack and Margo for this residency," Avery is saying now, "you just . . . *bailed.*"

I was very much myself that day. I just . . . couldn't return to that house off Old Topanga Canyon Road. Instead, I drove to Ventura and ate fish and chips on the pier. In the past, I've run to Carbon Canyon down in Orange County, cozying up against a redwood and reading *The Hobbit.* I've run to Cooper Canyon Falls in Angeles National Forest and found peace at a waterfall. But I never returned to the wilds of Topanga, even for a client, because that was . . . too much. Yeah, I was aware during those moments. Willfully bailing out.

And every time I left, Avery would go back to checking the morgues for unclaimed Jane Does just so that he could give me some news. None of them were ever Theresa Morris. Then, together, we'd drive to Skid Row and homeless camps all over this city and look for Jodie Turner, Avery's oldest daughter. She's been missing since 1988.

But investigators finally identified Jane Doe #78. Once I had my mother back, both Avery and I thought I'd settle down, but no . . . Leesa came to me with that Facebook tip, and I could no longer avoid returning to Topanga.

"It isn't like you to flake," Avery says, "except when it comes to *this* place. Your compass goes haywire. Makes sense. What you were about to do . . ." He shakes his head. "I'd get cold feet, too. I'd want to enjoy my last few days enjoying life, since we didn't know what would happen once you got here. Margo was kind—she changed your start date, gave Jack some excuse—COVID, probably—and you showed up right on time."

"Seems like it worked out," I say.

Avery had started laying the foundation of the investigation, taking on a new cover with the help of his old partners. They run Privatas Security, and they've allowed undercover detectives like Avery to dip in as security guards.

"I was wrong to doubt you." He shrugs. "You *did* get lost, just like I said you would. *Twice.* You're lucky I found you. You'd still be out there wandering the forest."

My heart still pinches beneath my skin. "But why didn't you try to contact me?"

His eyebrows furrow. "I *did* try to contact you. First of all, you kept blocking my phone number—"

"No way. I wouldn't have blocked your 626 number. I marked it as AAT."

"But I didn't use that number all the time," he says. "I told you I couldn't. This is an undercover operation, Sam. If someone saw AAT, they could've called that number and . . . guess where that number ends?"

You have reached the Missing Persons Unit of the Los Angeles Police Department.

"So, I used other numbers," he continues. "You texted me after your allergic reaction—"

"My . . . *what?*"

"You ate something with coconut," Avery tells me, "and you texted me, and I called, but the canyon kept dropping the signal. So I came up with that plan to see you in person."

I blink at him.

"You and Beckham were eating at the café, remember? I stopped by, said that you'd dropped a red scarf? A complete lie, but I got to see that you were okay."

I place a hand over my heart to slow its pounding. Red scarf. Me and Beckham. Coconut . . .

"But then I got a little too concerned," Avery says. "You acted like you didn't know me there at the café *and* when I picked you up at the trailhead."

Trail . . . head?

Avery nods, chuckles. "You went for it. All in. I know how that feels, being undercover, working and living as this whole other person. And I didn't want to disrupt the process. You were *supposed* to be Bailey, this other person. Like I said: it's happened to me a few times, so I understand."

I gape at him, clueless about everything he's talked about.

Avery swallows and tries to push back the tears now shining in his eyes. "And I came *here, now*, because you told me to come get you. And with the fire and what Beckham would do, I couldn't just let you . . . figure shit out. Didn't care that you'd be pissed with me calling it, but . . . it's just too dangerous."

Ice spreads across my scalp, and I close my eyes so tightly that stars spin and burn in my temples. I pinch the bridge of my nose—it's swollen, how'd that happen? I turn to see my suitcase and duffel bag in the hallway. A pair of binoculars pokes from the duffel bag. Though I can't see it from where I'm standing, there is an inscription on the binoculars' plastic barrel. *To Mom on her birthday.* I'd bought those glasses for Mom as a gift on her twenty-ninth birthday, using money I'd saved from gardening, babysitting, and collecting spare change found in couch cushions, in washing machines, and in the hand-me-down purses of our landlord, Miss Dorothy.

Mom and I had come here, back on the second of November in 1993, in her burgundy Honda Civic. That car . . . there was an ink stain in the seat—I'd dropped my calligraphy pen there once. There was a seashell hanging from the rearview mirror—Mom had won that trinket at the Santa Monica Pier.

"Sam," Avery says now, distress in his eyes. "I don't think you're okay."

"Just . . . give me a minute," I say, my mouth slick and funky tasting.

He shakes his head. "I think the stress of doing this high-stakes shit—" He spreads his arms. "You tweaked out a little—"

"Margo," I say.

We needed someone to help on the inside—that was Margo and, eventually, private investigator Ro Patrick. He'd been following Leesa around the city on Jack's retainer—he thought that *she* was Avery.

Avery told Ro about our investigation. Avery also told Ro that he knew that Ro's PI firm was not the most . . . *honest* PI firm. Avery didn't need to do a lot after that to *persuade* Ro to help us. Unless the situation has changed, Jack wouldn't know that his manager and his private investigator are now LAPD confidential informants.

"Eddie Skinner did a good job this time," Avery says now, grinning.

A master forger, Skinner worked with The Way Home and LAPD, providing fake identification and other personal documents for assignments like this.

"That driver's license in your wallet," Avery says, then whistles. "Even *I* couldn't tell that it's a fake. Glad to know that kid's on our side now. This fire, though. Everything's about to be destroyed. Any evidence we need will be ashes come Monday."

"Give me ten minutes," I say. "I'll get both Luann and Jack on this." I lift my phone. "Then, I'll find you—*where?*"

"Down at Leesa's tent—we have a route using fire roads, but—"

"But what?" I ask. "I'm good. I'm here. I'll be at the tent in ten."

Avery swipes his sweaty face with his shirtsleeve. "You know the rule, Sam. Never get desperate to complete an investigation."

"But if there's ever one time to break that rule," I say, "it's right now. I gotta keep going until I can't. Ten minutes. I'm not asking."

"I can arrest you," he threatens.

"I won't let you," I say, shrugging.

Once he sighs, I know that I've won.

I follow Avery to the kitchen, dull pain still working down my back. He lifts the window sash. Immediately smoke billows into the cottage along with all the sounds of the canyon on fire, so much noise that blends to become a mass of booms and roars. Avery knocks out the window screen and hops onto the sink.

I swallow the tears rising up my throat to say, "Hey, Zeus. Persephone here. Just picking some apples."

Avery sags a bit, comforted that, yes, I'm *here*, that I know our passcode, that all is well, and that we can carry on without interruption.

"Maybe Jack and Luann didn't see you enter," I say, "but they definitely have to be paying attention now. Please be careful."

"You know," he says, "once we go to court, and you tell people this story, folks are gonna blame you for everything. Some people are gonna feel sorry for *him*. They won't 'relate' to you or to Terri because you're . . . you're . . ."

"Yeah." I bite my upper lip and drop my head. "Doesn't make my experience less true, though. And really: fuck those people. Fuck all of 'em."

Avery says, "Bailey didn't curse this much."

I smirk. "That's because she didn't watch some psychopath rape her mother in this very house. If she had, bitch would've given zero fucks about fucking good manners."

Avery says, "Heard," then climbs through the window. "Ten minutes, meet me down at Leesa's tent." And then, he dips into the darkness.

◆ ◆ ◆

November 2, 1993
Topanga Canyon Boulevard

The smoke burned my eyes.

Mom tore her T-shirt in half, then wet both halves with the bottled water we shoved into our gray backpack before leaving the car. We had also stowed in that bag: potato chips, champagne, a few winning scratchers. "Tie it around your nose and mouth," she told me, sounding calm even as the muscles above her eyes jumped.

No other hikers had joined us on the Santa Ynez Trail, and so we couldn't gauge anyone else's reactions to those first whiffs of fire and that smoke climbing the sky on the other side of the hill. The canyon now smelled of acrid-burning wood, burning plastic, and melting rubber. Mom froze as she listened to the crackle and snap—trees splitting, trees falling. As a member of the all-female inmates camp that had helped manage the park and helped fight wildfires, Mom had become familiar with the sounds of normal tree fall and . . . *this*.

This made my heartbeat splutter in my chest and made tears fill my eyes.

"It's gonna be all right," Mom said, squeezing my hand. "Let's keep moving."

And we marched. Backtracking, we'd hoped, in the direction of the parking lot. Nothing looked familiar, though—smoke grayed out all color and every distinction.

"Terri!" The man's voice sounded like s'mores and cashmere.

"We're here!" Mom shouted.

I saw his denim work shirt as he ran to us, as we raced toward him. And then, he was right there on the path. Mom and I wrapped our arms around him out of relief.

"We're so glad to see you," Terri cried.

"And I'm glad to see you." Jack Beckham Senior kissed the top of Mom's head as though they'd known each other back in the day, and now, *finally*, they could be something.

"Come on," he said. "I know the way."

"You sure?" Mom asked.

"This park is my backyard," he said. "And every boy knows his backyard, right?" He winked at me.

We followed him, racing away from that smoke and away from our car, hiking up a trail winding between pink flowers and blue flowers, laurel trees and majestic oaks, passing a fireplace and a chimney with no house. Hiking up, up, up until we crossed through dense shrubs and stepped onto a tiled patio.

Mom said, "Wow," and gawked at the Spanish-style cottage and the rectangular swimming pool that shimmered blue, and the larger house with a red-clay tile roof that lorded over all the land like a watchtower.

I could still smell fire, but it reminded me of Christmas smoke, contained and fed by cords of wood bought at the grocery store. I also smelled honeysuckle, pine, and chlorine, and all of these smells offered comfort in the chaos.

"Aren't we gonna evacuate, though?" I asked. "The fire . . ." I pointed to the plume of smoke rising behind us.

"Too late for that," Jack said. "I missed the window to evacuate coming to search for you."

Mom touched her heart. "You shouldn't have done that."

"And let the fire take you?" He shook his head. "Nope. No way. And we have a bunker if it gets too close. Jack Junior's already down there. Come on." He led us over to the cottage.

Mom took my hand and kissed it. "We'll be okay."

But my heart kept losing its rhythm. Too much—*and not enough*—was happening.

"When are we going to the bunker?" I asked.

"Soon," Jack said. "Before we go . . ."

A pitcher of lemonade sat on a shelf in the refrigerator, and Jack poured us each a glass.

"There aren't any icy drinks down in the bunker," he said. "Enjoy while you can."

Mom chugged her lemonade, and Jack refilled her glass. I sipped mine and tore into the chocolate chip cookies left out on a plate. I settled on the couch, took a deep breath, and let out an exhausted sigh.

The floors were wood and the walls covered with framed black-and-white photographs of the canyon. That couch, busy with flowers and paisley, could hide any stain—my eyes couldn't land on one patch of fabric for too long. I smelled Pine-Sol and thought of hospitals and old-people homes I'd visited with Miss Dorothy on Tuesdays after school.

Mom and Jack stood at the living room window and watched the hills for fire. His gray eyes now bloodshot, he looked back at me and winked again. "A Beckham man has lived on this property for one hundred years," he said, "and will continue to live here for a hundred more."

I settled deeper in the couch cushions, fatigue settling over me like a weighted blanket. I yawned and fell asleep.

It was a woman's scream that pulled me from deep sleep.

I sat up on that busy-patterned couch, nausea foaming in my stomach.

Thick silence now.

My eyes skipped from the photos on the wall to the turntable and cabinet of vinyl albums. It was now dark outside—the only change my mind recognized.

Where am I?

The famous writer's cottage, the one who saved us.

My mind swam and my mouth tasted bitter. A coat of white, dried grit stuck to the insides of my lemonade glass. Was that sugar or . . . ?

"Mom," I called out.

The clock on the microwave said that it was almost eight o'clock.

How long was I asleep?

"Mom," I shouted again, spiders skittering over my heart.

My mother wasn't standing at the window, nor was she planted at the dining table.

Something was wrong—and it wasn't that fire raging outside in the canyon. No, something was wrong *inside this cottage.*

"No," Mom squeaked.

She was still here!

I hopped up from the couch. Beyond my heart jackhammering in my ears, I heard heavy breathing. I crept toward that sound of struggling, toward the sounds of slapping, smacking, and one throaty "Fuck!"

from Jack Beckham Senior. His voice wasn't warm and soft now. No, it was now hard and stone cold, a voice that chilled my blood.

Something crashed and shattered on the hardwood floor.

I crept closer . . .

Fear blistered the lining of my stomach—I wanted to vomit fire.

I crept closer . . . closer . . .

Until I stood in the doorway of the cottage's only bedroom.

My mother lay on the ground, her khaki shorts around her thighs. The famous writer was sprawled on top of her, one of his hands clamped over her mouth, the other hand clawing at her panties.

My belly shrank in on itself, and I wanted to scream.

Mom's eyes widened, seeing me standing there.

I ran back to the living room and grabbed an iron fire poker from the stand of fireplace tools. I ran back to the bedroom and swung at the man's head once . . . twice . . .

He slumped.

Mom shouted, "Go! I'm right behind you!"

I jammed out of that cottage, throwing a glance behind me to make sure that Mom was running with me. And she was there, fanny pack buckled around her waist, our gray knapsack back on her shoulders.

And we ran down that trail and into the smoky air, air so hot I thought my hair had caught fire. I tasted bitter smoke before it invaded my lungs, ready to choke me and steal all the oxygen I had just so that it could survive and grow. *Fire is a mean bitch,* my mother once said. *Even if you don't fuck with her, she gon' hunt your ass down—she didn't ask to be here.* You *the dumbass for bringing her to the party.* Then, Mom had laughed and offered me a salted plum pit.

And now, here we were, not only running from that mean bitch but also a rapist on two legs.

Mom shouted, "To the right," at the fork in the trail.

I hooked a right and ran, passing that fireplace and chimney without a house, racing deeper into smoke thicker than gravy. All I could hear were branches and trees and helicopters and my chaotic pulse and . . .

"Where to now?" I shot a glance behind me.

Mom wasn't there.

"Mom!" I cried out.

Fire caught in the treetops and hopscotched across the branches all around me.

Run, Simone! Go!

And I ran, alone, until I heard the grumbles of diesel engines and big men yelling.

A soot-faced firefighter shouted, "A girl!" He stopped me from running by crouching before me. "What are you doing back there?"

I gaped at him.

"Are you alone?" he asked.

Unable to speak, I sucked in a breath, my eyes feeling stuffed with cotton and water.

He guided me to an engine so bright red I could still see it with closed eyes. "What's your name?" he asked.

I shook my head.

The blood in my veins had muddied, and I tasted metal again. My name . . . *What is my name?*

I didn't know me back then, and years would pass before I remembered that I hadn't been alone that day in November. That I hadn't been abandoned by my parents. That Jane Doe #78, who'd been found in that fireplace without a house, who'd been found with a blue JanSport backpack over her head—not our gray one—would eventually be identified as my mother.

32.

Ten minutes will pass quickly if I don't act right now.

My face still feels swollen, but I don't have time to look or worry about what's broken and how it came to be that way.

Because the glow of the encroaching wildfire is blazing higher, closer, a red-and-orange inferno that crackles and pops with each snapping branch and tuft of grass that feed it. Even with the wet towels at the bottom of the front door, the smell of the burning trees and burning grass and dead animals seeps into the cottage. I return to the bedroom to pick up all the files that were spilled around me when I . . . *woke up*.

How is it that I've lived here since Wednesday night and have no recollection of anything that's happened or even how Margarita Duran ended up beneath this comforter mere minutes ago? I didn't shoot her—my hands don't vibrate like they do anytime I fire a gun at the range.

I stop at the bedroom's threshold . . . this is . . . this is where Big Jack Beckham . . . this is where he . . .

I take a deep breath, and it feels thick and crunchy in my lungs. I lift my phone and snap a few photos of this bedroom. It may never look like this again. Then, I swipe back in my phone's digital album—Jack Beckham Junior and mule deer, yellow and purple and orange flowers, a smoky sky, butterflies . . .

And there are pictures I took before my arrival in Topanga Canyon. A menu from Café Eritrea and Merritt Lake and an Oakland Police Department patrol car and a University of Oregon building sign and their duck mascot and a latte with a foamy heart . . . following leads on Kadence's movements after she left Baker, California.

I stop at the picture of me and my landlord, Miss Dorothy, standing in front of her smoky-lavender Barbra Streisand rosebushes. I've lived in her Baldwin Hills duplex since . . . *forever*, my mom and I living in the bottom unit. Miss Dorothy made the best crawfish étouffée, lima beans, and iced lemon cake, and she'd play her Miles Davis albums after church on Sundays. And now, I close my eyes, click my heels three times, and wish that I was back home on Miss Dorothy's couch, eating a hefty bowl of something good and watching *Judge Judy* with that old lady and my mom again.

I'm so far away from home, so far away from those days.

Oh.

Crap.

What if Avery runs into Jack Beckham on his way back to the tent and Jack Beckham kills him?

What if Avery runs into the fire instead?

What if I find myself all alone again?

My chest tightens, and I'm pushed closer to the edge . . .

No, I can't lose it yet, but I know—from the frizzy edges of my vision and the frizzy edges of my nerves—that I *will* lose it. *Soon.*

What happened to my mother and me on November 2, 1993? That question has always haunted me.

According to the autopsy report, Mom had been shot and killed. By whom, though? Big Jack Beckham. *Prove it.*

Mom's binoculars are in my duffel bag—Beckham actually had the *nerve* to keep them after we'd left them in this living room? And what did he do with our Honda? Trash it? Sell it? Drive it down to Mexico and leave the keys in the ignition? Has Jack Beckham Junior recognized me from Harvard-Westlake? Why would he, though? He was two years younger than me, so we never sat in the same classes or joined the same clubs. I was a no one, a scholarship kid and a geek who couldn't afford ski trips or car insurance or designer clothes or concert tickets to see No

Doubt that time or Janet Jackson that other time and *not even Bruce Springsteen?*

Investigators knew that Mom and I had come here to Topanga Canyon—they found her here, of course. And they knew we were hiking—the Thomas Guide showed highlighted maps and trails. The clerk at Hidden Treasures also confirmed that Mom and I had visited the store, and that we'd been lost. She also told detectives that Big Jack Beckham had offered to take us up to the trail. Beckham confirmed that he led us to the parking lot closest to Santa Ynez Trail, and he left us there and went on about his day.

Forensic techs found unidentified DNA in Mom's vaginal cavity when she arrived at the morgue as Jane Doe. But there hadn't been a man in the database that matched that DNA. Several years passed. Big Jack Beckham had been dead for a while, but his son, Jack Junior, was still alive and living in Topanga Canyon. The science of forensics had advanced since 1993, and now investigators were utilizing familial DNA—matching the unidentified DNA to biological relatives—successfully using it to catch the Golden State Killer, the Grim Sleeper, BTK . . .

I rummage through the contents of my suitcase.

A half-eaten Twix candy bar in a plastic bag. Jack Beckham Junior had been chomping on this Twix as I watched him at Cafe on 27, not far from here. He'd tossed the candy bar into the trash, taking only his cup of coffee before leaving to hop in his Porsche. I'd plucked the Twix from the trash can, hoping that his DNA remained on the chocolate cookie he didn't finish.

In case it didn't, though, I wanted more items either worn by him, half eaten by him, or spat on by him.

Did I find something? Hopefully—and it's in this suitcase and documented in this digital photo album. I swipe back . . .

Pictures of the Royal Hawaiian Motel in Baker, California, off Highway 15. Back in 2015, Finley, Kadence's old dormmate, had offered to help Kadence check into a nice rehab center in Malibu. But Kadence Hatfield flew out of Nebraska and landed at Ontario Airport instead of LAX. She drove from Ontario to Baker and stayed at the Royal Hawaiian. Extra wrinkle: Leesa Hatfield thought her daughter also flew into Oregon but didn't know when. Kadence returned to Southern California, but she never reunited with Finley nor checked into rehab. Finley didn't know where Kadence was—she figured Kadence had either changed her mind or had fallen back into drugs. Hikers, though, had claimed to have spotted Kadence at the Overlook, Red Rock, and near the Beckham estate.

The gray pickup truck . . . just a randomly parked pickup truck. Kadence drove a maroon Toyota Corolla.

I'd conferred with my contacts all around Los Angeles. Madelynn Stafford at LA County Registrar-Recorder records office. Forensic accountant Payton Wiggins for credit and debit card transactions. Realtor Javion May for apartments rented under Kadence's name or Finley's. Making every effort to find any trail left by her. I'd found nothing—Kadence had been raptured along with the other 521,705 people missing in America.

I need more to prove Jack Beckham's father killed my mother at this estate. If I leave and retreat to the tent right now, I may never have enough solid proof that some wicked shit has happened here, all of it involving Big Jack Beckham. Even if I've helped more than one hundred families reconnect with their loved ones, and even though I've received commendations from the city's fathers and mothers . . . no one will believe me, a woman who'd just experienced a fugue during this highly stressful situation.

My phone—the glass is cracked. Looks like a small hammer hit it. There's another cracked phone in my hoodie pocket. Both have enough battery to record. I will record Jack admitting this about his father and pray that either phone won't slip from my hands or out of my pockets.

I check the Glock—a full clip—then tap RECORD on both phones. I slip the mystery phone into my back pocket, and my phone in the hoodie.

There's a plastic card in the hoodie pocket—it's Jack's expired driver's license. How did I get this? I scan the demographics . . . *last name, date of birth, address—here, height—tall, weight—lean, eyes—blue . . . Why . . . ?*

I chew on this as I slip a thin-bladed boning knife from the block on the kitchen counter into my sock.

Beneath the kitchen sink, I find a box of face masks and a pair of plastic swimming goggles. I pull both on and head to the door.

Time to go.

I push the couch away and open the door.

Ohmigod . . .

The flames rage so close—the hillsides beyond the estate are glowing orange with embers. So dark out here now that I can't even see smoke, just that glow. I can't see the main house, either. I'm standing in another dimension of space and time, a place made of smoke and ash, where trees groan and cry as they fall into each other and add to the rolling booms that would make the bravest person shudder.

This world resembles the world back on that day in November 1993 . . .

I was a rat in a maze back then, and I'm a rat in a maze right now. I pluck out my journal and flip to the last filled page. A hand-drawn map of the Beckham estate. *Good job, Bailey.* This place is less of a maze now. I study the drawing, memorizing blocks labeled "Jack's office" and "library."

Where's the bunker?

Bailey didn't find the bunker?

I use the phone's flashlight to brighten my way through the darkness. Smoke and ashes blanket the stepping stones, the surface of the swimming pool, the world. Every step I take kicks up mini whirlwinds of what used to be just a week ago.

Slowly . . . slowly . . . I find the patio—the glass door is cracked open.

Remembering the floor plan, I creep down the hallway until I reach Jack Beckham's office.

No one is sitting at the desk or is curled up on the couch.

From here I can see out the windows and at that hillside across from the driveway in flames. From here, I can also see . . .

A square hole in the ground surrounded by high grass. There's a crumpled-up tarp covered with glued-on grass that is now pushed to the side. Not a blocky concrete aboveground bunker but an *underground shelter!* Does this mean that the bunker is unlocked?

Margo was supposed to leave the key to the bunker in my handbag. Did she? No—I didn't see *any* keys in my purse.

I open the bottom desk drawer—in one of her entries, Bailey had noted taking pictures of documents in these drawers.

Which?

I open the bottom drawer and grab an expandable folder filled with stapled papers, loose papers, and folded papers. But I can't carry this folder and keep my hands free. Maybe they'll have a better chance of surviving the fire if I keep them in this heavy wood desk.

I tiptoe over to the closet. A banker's box sits on the top of a stack of three cardboard boxes. I open the banker's box.

Manila envelopes . . .

There's a large, sealed envelope marked "Kad."

Kadence?

I tear it open: a silver class ring with a red stone in its center, a stormtrooper chess piece, and a miniature honey dipper.

In Jack's novel *The Overlook*, the main character had loved *Star Wars* so much that she owned a chess set with pieces resembling Han and Leia, Darth Vader and Luke, stormtroopers, and Chewbacca. She also loved tea and used a honey dipper, and she wore a class ring with a red stone.

Details all included in his novel . . .

I paw through the box again and find another envelope, this one marked "FB."

Finley Beckham?

There's a fountain pen, a puka shell necklace, and a pair of sunglasses.

Didn't another character from another of Jack's books *also* wear a necklace like Finley's? Didn't she also use a fountain pen to write angsty poems like Finley did? *Famished fiends as bright as galaxies ripping apart, a crackling symphony of sound . . .*

There's another big envelope in the banker's box, and it's marked "TM."

Inside, there's a single trinket: a short key chain with a small red plastic picture viewer from Magic Mountain.

I peek into the viewing window, and tears seize my throat.

In this picture, Mom and six-year-old me are wearing matching airbrushed jean jackets. We both have our hands on our hips—growing up together since she'd been only sixteen when she had me.

I stare at the viewer's yellowing picture until my vision clouds.

This fucker stole this from my mother.

I drop the viewer back into its envelope and fold it over until it's small enough to fit into one of my pants pockets. I now have proof that my mother and I were here back in 1993.

Ten minutes have come and gone.

Avery may still be waiting at the tent.

Or . . . Avery may be dead.

The bunker is my best choice for survival. I will shoot first, ask questions later. Jack won't get the drop on me.

Fucker.

I run back outside in the direction of the bunker.

Burning palm fronds from other properties drift from the sky and settle in the swimming pool. Other items that used to be something make fingers of flame in midair as they clunk onto the decks and patios of the Beckham house.

There! The rolled-up, camouflaged, and grassy tarp.

I pull at the large steel door.

Unlocked!

A ribbon of hope twirls in my heart. I've gone into dim, dark spaces before, searching for runaways and the abducted. I've survived those times. *Maybe I* will *survive this time, too.*

Gun in one hand, phone clenched between my teeth, I step down the ladder into the gloom.

The ladder ends, and after taking two steps, I'm in a dark room that smells stagnant and sickly. The walls feel close—and once I turn the flashlight back on, the walls *are* close—but the room is larger than it feels.

I allow my eyes to adjust to the bleakness and realize that it's not entirely pitch-black down here—a weak yellow emergency light shines from a corner.

"If you're in here, Jack," I shout, "pray now for forgiveness." The sound of my voice doesn't travel, and simply drops to my feet.

"Hello?"

Not Jack.

A woman. She sounds weak, craggy.

"Who's there?" I say, my breath tattered in my chest.

"Help us," she whimpers.

Us?

I step forward. The floor crunches beneath the soles of my shoes. I fish out the mysterious cracked phone—it's still recording. But now, I use it for video as I shine my phone's light on the stone floor. I turn, taking in this space slowly . . . slowly . . .

Filthy bare feet and . . . thin, bare legs . . . bony knees and stringy hair. The woman turns away from my light, covering her face in the lank hair of another woman, who is now staring at me with hollowed-out eyes. Both women are tied together with twine.

My heart chills. *What the . . . ?*

With her head still turned, the woman with the hollowed-out eyes asks, "Who are you? Police?"

"No," I say. "I'm Sam Morris. Just a person looking for other people. And who are you?"

A sob breaks from the woman's chest, and through her tears, she says, "Kadence Hatfield. And this—" She inclines her head toward the woman hiding her face from the light. "This is Finley. Please tell us that they're dead."

Finley?

I take a deep breath, and my lungs feel like they're contaminated with shards of glass. My mind feels swollen, ready to burst because *fuck me*—Finley Beckham is alive. Jack Junior . . . Why? How . . . did she return to the US without anyone knowing?

"I can't believe he did this," Kadence whimpers, her voice raspy. "He was good, but we found out . . . he said . . . he couldn't let us leave cuz we knew . . ."

"Knew what?" I ask, kneeling before them.

Kadence's mouth moves, but no words come. Tears bubble in her eyes.

Finley finally looks at me and whispers, "Who he truly is." She gulps back tears to say, "He . . . *changed*." Her eyes glaze as she peers past me and into her memory.

"No one cared that I was gone," Kadence says. "I'd already dropped out and . . . but he . . . on the trail . . ."

Finley shakes her head and meets my gaze with her big, wet eyes. "He forced me down into this hole, and Kay was already here. I didn't think it would get this far," she whispers. "I thought that he'd stop being so angry and let me go. Maybe he'd disappear or something, but he didn't. He lost his mind, and I knew he was gonna kill me, but he didn't. He did something worse. He left me, the woman he said he loved, *languishing* down here like I'm . . . like I'm *trash*."

She swallows her grief, and a fat teardrop rolls down her cheek. "He's not the man I thought I'd married."

I throw light from the phone all around the room. There is discarded twine over there. Plastic binds over there. And right here, there are rags that used to be shirts and shorts and . . .

In the corner of the room, something small, round, and gold catches my phone's light.

I step over to retrieve it.

"Please don't leave us," Finley begs.

"I'm not leaving anyone behind." I pluck the object from the ground and shine light . . .

A gold wedding band with barely there engraving:

To Lil on our day.

33.

Lil.

Liliana. Big Jack's wife. Junior's mother. Missing in Montana or . . . not missing at all. If the wedding band is any indicator of Liliana's last location, then . . . she had been kept here. But by which Jack? By both Jacks?

Change of plans.

I no longer need to catch Jack or Luann on tape.

DNA would've been nice, but Kadence and Finley are all the proof I need.

And we need to leave, because there is fire everywhere.

I have a car, though. I must have driven the Volvo here.

And it must be parked in the garage. I still need my keys.

And Jack Beckham—he may find us, kill us, and hide our bodies in this shelter until forever comes.

Unless I find him and end him first.

Find car keys. Call 9-1-1. Look out for Jack.

The shelter's smell makes me gag even though my face is covered by a mask and goggles. Death and dying hangs in the air heavier than the smoke out in the canyons.

The bonds around the women's wrists and feet are simple square knots, the first knot you learn as a scout—and whoever tied these knots learned at YouTube University. Still, these janky knots were obviously strong enough to keep two women captive for years. As I unloosen the ligatures around Kadence's ankles, I continue to scan this space.

Puddles of liquid—I don't wanna guess what those liquids are—wet the bunker's stone ground. The eerie glow of that single security light makes long shadows against the shelves of canned and boxed foods. There's a toilet and small sink stationed at the end of a short hallway. There's a mattress in the corner with spotless sheets and folded blankets, but I'm sure neither of these women have slept in that bed.

The asshole in Cleveland kept three women in his basement for *ten years*. The monster in upstate New York imprisoned five women and girls in his basement for over *fifteen years*. The Austrian—he hid his own daughter in the basement for *twenty-four years*.

And now . . . here we go again.

I blink at the prisoners, unable to understand . . . "You've been down here for . . . ?"

"What day is it?" Finley asks.

"Don't know the day," I say, "but I *think* it's sometime in mid-May 2021."

Horror clicks at the back of her throat and steals her words. Her big eyes fill with tears. "I've been down here since . . . Costa Rica," she croaks.

Six years.

She nods at Kadence, still too weak to talk. "Kay's been here since . . . Big Jack . . . he . . ." Finley blinks, and the tug of her mouth and the glaze in her eyes—she's overwhelmed, confused.

"But how did he get you back to the States?" I ask.

"Private plane," she says. "My *family's* private plane. He didn't list me on the passenger manifest. They had no idea . . ."

So he *did* sneak her back here—I *told* Avery my theory, but he didn't think it was possible. My mind wants to capsize. My hands want to strangle the monster who owns this land.

Kadence winces as she bends her knees—her calves lack muscle definition and resemble long, pale sticks. How often has she stood during her captivity? "Skin and bones" sounds like an easy description, but that's what she is. Both women have skin that resembles taut leather stretched to a tearing point. Thin, muddy-brown hair hacked short. Pipe-cleaner necks. Wearing T-shirts that have become nightgowns.

"Are you strong enough to walk?" I ask.

Both women shake their heads.

"He kept me alive on purpose," Finley says. "He gave me my pills every day so that I'd live."

Oh no.

"Your . . . *pills?*" I say.

"For my heart," she says. "I have a condition."

"Did you take your meds today?"

She shakes her head, eyes bright with tears.

"And you need them," I say.

She nods, close to sobbing.

Fuck me.

"Okay," I say, my heart twisting beneath my breast. "Umm . . . this is probably the safest place to be right now. There's a huge wildfire up there."

Finley rubs her free arms. "My medications . . . they could burn . . . I . . . need . . ." Words fail her.

"I know."

Shit.

I touch her ankle to assure her that I understand all that she's scared to say, to assure her that she's not alone, not anymore. I hand her that blanket off the bed and give her the knife I took from the cottage. "For protection, okay? Just start stabbing if Jack or Luann come down here, got it? I'll be back. You're gonna be okay now."

That belief—*you're gonna be okay now*—quakes beneath my ribs. It *has* to be okay now or else . . .

It has to be okay.

Finley whispers in her dry-bean voice, "Thank you." She pulls the blanket up to her neck, using claws that had been fully functioning hands once upon a time. Hands that took selfies and squeezed limes. Plump hands that brushed hair and clutched margarita glasses. Simple gestures—flicking away a ladybug, picking lint from a collar—stolen from her because, *Why?* He got bored with her or she left wet towels on the ground? *Because he changed*—that's what Finley said.

A monster—that's who he is now. A violent bully just like his father.

My mind whirls from scenario to scenario of Jack Beckham or his cook crouched near the bunker door. What will I do if they are?

Violence.

But Jack Beckham isn't standing at the top of the ladder, waiting for me, gun ready to end me once and for all. The world outside continues to burn, though, so there's still danger here. Those drifty palm fronds on fire now land with gentle splashes into the pool. The air out here is no longer air but something solid and deadly.

We could stay here and wait until the fire sweeps past us. But then, Finley wouldn't have her meds, which could burn in the fire, and she ends up dying anyway.

I hustle away from the bunker, my legs and lungs pinched and hurting from the lack of clean, breathable oxygen. No lights shine in the big house or in the pool—the fire has burned away the power lines to this grid. Just one ember landing in one perfect place . . .

I hurry to the main house to find Finley's heart medication.

No one is standing in the kitchen. A platter of bacon and strawberries sits on the breakfast bar. Maybe Jack evacuated and he's now watching me via security camera on his phone from a hotel room in Santa Monica.

Wiping sweat from my forehead, I take a moment to breathe and pull any kind of oxygen into my body. My nerves beat across my jaw, and I twitch like I've short-circuited. One at a time, I rub my clammy hands against my grimy jeans, and then clutch the Glock with both hands. Either the gun now weighs a thousand pounds, or my muscles have weakened.

Maybe both.

I throw open the fridge after realizing that I didn't ask Finley if her medication was refrigerated, liquid or tablet, capsule or . . . there are condiments, creamers, white wine, and produce on the fridge shelves. Nothing that looks medicinal.

Where else could they be?

Bathroom medicine cabinet. Bedroom nightstand. His office.

Back through the house and up the stairs I go, my gaze jumping from those pictures on the hallway walls to those shelves of books in the library. Just three days ago, I'd come here. Was that the patio where I sat with Jack for lunch and consumed something with coconut? What stories has he told Bailey? What lies did he push? What lies of my own did I push back? I'd memorized and written the story of who I was in this now-bloodstained journal. I'd started drinking a different coffee than my regular order—Bailey liked seasonal coffees like pumpkin spice and crème brûlée, or blonde roast with two pumps of sweetener and oat milk. Her signature was different—big "B" and "I" in her first name. Angular "M" for "Meadows." I'd changed my wardrobe—Bailey favored affordable, yet chic, woman's wear from international brands. I stopped cussing—that change tripped Avery out the most.

There's no one in Jack's office. I slip into the bathroom, open the medicine cabinet. Tylenol . . . floss . . . Gas-X. I take all of those things and distribute them throughout my pockets.

I return to the desk.

A single sheet of paper has been left on the otherwise clean blotter. It's a handwritten letter.

> *What's old is new again. He would have never been as epic as me. He was mine to take. Recycle Reuse Renew. There are only 7 basic plots—our personal story encompasses 5 of them, 6 maybe because if I'm being honest life is nothing but a comedy. That leaves the 7th—Rags to Riches,*

*except in this story, the opposite is true. Riches
to Rags. And I have nothing left to give.*
  Jackson "Big Jack" Beckham
  May 15, 2021

Is this Big Jack's suicide note? Written before he took his life down
in Costa Rica?

No—that date. I do not know today's exact day, but I *do* know that
it is May 2021.

But this doesn't make sense. Big Jack died in Belize years ago.

I pluck the letter from the blotter and slip it into my hoodie pocket.
Can't let it burn in the fire.

I open the drawers, searching for Finley's medication.

Nothing here.

I step into the biggest bedroom of the four on this floor.

What in the hell . . . ?

A Peloton bike, a rower, and a treadmill lined up beside each
other and in front of the large windows. On the dresser, an LED
skin-regenerating and antiaging face mask. Vials of Botox. Bottles
of hyaluronic acid. Needles. A pair of gloves for LED light therapy.
Compounds and vitamins and tonics and . . . so much. Who *needs*
all of this?

I hurry over to the nightstand and open the top drawer—I take all
six tubs of pills, any of which could be Finley's since her name wouldn't
be on the prescription. Because she's dead or missing. He must've found
a doctor who sells bootleg meds.

There are no pills in this bathroom. But I do take a toothbrush, a
comb and brush, and a tongue scraper. I wrap all of it in toilet paper
and shove the bundle into my hoodie pocket.

I dart from bedroom to bathroom, peeking in nightstands and medicine cabinets. Pepto Bismol, Advil, hydrochloro-this, dioxi-that, pred-
ni-something, and statin—who knows. I'm weighted down, a drug mule.

"You steal enough of my shit?" a man shouts from the hallway.

I spin around, forgetting immediately about the contents of the final drawer.

"Where are you going with all that?" he shouts.

My mouth fills with pasty spit.

Footsteps . . . coming up the hallway . . . closer . . .

My hands hold a tub of amoxicillin and a tub of pills with no label. My gun . . . it's in my bottom—

Jack Beckham stands in the doorway on the other side of the bedroom, looking haggard and grim, far from the Golden Boy I've followed around Southern California. He's wearing track pants and soccer shoes as though he's just returned from goalie camp.

He says nothing as he waggles a white tub of pills. "Looking for these, right?"

Shit.

I drop the meds in my hand and reach for my Glock.

He's gone before the shot explodes.

Damn it.

I need Finley's pills. The fire will be here soon. The smoke will kill me if the flames don't. I can't die.

Not yet.

I've failed Kadence—I didn't bring her home. I didn't know that I needed to bring Finley home, too.

No—you *didn't fail.* Jack *did this to these women. You're trying to save them.*

I take deep breaths in, and I push deep breaths out.

Hold on, Sam. You gotta push through. You've done it before.

The times I pushed through to survive, though, I came out slightly diminished, more disappointed than before. *Never get desperate . . . don't get desperate . . .*

Too late.

34.

From the bedroom window, I see that those embers on the hills on the other side of Topanga Canyon Road are transforming into flickers of flame.

Gun ready, I creep down the hallway to the staircase. Ice hardens around my spine as I realize that I may die tonight—by fire or man.

But I'm determined to leave this place knowing who I am.

I am Simone Alaina Morris, daughter of Theresa Morris. Graduate of UC Santa Cruz with a degree in history. Vice president of The Way Home, a partner of the LAPD. We've helped solve 106 missing persons cases, and I've come to Topanga Canyon to investigate what happened on the night my mother and I tried to escape this place—only for her to be found dead from a bullet in her head and a bullet in her neck after the Old Topanga Incident in November 1993. Jack Beckham Senior had claimed that he had rescued us, and in a second interview with detectives, he added that my mother had tried to rob him at the house, and that he'd kicked us out. And the police had believed him—my mother was an ex-con, and Jack Beckham Senior was a bestselling novelist and a prince of Topanga.

The last thing I remember my mother telling me was . . . *You need to get that eighties action-movie heart, boo. Blow some muthafuckas up.*

DNA—I'm here for that, too. Unidentified male DNA. *Beckham* DNA. And it has to be present in one of the personal items now wrapped in tissue and stored in my hoodie pocket.

Thinking about Mom . . . a single hot teardrop rolls past my goggles and down my cheek, soaking into a face mask that protects nothing, not anymore. I hear Mom's voice in my head, and I remember her Wet N Wild sticky-glossy lips pecking my forehead.

One last shiver cuts up my spine right as I reach the top of the staircase landing.

Got my Glock. Got my wits, and most important, I got *me*. I *know* who I am. And now?

Let's blow some muthafuckas up.

From the top of the staircase, I spot a woman's head poking up from behind the breakfast bar. She's hiding but doing a piss-poor job at it. She's wearing an orange sweatshirt—the worst color for hiding—and holding a big-ass silver gun that twinkles in the dark.

That must be Luann the cook.

I crouch and creep down the stairs. Then, I creep through the living room . . . and stop before reaching the kitchen. I bring air into my lungs, push it through the face mask with clenched teeth.

Ready, Sam?

I quietly pluck out the bottle of Pepto Bismol and throw it near the breakfast bar.

The woman pops up, aiming her silver gun in the direction of the plastic bottle.

I pull the trigger.

BOOP.

One shot.

The slug hits her ear, and its impact knocks her head into the microwave oven before she crumples back to the floor.

I hurry over to grab the bottle of pink stuff—we may need it down in the bunker.

Did Jack Beckham hear that gunshot? Will he rush to see who's been hit?

I hope he does—I need the vial still in his possession. The over-the-counter remedies won't help regulate the electric activity of Finley's heart.

Onward.

I pass the personal chef now slumped against the range top, pieces of her now back-splashed against the backsplash.

I grab a dish towel and pluck the gun from her lifeless hands.

Outside, there is no more up or down—the fire and the smoke have stolen that and given, in return, ash, soot, and embers destroying centuries of landscape, centuries of unspoiled beauty. "I really do admire you." His voice comes from somewhere in front of me.

In my right hand, I hold my gun up and out. Then, I hold up the dead woman's gun, the towel still a barrier between my hand and the gun's wooden grip.

Jack Beckham emerges like a wizard from a column of smoke. He is made of ash—it covers his hair, his clothes, his eyelashes, and the tip of his nose. He holds the binoculars in one hand and a silver .357 that resembles the gun I'd taken from the dead woman's hand back in the kitchen. Surprise lights his face, seeing that .357 in my possession. He blinks, then moves his head a bit to peer back at the kitchen.

"Yeah," I say. "Whoever the fuck that was didn't do so well back there."

"That's awful," he says. "And wow: you turned out to be smarter than we expected. You're probably the strongest woman I've ever met. Mentally. Physically."

"I'll accept my trophy later."

A mix of expressions—the scrunched brows of confusion, surprise that lifts those brows, angry Vs and tight lips—pass over his face until it relaxes back into Nordic cool. Flat gray eyes, flat jaw, ice and stone. "Why did you kill my beautiful Luann?"

"She started it." My finger rests against the Glock's trigger. "FYI: I know how to use this. I got a certificate and a box of complimentary bullets and everything. And I'm taking my mother's binoculars. They were never yours to keep."

He smiles, then shouts, "I made a good choice when I selected you, and really, it will be fun writing this story. I'm inspired again. And you're delusional if you think I'm going to jail."

"*You're* delusional if you think you know the ending to this story, Beckham," I shout back.

"*Beckham?* It's like you don't even know me."

"I *don't* know you," I say. "Not in the way you want me to. Not in the way you *expect* me to."

His head falls back, and he lets ashes drift onto his face.

The roar of the burning forest intensifies.

"The fire is on the other side of your house," I shout, "and I need Finley's medication. I'm not gonna be here when that fire crunches over to this side, but I *will* take those pills first."

He says, "Wanna bet?"

"I'd put money on it," I say, "but I can't trust that you'll pay up when it's time for me to collect. You're a fucking liar."

"Is this code-switching?" he asks, looking at me again. "Because you don't sound like my Bailey Rose anymore."

"That's because I was *never* 'your Bailey Rose.' Throw me the pills, Jack, or else."

"If you're not Bailey Rose, then who are you?" he asks, tipping his head and ignoring my demand. "Really? What should I call you?"

"Call me Sam." I wait a beat—*he's changed*—then ask, "And who are *you*? *Really?*"

He says nothing for a moment.

Jack Junior's driver's license in my pocket . . .

Date of birth . . . weight . . . eyes . . . blue.

The eyes of the man before me . . .

"Do you know how much a black-market morgue charges for a body?" He pretends to wait for my guess, then says, "Five thousand dollars in the Philippines. Seven grand in Belize—that comes with having more white Americans saving souls and whatnot. But it's a bargain. Comes with a death certificate, police and coroner's reports, everything watermarked and authentic."

"Are you Jack Beckham?" I ask.

"Of course I am," he says.

That letter from Big Jack on the desk in the office upstairs . . .

What's old is new again.

Renew Recycle Reuse

Rebirth

The quest

Overcoming the monster

Voyage and return . . . to Belize and then back to the US after . . .

That date, though. *May 15, 2021* . . . ah.

The expired driver's license . . .

Oh . . . shit.

Jack Junior's eyes are blue.

Big Jack's eyes are gray.

The man standing before me . . . his eyes . . .

"Nice place you got here, Big Jack," I say, my skin crawling. "Fancier than when I was here the last time."

He chuckles. "You've never been here before. But I'm burning it all down anyway, and then I will be free to leave this fucking forest. *Finally.*" He scans the smoky world around him. "You know, I could never leave this plot of land. I've been living as him since . . . 2015? Wow. My son's been gone *that* long?"

His eyes land on the ceramic pot beside the swimming pool. "It's a fascinating prison, don't you think?" He scratches his jaw with the barrel of the gun, and then his eyes wander back to me. "Sometimes I miss them. Lil and Jack. My boy knew what I'd done to his mother, and he threatened to call the police and tell them . . ." He shakes his head. "I couldn't let that happen. I prefer this jail instead of theirs."

Anger builds in my chest, and it takes self-control to keep from pulling the trigger and blasting this bastard until he's just a memory and a stain on the tile.

"I know who you are," I say. "You preyed on my mother and me that day when we met you at Hidden Treasures. You drugged us in that hellhole behind you. You raped my mother. You *killed* my mother, left her in that chimney off the Santa Ynez Trail with a fucking backpack over her head, like she was a character in one of your stupid novels. You were counting on the fire to burn it all and cover up what you did. But the fire didn't burn it all. Theresa Morris came back to me, and now I've come back for *her*."

He squares his shoulders. "I don't know Theresa Morris. I don't remember meeting her or meeting you, and I don't frequent that tacky store."

"Oh, so she's not important enough to remember?" I spit. "I remember *you*, though, and I've been watching you for the last six months now. That old security guard, Russell Walker? He's an undercover cop. Your private investigator, Ro Patrick—he's a CI for the LAPD. He's a crappy private detective, but a great liar.

"And speaking of lies," I continue. "He's a con, and he lands rich clients like you and tells them what they wanna hear. The money you gave him to cover his kid's heart surgery? He has no kid. He bought a Maserati with that money. All the reports that he sent you? Some of it was right—I *did* see a therapist for PTSD—but I'm not Avery Turner. Ro *was* following a woman he saw parked in my office parking lot over in Culver City, but he got bored and started making shit up.

"Ro called her 'Avery A. Turner' since that was the name you'd connected to the Acura's license plate. And that car *did* belong to a member of my team—a *male* member, that undercover cop you know as 'Russell' and I know as 'Avery.' See? That's what happens when you assume. Once we told Ro that we knew he was actively scamming you and two other rich fucks, he quickly agreed to help us.

"And since we're here," I say. "I might as well tell you: Margo also lied to you. She knows *exactly* who I am and why I came here. Kadence and Finley—"

"Should've minded their fucking business," Big Jack shouts. "They thought I'd just let them run and tell the world about me? If they'd just accepted that I was my son . . ."

He drops his head. "We had a good time together, you and me. We've lived a whole life since Wednesday night, you and me."

I shrug. "I don't remember a damn thing."

He smirks. "You left scratches on my back. The neighbors across the canyon heard us going at it on Thursday night. You told me that you've never come so hard—"

"See," I say, shaking my head, "now you've gone and overwritten your little story, and you've made it *completely* unbelievable."

His eyebrows dart down into those Vs again. "You're pretending to forget right now."

I shake my head. "Nope. I will never have the capacity to ponder and wonder, 'What if,' in whatever happened these past few days. Heartbreaking, I know. The last thing a man like you wants is to be forgettable in his own story. Yet here we are."

I pause, then add: "This day, though . . . I'll remember all of this. The ashes. The *Apocalypse Now* helicopters. How you lied and carved your face and exercised and lasered and popped thousands of vitamins to look young. And your very sad face and those very sad eyes, the ones glaring at me right now. I'll remember *that* the most."

Up at the driveway, glass shatters the windows of the main house. *She's here.* The fire shrieks, a gleeful rioter. *Burn, baby, burn!* Burning palm fronds fall upon the rooftop of the main house.

"You'll never know enough," Big Jack tells me. "I know it all."

"No," I say. "Not all. Because I never told you the ending. *Sam's* ending, not Bailey's. Bailey didn't have Ripley's heart or Sarah Connor's strength. She wasn't a fighter like Theresa Morris. You . . . you were a hack who needed to kill everyone around you because you ran out of ideas and they found out that *you* were a monster at the end of the book."

Big Jack drops his head, but a smile stays on his lips. "That's it, then," he says. "You know it all. And she lived happily ever after. The end." He lifts the hand holding the gun.

I pull the trigger.

He pulls the trigger.

The pill vial drops to the ground.

The shots aren't as deafening as the rioting fire, but the terrible splash he makes falling into the swimming pool snaps me out of my trance.

Run, girl!

And so I grab the medication from the ashes, then run to the bunker as the ornamental trees on the patio catch fire, as more glass shatters, as the heat steals some of my energy. My lungs tighten as smoke fills them, and my head swims . . . the bunker door is still open, and I duck in and pull the door down behind me. I barely hear the crash and booms and breaks over my raging heartbeat from my pulse banging in my skull. My breath rattles violently in my chest and makes me cough and gag and spit.

"Simone!" a man shouts.

"Sam!" a woman shouts.

My legs have lost all feeling as I climb down the ladder, careful not to trip and break my neck in this last moment. The bunker is crowded with people.

Avery Turner is here.

Ro Patrick is here.

And so is Finley Beckham and Kadence Hatfield and Leesa Hatfield, Kadence's mother. She's holding her still-living daughter in her arms and smiling through her tears. Back together again.

I hold up the grimy pill vial and offer a tired smile. "Someone needed these?"

Soon, the fire will burn itself out.

Soon, the smoke will clear.

But there will still be danger. That's because the most dangerous animal will have survived. Maybe not Big Jack Beckham this time, but there are others just like him roaming the world. And they'll destroy people like my mother and me, and they'll tear people away from their homes, away from their loved ones.

My team and I will be there to guide the lost ones home.

But first, though?

I'm gonna get out of this bunker.

And once I do?

I'm gonna *keep* blowin' muthafuckas up.

EPILOGUE

Friday, May 21, 2021

The sky was the color of dragons and despair—oranges and purples, smoke and end-of-everything darkness. Ragged, ash-filled clouds hung low in the sky, close enough to touch. Above him, the sun hid, its light barely penetrating the veil of smoke. Even with the wildfire contained at almost 84 percent, he still couldn't breathe this debris-filled air. Even wearing protective goggles and an N65 respirator, his eyes and lungs still burned. Even with a decade of experience, his stomach still filled with sour-milk queasiness.

Detective Ean Rusch had a job to do.

The helicopter pilot up in the yellow-and-green sheriff's department helicopter said that he'd spotted a body floating down here in a swimming pool.

Probably a nutjob who didn't wanna leave his (almost always a "his") house during the brushfire. People like that were as dangerous as the blaze itself. They always thought that a garden hose from Home Depot could put out a fire that was being fed oily, dry chaparral that had grown unchecked through these canyons for the last fifty years.

Typically, fire season in Los Angeles County didn't start this early in the year. In Ean's lifetime, Angelenos started watching the hillsides and smelling smoke around September, August at the earliest. As a teenager, during summertime trips to Six Flags Magic Mountain, Ean had watched flames lick the dry Santa Clarita hillsides, just as he crested the Colossus roller coaster.

But today was May 21, three months too soon for a fire this astronomical. Last year? A landmark twelve months with nearly ten thousand blazes, including that Complex fire up in Humboldt and Mendocino, a fire caused by lightning, with the burn area over a million acres and larger than Rhode Island. Combine those thunderstorms with Diablo and Santa Ana winds . . . those ten thousand fires had killed thirty-three people and had destroyed over eleven thousand structures.

This fire in Topanga Canyon had burned over the last week. An arsonist had ignited the blaze near a trail leading into the Santa Monica Mountains.

Fucker.

No one had been reported dead so far. Thank the stars for that. Well, maybe that luck was about to change . . .

As an LAPD cop for more than twenty years now, Ean had seen a lot—overdoses, hit-and-runs, bodies caught in sewer drains, PVC pipes caught in people, stalkers, loan sharks, that dude's head found on a trail near the Hollywood sign—but nothing freaked him out more than a human charred to a crisp. Like the swimmer he was about to meet.

Ean acknowledged the passing firefighters working to clear the rest of the brush around the property. Since the early 1980s, the owner had been fined six times for not taking better care of—hell, *no* care of—the overgrown, dry brush that spanned nearly three acres. Ean had never met the family who lived here—the Beckhams weren't *those* kind of troublemakers—but he knew that the family absolutely had the means to hire gardeners to clear the land.

This time, nature got to that land first.

And now, someone was floating face down in the swimming pool.

Ean's breath turned shallow as he neared the patio area. He took a deep breath of cleaner air just in case the air near the pool water reeked of wet burned flesh, a stink strong enough to penetrate his mask.

Here we go.

Yeah, the air smelled of burning, and yeah, the air tasted of burning, but there was also a taste and a smell he couldn't identify. Didn't need to identify anything except . . . his newest Doe, floating on their stomach, arms and legs stretched like a starfish. Couldn't see the victim's clothes beneath the fallen branches and soup of ashes and debris.

The *click click click* from the photographer's camera rose above the grumble of fire engines, the hypnotic thrum of helicopter blades, the hacking axes, the mumbling sheriff's deputies, and splashing divers working to carry Doe over to the terra-cotta-tiled patio. With echoes of the fire still crackling and raging, and 84 percent of it contained, the last 16 percent still crunched across the canyon somewhere, still consuming everything, still destroying.

Fire music.

Wait.

This Doe . . .

Floated.

Air had still been in their lungs before they'd landed in the swimming pool.

The queasy sour-milk feeling in Ean's stomach formed into a brick—he needed to burp.

He'd have to track down witnesses and drive over all Los Angeles to figure out whodunit. Because bodies just don't . . . *go dead* unless helped along by nature (maybe smoke from the fire in this case), their own body (heart attack, perhaps), or another living, angry body.

Maybe whoever this was hopped into the swimming pool and watched as flames crawled over the gardens, burned through the grove of live oaks and sycamores, then watched the flames travel up the hill on the backs of chaparral, leaping onto the patio to consume the furniture and the potted plants, running up the sides of the cottage and racing along more trees up to the main house. The terra-cotta tiles surrounding the swimming pool may have stopped the fire's descent, but the smoke . . .

Smoke gets in your eyes . . . and your lungs.

"This is the third body we've found on this property," his partner, Giada Scalise, said. "Can't all be from the fire, right?" Her eyes looked watery behind her goggles.

Wearing these shields and masks, they all looked like astronauts but stationed here on Earth, where the landscape changed again and again from flame and wind, water and violent shaking from faults seen and unseen.

Giada moved aside her N65 to stick a piece of chewing gum into her mouth. "The vic in the kitchen maybe took a bullet here—" She pointed to her ear.

"Yeah," Ean said, "and I don't believe the actual fire had anything to do with whoever this is floating in this pool."

"A John or a Jane?" she asked.

Ean shrugged, then wondered, "How did they get in this pool?"

"Dunno." She clapped him on the back. "That's your job. It's mine, too, but you're the lead. Guess you need to pull out that little memo pad tucked in your pocket, right? Or are you still carrying around that cute iPad mini?"

"Ha ha." His nerves pulled across his scalp as he reached into his jacket pocket for a traditional memo pad. Stacy, his ex-girlfriend, had given him the iPad mini, so he *had* to use it. A disaster—both the iPad mini and Stacy. And now, his nephew used the damned thing to play *Fruit Ninja*.

Anyway, forensic techs had already plopped yellow evidence tents leading from the main house up front back down to the swimming pool and to the cottage. Ean followed the yellow tent road.

A cell phone with a shattered screen—tent 3.

A spent shell casing—tent 7.

A silver .357 with a black grip—tent 8.

A pair of binoculars—tent 12.

All of it still being dusted—not by his team but with falling ashes.

"What happened up here?" he whispered to himself.

Ean walked until he reached the cottage on the other side of the swimming pool. There, he took a soggy breath filled with wonder and anxiety. Ash continued to settle on his exposed skin, over his clothing, in his hair. Like after every fire in Los Angeles, the remains would become another layer of ash and grime against his skin, a new coating of urban armor that had clung to him now for fifty-one years.

He used to like the smell of burning wood and pine needles. That aroma reminded him of family trips over the hill to Angeles National Forest. Reminded him of camp stove–cooked bacon and breakfast potatoes in the morning and campfire s'mores at night. That smell—the best smell ever—reminded him of summer in LA.

And it still did. Except now, fires raced beyond the campsites and went full-on Rambo up and down the state of California.

Ean pushed out a long breath. *Man, this view . . .*

Fire burning over there. Ocean glistening over there. Downtown twinkling over there.

Those final flames still raced over Topanga Canyon, coloring the sky and throwing soot in the air to make LA snow. But it was the kind of snow that burned your eyes, filled your lungs with cancer-in-waiting, the kind of snow that got you dead in this city. There'd be no more blue sky for the rest of the month—the fire had deprived the citizens of Los Angeles County of clear skies. *No,* the *asshole arsonist* had deprived the citizens of Los Angeles County. One person in a town of almost four million people in the city alone—almost ten million in the county. One person who'd fucked it up for a place bigger than the country of Albania and with more people than forty states.

And one person may have fucked it up for Citizen Doe now being eased out of this canyon-side swimming pool.

Well, goddamn.

"We got fire, a pandemic . . . all we need *now* is an earthquake." Ean immediately knocked on the garden bench. It had burned, but it was still wood. "That was sarcasm," he said to the sky, his voice tight. "No earthquakes, please. Don't make it harder than it already is."

Nothing in Los Angeles was ever easy. Except for finding a great burger. And knowing a murder—bullet in the head, another bullet in the neck—when you see one.

And what more am I about to see? "I'm just eyeballing," Ean said, squinting, "but these gunshot wounds . . . both can't be self-inflicted, can they?"

Hundreds of burned palm fronds floated in the pool along with dead birds, a dead squirrel, and a patio chair.

"You know who this resembles?" The photographer snapped pictures of the floater. "Jack Beckham. Makes sense, right? This *is* his property."

"Didn't his old man bump himself off back in the day?" Ean asked.

"Sure did. Somewhere down in Central America."

As the divers brought the John Doe over to the edge of the pool, Ean inspected the gunk bobbing around the water, then headed over to the unscathed cottage. Most of the main house on the exterior had stood up to the flames, the wood catching fire while the stucco resisted. With new coats of paint, the property would be fine. *Inside*, though? The office and kitchen—both places *still* reeked of starter fluid. Needed more than paint and spackle.

On his drive up, Ean had spotted pink flowers pushing up from the burned earth. A hawk soared above a gorge—there was still prey to hunt in the canyons. Whole groves of trees still stood, scenting the air with fresh pine and fir. How the hell was all that possible?

By rough estimations, this fire—caused by an arsonist—burned over twelve hundred acres, starting in a canyon that hadn't burned in over fifty years. And the fire that had roared across the Beckham estate . . . that fire had also been set—but it wasn't part of the original canyon blaze. No other structures burned or were damaged in the original conflagration fire officials had named the Palisades Fire. Just . . . *this* structure, the Beckham house.

Only one firefighter had suffered a minor injury to his eye. But at the Beckham estate, firefighters had found . . . Ean counted on his fingers . . . *six living souls, two of them women who'd been missing for years.* Alive.

Brown-and-black-winged butterflies fluttered above the trashed swimming pool. Beauty even in the wreckage.

"What the hell happened here?" Ean whispered, surveying the little yellow plastic tents dropped all across the estate.

The sneaker—a man's size 12.

The black ink pen left on the flagstone, a yellow evidence tent beside it, dusted with ash like everything else. No ordinary ink pen, not with that cracked ceramic barrel.

And the gun. The .357 is on the tile, far from the swimming pool. How did he fall into the pool if he was standing over . . . *there*?

If this was Jack Beckham in the swimming pool, and if his wounds were self-inflicted . . . ?

Why did he do it?

Depression? He'd lost his mother and his father. Maybe he'd been trapped by the flames and feared being burned alive?

Goose bumps marched across Ean's bare neck. Yeah—this was a murder scene.

Back in the driveway, Detective Avery Turner sat in the passenger seat of a black-and-white patrol car. Simone Morris hunkered on the back gate of an ambulance. Their confidential informant, private investigator Ro Patrick, stood at the edge of the driveway, being interviewed by Giada Scalise, now explaining how he'd helped Detective Turner set up a photo shoot of the woman that Jack Beckham had believed to be Avery Turner. A woman that Ro Patrick had chosen to cast as Beckham's stalker.

"Who was she?" Ean asked.

"My former partner, Winona," Avery said. "She'd started on the Beckham investigation, but she caught COVID and had to leave the team. But before he switched sides, Ro thought *she* was Avery Turner.

"To trick Jack into believing that Ro had carried out the hit, Winona posed as the dead Avery Turner." The old detective chuckled.

"We staged the entire thing with fake blood, a fake bullet hole, Winona playing dead in my Acura. Beckham was happy—his stalker was dead. And we were happy—another criminal charge would eventually be added to the arrest warrant. One more crime to ensure he'd land in jail for *something*."

"And Winona?" Ean asked.

"Makes homemade soap now," Avery Turner said. "She never came back to being a cop after recovering."

"Hey," Ean said now to Avery. "Mind if I go over and chat with Sam?"

Avery eyed him warily. "Umm . . ."

Ean blanched. "What? I *shouldn't* go over or . . . ?"

Avery slumped in the front seat of the patrol car. "Sure. *Just* . . . come find me afterward. We were in that fire bunker for days, and a lot changed down there. It was touch and go, at times. So . . . remember that as you're asking her questions."

Ean strode over to the ambulance, where Simone Morris sat on the back liftgate. He held out his hand. "Detective Ean Rusch, Robbery-Homicide Division. Avery was my training officer. Extraordinary guy. I've heard a great deal about you and The Way Home. A wonderful organization. You all do brilliant work. *Hard* work."

Simone took note of him and accepted his handshake. "Do we know . . . ?"

Ean blushed. "No. No. We've never met."

She flashed her teeth. "Well, nice to meet you now, Detective."

Firm grip. Bloodied, battered, and bruised, but she was still a stunner.

"For the record," he said, taking out his memo pad. "Your full name is . . . ?"

She stared at the blood in the soles of her cross-trainers. "Bailey Rose Meadows."

A shot of color hit Ean's cheeks, and that flush tugged at his scalp.

He appraised her, then peeped at the sheet in his memo pad. He'd written:

Sam A. Morris, The Way Home

"Bailey Rose Meadows," he said, writing in his memo pad again. "Do you have your identification on you?"

The woman before him fished in her red purse and pulled out a wine-colored wallet. She pulled the driver's license from its slot, then offered him the card. Her eyes then roamed to a spot in the distance until her glassy gaze fixed on brown butterflies fluttering above a surviving oak tree.

"Can I ask a favor?" she asked. "Could you have someone get me a pastrami burrito, fries with seasoned salt, and a strawberry soda. Please? I wouldn't request this, but I'm really hungry. I feel like . . . like . . . I'm coming undone."

"Sure," he said, handing her back the driver's license with a shaky hand.

What in the actual fuck?

"What happened here?" Bailey Rose Meadows asked. "Detective Turner told me that there was a fire, but . . ." She shook her head. "I saw a gun back on the patio, and a body floating in the pool."

Ean said, "Yeah. It's . . . it's . . . I'm gonna go check on something. See who can do a quick pastrami burrito run for you. Don't want you coming undone."

She said nothing and continued to watch those butterflies dance over hot spots around the Beckham estate.

Avery was still recuperating in the front seat of the patrol car, chewing now on a granola bar and drinking from a bottled water.

"That *is* Sam, right?" Ean asked. "Simone Morris, yeah?"

"Yeah," Avery said.

"But she said—"

"That her name was Bailey Meadows?"

"Uh-huh." Ean tapped his memo pad against his thigh. "What the fuck is going on?"

"Confabulation—she doesn't know that she's making shit up," Avery said. "And then, there's *trauma*. In the bunker, she read some of the journal she kept as Bailey Meadows, and she has a wallet full of IDs that say she's Bailey Meadows—and that's who she is right now. These episodes—dissociative fugues are her mind's way of dealing with all this shit that's swirled around her since she and her mother were kidnapped by Big Jack Beckham back in '93."

"Fugues," Ean said. "That's when you just . . . *zone out* and wander away, right? Like that woman in New York, the one they found floating in the harbor?"

Avery jabbed his chest. "Exactly. And like *that* young woman, Sam probably doesn't have any neurological illness. Nothing showed up on that woman's MRI or EEG. Probably won't for Sam." He shook his head, then rubbed his weary eyes. "There's a good chance that she'll never fully recall any memories made during this last fugue."

"How about hypnosis?" Ean asked. "Or what if you, like, locked her in somewhere? Not as punishment but just to keep her safe."

"Safe?" Avery said. "She made it out of here alive while three other people who *didn't* experience fugues are dead. I don't want to force her to stay anywhere, because I don't think that would work. But who knows? I haven't had a chance to learn much about it. And it wasn't like I could really tell she was completely lost. Bailey Meadows was just as by the book as Sam."

"Leesa Hatfield," Ean said.

"She knew that Jack was hiding Kadence somewhere, but she couldn't prove it. We knew there was a bunker around here, but we couldn't ever find it. Didn't know we weren't *supposed* to find it. There was fake grass glued to the bunker's hatch door."

"And that writing pen by the swimming pool?" Ean asked. "It's one of those new spy deals, right?"

"Sam's idea. And she took a lot of notes and recorded a lot of video and snapped a lot of pictures since she got here. All that went into the cloud. It's proof that can't be denied, that won't need a person to explain any of it."

"Especially since you can't put her on a witness stand," Ean said, nodding.

"Not that there will be a trial," Avery said. "There's no one left to try."

Ean peered at the older man. "You really think that's Big Jack Beckham floating in the pool?"

"I do. Sam grabbed a few things from the house—toothbrush and tongue scraper. Besides the body, those things will help tell us if we're right or not. We think he shot and killed his son. We think that he's had extensive surgeries to hide his age. Obsessed with vitamins and diet and exercise to look young. We *do* know that his prints don't match the prints that Jack Junior gave to the county when he was a junior lifeguard."

Ean rubbed his neck, still uncertain. "You told me yourself. Beckham pulled a disappearing act before, right in front of the audience, and now, here we are, expecting him to be . . . *him*."

Avery Turner ran his nails across his scalp. "I know."

"Who's to say he isn't somewhere else at this very moment, pretending to be Cousin Beckham right now? Who's to say he hasn't taken a whole new identity? That he's now Charlie Cooper from Philadelphia, or some shit?"

Avery shrugged. "We won't know for sure until the autopsy and DNA returns."

"How will Sam stop . . . *doing this*?" Ean asked.

"Therapy. Meds. Someone monitoring her constantly, even though we stayed in that bunker together, and I couldn't stop what eventually happened. But without therapy to address her PTSD and other interventions . . ." He shook his head.

Ean watched Avery for a long time, then said, "So what do I call her?"

"Call her 'Sam,'" he said. "She'll come out of it soon. Once she's ready to face it all."

"This shit is wild," Ean said.

"You have no idea," Avery said, smirking. "Buy me a chicken-fried steak at Norms, and I'll tell you every weird piece of shit about this case. You won't believe it, but it's all true."

"The truth *is* out there," Ean said.

"Yeah. In that bunker and in that maroon Honda, and up in that house, and back in that cottage, and buried all over this property. The truth is the size of the moon, my friend."

"The *moon?*"

Avery's forehead wrinkled. "You're lucky that I didn't say 'Jupiter.'"

Ean tapped the top of the patrol car—this shit was *wild*—then pivoted to return to Simone Morris.

But the back of the ambulance was deserted.

Ean spun around, his heart in his throat. He saw, though, that he'd come to rig *719*, not rig *331*, where he'd left her.

Ah. *Phew.*

Ean strolled over to the next ambulance, his legs watery, his knees pulpy.

The size of Jupiter . . .

But Simone Morris wasn't seated on the tailgate of rig 331, either.

Nor was she receiving treatment in the back of the other ambulances parked in the driveway.

His eyes skipped around—the maroon Honda Civic was now being processed. The driveway was filled with fire trucks and marked and unmarked police sedans. Detective Avery Turner from Missing Persons smiled at him from the front seat of the Ford sedan and threw him a shrug.

Ean shrugged back at him, then muttered, "Shit." He retreated to the side of the house to reach the swimming pool. *Maybe she's back here.* His breath stuttered as he peered at the charred landscape, at that guesthouse, at the hot spots beyond the bunker.

No Sam Morris.

No Bailey Meadows.

Even those brown-and-black-winged butterflies had disappeared.

ACKNOWLEDGMENTS

For the first time in my writing career, I missed a deadline. For the first time in my writing career, I needed more time. My in-laws, my dog, and then my father passed as I was trying to write this novel. Exhaustion. Grief. Depression. Moments of "I got this." Then, sadness again. Then, snaps of, "This is so good." And then, exhaustion again. With all that going on in my very-real life, it became a challenge to write the types of stories I love to write, the ones with red herrings, misdirection, pinhead twists, location as character . . . From June 2022 to December 2023, my mind looked like the junk drawer in the hallway, filled with batteries that don't work, expired driver's licenses, and keys to locks that no longer open anything. Beneficiaries. Life insurance. The costs of grave sites. The left-behind dog leash and Kong. Ugh.

I'm sharing all this because you're reading a book that may not have survived had it not been for my village. I've thanked these folks before, but right now I want to say it again. Thank you for being there. For being understanding and giving me time. For holding my hand, either virtually or in real life, as I tried to adjust to so much in so little time. Thank you for the flowers, candles, wine, late-night texts, early-morning texts, phone calls, wonderful distractions, long hugs, silence.

Jill, Jessica, Clarence, Crystal, Taylor, Grace, Liz, Alice, Jess, Kellye, Yasmin, Naomi, Arielle, Shawna, Patty, Camille, Rachel, Zahra, Andre, Toni, Judson, Monica, Gigi, Richard, Ema, Karlton, Daniel, Twila, and

Santoy: I love and appreciate each of you for your kindness, thought-fulness, and patience. You mean so much to me.

My family, got-damn, we been through it, and in some ways, we're still going through it. But! Well. Umm. What a helluva story, right? Mom, Terry, Gretchen, Jason, here we are. I love you. Lucille, Mike, Jeffrey, Duania, I couldn't ask for better in-laws, and I love you, too.

David and Maya, my loves, my besties, my support. We were already a tight little threesome. From one crisis to the next, we held on to each other. I'm convinced that we can't get any tighter. I'm glad I could be there for you through everything—and I'm so grateful that you were there for me when I needed you.

To the geniuses behind Orville Redenbacher's popcorn, *Elden Ring*, *Fallout 4*, *The Golden Girls*, *90 Day Fiancé*, Josh and Joel Cabernet Sauvignons, Grubhub, Uber Eats, truffle butter, Topo Chico, Xbox, PlayStation, Molly Maid, Jeni's Splendid Ice Creams, scented candles, and an assortment of office supply stores: Thank you for providing necessary addictions. You all were delicious and entertaining, restorative and distracting.

For my readers and those who I may have neglected to name, please know that I hold each of you in my heart and I'm forever grateful.

RHH

ABOUT THE AUTHOR

Photo © 2023 Andre Ellis

Rachel Howzell Hall is the *New York Times* bestselling author of *The Last One*; *What Never Happened*; *We Lie Here*; *These Toxic Things*; *And Now She's Gone*; *They All Fall Down*; and, with James Patterson, *The Good Sister*, which was included in Patterson's collection *The Family Lawyer*. A two-time *Los Angeles Times* Book Prize finalist as well as an Anthony, Edgar, International Thriller Writers, and Lefty Award nominee, Rachel is also the author of *Land of Shadows*, *Skies of Ash*, *Trail of Echoes*, and *City of Saviors* in the Detective Elouise Norton series. A past member of the board of directors for Mystery Writers of America, Rachel has been a featured writer on NPR's acclaimed *Crime in the City* series and the National Endowment for the Arts weekly podcast; she has also served as a mentor in Pitch Wars and the Association of Writers & Writing Programs. Rachel lives in Los Angeles with her husband and daughter. For more information, visit www.rachelhowzell.com.